THE
FLOOD

Other Novels by

John Broderick

THE PILGRIMAGE
THE FUGITIVES
DON JUANEEN
THE WAKING OF WILLIE RYAN
AN APOLOGY FOR ROSES
THE PRIDE OF SUMMER
LONDON IRISH
THE TRIAL OF FATHER DILLINGHAM
A PRAYER FOR FAIR WEATHER
THE ROSE TREE

Plays

THE ENEMIES OF ROME
A SHARE OF THE LIGHT

JOHN BRODERICK

THE
FLOOD

A NOVEL

Marion Boyars

London · New York

Published in Great Britain and the United States
in 1987 by Marion Boyars Publishers
24 Lacy Road, London SW15 1NL and
26 East 33rd Street, New York, NY 10016

Distributed in the United States by
Kampmann and Co, New York

Distributed in Canada by
Book Center Inc, Montreal

Distributed in Australia by
Wild and Woolley, Glebe, N.S.W.

British Library Cataloguing in Publication Data

Broderick, John
  The flood.
  I. Title
  823'.914[F]   PR6052.R5

Library of Congress Cataloging in Publication Data

Broderick, John.
  The flood.
  I. Title.
PR6052.R5F5   1987   823'.914   86–31673

ISBN 0-7145-2867-6 Cloth

Typeset by Ann Buchan (Typesetters)
in 11/13 Baskerville and Garamond
Printed and bound in Great Britain by
Biddles Ltd, Guildford and King's Lynn

Part
One

NOVEMBER 1933

Most of the seven o'clock women woke with the first ting of the alarm beside the bed, and smothered it with a moist hand before sitting up and dragging their feet out of the deep tunnel of the blankets, but there were others who rose slowly out of the buried night and lingered for a while in the warm and murmuring depths.

Not a stir is that the wind outside and the dog barking no dog something else god in heaven could there be a stranger creeping over the hill someone saw a line of men on the top of the corrigeen but no glint not a glimmer they were only our own back from another townland maybe the one beyond here but where is the dog and the pig and the few coppers I hid under the stone and give us this day our daily bread.

Ellen O'Farrell always dressed quickly and tidily by the light of one candle in a little enamel holder on the dressing table. She prepared now only a little less quickly than usual, her five months pregnancy not yet a real burden. But she had never been delayed by these stray thoughts which came and went in her half-conscious mind. Like the other women, most of whom had experienced the same waking terrors, she was up and dressing by twenty to seven.

Ben, her husband, was never unaware of her stealing across the bottom of the big bed and dropping silently like a ripe plum to the floor, but he no longer grunted and complained and blew through his out-turned lips.

'Take care, Nellie, don't trip,' he murmured to himself as Ellen opened the drawer of the tallboy in which she kept her most precious possessions: fine wool vests, silk slips and stockings, two pairs of satin knickers for an occasion that had never arisen, her best pig-skin gloves and pure silk blouses. Above all, in their own secret place at the back of the drawer, her collection of satin, velour and heavy silk garters. They lay, gleaming even in the feeble candlelight with their splendid winking bows in rich and varied liturgical colours. White and red and green and violet and black: there was not a feast day in the calendar of the ecclesiastical year that she could not match with an apt, snapping garter.

But in time Ellen developed scruples over this, and now she wore whatever colour her mood dictated, so that no one, not even her husband, could accuse her of irreverence. Not that he ever would. The idea of his wife wearing a garter to suit the season had delighted him. For a while after their marriage he teased her about it: 'red for martyrs, green for hope, violet for Lent and Ember days, black for the holy souls, and white for everything, even me, what?' After a few weeks of this Ellen no longer allowed herself to match her garters with the saints and the seasons. Ben regretted this and often watched her sleepy-eyed, as she dressed.

Today she wore red, a bright crimson garter with rhinestones sewn into its flouncy bows. Then she tiptoed over to the marble-topped table on which the ewer and basin of water had been laid out overnight, covered with a towel. This helped to keep out the dust that, in that old house, was forever settling on everything, like flour in a bakery. Ellen was sure that if she stood in the middle of any of the rooms long enough, she would be turned into something like a statue.

Her face washed, a comb through the thick hair faintly streaked with grey, a little silent shake as she picked out her bulky tweed coat, hat, gloves, scarf, prayer-book, and the tiny rosary beads she always carried in a pouch hung round her neck when going out: one must always be prepared. This accomplished, she looked at her husband who seemed peacefully asleep again.

'Now,' she said to herself looking at the heavy, dark red curtains that hung in frozen folds over the front and back windows. She knew and everybody knew and Benedict knew, and everybody knew that he knew that the curtains were never drawn until mid-afternoon, when Ben had been already several hours in the bar. No one in that town was going to know when he rose. Some said eleven, others, the majority, twelve; others later still. It was nothing new. In some houses bedroom curtains were never drawn back at all, except for a wake.

Ellen opened the door silently and stepped down into the big parlour that stretched the full length of the shop below, the O'Farrell's bedroom being over an arched passage to the yard behind. She made her way as surely as an acrobat on a high wire between the huge lumps of furniture that made the room almost impassable to those who did not know it. A further hazard were the ornamental sprinklings from visits to Galway, Dublin, Tramore, New York, and Belfast which lay on the various tables like wreaths on war memorials.

When she reached the thick lace curtains she grasped them firmly, and drew them back as silently and carefully as she had done everything that morning: the curtain rings had to be greased occasionally. Then she let up the Holland blinds, patched like elderly hands with dark spots.

For a moment she waited at the end window. A second later the sound came, *tap-tock-tap-tock* down the street on the other side. Miss Hosannah Braiden was on her way to mass, as she had every morning in the twelve years since Ellen McCarthy had come to O'Farrell's as a young bride. The time of the drawing of the curtains, the letting up of the Holland blinds had not altered by more than a few seconds in all these years, except that recently Hosannah had broken the heel of one of her shoes, and the *tap-tappity-tap* of former years had become the *tap-tock* of the past few months.

'Bloody hell, why doesn't she get it fixed?' Ben grunted when told this significant piece of news. It altered the whole rhythm of the street.

'She hasn't the money,' Ellen shook her head and smiled sadly.

'Doesn't she make wedding cakes? Doesn't she do a bit of dress-making? Doesn't she get a handout from her American cousins an odd time? Doesn't she? Oh yes, she does.' He had paused as was his usual manner when he wanted to make a special effect. Ellen always awaited these with her eyes wide open and interested. It was a small price to pay for the only boring mannerism that Ben had, and even then he often came out with something interesting or amusing.

'If the old faggot didn't spend all her money lighting bloody candles in the church, she'd be able to buy herself a new pair of shoes.'

'Oh Ben, it's another cross, she's lame now as well as

everything else, caught in the chest, and bent down with a growth.'

'Growth, me arse!' He gave his wife a sharp look. Ellen was gazing at him with wide, innocent eyes. 'I don't know what it is that regular mass-going does to women, but it turns them into a bunch of unholy bitches.'

Ellen thought of that remark now as she turned from the window and made her way towards the door. The gaslight flickering through the window spread over the half-shaped mass of chairs and tables like a covering of decayed yellow lace. She went carefully downstairs and along the passage to the hall door. From the entrance to the shop at the bottom of the stairs the rich smell of beer, spices and oranges made the hallway a place of generous anticipation and cosy warmth. Ellen remembered the first time she had ever been there, and always at this time of the morning, that memorable day came back to her as she pulled the bolt on the hall door, usually in a hurry.

There was no need for hurry today. Since her pregnancy she had risen a few minutes earlier, although Ben had for some time now been trying to persuade her to lie in. But her condition was an unusual one, hardly to be hoped for a year ago, and she felt the need to continue the seven mass to thank God for His goodness to her.

Outside, the shop fronts opposite were clear or dim or glimmering 'accordingly as the lamps caught them. The wooden shutters were still up, giving the windows a blind, bandaged air. Yellow circles were drawn around the bottom of the lamp posts; the street, after rain yesterday, was muddy and still smelled thickly of horse manure and damp straw.

There was no need to wait for any more footsteps.

Miss McLurry, who kept the sweet shop seven doors down from Ellen, always waited until Hosannah passed before setting out in her leisurely fashion twenty or thirty paces between Ellen and Miss Braiden. Ellen had often wished that Miss McLurry would get a move on, for her ambling progress led to Ellen's having to walk slower than was natural for her, even in her present condition, and was a serious matter on wet mornings. But the procession, with its minute timings, had been instituted long before her time, and she respected it. None of the Connaught Street women ever walked to mass together.

The last of the seven o'clock women was Mrs 'Pig'

Prendergast, the big Kerry woman who sold pigs' feet —
crubeens — in her dark and cavernous shop, and had been
married to the biggest pig dealer in town. Having small use for
local protocol, she dropped into the church in her own time and
stayed on sometimes after it was over, fast asleep in the back
row, wrapped in her late husband's thick frieze overcoat.

It was a good twenty minutes walk to the Friary from
Connaught Street, and one had to face the bridge, a fearsome
place on a wet and windy morning. But as Ellen walked across
the market square between the military barracks and King
John's castle on the other side at the end of the bridge, she was
relieved to see that this morning promised a fair crossing,
middle of November though it was. The gas lights flared on the
parapets, and threw down little islands of light, which made
pedestrians and pilgrims feel that they were hopping from one
small stone foothold to another, as in the days when the
Shannon at that place was a famous, dangerous and warlike
ford. It was the border between two provinces, between east
and west. The Connaught women, following their seven o'clock
routine, separated by so many exact minutes as they crossed
into Leinster under the hissing lamps, were aware in their
hearts of immemorial things.

*It's a fearful place child dear but tis the only place to cross the river and
it's full of demons and dead men's bones and they forever killing for the
ford the bed of that river is white as death don't look down when the lights
is out and hurry on home our side is safest.*

There were two ways of getting to the Friary after crossing
the swollen river that was as 'wide as half the world.' One was
straight ahead through Church Street, named after the
Protestant church that stood in the middle of it, and down you
went like a sack of potatoes if you slipped on the steep incline of
the Friary Lane. Hosannah and Miss McLurry always went
this way, with Hosannah always first to huddle in her corner of
the doorway, until the holy place was opened by sardonic
Brother Ulick, who always looked at the famished woman with
a forbidden glance, and murmured 'glory be' with no little
sarcasm.

'Amen, Brudder,' Hosannah quavered, getting her oar into
the holy tide.

The other women took the low road that forked down a few
yards beyond the bridge, and led through a maze of small lanes

and houses by the side of the river and the opening onto the docks. A line of tall eighteenth century houses stood at the top of the lanes.

It was while passing one of the narrow lanes which led directly to the embankment, partially lighted by a lamp at the corner, that Ellen saw something out of the corner of her eye. She would have passed on, quickening her step, but for some reason she paused that morning, although it was the last thing she should have done in her condition. The man was lying on his back outside the end house, with his legs sprawling across the path. She could have avoided him by stepping a little to the right. But she bent down, saw the blood on his forehead and heard his rasping breath. She did not wait, but hurried as fast as she was able to the Friary door and rang the bell long and hard. It was answered by Brother Ulick who looked anything but pleased. Life was difficult enough, what with getting old Father Pacificus dressed and vested for mass, opening the door to the two humbugs, Hosannah and Miss McLurry, whose woe-begone faces made him want to puke. And now a hysterical ring at the convent door.

'Well, what is it?' he demanded in his sharpest tones, but when the woman answered, he knew the call was genuine. Nice Mrs O'Farrell was one of his favourite mass-goers; pretty, quiet, thoughtful, and now apparently and almost miraculously, pregnant.

'I'm terribly sorry to disturb you, Brother, but there's a man lying on the path at the corner of Barnett Street and he has a gash on his forehead and — '

'Oh, Mrs O'Farrell, I didn't know it was you. It's one of the men out of that god-forsaken county club, I suppose?'

'God help him, I'm afraid so. Isn't it awful?' Ellen felt a genuine alarm, touched by fear at the mention of the drinking, card-playing, billiard and dice club, known locally as the 'dogs' home', where fathers of families often disappeared for days on end, while the women who were not allowed to cross its threshold, fretted and prayed and muttered and were helpless.

'And more than awful,' said Brother Ulick grimly. 'Aren't you the good woman to stop and look?' He gave her a glance which did not include her body, but she knew from the unusual tenderness of his voice, which he kept for the sick and the pregnant, that he was aware of her state. 'Several others passed that way this morning too, and in the night you may be sure. They throw them out of that place when the money runs out, you know.' Ellen remained silent and stared down at his bare toes in their heavy sandals. She was always embarrassed when anyone referred to her condition, even silently by a look.

'Now, you don't bother your head, Mrs O'Farrell, I'll see to it.'

'Oh you are good, Brother — '

'Nonsense. Would you want him to stumble into the river, if he got to his knees and crawled that way? You know there are at least two or three drownings in the Shannon from that same club every year, unfortunates that don't know where they're going. And to think that most of the club committee are in the Third Order!'

'I'll be late for mass, Brother,' said Ellen nervously. Ben had spent a few days in the club in his time.

'No, you won't. Father Pax is just about ready to move now, having been wound up, we had a terrible time with him this morning. Cross as a chained dog, he was.'

The great beauty of seven mass was that it had never been known to start before ten minutes past: plenty of time on frosty winter mornings. But Ellen had never got used to the way priests talked about one another.

'I'll have him down in the hospital in two shakes of a ram's tail'. He held up his huge workman's hands and laughed lightly.

Ellen smiled and hurried across to the church door. Brother Ulick watched her go, then took down his cloak from a peg in the hall, threw it over his big shoulders, and went off to carry the drunk back into the Friary, if necessary. As he went out of the gate and made for the river, he could see the height of it, already lapping angrily against the quay wall. Some houses facing the docks were keeping a lamp lit all night, something they could ill afford, in case the baleful river, the great arbiter of the district, rose up in the small hours and invaded their kitchen floors.

'God grant I don't get my death from wet feet,' said Brother Ulick to himself, thinking of the 'questing' he had to do before Christmas, those long tramps through the hospitable country-side, begging for alms from those who had little to give and gave of it freely. He thought of his bare feet and the thick brown tea and the turf fires and the fowls he was loaded with by the people, as he made his wintry way to the man lying in his own bright blood on the road.

Father Pacificus shuffled towards the altar, closely supported by two altar-servers who had been trained with great patience by Brother Ulick to wedge their shoulders under the old man's elbows, and to hold him up by the arms when he ascended the steps to the altar.

At first the old man reacted violently to this aid and boxed the boys' ears for daring to touch him, but necessity had reconciled him to the idea of having some support, however unwelcome, against falling. It had not reconciled him to the congregation, on whom he cast a baleful glance as he made his way out from the sacristy. Later, when reading the announcements, he would get his own back on them by mumbling through the notices, having first slipped his false teeth into a big check handkerchief in order to do so the more inaudibly.

This had led to some restlessness on the part of mass-goers, and once, some years ago, they had expressed their disapproval by coughing, sighing and moving their feet while the old man croaked on. He had looked at them venomously over his spectacles, put back his teeth, and in a clear voice told them to keep quiet in the house of God.

'Pack of heathens, I don't know why St Patrick bothered with the likes of you. Stop that noise at once, you're not at a pagan, drunken wake now. And as for the announcements, d'ye think I don't know that you already know who's dead, or dying, or about to die, far better than I do? And the anniversaries too.' Then he took out his teeth again and went on reading to himself.

But the congregation was now long used to Father Pax, who was, they all agreed, a saint, and too good for this life.

This morning however, even though the old man seemed more unaware of his surroundings than ever, the very length of his mass brought with it a thrilling experience which the congregation did not often enjoy at this time of the morning.

Just before the *ita missa est*, when Father Pax had given his last dirty look at the people, Brother Ulick came hurrying out from the sacristy with a little note which he handed to the old man. They studied it together for a few moments, Brother Ulick whispering into the priest's ear. After a pause for reflection, the celebrant turned to face his congregation again. This time he had put his teeth in and was looking quite benign.

'I have just been handed a death notice,' he began in a loud, harsh voice which could be heard down to the middle of the church. 'A poor unfortunate by the name of Michael Sweetman, from Ballinasloe. May God have mercy on his soul. Amen.' Father Pacificus paused and looked over the top of his spectacles. 'Dragged out of a pub and found on the path, dying.' He cleared his throat noisily. 'It could happen to any of you. One false step and you're buried in a watery grave. And —' he raised his voice to a bellow — 'every one of your past sins, including those you think you have forgotten, will rise up in front of your eyes, and their weight will be like a millstone tied round your feet. Maybe your necks. Repent, while ye have the time, and keep away from the river for God's sake, there's enough in Hell as it is. Amen.'

Outside the church, as soon as they could decently rush away, a little group of regulars huddled together to discuss the exciting news.

'Drunk, I suppose.'

'Imagine facing your God after a drunken brawl. O God!'

'Sweet Jasus, isn't it awful.'

'He might have been sober. A stroke or a heart attack on the brink — '

'Or gone to a shadow from cancer.'

'Oh, me poor sister seven years dyin', eaten alive with it she was.'

'It's that county club of course,' said Mrs 'Pig' Prendergast, who had woken up just in time for Father Pacificus's announcement. 'What else? I passed him on me way here, but d'ye think I'd touch him?' She squared her shoulders and glared about her. There was a muted chorus of agreement.

'He mightn't be full out at all. Them drunks have a shockin' queer way of comin' to when anywan bends down to help them. Pull the hat offa ye he would, so he would.'

'And more.'

'Save us, amen.'

'He wasn't local, well we heard dat, but I happen to know all dat's inside at de moment, and I took a dippin' look at him when I was passin', and no, he was no one. Did you take a peep, Mrs Prendergast?'

'Egad, no. A drunk once bit Lizzie Egan, a girl from Lyracrumpane, a mountainy place in Kerry, and she festered.'

'Dat is perfectly true,' said Miss Hosannah Braiden, speaking with great difficulty through a fit of coughing. 'Oh me last gasp! But de poison gets inta dere blood, and if dere cut and bleedin' an' if ye get it on yer hans, and den in a fit of forgetfulness wiped yer mout' wid de spot, well, ye could be done for life. Me poor mudder, Lord have mercy upon her, thirty-two years dead the fourth a' August, always tole me, "Susannah," she said, "never, never go near a drunken man, and don't touch him." Oh, me mudder!'

'Bite the tail off ye he would,' cut in Mrs Pig coarsely, 'and give ye the piles. Does anywan know who the dirty eejit was?'

'He was from Ballinasloe. I couldn't hear Father Pax right.'

'Sweetman was his name, I got that. O Father Pax!'

'Does anywan know him?'

There was a mute but shocked chorus of denials. This embarrassment was broken by a little movement of the women as Ellen O'Farrell pushed the side door of the porch open, and purposefully slipped out through the front door with a smile for those who caught her eye.

The women looked after her with curious eyes, but remained silent. Her pregnancy had been a matter of hot gossip in the porch for weeks, but it had died down now. Yet they still measured her, for it was a remarkable occurrence after twelve barren years, and they were a little overawed by it. It might just be the result of prayers. On the other hand, it was perilous, and they had a feeling that a miscarriage might happen at anytime, even in the church.

There was a genteel cough at the edge of the little group. Miss Sarah Jane McLurry moved forward a few inches and prepared herself for speech. This meant settling her flat mass-hat firmly on her crisp grey curls and fussing with her woollen gloves.

'I'm surprised that someone here doesn't know, even if they didn't hear poor Father Pacificus. I don't have to tell you that I always come down the Friary Lane and go home the same way, a habit. But if I had gone the other way I think I'd have stopped. I wouldn't have passed him by.' She looked about her with bright brave cheeks.

'He might have had money on him,' said Mrs Pig.

'He might, and someone might have robbed him,' went on Miss McLurry with more firmness. 'No one ought to pass a poor, injured man —'

'Our Lady of Perpetual Succour,' said Mrs Pig, whose friends, few as they were, brought out the worst in her.

'She wouldn't have passed him by,' went on Miss McLurry doggedly, ignoring Mrs Pig, and addressing herself to the others. Miss McLurry knew that Mrs Pig's bark was worse than her bite. In her heart she knew Mrs Pig had probably not even seen him, striding along as she did, staring at the ground and walking in the middle of the road. Besides, she often changed routes and sometimes came down the lane like herself. 'None of you would like it if one of your own was lying on the public path, and all the neighbours passed him by.'

'Dey wudden,' piped Hosannah. 'It's because he was a stranger.'

'True for ye,' said Mrs Pig, who regretted the remark she had passed on Sarah Jane's contribution.

For a moment the women said nothing, and in the silence Miss McLurry, having adjusted her gloves, which were too big for her, and grasped her umbrella, went out and began to climb up the hill.

'She has her own troubles,' said one of the women.

'The poor unfortunate,' said another.

'I pity her.'

'I pray for her and her trouble.'

'She's a good woman,' concluded Mrs Pig firmly, and they all nodded in agreement. But no one made a move to go. Perhaps on such a morning, when one thrilling event had happened, another might luckily occur.

'But the man is dead, isn't he?' said someone, and this might have given rise to many more speculations, but Hosannah piped up again.

'Whist, whist,' she whispered, 'Brudder Ulick is comin' down d'aisle and he'll murder us all.'

Donie Donnelly, the night-and-day porter at the Duke of

Clarence Hotel, opened his eyes so abruptly that anyone watching him would have half expected them to click. The occupant of the other bed was snoring loudly on his back with his mouth open. Donie gave him a glance and sniffed, but the explosion of wind which sometimes accompanied the disturbed slumber of his companion did not occur. Donie leaned forward carefully and dusted his boots gently with a dirty handkerchief which he kept under the pillow. His morning task completed, he stuffed the handkerchief into his trouser pocket and slid off the bed.

Standing up on the place where the boards did not creak under the bedside rug, he reached for his brown tunic, put it on and tiptoed towards the door. Even if the room was not delicately lit from the gaslight in the corridor, seeping in through a large glass panel over the door, Donie would have been perfectly able to dress in the dark. It was many a long year since he had slept with his boots off — not since his honeymoon in fact — and he did not have to shave twice or three times a week because of his fair hair. It was not the uncomplicated act of rising and making himself ready to face the day that worried Donie: it was Willie Wickham asleep on the other bed.

Willie had drunk nearly three bottles of whiskey the day before, and had a half-filled bottle by the side of the bed to aid him when consciousness returned. Donie had had a terrible time getting him to bed last night. A few fellows who were reasonably sober helped to pick him up and drag him down the hall and along the corridor to the Lock Hospital, as the room where Donie slept, often accompanied by Willie and a few other drunks, was known. It was sometimes, especially in the summer, occupied by genuine guests, often American.

Donie was of course 'up all night' officially, as he constantly reminded Mrs Katie Daly, the proprietress of The Duke of Clarence.

'I'm d'ony man in Ireland who works twenty hours a day,' he would complain, closing his eyes and letting his mouth droop open.

'Yes, yes, we all know that,' his employer would reply with a snap of her fingers, a horrid habit she had which always twanged on Donie's nerves and sometimes gave him a tic which lasted half an hour, so that he had to go round with one hand covering his jaw. This gesture was known as 'Donie's toothache' and it let the whole world know that Mrs Daly, the slave driver, had been at him again.

'A course d'aul faggot knows ye have a bit of a snoozeen after two or three when de bar closes,' one of his cronies would say, 'But did anywan ever knock on de door, and was sent away?'

'Never wanst.'

'How would *you* know?' Mrs Daly had once demanded when she was in a particularly nasty mood. 'And you snoring to beat the band in the invalid guest room. A room that's famous in all Ireland — and beyond — for the luxury accommodation it provides for visitors with weak hearts, high blood pressure, or any ailment that prevents them climbing stairs. Old age too. You know how many letters I get about that room, thanking me?'

'Well,' said Donie to himself as he gave a last look at Willie, 'it can't be said dere's any breakin' boards between you an' Maud, ye might as well be De Profundis. God an' all if I had yer looks, lad, I'd have her up de pole an' she runnin'.'

Donie successfully negotiated the corridor outside the Lock Hospital, where he noticed, on tiptoes as he was, that no one was locked in the miscellaneous lavatories at the other end of the passage; that the frosted glass window giving out onto the kitchen yard was untouched; that the piece of paper on the bottom step of the back stairs at the end of the corridor was unmoved; and that the door into the bathroom attached to the famous downstairs bedroom, where he had just slept, was still locked. When 'the suite', as Mrs Daly often described it, was occupied by paying guests, this outer door was always kept locked and bolted for the customer's privacy and convenience.

'Ground floor suite, all de luxe, personal fire, private bathroom', was how Mrs Daly had advertised this celebrated amenity in the three Dublin newspapers at the beginning of the season, six years ago. She had continued the advertisement ever since, and a strict watch had to be kept on the corridor, including the back stairs, because the locals, few of whom had ever seen a bathroom, would invent the most amazing excuses just for a glimpse of it.

'Me daughter left a note on the table to say she was having a baby in the Duke of Clarence bathroom and I was to come quick,' protested one lady, caught with her knickers down by Donie, who had crept in through the other door, opening onto the bedroom itself, which she had neglected to lock. And a very respectable woman too, he always said, refusing to give her name, for which silence he was paid two whole pounds.

This morning Donie decided that all was well on that side of the house. But he was wrong. As he turned away, a shadow had hovered and stopped on the upper wall of the back stairs, slowly moved and began to descend as Donie rounded the corner in the other direction and made for the front hall in search of his helper, Hamlet.

Hamlet, an orphan boy picked specially for Mrs Daly's use by the Brothers of Mercy, slept, when he was allowed, in a dark space under the main stairs among the mops, the coal shuttles, the empty polishing tins, the twigs, brushes and mislaid waterproofs, the frayed cloth caps and old newspapers, the sudden, sharp tin boxes and softer cardboard boxes, the wet rags and stiff dry ones, a broken painting of a red setter, the dust long turned to fust, an uneaten wedding cake in a box (still to be called for) that had begun to stir several years before, empty tobacco tins, a cracked chamber pot, heaps of old bills dating back to 1870, and everything else as well.

Hamlet was used to living among debris and was not alarmed by either rats or mice. At one time he had tamed a rat, but found he had not time to keep the friendship up as he grew into his job in the hotel. He was a long, lanky consumptive boy, with red hair and freckles, an unshaped mouth, a receding chin, huge spotted hands, and a pair of very sharp blue eyes of a quite unusual brilliance, staring out of a face of peculiar pallor. He was dressed in the same suit as the Brothers had delivered him in two years before, when he was thought to be fourteen. Although he was never seen washing himself, he managed to keep himself fairly well. Even Mrs Daly admitted that he did not stink. But Donie would have none of this.

'Get outa dere ye dirty filtee smelly ting. Oh!' He pinched his nose and turned his head away, thus allowing a flicker of sly amusement to waver across the boy's eyes. 'Oh, suff! O phew! O God in Heaven!'

Hamlet ducked his head and came half-way out into the passage, blinking, for he existed much in darkness, and even a flickering gas jet at the bottom of the stairs troubled his eyes. Donie gave him a wrist over the ear, which was not exactly a blow, but what he called himself 'a clip over de glue-hole'.

Hamlet crossed his arms over his upper chest in an instinctive gesture of self-protection, but he did not fear Donie who was mean, but not violent as the boy understood violence.

'Did anyone knock at de door while I was sayin' me prayers?' demanded Donie. Not even two years ago did Hamlet believe that Donie spent the hours between three and seven in the morning saying his prayers.

'Umm,' said Hamlet, a word that with him could mean both yes and no. But Donie had mastered the idiom.

'Where did ye bud dem?'

'Number 47,' Hamlet shuffled the old carpet slippers which he wore on duty at night.

'Were dey long waitin' at de door, ye lazzy houn'?'

'Umm.' Hamlet shook his head.

Hamlet could sleep at will and wake up at the slightest sound. Donie in his youth had also had this acute animal sense, but years of rich eating and drinking, and even more the growth of his own self-esteem, had made him slack. He could not now manage without his young assistant, and for this he gave him another clip over the glue.

'I bet ye leff dem waitin' out dere in the cold and wet, ye mangy cur, o de smell of ye! I have to pray ad night dat I can overcum me natural, tenderbred nose so dat I can even speak to ye. Did de sign in?'

'Umm.'

'How many?'

Hamlet held up one dirty forefinger, and Donie took a step backwards, closing his eyes in long-suffering patience.

'Wan lousy jest an' ye have me up at de crack a' dawn, runnin' up de passages, cuttin' corners like a hare before de houns. O look at me, splayin' me pashun with patience to save yer life.' These flights of fancy were always expressed by Donie in a high, quavering voice — his operatic tone. But he always ended them with a short, sharp, and entirely unmusical question. 'Is he a reglur?'

Hamlet looked at Donie's chest for a moment. It did not occur to either that the visitor might be female. No decent woman would come knocking at the door of The Duke of Clarence at three o'clock in the morning. Such a thing was outside the wildest flights of fancy.

'Umm. Yes and no. I dunno. He was here in the summer.'

There was something in the boy's tone which only Donie, who had retained his native sharpness while on his feet, recognized as clouded with inner meanings. Was the little bastard laughing at him? There were times when Donie suspected that he was. So he gave him another clip over the glue.

'Go down to de kitjen an' cut yerself two slices a' plain bread, d'ye hear me? And no jam or I'll know, an' yer ta wait til Mrs O'Flaherty Flynn comes down before ye start biling a kettle.'

Hamlet scuttled off like a young horse in a half-fright, and Donie hurried back across the hall in front of the main stairs to the reception desk just inside the street door. The wooden flap over this hole in the wall was fastened, and the big book with its pencil attached left as usual on the ledge below. This was done every evening at eight o'clock, when Miss Moffam and her assistant Miss Cutler, known far and wide as Mutton and Cutlet, closed their office and went home.

Years of signing in visitors, of finding the book in the right position in the morning, something in the air itself — for single travellers late at night always disturbed the flaccid air of the hall and left their own vibrations — all this had given Donie a kind of second sight. Before he looked at the entry on that fatal morning of Tuesday, the 11th November, 1933, he knew who it was that had come.

Willie Wickham, Willie Willie Wick as ever was, naked and sweating whiskey, was lying on the floor, face downward, with his eyes gummed together. 'I'm honey-eyed, I am', he used to say gaily, just before the booze took over and deprived him of coherent speech. He was literally floored this time, after five days and nights of steady, relentless drinking. Maud Daly had refused him again, and he wanted to anaesthetize every aching thought of her. In and out of the hotel he swayed, like a large chunk of music played out of tune; in and out of a dozen pubs in Church Street, pausing only to vomit on the way. But eventually, hands shaking, knees crumpling, morose and tearful, he shouldered his way back to The Duke of Clarence, where he always ended up. There his treasure lay, a great deal of it in Mrs Daly's bar till, and a few grains of finest gold in the heart of her daughter.

Donie had put him to bed in the Lock Hospital for three nights: another night was lost behind Willie's glazed eyes.

Now, hearing as from a great abyss, at the bottom of which mighty waters beat against the rocks, he had become aware that Donie was no longer in the room. A little while later he managed to roll off the bed and lie on his stomach on the floor where, with his nose in the carpet, he felt some relief from the burning of his body. But the thick, dusty pile soon warmed under him as it always did, so he crawled slowly under the bed, where it was cooler than the rest of the room. But even this haven, an algid creek in a coastline ravaged by the sun, quickly became stifling, and dimly in his mind, while his body burned, he began to thirst for water. Sluglike, sniffling and turning his baked head from side to side, he began the long, long trek on hands and knees over the parched desert of the carpet, towards the oasis of the distant bathroom.

Once, in his apprentice days, when he had not yet achieved the status of a bottle-a-day man, and two or three when on the twist, a barber in Dublin (round the corner from the Hibernian Hotel) took pity on him, and applied the end of an ice-cold towel to the throbbing veins behind Willie's ears. That sensation, the keenest he had yet experienced in a fairly sheltered life — drink was as respectable as going to church — had caused him to rear up in the chair and gasp with relief and pleasure.

'O Mother of God,' he moaned, shivering indecently, and wriggling his feet two inches over the floor.

'Steady on there now, auld son,' said the barber, who knew his trade from the inside out and, more importantly, from the outside in: it was worth half-a-crown from this well-dressed and innocent eejit.

Now, nine years on, Willie paused at the bathroom door for breath. The treasure of the Indies, the gold of King Solomon's mines, the diamonds of Kimberley, the spices of Asia and all the tin in Colombia were as nothing to him beside the imminent prospect of cold water on his face, neck and wrists.

He put his head against the door which, fortunately, opened. There was a sound of gurgling water, splashing, running, rejoicing in its own half-human language, which got straight through to Willie's befuddled mind as quickly as a new theory of healing might penetrate and flower in the brain of a hyper-intelligent medical scientist.

In he went on all fours across the rubber floor — a great innovation, and one that all Bridgeford longed to see — until he reached the haven of the washbasin. This was a magnificent Victorian piece in mahogany with florid but indestructible ironwork. Clutching it, and whimpering with thirst, Willie managed to haul himself to his feet, supporting his sagging knees by gripping the edge of the basin. Then slowly, trembling like a nervous dog, he managed to turn the big brass handle of the cold water tap. It seemed to him that the effort took every drop of strength out of him, and for a few minutes he stood there, wobbling and hanging on to the porcelain rim, gazing through sticky lids at the life-giving water.

A few minutes later, after groping about for the plug, he plunged his hands into the miraculous spring and panted with relief. He dipped his arms in as far as they would go. He soaked a face towel which, also miraculously, was laid across the side of the basin: he applied it to the backs of his ears, his burning nose and cheeks, and his half-sealed eyes.

Almost immediately he felt relief. If only the water were colder, cooler, icy. He was still shaking in every limb, but at least he could see, and the wet towel, if not as burning cold as he would wish, was as welcome as a ham sandwich to a starving man. Then he looked up and, with the courage of the condemned, peered at his image in the glass. It was slightly damp, and Willie knew that his sight was not quite perfect yet, as he had many times had the experience of seeing himself reflected in a glass twice, even using only one eye. But the double or triple image had at least always been that of himself: what he was seeing now bore no resemblance to himself at all. It was the face of a man, much older, with something on his head which Willie in the heat and cold of the moment took to be a pair of horns.

His voice had not always come when called at this stage of a hangover, but he did make a weak, hoarse sound, and hanging onto the basin, poised on the very brink of Hell, he began to mutter his prayers. At last it had happened. His soul had left his body and he was *damned*, devil and all, down in the deepest pit where he would burn forever as he was burning now. The cold towel would be taken away and the torture would begin.

'Jesus, Mary and Joseph and Holy John the Baptist — '

'Please,' said a voice with a very high-toned whine, 'there is no need to curse.'

'Curse! Oh Sacred Heart, I'm only saying my prayers.'

'Oh, I see.' The voice was quite sympathetic, even kind.

But the shock of finding himself where he thought he was had sobered up Willie a great deal: it was at least as good as a large pot of black coffee, raw eggs and Fernet Branca, aspirin and a teaspoon of poteen, the black syrup the chemist down the street sold, and the pound of raw beef that Mrs Daly had once made him swallow. Where was she now? Where was his own mother in his hour of need? Why didn't somebody do something?

Suddenly, as intimations of death and immortality flitted through his subconscious, always muddily stirred up by booze, Willie became aware that he was facing the devil stark naked. He groped wildly on either side and grasped the towel hanging on the rim of the basin. O blessed towel, more than Adam had to cover his shame. He dragged it over his stomach, making him respectable at least in the presence of Lucifer, Son of the Morning, far fallen, but still a prince.

'I'm awfully sorry old boy, but I'm afraid that's my towel.'

Moaning, Willie thrust it from him in the general direction of the evil one, then bringing back his hand with great effort, his fingers touching more towelling material, he grabbed it and pulled it in front of his loins. The sweat was pouring down the inside of his legs, and his back felt like a wet tent.

'Sorry again, old man, I'm afraid that's mine too. It's a bore, quite a mix-up. But there *is* a hotel towel — of sorts — just below the other side of the basin, on a rail. Fine piece of Victoriana, that washstand, wouldn't mind bidding for it, but that's only a passing temptation.'

'Temptation?' croaked Willie, finding the towel on the rail at last, and wrapping it round his middle. It felt coarse, rasping and prickly — was this the sort of thing they wore down here?

'I always resisted it. I always said my prayers. I never gave into anything at once. O God, temptation isn't my fault.'

Instead of an answer, Willie was conscious of a splashing noise and the movement of something large and pinkish, a bit blurred along the edges, and for a moment seeming to possess two right arms. But what was clearly evident, even to Willie's befuddled eyes, was the fact that this man or devil or apparition or whatever he was, was bare naked also.

'Thought I'd pick up the towel, floor's a trifle wet there, and thank you so much for the face-cloth, I always use it before shaving, softens the beard, don't you know.' The figure moved, bent, turned, arranged things while Willie, clutching his towel, began to make a slow, shaky exit towards where he thought the door was.

'So you were tempted too,' said the voice in a friendly tone. (O beware of him when he smiles, son.) 'Well, of course, one often is if one is a true collector, but it would take a small regiment to move this massive construction.' He turned towards Willie who could now see a good deal clearer than before. What he had taken for horns on the man's head were the ends of a large handkerchief knotted over his forehead. And he had obviously been taking a bath.

Willie had another revelation on this apocalyptic morning. That voice, which he had taken to be the devil's, was English. A memory from long ago came back to him: old Jack Nugent, who had first put him on a pony and taught him to ride, used to say: 'Always be civil to the English, Master Willie, for the Divil is always on their side. He talks with an English accent.'

'By the way,' the large, pink, naked Englishman said, wrapping his own towel round his middle, 'I must apologize for making use of your bathroom. You see, they always put me in 47, which is just at the top of the back stairs, and I rather got into the habit of coming down here for my bath. I had no idea there was someone in the bedroom. I looked in before I ran my bath, and there was no one in the beds.'

The steam from the bath which, although not thick, had seemed to Willie so much like smoke, had cleared. He now saw that the man, who was as tall as himself, but rather more heavily built, had a familiar pink face, agreeable and friendly, and was no devil, even if English.

'It's quite all right,' said Willie, clutching his damp towel and nodding his head, 'I didn't know you were in here either.'

'But the point is, I shouldn't be here at all, this bathroom is attached to your suite. I do apologize.'

'Not at all, not at all,' Willie gabbled, feeling for the handle of the door behind his back. The towel, wet as it was, began to slip from its moorings and he made a quick grab for the edge of it.

'But, you see,' went on the stranger relentlessly, 'Donie wasn't about when I got in late last night, shockingly late, but there was a bad fog all the way from Dublin to Rochfortbridge. Very tiresome.'

'Was there?' This man seemed to Willie, whose brain, if not his hands and knees, was beginning to work again, at least in relation to the matter in hand, this curious stranger appeared to be much associated with areas where visibility was bad. 'Imagine that. A lot of steam around in this weather.'

'I beg your pardon?'

'Did you have a nice bath?' was all Willie could think of saying. He found he was staring at the handkerchief on the man's head. The stranger put up his hands and began to unfold it. He looked around for somewhere to put it, and finally tucked it into the towel around his middle. His hair was revealed, not black and pointed as one might expect from the Evil One, but thick, healthy, well-cut, and bright Anglo-Saxon yellow.

'A woman friend gave me this bandana,' he explained, 'and taught me to tie it mulatto fashion. It keeps the steam from getting into the hair, but I wear it out of habit really, as I generally have a shower rather than a bath, and the habit sticks, even though I know there's no shower here. But thank you so much for my bath. I shall clean it, of course, and leave it for you.'

Willie nodded in a preoccupied way. Another thought, almost as alarming as his fear of the devil, had come into his mind with the taking off of the bandana. He had met this man before, and his appearance now stirred some strange atavistic instincts in his clouded mind. It also affected his stomach, which began to make highly embarrassing noises. But the stranger did not appear to notice.

'I do believe we've met before,' he said with a smile, unloosening his towel and wiping the back of his neck. The bandana he had plucked out adroitly as he made his move, and it was held in casual decency in the right place. His control of his movements, even in this simple exercise, affected Willie deeply. It seemed to him that this Englishman was enormously powerful, skilful, healthy, and well balanced, whereas he could not stand up without holding onto the door-knob, or something else stationary like the wall, in a world completely fluid and buckled at the corners.

'I believe we have,' repeated Willie automatically as wind gathered like thunder clouds in his bowels. He wanted to flee into the bedroom, but was unable to move for fear of his knees giving. So he broke wind with a jagged report, like the sound of untrained rifle fire in the hills. And worse, he knew, was on the way. He wanted to weep, run to his poor dead mother's knee, to Mrs Daly, to almost any plump and maternal woman, but not Maud, not ever Maud. He was mortified.

'Sorry I haven't my card here, but in the circumstances, perhaps I'll be excused, ha ha. The name's Slyne, Hector Slyne. I stayed here last summer. Probably met in the bar, what?'

'How d'you do?' said Willie, remembering his manners automatically, in spite of the fusiliering of his bowels. All hell was breaking loose from him; a sudden explosion in the garrison.

'How d'you do?' replied Slyne politely.

Then suddenly, his wits shaken by shame, fear and embarrassment, his body swollen by excess and his stomach beginning to heave, while sweat ran down his chest and loins, and stood out like raindrops on his forehead, with all this physical deterioration making him an object of shame to himself, Willie Wickham, squireen grandson of a land agent, who had started with nothing but ambition, and ended up owning a large chunk of his employer's property, began to think of land, money, acquisition as he slowly and dimly remembered something about Hector Slyne. This was the man Maud and her mother had not allowed him to meet. In the pubs he had heard talk about him: he was buying up land and cheating the people of their few bog acres. Or was it the other way round? Willie was recollecting with his nerves. His instinct was not yet completely focused, but something told him to avoid this man. Maud would not like it.

'Yes, you probably did,' he replied slowly, feeling the wind dying down like a wet breeze in his bowels. 'One meets so many people there.' He unloosened his towel, threw it on the floor, held himself up with both hands on the knob of the door, which he had at last found, and slowly, carefully began to turn it. He managed to nod at Slyne.

'Mum's the word,' said Slyne, who knew the form.

Willie nodded again, but a trifle coldly. He did not want to get mixed up with this man and the small-holders, and he remembered faintly that something odd had been going on. He did not want to be involved.

'My name is Murphy,' he lied, slowly backing into the bedroom.

'Of course, I remember perfectly,' said Slyne, stooping quickly and picking up a towel, which he replaced on the basin. When he turned back Willie had disappeared behind the closed door, which he had managed to negotiate by clinging to the knob. Slyne went over to it and turned the key in the lock. Then, picking up his things, he got into his red-white-and-blue bathrobe and marched out, carrying his loofah like a national emblem, through the other door.

When Donie saw Hector Slyne's name written in the book he lost his head for a few minutes, and sculled about flapping his short arms like a small craft in troubled waters. He made as if to run upstairs, but Mrs Daly and Maud were not yet awake. He ran towards the Lock Hospital, then remembered that Willie was a total loss in this business, even when sober. He trotted back to the front door and peered out, but mass was not yet over, and the Friary Lane was deserted under the black and tan shadows thrown by the street light at the top of the lane.

Then, instinctively, he made off at a cracking pace for the kitchen. Hamlet had just time to hide the thick sandwich of bread and jam, which kind-hearted Mrs O'Flaherty Flynn always left for him at the back of the linen drawer in the pantry, where it was well protected from mice by a small tin box. He thrust the remains of the breakfast into the box, hid it in one of the drawers under the big kitchen table, and buried his head in the cup of water which he was allowed to have with his plain bread.

The cup was knocked out of his hand and sent into little bits on the flagged floor with the force of Donie's assault. He came into the kitchen like a small bull charging into an arena, head down, hooves flying and tail swishing. Donie, although he possessed a backside as fine as any man's in Bridgeford, could not be said to boast of a tail which he could really brandish, but he had picked up a riding crop, which someone had left in the hall stand twenty years before, and this he flicked behind him as if he were lashing his tail.

'Get up outa dat, ye lazy liddle basturd, take dat and dat and dat an' yer mudder an' fadder along wid ye!' Donie's flat Bridgeford accent, with its big-tongued elision of the *th* sound, and its soupy vowels, always came out with extra force when he was angry or uncertain of himself. But the hammering of Hamlet afforded him little satisfaction this morning. What he really needed was someone to share his dreadful secret with. So, whirling around like a plump dancing master, who has preserved the steps of his youth but not the figure, he dashed about the kitchen and out of it as wildly as he had come in.

Hamlet was accustomed to blows, and at one time had taken them as a natural part of the scheme of things, like storms and heavy rain. But recently under the influence of three people who made him feel he was doing what he had to do well, he had begun to resent Donie's blustering bossiness. The young stag was beginning to feel his horns and was eyeing the ageing leader of the herd.

But Hamlet did not allow his longings to interfere with his duty. He was planning to take over from Donie in ten or twelve years' time. So he rushed up three flights of stairs to Mrs O'Flaherty Flynn's room and knocked on the door in a certain way.

In the middle of winter the cook established in The Duke of Clarence Hotel did not expect to be called out of her warm bed at half-seven in the morning. Wasn't the slut Maureen, Polly Pox's sister — God bless the mark — there to cook and fry for anyone who might want to be fed at such an unearthly hour? Mrs O'Flaherty Flynn was not a breakfast woman: she was an artist who fulfilled herself at lunch-time, and even more when the occasional dinner at eight was requested. Then she was seen in her fullest flight, a flamingo of food, well aware that any scrawny bird could throw a handful of bacon, sausages and eggs into a pan, and fry the hell out of them steeped in dripping.

'Travel on', she muttered drowsily, preparing to turn over.

'It's the Englishman, Slyne,' whispered Hamlet through the keyhole, on which instrument he was a virtuoso. Hamlet had once given a demonstration of his genius to Miss Maud, his beloved one, and Mr MacDonnell, his patron, and they had been astounded at the sounds he could produce, and even more at the distance he was able to project them.

Although the cook was one of the three who had befriended

him, he did not judge it prudent to give her a like concert. She had her own door and liked to think it yielded itself, together with its keyhole, only to her.

But now she was up and across the room to the door as fast as if someone had yelled 'fire'. She opened it wide, for she, like Donie, Mrs Daly herself and most other people, thought of Hamlet as a child still. The cook slept in her shift which came down to her knees, and displayed more of her massy breasts, solid buttresses of virtue, than she would have allowed any man to see. Hamlet, who knew his place, kept his eyes covered, since the sight of such feminine amplitude filled him with lusty confusion. Mrs O'Flaherty Flynn thought him a well-mannered, pure boy, unfortunate though he was.

'Slyne?' she whispered, her great hands tugging at the two pig-tails into which she plaited her red-brown hair.

'Yes, mussus. That's what Donie told me. I couldn't read the way he wrote in the book.' No one wanted to admit to meeting Slyne first.

'Isn't he de Divil an' all dat Donie,' gasped Mrs O'Flaherty Flynn, who was born a mere street away from the night-and-day porter. 'Well, go down, child, an' keep im — d'Englishman, I mane — in sweet talk til I get me close on. Tell im I said he can have anyting he likes fur breakfast, even if it's talkin' ram wid tree legs. We haven't got anyting in de kitjun bud id's all in d'askin'. I'll do im a porched egg and serve id mesel'. I'll tell im him id laid it specially for him and ruptured hersel' wid it. Now, run, chile, run run run.'

Hamlet ran, racing down the stairs in great soundless leaps, a skill acquired, among many others, in the orphanage. When he reached the kitchen, he took a clean table-cloth out of a drawer and flew towards the dining-room — huge, dim and smelling of bread and mice — and threw it over a table even before he lit the lamps.

Miss McLurry was never afterwards able to explain to herself just how she went up the Friary Lane, as she always did, and then crossed the road. It was her habit to turn left at the top of the lane and go along the path on the Friary side of Church Street.

She was a little upset by what she had said to the other

woman. She had rarely had a disagreement with any of the seven-o'clockers. Her nature was hardly a passionate one. She did not express herself with the newly-forged inspiration of the moment, as Mrs Pig did, aware that her Kerry friend was quite capable of expressing the opposite opinion the next day, and often a great deal sooner, with equal force. The hammer fell, sparks flew and a brand new shoe was gleaming on the smithy's anvil. It was often melted down and re-fashioned the following day with many a thump on the metal.

Nevertheless, the fact remained that Miss McLurry walked up the steep incline, with its iron rail along the walls for the old and infirm, the drunk and the sufferers from the scourge of the imagination, their knees weakened by dreams, fancies and bits of long-and-gory. The Friars catered for all.

'Well, here I am,' murmured Miss McLurry to herself in sheer surprise, and 'what's that awful man Donnelly doing behind the door of the hotel?'

'Oh, Miss McLurry, miss, if I'm not keepin' ye, but would ye step in here for a minnit?' Donie had stuck his head out and was taking a quick glance up and down the street. Miss McLurry halted and stepped back a pace to the edge of the path. Could he be letting drunks out at this time of the morning, when people were coming back from mass? Or could he be drunk himself?

'Indeed I will not, Mr Donnelly, thank you very much. I have business to do at home and don't spend my nights — ' her voice failed her. It was unlucky to call a drunk a drunk. She grasped her rosary purse and felt the comforting little tangle of prayer inside.

But the next minute she was grasping it with quite a different emotion. It was like a little heap of grain now, her old rosary, and that was what it was: seed sown in the heart.

Donie came out, and before she could defend herself was whispering something in her ear.

'Id's Mr Slyne, miss. He arrived lass nite.' Then he was back behind the hotel door again. Snipers abound.

Miss McLurry was stunned for a few moments, but God came to her aid, as He always did when she hung onto her rosary.

'I'm going into Hogan's, Mr Donnelly, to buy *The Messenger of the Sacred Heart*. I'll talk to you there. At the door, or just inside it.'

What Donie told her in Hogan's doorway was soon all over the town. And particularly in Connaught Street, home of the people most affected by the sudden and unexpected appearance of Hector Slyne.

All those involved in Connaught Street said, as the news flew out of McLurry's and up the curving path and across the road and in and out of the houses like a loaded fuse, that they would meet at old MacDonnell's that evening, after tea-time, and before the drinking men began drifting into pubs. That was what they said.

'Is that what you heard?' said Benny O'Farrell — known to one and always as Fenny O'Barrell — to his wife when she came upstairs with the news at eleven o'clock.

'Wouldn't it be the natural thing to do?' Ellen went over to the looking-glass and flicked it with her handkerchief. O the dust! The Church was right.

Fenny, who was sitting on the side of the bed in his nightshirt, sunk his fists into the mattress and slowly rose to his feet. The flannel nightshirt draped itself over his enormous belly and fell in speechless folds to the middle of his calves in front, and almost to his ankles behind. Since he rarely stood for any length of time for anything or anybody, except for pulling a pint majestically, his legs were smooth and quite free from swelling veins, while his ankles, like his hands, were slender and finely shaped.

There was something of the mandarin about Benedict O'Farrell. Ellen, catching a glimpse of her husband's pink features in the glass, turned and smiled at him. He smiled back, and the youth, which the rich amplitude of his fifty years had clouded with something more than a gleaming patina but had not altogether erased, could be glimpsed again, outlined like a watermark on paper held up to the light.

'If I hadn't this bloody business on my hands, Ellen MacCarthy, I'd — '

When Fenny called his wife by her maiden name it meant he was in amorous mood. Ellen knew exactly when his affection could be acknowledged for what it was. And the idea he was expressing now was, she knew, a compliment that called for special emphasis.

'Oh, Benedict,' she said softly, blushing candidly.

'Let me see that blush again,' said her husband rosily.

Ellen stood quite still for a moment, then covered her warm cheeks with her hands.

'Now, Benedict, the shop is open,' she warned at last when she felt he had gazed his fill. 'When are you all going to old MacDonnell's?'

Fenny began to put on his long woollen underwear and picked up his socks which Ellen always thoughtfully put on a chair by the bed so that he would not have to stoop. Otherwise he dressed with speed; shirt, trousers, tie and pullover. The boots he managed to get into without difficulty because of his old shoehorn, which had a long handle and saved him bending over.

When he was finished, with his red hair brushed and his tweed jacket on, well made to cover his belly, he turned his attention to the startling news Ellen had brought up.

'You know, Nell, like I always say, it's easy to see that you're a country girl, and from another county too, for you've never got in on the way things are done here.'

'I mind my business,' said Ellen firmly.

'That's what I mean.' He chuckled and she smiled faintly. But when he reached out suddenly, like a big bird shooting a wing, to snap his wife's garter, an exercise that delighted him hugely, Ellen slapped his hand and moved out of range. Gartering at eleven in the morning, and in her condition, was downright indecent.

'They have no intention of going, not like that, not all of them at once. Everybody in the whole town and country knows about Slyne's return by now. But people who haven't dealt with him are not going to speak about him. It's not supposed to have happened, for one thing, and they'll wait and see which way, well, which way the waters are flowing. And if we all trooped up to MacDonnell's tonight, we'd be making the whole thing public, almost inviting the town to join in, as it were.'

He paused and looked at Ellen who was frowning and stroking her lip thoughtfully. She had indeed never quite got used to the Byzantine intricacy of the Bridgeford mind.

'But surely Mrs Prendergast and Hosannah and Miss McLurry and the rest of them will talk about it?'

'Of course. They'll talk and think about nothing else. But not with those outside the deal, no matter how well we know them. They know that I usually drop in for a chat with MacDonnell on a Wednesday or Thursday evening. Now, if I didn't go to MacDonnell, that would cause comment. You see?' He looked in the glass and stuck his tongue out at his reflection. His tongue was moistly pink and uncoated.

She sighed and shook her head with a smile. Ellen did in fact see quite plainly, and she thought it all a great waste of time. But she understood the anxiety that her neighbours must be feeling.

'Is it very serious, Ben?' she said softly.

Her husband walked slowly and with intent, indicated by the folding back of his shoulders, to the back window, and drew the curtains, something she had never known him do before.

'Come over here, Nell.'

From behind this window they had an uninterrupted view over the back yard, the sheds, the little lane with its row of cottages at the side of the house, and of the river as it curved southward below the town. Ellen often paused for a few minutes in the afternoon when she was drawing the curtains, but in the winter she did not look long at the Shannon. She gazed lovingly at the big orchard behind the yard that Fenny also owned; bare, leafless trees, chilly walls and rough, damp grass. It nevertheless brought back memories of warm summer days, rich autumns with gleaming apples and the wonder of old walls in the heat.

'Well, what do you think of it?' he said, pointing to the river.

She looked at the great expanse of water which ended only with the horizon, and spread out on either side of the town. A ragged line of bushes here and there indicated the presence of fields under the flood. There were the roofs of a few tin sheds also, and if Ellen leaned her head against the side of the window, she could see the thatched roof of one of the small cottages that were inundated every year, and the top of a tiny window and a segment of the white-washed wall below against which the waters lapped.

'It's like a lake without a shore,' Ellen said quietly at last. She was conscious of her husband's arm, warm and firm about her back, and his hand resting like a bird in the crook of her arm. Everything was familiar, well-loved. The room itself, maternally enclosed; Benedict's masculine presence, his constant use of Lifebuoy soap, the leather of his shoes, boots and belt, her own little stock of good scent, 4711 rose soap, the fresh linen that she brought from the hot press and put into one of the dressing-table drawers, always leaving it a few inches open to let the air in. But the damp could be smelled too, lurking in the background like stains on the wall paper. Boot polish was the only thing that banished the nagging smell of damp; but who could leave a tin of that open all the time?

'A shoreless lake', he repeated it twice, and Ellen felt his arm grow a little tense, and the bird moved in the nest in her arm.

'That's good, Nell, bloody good. The reason I ask you so often is that I don't really see it anymore. It's just the flood, and I forget what I thought of it the first time I saw it. It wasn't so bad then, the government hadn't made the big dam near Limerick for the electricity. So in a way it's your flood, you've had it since you came here.'

'I can't help thinking of what's under it, Benedict,' said Ellen solemnly.

'Oh ho! You and your conscience.' He leaned forward, drawing her with him, and looked down at their own back yard and the cottages in the lane. Immediately they both became aware of the noises that were part of the day and night here.

'Funny, isn't it — ' she began.

'Yes, I know. When you look down at the flood it seems to smother all the sounds between it and us.'

'I noticed that the first year,' she said proudly.

He patted her arm, the bird ruffling its plumage.

'You were taking in everything. I could see you, and not only that, I could feel — '

'Oh, I know.' She stiffened a little under his arm in spite of the support it gave her, now that her spine ached so often. He patted the small of her back gently. 'I was — '

'Counting the house? Well, it's your house. And the yard, everything we see from here is your view, our view, even the river.'

She was silent, listening to the noises she had begun to speak about. They often conversed like this, one knowing what the other was about to say. Especially in the last few months.

The clucking of the hens, owned by a few women in the cottages, came up from the yard below, where most of them spent their time, and where the pickings were rich; Indian meal, wheaten flour, an occasional burst bag of Quaker oats, and as always, potato peelings and crusts of bread from the kitchen. The barking of dogs, the screams of children — fourteen of them in one cottage alone — the yells of demented mothers, the occasional shouts of their menfolk: a bustling, bumbling, raucous, hit-me-now-and-the-chile-in-me-arms way of life, with nowhere on anyone a seam that was neat and unstrained and tidy. Seams, straight and purposeful, were sometimes to be seen on the street above, where the ladies and gents how-are-ye lived; or so said the laners, sometimes bellowing it out on Saturday nights, full of windy spirits and not a secret, good or bad, between them and the pawnshop.

'Isn't it queer, when you come to think of it,' said Fenny thoughtfully, 'that I've never heard anyone in this street complain that the lanes are an eyesore and a disgrace to us all? Which, sweet Nelly, they are.' He stared down at the hovels, all of which belonged to an old lady outside the town, who sent her agent in to collect the rents every week.

'Did ye ever hear of the time Miss Frayn's corpse-twisting bailiff came back twice in one week to collect ten pence from old Mrs Fogarty, the present woman's mother-in-law? "Aren't ye workin'?" he said to her. "Aye," she yelled at him, "makin' bonnets for bees." '

Ellen laughed softly and carefully, for to be seen laughing down at the laners was fatal. Yet she too had never questioned their plight, their marvellous triumph, like roosters on a dung heap, over the conditions of their lives. But before she could say anything, she gave a little start and drew back from the window, Fenny's encircling arm being too light to restrain her. Yet he kept his hand in the small of her back; a comforting pressure.

'That one,' she whispered, 'Mrs Fogarty's child with the big head. She's looking straight up here at us. O, and look, her mother's come out too — '

The Fogarty child had an underdeveloped body which made its head appear huge. The mother, a tiny bird-boned woman almost always pregnant, clutched the child's head against her swollen belly and began to drag her into the dank, dip-roofed dwelling. Instead of stepping back, as his wife had done, Fenny leaned forward and raised his hand in a friendly gesture to Mrs Fogarty. She shouted something back, and grinned. She had no teeth, was white-haired, limped from a consumptive hip and could eat very little because of a malformed gullet.

'Why did you do that?' said Ellen when her husband finally stepped back from the window, patting his own big belly, and smiling at his good little wife who knew so little of Bridgeford ways.

'Well, if we both started back, the laners would say we were spying on them, and if Miss Frayn took it into her head to press her back rent, or even increase it by tuppence a week, and believe me she's capable of it, we'd be blamed for sizing up the place, and thus knowing in advance. And we'd be even worse in their eyes than the pain Frayn.'

'Oh.' Ellen covered her mouth with her fingers. 'I never thought of that.' Then, woman-like, for it drew attention away from her total ignorance of local politics, she nodded her head at the curtains. 'Will I draw them back again?'

'No love, they're back now for the day. Drawing them again would cause comment, puzzlement, what-were-we-up-to-this-time talk? And the less of that the better.'

'There's no one in the shop,' she said anxiously, plucking at the heavy repp of the curtains.

'If someone we know comes in, they'll either wait or shout up from the bottom of the stairs. If a stranger — and that's not likely at this time of year — they'll either wait or walk out again. And what about Gummy, *acushla machree*, as John McCormick says in the song? Life is really very simple round here.' Fenny beamed, and not for the first time seemed to effect a change of atmosphere: his blue eyes shone, his lips revealed all his own strong teeth, well washed every night with soot, and he looked ten years younger: a big chuckling-puckling young fellow, who could make a dismal room seem warm, or banish the presence of November outside.

He gave his wife a quick peck on the back of the neck, put his hand firmly against the small of her back and gently propelled her forward across the room. Together they went down into the drawing-room, and with slow and careful steps, placing their toes precisely in the spots appointed by nature, custom and wear, they descended the winding staircase, which both had agreed would necessitate their coffins being taken out by the front windows when their time came.

In the shop, the high ceiling, darkened by the smoke and dust of years, seemed above a cloud, but was sometimes revealed in all its embossed glory by the sun pouring in through the glass of the double-door, and the well-polished expanse of Ellen's grocery window. The bar window, behind which Fenny presided, was covered to half-way up by a brown, sun-mottled 'shade', upon which might be faintly read the name of the establishment, over the style and emblem of a famous brand of whiskey.

Shutters covered the door and windows for the night and were taken down first thing in the morning by a small boy from the lane, who varied from time to time, as even Ellen could see, but whose name 'Piper' had not changed in living memory. His real name had never been investigated: he had been born in Pipe Lane a long, long time ago.

Ellen and her husband took up their stations behind their respective counters, and the ritual of the day began. It never varied. A minute or two after Ellen's re-appearance in the shop after her mid-morning visit to her husband's room — there were two visits, the first with his breakfast tray at nine, and the second between eleven and half-eleven — Mrs O'Brien would sidle in.

She was a thin little woman with no teeth and wispy strands of dull grey hair, who looked seventy to Ellen, but who was forty-seven or thereabouts according to Fenny, with a year-old child to prove it. She was the only woman in the lane who never put in an appearance at the O'Farrell's kitchen door. Her pride, she had explained to Ellen, would not allow her to do this, since she was superior in breeding to the other women in Pipe Lane. Her sister had married a man with a big shop in Coalville in England; an enormous city, Mrs O'Brien would explain, ten, twenty, a hundred times the size of Bridgeford. 'All de coal is named afther id, ye know,' she had assured Ellen.

Now, she made a little dip in her shawl in Fenny's direction, like a bird with a wounded wing. Then, lowering her shawl from her mouth to the tip of her chin, she scuttled over to Ellen's counter, and in a surprisingly loud voice said: 'Me groceraries, Mrs O'Farrell, please.'

These items consisted of a tiny packet of tea folded in a triangular piece of white paper; a little sugar done up the same way; half a loaf of plain bread, and enough margarine 'to butter it,' as the saying went. These were accepted with a grave inclination of the head and put into a big paper bag which was produced as if by magic from under the frayed shawl, and disappeared as unexpectedly. A murmur of thanks, another little dip towards the man of the house, and she was at the door, where the most important of all the moves in this particular ritual was played. Somehow, from somewhere, Mrs O'Brien would produce a few pennies, count them carefully from one palm to another, nod her head wisely, produce her large shopping bag and disappear round the corner of the lane, having demonstrated to the entire street, and to her own satisfaction, that she was a woman who paid for her 'groceraries' out of the large sums of paper money her sister sent from the big shop in Coalville, the metropolis that had given the name to every coal fire in the whole world.

'Does she really believe it?' Ellen had asked her husband shortly after their marriage, when these mysteries had to be explained to her.

'Well, the bit about Coalville is true. The sister got someone to write on the grocer's bill-head. She's in service there. Another Bridgeford woman passed through Coalville, and made it her business to find out.'

Ellen thought this was a pity and showed definite malice, but said nothing. Mrs O'Brien's 'groceraries' had been established for a long time; inaugurated with due solemnity by Fenny's mother and therefore sacrosanct.

Fenny was now ensconced in his special high chair behind the bar, well placed out of draughts in the angle of the wall, surrounded on two sides by shelves of various potions, local and foreign, and with a wide ledge on which he might rest his hand, put down his own drink or place his letters, bills, invoices and newspapers. The chair had a high back with a harp and a shamrock cut into the wood near the top, with a special stool on which Fenny could rest his feet, and climb up and down from his throne with ease and dignity. But most important of all, the chair had a wide, wide seat to accommodate the master's barrel-elegant posterior. This chair of majesty, the throne of scone-mahone, as Mahon the carpenter had called it, was in spite of him and his craftsmanship universally known as 'Benny's bum-boat.' The locals could not resist the alliteration which might very well have become his pet name, the nick by which he was notched by his friends and customers, had it not ceased to circulate like the sovereigns which predeceased it by a few years, when Benny, as he still was then, reached his thirty-fifth year and had already developed the stomach, mien and countenance appropriate to his state and position, which forced his customers by a spontaneous combustion of inspiration to dub him Fenny O'Barrell. That happened in the year of Our Lord 1918, and the bum-boat had been constructed with loving care three years earlier, when the golden coins had been withdrawn from circulation. Benny Bumboat would not have been a bad name, but the one that followed was infinitely more apt, and it left the great chair with its own title, which had so far outlasted the golden profile of King George V.

Fenny was always seated for Mrs O'Brien's visit. For the next mid-morning advent he had contrived to move a little forward in his seat so that the wide shelf under the counter, invisible to customers and butties, was under his hand.

Ellen opened her mouth to say something about Slyne, when the door opened, and a long thin dark 'article', as Fenny called him, slipped in. This was the second mid-morning fixture, and Ellen, try as she might was never able to say a word to her husband between Mrs O'Brien and the arrival of Sonny Boy. He flickered his fingers against the jagged peak of his cap in Ellen's direction, raised it more by intimation than operation to Fenny, leaned his arm on the counter, allowing one shoulder to disappear into his body and stuck out his long neck, white face and pursed, whispering lips to repeat his morning litany:

'Give us de cut o' half a Woodbind, Mr O'Farrelld in d' oner o' God, an one for me mudder.'

Fenny who would never cut a cigarette in two in his life, produced two whole Woodbines from a loose packet under the counter, and handed them with considerable solemnity and great civility to Sonny Boy.

'Oh, is it two whole wans? Mr O'Farrelld, I never never axed for two, ony two butteens, an' for me mudder because her chest is bad an she fines d'aul Woodbind powerful for blastin' de pipes.'

While he was saying this Sonny Boy retreated step by step towards the door, facing Fenny all the way. One never knew with shopkeepers; civil and all, one day he might ask for payment. Wasn't it well known that half the pubs in Connaught Street sold half-fags at double the price of one?

'She's always axin' for ye, Mr O'Farrelld, and prayin' too a course, Mornin' mn — ' and he was gone. Disappeared backwards.

'Does he ever do any work at all?' said Ellen, getting ready to bring up the subject of Slyne. Fenny had taken up his pipe, which he only smoked in the shop to clear the air of germs. He was now pressing and repressing the tobacco mixture in the bowl.

'Isn't he killed working as it is?' Fenny paused for some delicate finger work on the bowl. 'Shovèlling light into dark rooms.'

Ellen began to giggle, and thus encouraged, Fenny used one of his riper stories about Sonny Boy and his father, who was exactly like him, and never did a stroke of work in his life. When asked by a well-meaning shopkeeper's wife what he would like to do if he got the chance to make money, he replied without taking his mournful eyes from her fat face: "I'd be a great hand at bottlin' farts, ma'am, an' you could sell them to d'Americoons". They had a bill with her of course, but she never pressed for it after that, a ringin' rip she was too.'

'Oh, Benedict,' said Ellen reprovingly. But nothing more was said that morning, what with the customers at the grocery counter, and the men who held low-toned conversations with Fenny over their Guinnesses, several of them glancing over their shoulders at Ellen before leaning even further in over the splendidly polished mahogany counter, with its three green-and-white china pint-pullers, the oldest and best in the town. An altar in its way.

There was a lull just before one. This was a time that husband and wife often discussed business, reasonably certain that 'Gummy' Hayes, their 'girl' in the kitchen, was in the last stages of cooking their lunch, and therefore absent from her post behind the door at the back of the shop leading to the dining-room and kitchen. She could hear very little, as the O'Farrells knew, but she had a genius for atmosphere. If it was tense or even silent when customers were present, she would risk a peep through the door, an inch or less would tell her all.

'Ben,' began Ellen firmly, 'about this Slyne business. What are you going to do?'

'I'm going to see old MacDonnell, like I told you, pet.' Fenny put in some more fancy finger work on his pipe; a sure sign that he was not facing up to whatever issue Ellen had raised.

'I know all about that, and he'll give you the best advice, I'm sure. But what about the other people?'

'What about them?' Fenny drew on his pipe, patted his belly to give himself confidence, and kept his face averted.

'You know perfectly well that poor Miss Braiden, and a few others, simply cannot afford to pay back the money he's paid them. They're in a terrible state.' She took a deep breath and went on regardless: 'And they all blame you.'

'No doubt. That's what they say to you. But when holy Hosannah meets Mrs Pig, the pair of them blame Donie Donnelly, and in the last hour or two a new school of thought has arisen — very subtle, very comprehensive, maybe a bit Jesuitical — which puts all the blame, every bit of it, on the pearly plump shoulders of Mrs Kitty-Kate Daly, who as you know talks to none of them, except Donie. Her cat has a bigger pedigree than any of her partners in crime — imagine, a pedigree cat! How do they keep the records?'

'You didn't sell all of your land to Mr Slyne,' Ellen went on. She recognized a red herring by now, even in the form of a cat of breeding.

'No.' Fenny got down slowly from his bum-boat, and spread his arms hands down on the counter. 'After all, I didn't know what he was up to. It seemed daft, but one never knows. And now he's come back, having told us all that he spent every winter in South Africa. So I was right to hold back the rest of the land, although of course the biteen I did sell is no good to him without the rest, I mean the others' bits.'

'That's all very well, but what about those who held nothing back? What are they going to do?'

'I hope,' said Fenny slowly, 'That I haven't married a saint, I've been accused of doing so.' He raised his long reddish-fawn eyelashes with considerable effect to meet Ellen's steady gaze across the boarded and sanded floor, where straw was added on fair days. 'It's not something you'd wish on any man.'

Ellen looked at him helplessly for a moment, then slowly began to shake her head, and the smallest smile that woman ever smiled, as Fenny once described it, trembled at the corners of her mouth.

'Why did you do it, Benedict?' she said softly. Immediately Fenny began to shake, almost imperceptibly at first, with the slightest of tremors about the belly-button — he always worked in his shirt and trousers in the shop — as subtle as his wife's smile: a flicker of mirth, which spread with an ever increasing heave and ho all over his body, until his shoulders began to shake, his jowls jiggled, and he gave himself over to mirth, like a pool in the middle of which a fresh spring has just broken the surface.

'I couldn't help it,' he chuckled at last, wiping his eyes and mouth. 'I just couldn't resist it. No one could. Not mortal man, Ellen love. By God, it would have made even Madame Daly's pedigree cat laugh. You never saw so solemn an Englishman in your life. And the bunch of twisters he was proposing to do business with, right in the middle of the bog on the finest day of June that ever was, all of us double-crossing one another like eels in a box.'

When he mentioned June, Ellen blushed a little and looked down at her joined hands on the counter. She did not look up as she continued:

'Yes, but poor Miss Braiden and Mrs Prendergast and Miss McLurry, and Donie's children — how many has he? — and his poor wife — '

'The same ladies and the hard Donie would between them face a charging bull and pull the horns off him with their bare hands, if they thought they'd make money out of it. Have you any idea of what that gang would do to Slyne if he demanded his money back? They'd disembowel him, and fry his guts for sausages.' Fenny thumped his belly, which sounded like a drum, for it was a fine, hard, solid belly, and had its own resonant music of which he was proud.

'You're acting guilty, Benedict,' murmured Ellen. 'And you know Mr Slyne has the law on his side, and he's no fool.'

'The law me arse! Wasn't it to get rid of that that we all died for Ireland?'

'Lunch,' said Ellen suddenly raising her voice. 'Lunch!'

'Dinner,' shouted 'Gummy' Hayes, opening the door where she had been listening for the last three minutes. 'Oh, that knob!' She had taken out her teeth, which she carried in her apron pocket, and now popped into her mouth. Then she adjusted her spectacles and directed her speech to Fenny, who had been bathed by her as an infant. 'Mr Benny, did I hear you using language while I wus wrestalin' wid dat door, and me rumoratics gone down to de tips a' me fingurs?'

Part
Two

JUNE 1933

'It's dat Donie Donnelly', Gummy had begun, in the middle of the month of June, just as Fenny and Ellen were sitting down to their lunch; an hour when no one — except a stray American — ever came into the shop. 'Dat has de forsaken wife an' eight unfortunated childer an' anuder on de way. Livin' in dat otel night an' day, don't tell me. Forsaken she wus and forsaken she'll be, excep' for de hape a childer. O glory in de dust, the draggin' down of a wummin, an' she comin' a' dacent people.'

'Lunch,' said Ellen firmly, 'we're having our lunch.'

'He *would* barge in at de dinner hour,' said Gummy, who had not taken kindly to Ellen's efforts to institute lunch at one and supper at half six. Gummy still stuck to the habit of dinner in the middle of the day, and tea in the evening. 'Settin' hersel' up like de bank people, dat ate at English times. Dinner, I axe ye, at eight in d'evenin', when de devotions are on, it's all pagan, Protestand an' English.'

'Well,' said Fenny mildly, 'I suppose I'll have to see him. He's probably dashed over from the hotel in a hurry. Mrs Daly doesn't allow much time off.'

'Dat fella,' went on Gummy, adjusting her steel spectacles, squaring her skinny shoulders and shaking her tangled mane of white curls. 'Livin' in ase with every kinda dog an' Divil in dat otel, open night an' day, an' drink flowin' like a horse wid weak kidneys — an' not much better quality either do dey give, I hear. Well, anyways, dat fella is up in de shop, dressed in a dickie bow, if ye don't mind, an' askin' fur you, Mr Benny, what lie am I goin' to tell him, for he doant know the trut'.'

Fenny, who had already heard about the strange visitor to The Duke of Clarence and something of his business, rose from his luncheon table, and would have gone directly to the shop if Gummy Hayes, who in spite of her age and emaciated appearance, retained a fairly strong arm, had not hit him sharply on the shoulder with the handle of a brush, and made him sit down again, more by surprise than weakness.

'Miss Hayes!' exclaimed Ellen, who had had reason before to complain of the way his old nurse treated her husband. 'Put that brush down!'

Gummy passed not the slightest heed, but she flung the twig into the corner of the room behind the massive mahogany sideboard, and confronted Fenny with her fists on her hips, or what passed for them. 'No Katie Maries, no hips, no bum,' a neighbour had once said wonderingly to Fenny. 'I mean, there's some women natural spinsters be the grace o' God, but she's built for the business as well, or lack of it. Janey!'

'Ye doan mane ta tell me, Mr Benny,' she went on now, raising her voice in the hope that Donie would hear it in the shop. (He did.) 'Ye're nod goin' ta get up from de gentlemanners dinner I cooked for ye wid me own two hans, and nod a kitten to help me, to rush up like a common shop-biy ta meet a fella like Donsheen Donnelly — ' she raised her voice higher to a screech — 'Donie-Phonie-de town balony.' She dropped her voice like an old window pane and reached her neck out, long and puckered as a plucked goose. 'Whoever heard a' de master a' de house gettin' up from his dinner ta go and see de likes a' him. No class before he wus born, and none atall now dat he has a face an' a reputashun ta show for it.'

Fenny knew Gummy well enough to lapse into diplomacy. There was, he knew, bad blood between the Hayes and the Donnellys, dating back to the Famine, and Gummy would gladly have poisoned the poor night-and-day porter if she had the means to do so. It was also said that his father had tried to heal the blood by making a bid for Gummy herself when she was sixteen; the lowest bid ever recorded in their respective clans.

'Well, it's not exactly himself, Annie agradh, it's a message he has for me from a visitor in the hotel. It's business and it's urgent. The visitor is an Englishman, you see.'

'Oh. Aw.' Gummy was taken aback. Then she transferred her attention to Ellen, who was used from time to time as a kind of outside arbiter. 'Well, why diden he tell me dat? How wus I ta know? De cheek a' dat fella, nudden more 'n a penny-boy, and he never goin' near de houseen he has dat belongs ta is wife, God pity er, never dere, ony ta put up de populariation, disgustin' liddle ferret. I'm surprised dat an Englishman, an' I hear de wan dat's stayin' at d'otel at de moment is well-spoken, an' wears blue suits wid turnips at de end i' de trowsers, well, I'm very surprised dat a gintleman like him id put any kind ofa message inta de hans a' dat low-down fella. Times is changin', dey certainly are.'

'Yes, yes, Annie, I know, too true, but I can't refuse a message from a respectable stranger.' Fenny faced for the door.

'An' his tuppeny-haypenny pinny-biy!' screamed Gummy after him.

In the shop Donie was looking ill at ease, as might be expected.

'God Almighty, Mr O'Farrell, but dat Gummy Hayes went an' tuk out her teet when she saw me, and threatened to put de end of a brush up me — ' he broke off, coughed and glanced quickly at the door. Gummy might be listening.

Fenny who was used to Gummy's methods with unwanted callers, smiled his 'that's life' smile, and got behind the counter. Donie had run across the town in his shirt and brown hotel trousers, and the famous dickie-bow which was blue-black. The little man was flustered, red-faced and obviously parched with the thirst. Fenny began pulling him a comforting pint.

He was just wiping the top flat, and Donie's eyes were popping with desire, when Gummy stuck her head into the shop, opening the door just wide enough to allow her to do so.

'Dat's right Donieen Donnelly, suck id up when ye get id fur noddin'. Did anywan ever see ye spendin' a penny a' money on de Connaught side a de town in all yer born nanny? Ye woudden come across de bridge from lousy aul Linster, fulla de lavings a' de British army, an' all de blow-ins in Ireland, an' all de tinkers outside a' Ballinasloe, if ye weren't upta some divilment or dudder. O Mister Benedict, you that wus born dacent, an' reared be hand, take heed from wan dat knows an' give no sorda conference or confiteoribus ta dat fella, are ye listin' ta me now?' And before Fenny could answer, she had disappeared again and banged the door after her. Ellen's voice was heard in the passage behind, and the two men relaxed. It meant that Gummy's attention would be diverted elsewhere for a short while at least.

'God reward ye for de drink, Mister O'Farrell, but me tongue is like a crumbling brick in me mout', and Lord save us, bud dat aul Gummy is terrible hard on her own. Ye know she's a second cousin wanst removed to de wife, but anyway an' how an' ever, I ran over ta tell ye about dis man Slyne.'

Donie took up his glass and waited politely while Fenny drew one with a long bow for himself, with the calm, sure and absolute touch that master barmen share with great pianists. The fact that Donie had not gone on to expound his connnection with the Hayes family and defend himself from Gummy's bitter tongue, was a sure sign that his business was of the very highest importance.

Both men raised their pints and toasted each other with a significant but subtle raising of the eyebrows. There was an elaborate etiquette in the matter of toasting; it was an art that concealed art. The greatest painters could not indicate a line of colour, or shade with a greater finesse, than Fenny and Donie achieved so exactly by a flicker of the eyebrow in a greeting that implied importance, but not yet the knowledge of it. The curve of the mouth, serious but not set, was also a throwaway gesture that the subtlest actor might envy.

'Ah God,' sighed Donie, touching the counter gently with his glass, 'that was — ' he did not venture to describe it by a mere word; it was too sacred. But every one of his mobile features, including his ears, which wriggled sensitively, and his one raised hand paid tribute to the presence of the divinity. 'Well, anyway,' he went on after a suitable hush, 'dis Mister Slyne wans ta buy lan' near de Shannon for holiday bungalows.'

Fenny did not get back into his bum-boat, but leaned on the counter and nodded. He knew all about it.

'Bud, bud d'ye know where he wans to build thim?' Donie drew back, one hand keeping in touch with his glass as if he were guarding a sacred relic, the other outspread, indicating momentous news.

'Up by the lake, I suppose,' Fenny knew something had to be said here to 'feed' Donie, who was a highly skilled artist in his own way.

'No, sir, no.' Donie shook his head and came slowly forward, following the length of his arm, until his face was half-way across the bar counter and almost touching Fenny's splendid, pink-hued nose. 'Nod so, Mister O'Farrell sir, nowhere near de lake, or de yawt-club, or d' islan's, or any a' de shores dat rise like pomes outa de bottom a' de lake.' He took a breath and paused to let Fenny relish his piece of tourist prose, learned by heart from an Irish-American journalist many years ago, and never forgotten. He paused also to allow expectation of his next offering to mount up through Fenny's rich blood stream. 'He wants t'erect dem up da bogs.'

'Up the bogs!' Fenny, who could be as impassive as a carving of the Buddha, leaned back abruptly and opened his mouth, like a young gull in the bar business for less than a year. It was a glorious impersonation.

'Up de bogs, Mister O'Farrell, me jewel. An' he axed me ta fin' im land stretchin' from de Queen's meadows, below yersel' dere, to de bend a' de river, half way ta Curranaghbull.'

'Half way to Curnabul,' repeated Fenny, giving the famous place it's true Connaught pronunciation.

'Half way dere. If id wur half way to Divils Island, ye couldn't have pushed me over easier.' He clasped his hand to his stomach, and squared his shoulders, all the while keeping in touch with the holy glass. 'But I recovered mesel', Mister O'Farrell, an' dat right quick, pretendatin' dat I had a sprained ankle. I recovered mesel', so quick Mister O'Farrell, dat I wus able ta tell im dat he had picked on a place dat people were feared to build on, for fear a' makin' a gomoshun in Paradise.'

'The devil you did, Donie, good man.' Fenny's eyes gleamed with admiration, and he too stood back a little, so that his magnificent belly, one of the finest and firmest in the country, was seen in its full splendour, with his two hands clasped against it at the sides. It made poor Donie, who was a bit miserable in the bulk, look like a tugboat under an ocean liner. But for a moment there was silence, a tribute to the business in hand, and both of them savoured that moment. After all, Donie had just related an exchange that would go down in Bridgeford history, taking its place with the Battle of the Bridge, the wars of the Kings of Connaught and Leinster, and the visit of the long-necked Duke of Clarence himself, the year before his death.

'I did,' went on Donie proudly, 'an when he pud de madder fudder, I wus able, very correctly, Mister O'Farrell, for I've larned to speak well ad d' aul Duke a Clarence, ta tell im dat I could, wid' — he paused and put on a solemn expression, indicating great strain — 'tact, an' de drop of a blink, put im in touch wid de people dat ownded de — ah — lan' he had his eyes on. A course I said dat some a' thim might be mortharly offended be even de whisp of an offer. Proud, like ye know.'

Fenny chuckled richly and stroked his well-shaped and very masculine nose. Elderly women who knew what to look for in men, steeped as they were in the lore of horses and dogs, always congratulated him on it.

'Me, you, Mrs Daly, Mrs Pig, Hosannah and Miss McLurry, am I right?'

'As right as robin's nest, an' all a' thim, 'cept Mrs Daly an' me, livin' here in Connaught Street.'

'Connaught people,' teased Fenny, pressing his belly against the counter, and slowly expelling air through his nostrils for the sheer pleasure of the exercise. 'You're the only Leinster man. Even Mrs Daly got her land from her aunt Halligan.'

'I hauld de flag a' de province, as glorioshus as any a' de four, an' more dan some, I hauld id alof' where no hangman will ever pull id down.' And Donie proudly thumped his chest.

'That's the spirit that made Leinster great,' said Fenny with delicate irony, 'whatever about the rest of Ireland. Did your Englishman spoil the poetry of the occasion by mentioning a price?'

'He mentioned sixty pounds an acre, according to situation.' Donie, whose Bridgeford patois came more easily to him than standard English, could also by speaking slowly and concentrating on some important event, speak with less of an accent if he thought the occasion called for it. This one certainly did.

'According to situation,' mused Fenny. He sipped his Guinness, rubbed his big, well-shaped nose again and struck his belly, as if he were saying the Confiteor in full view of priest and people. 'That constitutes a refinement, a get-out, a rabbit in the hat. And of course you know no Englishman can be trusted. They can twist words like a man with a forked tongue.'

'Don't I know id?' exclaimed Donie. 'Dere nod straight. I suppose id's because dey have no religun.'

'No, it's something else. They never had any religion, not even when they were supposed to be Catholics. Did you have a witness to this offer?'

Donie thought it was time to drain his pint. And drain the half-empty glass he did in one long breathless swallow, a performance as great in its own way as that of an admired singer's command of long-breathing phrases in Mozart. But Donie's effort with a full glass, and then another three immediately following, was in a class of its own. The greatest thing since the invention of lips for glasses.

'Whada ye take me fur?' He put down his empty glass, and Fenny, like the gentleman he was, immediately began to refuel it. 'I had young Maud within ear-shot when I wus speakin' ta'im privaciously in his own room.'

'Was Maud in the same room as you?' Fenny's pale eyebrows went up like flicks of flame.

'Course not. De liddle lady wus posted in de nex' room.'

'Ah.' Fenny waited for the glass to fill, a movement as simple and exquisitely co-ordinated as a gesture in ballet.

'Well, OK,' he said after Donie had thanked him at some length. 'How do you know that Hosannah, Mrs Pig and Miss McLurry are prepared to sell?'

'I tole Miss McLurry de noos dis mornin' before eight,' said Donie with the quiet authority of a great advocate. 'When did you hear id?'

Fenny hesitated for a second. Ellen had heard it long before she deemed it time to tell him at eleven. But this was one of the secrets of his private life, or so he fondly half-believed.

'Nine, or a few minutes before. Ellen came up with it. I was keeping my sore leg up.'

'Who tole er?' Donie was uninterested in significant details. Fenny O'Barrell could have two legs up and his head in a sling for all he cared.

'Mrs Pig. She often comes across the street before breakfast to get her tea. Normally, I'd hear it from her myself.' Not since his mother's death had Fenny seen nine in the morning in an upright position, and his legs were as smooth and as healthy as those of a youth.

'You mane she buys it be de cup?' Donie had never heard anything like this before. Connaught Street.

'No, by the quarter pound, she puts it in in handfuls.'

'Oooh aah. Kerry.' Donie relaxed. 'Well, ye see, she's prepared to do bisness. Mrs Pig is very friendly wid Miss McLurry isn't she? An' has Hosannah dropped in fur a liddle chat wid yer wife dis mornin' yet?'

'Yes,' said Fenny equivocally, looking at Donie thoughtfully for a moment. His visitor looked back. Both of them knew exactly what the other was thinking. None of the ladies involved would condescend to do business with Donie Donnelly. They would come to Fenny, since he represented an old and respectable family, none of whose skeletons had been publicly exposed. There were other refinements too, which Donie was not suitably placed, geographically, to deal with.

Donie knew that no further speeches were needed, and that the Connaught end of the business could be safely left in his host's hands. He and Fenny parted with many mutual exchanges of goodwill. Fenny saw him off in style by raising the flap of his counter and bidding farewell from the middle of the shop floor, a courtesy Donie appreciated as that of a gentleman.

Fenny acted quickly the moment Donie had passed out of earshot. He went to the passage door and called his wife softly. A few moments later, knowing all, she was back in the shop, addressing herself to dusting the grocery shelves. Fenny returned to his bum-boat to await events.

Mrs Pig was the first to come, as he expected; about twenty minutes after Donie's departure. In the interval no one had come into the shop. Not one. Fenny was well aware that the whole street was watching. But, of course, he also knew that it was well established that Mrs Pig not only came in the morning for her tea, but also during the day as well, for this and that. This could not be said of either Hosannah or Miss McLurry.

In she marched, her hands deep in her pockets — it was thought that she took off the big frieze coat only at bedtime — her wild hair still held down under her husband's squashed hat, her big boots thumping like Orange drums across the floor to the bar counter. Ellen did not look around.

'Heard de news?' she grunted, rapping the counter with the edge of a penny. It made much the same sound as a two-shilling piece; she could be in the shop for the purpose of buying a small cup-full of whiskey for a cold on a wet night.

Fenny took the pipe out of his mouth and nodded sagely.

'Where are we goin' to meet dis fella, dis English whats-his-name?'

Fenny was prepared for this. Quite apart from not dealing through the likes of Donie, Fenny knew that none of them would meet Slyne in their homes. Hosannah's was not fit to be seen, Mrs Pig's was even worse, while Miss McLurry had a handicapped brother locked up in the house, which no one was supposed to know of. And of course none of the ladies would be seen dead in The Duke of Clarence. Only fast women died there, as Fenny had once remarked drily.

Fenny thought for a while and, instead of visiting old MacDonnell, had a brilliant idea. But he went on thinking for some minutes. A quick answer in grave matters was always suspect.

'Tomorrow is Thursday,' he said at last, and they both nodded. To meet anyone today would display undue eagerness. 'There's a big political meeting in the square at eight. And the two parties are going to speak. They couldn't agree on separate dates.' Fenny knew that Susannah and Miss McLurry were always out at this time, going or coming to their parish church, which was situated in a narrow street not far from the town square. What more natural than that they should stroll back, after doing the Stations of the Cross, on the footpath on one side of the square, to see how the meetings were going. This was how they always went to meetings, since it was not thought proper for ladies to mingle with a crowd of men. Mrs Pig, being a law unto herself and a fanatical supporter of 'The Chief', always attended these jamborees to cheer her hero on.

'The Chief himself is unable to be present,' she said now. 'Affairs a' state, ye know. He's got de whole country to look after. It's ony a minister dat's comin'.'

Like a true follower of The Chief she did not even acknowledge the existence of the other party. She had, to Fenny's knowledge, commented once on the opposition, when she described a neighbour she did not like as 'a Free Stater, a murderer, a wife-beater, a child-walloper, a wholesale short-weight merchant, a rapist,' — all of which could be overlooked in a decent man who voted the right way — but in addition he was also 'a total abstainer, a miser that's rearing rats for their meat, and tight as a fish's elbow.'

'I expect Mr Slyne will be at the meeting,' said Fenny, who had just thought of it. He would have to send word to Donie.

'I see,' said Mrs Pig, assuming that all had been arranged beforehand. 'Did d'Englishman mention any figure?' she enquired delicately, clearing her throat softly, and crooking her sooty little finger as she covered her mouth with her big fist.

'Sixty quid an acre, according to situation.'

Mrs Pig did not move a muscle. She dug her fists into her overcoat pockets, straddled a little in her boots and drew her chin in against her neck, or what was taken for it. Summer and winter, Mrs Pig wore a tattered navy blue scarf, which like her coat and boots, also belonged to her late husband. It was generally believed that she wore his shirts also. But no one, not even a doctor, had ever seen this hardy woman without clothes. And her face, like Hosannah's, was finely powdered by a delicate layer of sooty dust, which disguised her age as effectually, and with a more natural make-up than the finest French rice powder. She had unwittingly discovered the secret of eternal middle age, which is essentially a matter of camouflage.

'I see.' She was not going to pursue this business one moment longer. She had been commissioned by her two land-owning neighbours to find out what the rate was, and where they could meet Slyne without compromising themselves.

'Give us baby powaer, will ye?' said Mrs Pig. She stuffed it into her pocket and stalked off.

'It's all right now, Ellen,' said Fenny. 'You can turn around.'

And soon after, the usual customers began to come in, all expressing shock at how late they were with everything that morning.

Bridgeford is an ancient town (population 8,767). There was a ford here crossing the river Shannon from the very earliest settlements of the Picts, Firbolgs and *fir na coill* (men of the woods), who made infrequent but bloody forays on the rude wattle huts of the less warlike Celts, who kept flocks of sheep and goats on either side of the ford. It was thought for many years that the *fir na coill* lived in the trees, or upon their branches, but modern research has proved that this was not the case. They wore their hair long and covered their women with the skins of sheep, deer and wolves.

The earliest town was built on the navigable extremity of the ford; it has a long history of commercial importance. But it was chiefly as a military settlement that Bridgeford is celebrated. A castle and a bridge were built by John de Grey, the famous one-handed, one-eyed Bishop of Norwich and Lord Chief Justice of Ireland, in 1210. It became the seat of the presidency of Connaught under Elizabeth I and withstood a siege in 1641. In the war of 1689 it sustained two sieges, the first by William III with one of his favourites disguised in feminine attire, and the second by General Godart van Ginkel, an illegitimate ancestor of the reigning house of Orange in Holland.

The first siege led by William himself failed, largely it is said, through the favourite's running off with a woman of the town, who had secreted the keys of the castle beneath her skirts. The second siege was successful, and as the Irish under James II were defeated, it has been the subject of many songs and ballads, mostly in Erse, but some also in that patois known as bog-latin.

In 1797 the town was heavily fortified on the Connaught side, but the works are now largely dismantled, the stones being broken up and used as road surface by gangs of men and women employed as relief workers during The Great Famine of 1847. Many others of the stones were exported to India, where they form the basis of some carvings of a licentious nature in a variety of Hindu temples.

Bridgeford was incorporated by James I, mistakenly, it was afterwards discovered, for Bridport in Dorset, famous for its hangman's nooses. Bridgeford returned two members (Left and Right bank) to the Irish parliament, and afterwards one member to the Imperial parliament. It is a known fact that three of the Imperial members of parliament for the borough were direct descendants of General van Ginkel by an unknown Irish mother, and all of them were members of the Dutch Reformed Church.

Hector Slyne read all this, and much more, in the official guidebook of Leinster published in 1884. He found the Guide, which he had read before his first visit to the town, interesting but not very useful to his purpose. Some of its statements seemed quite incomprehensible to him, although he was assured in the Dublin bookshop that it had been accepted by the most eminent scholars as the best guidebook ever published about any part of Ireland.

There was a knock on his door, and Donie poked his head in.

Slyne put down the Guide on top of another, and much weightier tome on a small table beside him. The leg of the table then quietly but indubitably buckled and collapsed under its load and settled on the linoleum floor in a heap of dust.

'Goodness gracious me,' cried Slyne, jumping up and staring at the table with horror. The guidebook had been upsetting enough with its men of the woods, its extraordinary Williamite officers and its lingam stones for India — if that was what they had become.

'God Almighty,' said Donie, picking up the books and putting them in the middle of a damp patch on the wash-basin table. 'I tole em never ta pud dat table in a jest's room. I mane ta say if ye had a bad heart or sometin id might kill ya. Are ye all right?' He fussed about the small, bare room with its iron bed, patchwork quilt, and battered old walnut furniture. And there was the much-stained bentwood chair on which Slyne had been sitting before the table collapsed. He was now looking at it with a suspicious eye.

'Dat's all right,' said Donie quickly. 'Everything else in dis room has stood de test a time. Id's sound.'

'It's certainly very old,' said Slyne, who had observed that the first time he had entered the room: Mrs Daly did not believe in pampering her guests.

'De testa time,' repeated Donie firmly. Then he noticed that the jerry-pot was obtruding itself a little too colourfully from under the bed. He picked it up, noticed that it was the one that had the bad crack, and quickly put it outside the door. 'Dat Hamlet,' he said crossly as he turned back. 'I tole im nod ta pud dat table, or dat articler in dis room, or take dem out ad wanse, which is de same ting, bud de liddle eejit never does whad he's toled, de yout' today is completely gone to hell, an beyond id.'

'I don't use that thing,' said Slyne, sitting down gingerly on the bed. It creaked and was as hard as the deck of a battleship, but it had held up, so far.

'A coarse nod,' declared Donie, 'haven we a lovely twilit at d'end a de corridor. Id's nod every hotel dat has dat sorta conveyance. Bud, a coarse, dere's some dat won't venturate out on de landin' in de dead a night. All de same I did tell dat Hamlet — '

'What happened to the table?' said Slyne, anxious to get off this subject, about which he suspected that Donie had a fund of stories.

'Well, it was like de time dat British officer — Oh what's his name? I can't remember it now — was laid out in dis room. It was during de British time, you see — ' When speaking of the Brits Donie automatically fell into something akin to their curious accents.

'Laid out!'

'Yesss, with the drink, don't ye know? Ah, sure, this 'otel is famus from Hong Kong to Ding Dong, aull the wey round the globe for the quality of its service and hospitality.' Donie stopped, screwing up his mouth to produce the refined accents he imagined he had heard from the great days of the British officers, and their private incomes. 'Well, anyways,' he went on, giving up the labial contortions and relapsing into his native tones, slurring, soft and infantile, 'dis wan wus laid out cold, an' he woke up in de middle a de night, got outa bed, and crawled over to a table like dat.' And he indicated the heap of dust.

'Yes, yes,' said Slyne, who did not want to be held up all evening with tales of drunken officers, 'laid out' or otherwise in every room of this terrible hotel. 'But what happened to that table just now?'

Donie gave it a sorrowful look. It was just such a table that Lord Edward Chatham-Wyle had attempted to mount and ride through the door, under the impression that it was his saddle. He often had his man bring his saddle into the hotel and set it up on a high chair, where, cheerfully astride, he would drink his way through the night, sometimes spurring his horse and waving an imaginary sword, as he led his troops into battle at Waterloo.

'Worm, wurum, dried rot, de beetles, everyting,' said Donie dolefully, for he dearly loved recounting his adventures with Lord Edward. 'De hole place is rodden wid id. A coarse, id wus ony de leg a dat table dat wus aeten. All de same.' He gazed at it for a moment, and then looked up.

'Some-un 'ill have ta brush id up and bring ye a noo wan.'

'That seems obvious to me,' said Slyne sharply.

'Bud ya doan't want a noo articler?' inquired Donie politely, for he could see that Mr Slyne was vexed. Not the same class, of course, as Lord Edward and his jolly brother officers.

'Certainly not,' snapped Slyne. Then he collected himself and remembered what he had been told about the Irish. They would talk about death, disaster and dry rot, until the cows came home with their horns missing; that was how a friend of his had put it. He must be gracious. After all, this was a very old hotel, the owner seemed eccentric, and for all he knew might suddenly accuse him of breaking her furnituure.

'What is Mrs Daly going to say when she finds out about that table?' Slyne demanded.

Donie looked down at it idly and shook his head.

'Nudden. She'll get somewan to pud a noo leg on id, an' id might lass fur anodder ten year, although de wurum is in de top too, underneat' like.'

'Well, you know I'm not responsible for it, I want you to be quite clear about that.' Slyne stood up and looked sternly down on Donie, who stared back at him with his mouth half open in surprise. The idea that Mrs Daly would kick up a row about a table that ought to have been burned in the yard years ago, while she was in the act of selling seven acres of bog land to this mad Englishman was something that Donie found absolutely cock-eyed. He began to giggle, covering his mouth with his hand and hunching his shoulders.

'What are you laughing at?'

'I'm nod laffin',' said Donie wiping the smile off his face literally with the back of his hand, 'id's de hickcoffs, I do suffer sometin' awful from dem.'

'Well, that table will have to be got out of this room, and another one brought back in, and Mrs Daly will have to be informed by you just exactly what happened. I will not have her think that I broke it, d'you hear me?'

Donie was amazed. The man seemed to be genuinely upset. What would he have said if he had seen what Donie had seen, sober and freshly-shriven by a newly ordained priest, with the holy oil almost dripping off him; the gable of an old house, not far from where his wife and sometimes he himself lived, slowly quiver, buckle and gently collapse in a shower of damp dust? He began to tell Slyne about this, when the Englishman abruptly told him that he had heard enough and repeated his demand that Mrs Daly be told the truth.

Never allow them to feel that you are trying to be nice to them civility is always suspect and they don't really like too much affability stare straight at them and keep your demands short sharp and simple as if you were training Labradors not that they're as dependable as dogs! o no wish they were just be prepared for anything never never show amazement close your eyes often and wearily yawn but hold your shoulder straight and in a manner of speaking never turn your back on them and leave it exposed for any length of time they'll knife you and always remember that in the last resort though we do speak the same language you will have to try and decipher the lingo as best you can they just don't think like we do it's very strange but as an old Irish hand Hector I can tell you that after a while you develop an instinct the same thing as I used to feel in India not in the jungles but in the streets very similar you know but different to us different

'Bud she wudden tink in a tousan' year that ye broke id, sir, we all know a gintleman here when we see wan, I know id mus' have been a shock ta ye ta see d'aul ting collapse like dat, but shure won' we all go like dat ourselves in de end, nuttin' bud dus' and' asshush, sure id's hardly wort' worryeean aboud dis life ad all ad all.'

Slyne listened to this speech with impatience, but was careful to close his eyes, smother a yawn and hold his hand to his brow. The effect was startling.

'I have all de landowners rounded up fur ye Mr Slyne, an' ye can meet ivry wan a dem dis very evenin' ad de politicle meetin' in de square. Bein' landowners, dey want ta know what de bloody aul politicklers are up ta, ye coulden watch dem, ye know, see whad I mean, sir?' Donie was all eagerness, impatient with himself for wasting time on an old table red rotten with worm, when he should have been doing business, which was the real purpose of his visit to the room.

'All of them?' said Slyne briskly. He was a large man, and had a full handsome face, rather florid, with piercing blue eyes. He wore a well-cut blue suit, expensive shoes and a white shirt with a discreet dark blue striped tie. The heat did not seem to affect him, he always appeared cool and unruffled, and his thick, blond saxon hair never seemed to run wild. All this, he knew, made a great impression on natives everywhere. It would be untrue to say that he had no nerves, but they were well sheathed.

'Well,' said Donie, screwing up his mouth, 'dere's wan man thad says he's nod innerested in sellin'.'

'Who is he?' Slyne took a notebook out of his pocket and opened it.

'He's a Mister MacDonnell, lives ad de top a Connaught Street, in a privad house, an' 'e 'as ten acres, more dan anywan. Isn't id de mercy a God he hassend de land in de centre a de whole lot?'

'It is indeed.' Slyne snapped his pocket book closed, and held it thoughtfully in his hands for a moment. MacDonnell. . .

'Bud id's in a beeootiful place, jus' on de bend a de river.' Donie was enthusiastic. Although he was in mortal dread of old MacDonnell, he knew there was always a percentage in it for anyone who did anything for him.

'Indeed.' Slyne put his little book back in his pocket, and stood staring down at Donie with his frank and piercing blue eyes for a moment. This impassive stare always helped to demoralize people, and indeed Donie felt the need to talk, about anything, it did not matter, when this icy glare was directed upon him.

'A coarse he's terrible rich, ole MacDonnell, wus in America an' made millions outa Toomany.'

'Tammany? Did he now?' Slyne repressed a smile at Donie's version of the great political machine.

'Yes, 'e did. Seventy if he's a day an' —' here Donie lowered his voice and looked about the room — 'stone mad about Miss Maud. Ye never saw anyting like it in yer life.'

'I thought Mr Wickham was the favourite there?' Slyne's well-shaped but set mouth softened by the end of a fraction.

'Arrah poor aul Willie,' said Donie with an indulgent smile.' "Me Passshun", he says when 'e's well oiled. Imagine usin' a holy word like dat about Miss Maud. I had to correct 'im a few times, you'd never believe id, bud 'e spends a lot a' his time readin' stinkin' novels.'

'What — ' Slyne was about to ask just exactly how the matter stood between the two young people, and how Mr MacDonnell proposed to deal with things after his Tammany experience, but he checked himself at the last minute. This was not the first time Donie had succeeded in taking his mind off business. He had been warned about this insidious aspect of the Irish, but no matter how wary one was, they always managed to draw what might be described as a red scroll across one's path, inviting one to view the illuminations. But he was not going to be drawn on MacDonnell.

'Well, id's hard ta know wha' Miss Maud intends ta do, bud dere's wan ting I can tell ya.'

'That's not what I was about to ask you,' cut in Slyne shortly. 'Mr MacDonnell's affairs have nothing to do with me. I was about to ask you what time do I meet these people in the square this evening?'

'Oh,' Donie was knocked off course. 'Well, now, de first meetin' is ad eight, an' begod so is de second wan too, dey cudden agree about slicing de time, mordal emenies dey are, Free Staters and Republicans, O biys!'

'Will the meeting start promptly at eight?'

Donie looked at Slyne with something like wonder. There were times when he asked himself if this man was real, was human, to be taken seriously.

'Aw now Mr Slyne, sir, shure no polidical meedin' ever started on time, id's agin de nature a' de ting, ye know. Dey do have ta come a long ways, and dey do have ta have a drink, an' dey have ta have dere tea, an' dey have ta meed dere friens, and dey have ta get themselves inta de mood for de meedin', and dey have — ' he broke off and wiped his forehead, which was beginning to bubble with sweat, 'an' when dere's two meedins, an' dey do have ta go ta diffrunt places before an' wash dere hans, like ye know an' — '

'Yes, yes, I know all about that. Would it be possible for me to see these people before the meeting?'

'Oh no, sir!' Donie was shocked. 'De ladies have ta go ta de church for de Stayshuns, like dey do every night, bud dere goin' earlier tonight juss so as ye woant have ta wait a minnit longer —'

'A minute longer than when?' Slyne went to the window, touched the edge of the faded and frayed curtains which had once been green, and were now a sort of mud-in-the-moonlight colour. He gazed out at the high wall of a church with two towers and a large flat tomb dominating the entrance to the side door.

'Dat church dates back ta 1640,' said Donie cheerfully, glad of a little respite from business. 'An' d'ye see dat tomb? Well id 'as a liddle gate an' ye can walk down intit, if yer smallish, and visit de coffins, all covered wid red velved dey are, lovely — '

Slyne turned back abruptly from the window.

'I expect if I get to the meeting at half-eight it will be all right?'

'Anytime ye like, sor, annytoime ad aall — ' Donie dragged out the vowels like a rug he was wrapping round himself, 'De'll fine ye, never fear.' He stopped and cocked an ear. 'Jasus, is dat de bell?'

Slyne stared back at him; he had heard nothing.

'Idis idis,' said Donie rushing to the door, 'an' de misstrace's bell too. I muss run or I'll be cut inta liddle bits.' And he dashed out the door, leaving Slyne staring after him with a bemused expression in his blue eyes. Then he looked at the collapsed table, and sat down slowly on the edge of the bed. There was nothing for it but to wait.

Mrs Katherine Anne Daly occupied two fine apartments in The Duke of Clarence: one was her sitting-room to the front, overlooking the street; the other, her bedroom, to the back, where it was quiet.

The sitting-room was generally accepted as being the finest in Bridgeford. It was very large, had two high windows to the front, and another to the side overlooking the Protestant church with its 'walk-in' tomb, so that there was little in Church Street that Mrs Daly did not see from three classically shaped and strategically placed look-outs. These windows were hung with heavy blue velvet curtains, trimmed with tiny gold tassels, and surmounted with pelmets of the same colour and design. The use of net curtains was scorned, and would moreover have blurred Mrs Daly's view. She had excellent sight — indeed, it had been said that she could pick a lock with a glance — and could survey her world from a comfortable armchair set well back from the windows, where she was a mere blur to the passers-by, or so she imagined. Occasionally, when something very special or convoluted was happening, like the time a visitor had a fit at the top of the Friary Lane, after coming from confession, and tried to tear all her clothes off, Mrs Daly would move to the glass and frankly stare; but these were moments when everybody else was staring too.

The room was high ceilinged, had a fine eighteenth century moulding, and a centrepiece from which hung a splendid Waterford glass chandelier. The carpet was worn but well preserved, old Persian and priceless, with shades of the most subtle hue blending one into the other in an elaborate and intricate design. It had been brought from India by a British officer in love with one of the Daly girls in the middle of the nineteenth century. She had taken the carpet, but married a Catholic.

The furniture of this superb room was in no way overshadowed by the carpet, the curtains or the eighteenth century chandelier. It was mostly George III and George IV. The end wall, facing the front windows, was filled by a magnificent mahogany breakfront bookcase of the late eighteenth century, and contained a collection of splendidly bound books which Mrs Daly never read, but which Canon Sharkey, who was the literary man of the town, pronounced to be of great value.

Mrs Daly did her accounts and wrote her letters on a George III bureau with walnut and satinwood stringing, and the chair she used for her desk was a George II library chair, while the saddle wing chair she sat in to look out of the window was of the same period.

Tables, chairs, a red lacquered cabinet on a silver stand, embroidered silk screens, delicate damask fire screens, tripod tables and Regency card tables, old Chinese bowls and heavy Irish silver candlesticks, trays and teapots, gleamed and shimmered in this gorgeous room. The few people who, greatly daring, had had a peep into it, after bribing Donie heavily while Mrs Daly was away, pronounced it as 'worth two fortunes and a sudden death.'

But the most prominent object in this room of muted old colours and rare old woods, dull satins and luminous silks, was the enormous scroll, magnificently framed in heavy gold leaf, and reaching from the carved mouldings down to the marble fireplace on which it almost rested. It was the illuminated family tree of the Dalys of Dalys Court and Kingswood. All the way from Murrough Mor O'Dalaigh and his bride, the Princess Emer of Dalchaise, both of whom flourished two centuries before Christ, according to this manuscript hand-painted by the nuns. Often would Mrs Daly stand in front of her Adam fireplace, which was genuine and extremely valuable, and gaze up in reverent awe at this tumescent family tree, which was neither. Heavily embossed and significantly writhing silver candlesticks were placed on either side of it, and a small but weighty gold plate stood under it with a gold spoon laid beside it; rather reminiscent of the paten and spoon used on the altars. Mrs Daly, a woman of strong Catholic principles, would have been horrified if anyone had suggested such a thing to her, but the gold plate nevertheless had a religious meaning for her in the broadest sense; upon it were engraved the arms and coat of the O'Dalys.

She herself was not of course a Daly: it was her husband and his father who had gone to the feverish lengths of having the family tree drawn up in the first place. It was also they who had got the collection of furniture together. Mrs Daly's name had been Slattery, and try as she might she could find no royal pedigree for her own clan. But she had completely identified herself with the Dalys. Her preoccupation with them was that of an enthusiastic convert to a new religion, although she thought rather of herself as a sort of queen dowager, carrying on the family traditions.

Today, she sat in one of her less rigid armchairs, waiting for her tea to be brought up. She glanced at her watch and frowned. Donie was late again. Five minutes after four: it was most provoking.

'Shall I run down and see?' said her daughter, Maud, who was seated on a little stool on the other side of the small coromandel table, now covered by a cobweb-light lace cloth, on which they took their tea.

'Of course not. How often have I told you not to go running up and down the stairs, and along the corridors too, like a wild girl let out of school for a half-day?'

Maud said nothing to this. Arguing with her mother was, she had discovered, a complete waste of time. Besides, she agreed with most of the things her mother told her: it was just that one disliked being told them. She flicked the paper from a box of chocolates lying on the carpet beside her, chose a caramel cream and popped it into her rosy mouth.

'You'll get fat, Maud,' frowned Mrs Daly. 'As big as Mulldowney, awful.' She ran both hands down her own slender waist.

'Who cares?' said Maud, munching happily.

Her mother sighed. She herself never put on weight, and she knew that her figure was good. But it never had been as good as her daughter's, and she was well aware that Maud had not inherited her brilliant beauty from her.

Maud Daly was just twenty, and such were her looks, her vitality and her charm that every man who saw her instinctively wanted to join his fingers about her waist. She had a mass of glinting blue-black curls, her blue eyes shone, her cheeks glowed, her small dimpled hands gleamed, and her ankles, encased in sheer silk stockings, flashed with youth and eagerness.

Her mother was small and dry, though only forty-seven, and her thick coarse hair was an unnatural black, which showed up to great disadvantage beside her daughter. Her ugly hands were beringed, and she wore a rope of heavy pearls about her neck; she was flattered by none of them.

'What on earth is keeping that Donie?' she grumbled. She got up and walked over to an old-fashioned bell-pull on the wall and tugged it viciously.

'It doesn't work if they don't want to hear,' said Maud. 'And that tapestry is very frayed. Someday it'll come away in your hand. I don't see what's wrong with standing on the top of the stairs and yelling.' She got up and seated herself at a chair before the table. Her movements emphasized the gleam and glow, the ripple and flow of her skin, hair and gestures, so that she seemed to dispense light by merely walking from one place to another.

'And Donie has been in that man Slyne's room for ages,' she went on, staring at the chocolate box. To pick it up or not to pick it up? She decided to wait for Donie: a sort of abstinence. She ran two fingers through her curls and smiled to herself. Her small teeth made another little point of light.

'Why didn't you tell me that?' Mrs Daly did not return to her chair, but stood in her favourite position under the family tree, snapping her fingers and occasionally also cracking the knuckles by pulling them out, a horrid habit she had, which she believed kept her hands supple.

'I thought you might know.'

'That makes no difference to tea-time. He could easily send Hamlet up with it.' Mrs Daly gave her daughter a vexed look.

'I suppose he could.' Maud looked at her pink nails, innocent of varnish, and rubbed them against her glowing cheek. Then she breathed lightly upon them and repeated the treatment.

Mrs Daly moved to one of the windows and looked out. There was silence for a moment, broken only by the ticking of a Meissen mantleclock set on a small table near the bookcase. No clock, however fine or valuable, was going to take away from the pedigree above the fire-place.

'Oh, look!' exclaimed Mrs Daly, 'there's Mr MacDonnell passing by — and he's looking up.' She waved and beckoned. 'He's coming over. Oh, I'm so glad. I'll take down another cup from the case.' She trotted over to a cabinet which housed a varied collection of Worcester, Spode, Derby and Sèvres. She picked out a Worcester cup, saucer and plate, then set them on the table in front of Maud. The girl moved them to the side, then moved them back again, a thought which pleased Mrs Daly. Maud had her heart in the right place: she put first things first. Then another thought struck Mrs Daly. One should not allow a guest to see that a place had obviously been made for him. She never allowed her good china to be washed in the kitchen, but cleaned them in her own bathroom, then took them out of the cabinet and sent them downstairs to be put on the tray and carried back up again.

'Maud,' she whispered, 'run down the back stairs with that cup and saucer, and put it on the tray, oh and the plate too, so that it can come up prepared for Mr MacDonnell. If Donie isn't back, get Hamlet to carry it.'

Maud rose quickly, picked up the china with a deft movement and tripped out of the room. Her mother smiled and patted her wiry hair in front of the pier glass set between the front windows. But she had plenty of time to prepare. Old Mac-Donnell was not a fast mover. He would have to have a word with acquaintances in the street, he would have to have a few words for the Misses Mutton and Cutlet in the office, he would exchange civilities with those who happened to be in the hotel lounge at the moment. Then he would make his slow, stiff-backed and stately progress up the main stairs, using his silver-mounted cane in such a way that no one could think he was reliant upon it. And finally he would pause before knocking at the door.

Today, however, he did not. He met Maud at the top of the stairs as she was coming back from the kitchen. As he always paused for breath before entering any room, he was pleased to be able to make a double use of the moment. It was a meeting that augured well.

Maud looked up at his smiling face. He was a tall man, and she was a small young lady: as he looked down at her with one thick grey eyebrow raised, she felt herself beginning to blush. It was a horrid sensation, and it made her want to scream with annoyance, but there was nothing she could do about it. In vain had she written away, both to England and America, for advertised remedies that were guaranteed to cure it. None of them worked, and if they had, old MacDonnell and most of the other males in Bridgeford would have been bitterly disappointed. There was something in Maud Daly's blush which, added to her other charms, made her as fresh and desirable as a ripe apple on the top of a tree. The transient beauty of black curls falling on a snow-white forehead, the shadow of long, dark lashes on tender blue-cream skin below the glowing eyes, the almost imperceptible dilation of a delicate nostril, the trembling of the small pink lips, all these were aspects of a kind that could only be observed by the naked eye: Maud, like many another beauty before her, took a bad photograph.

Old MacDonnell always did the same thing when he found Maud blushing. He reached out the silver head of his cane and touched her cheek lightly.

'Oh, Mr MacDonnell,' she always said, taking the knob of the cane and reading the inscription on it. His name, and a date in May 1905. It was a perfect way of subduing the embarrassment of reddened cheeks, and both of them knew it.

'That's when Mr O'Conor was made a senator, wasn't it?' she said.

'Yes, indeed. He always said he'd never have made it but for me. He would have made a great President.'

At other times, especially when her mother was not with them, she would ask for the political history of Patrick Joseph O'Conor, Senator for the City of New York. MacDonnell told this tale in a wonderful way. He was a born story-teller.

'Mammy is expecting you.'

'Yes, I know.' He smiled down on her again. It could not be denied that at sixty-eight — it was commonly rumoured that he was seventy-five, eighty, ninety — MacDonnell was a credit to Ireland and the U.S.A. A handsome, white-haired, broad-shouldered man with patrician features, he looked lavishly well in his grey tailored suit, his gleaming white shirt and thick silk tie. He held his Panama hat in his hand.

'You know, Maud dear,' her mother was apt to say, 'if I were your age, I'd go for MacDonnell like a pin to a magnet. He's so handsome, so well-preserved — his hands, did you notice? Hardly any liver spots at all, most unusual in anyone who's lived in America, he could be fifty as far as his figure is concerned. I must say I think he's divine.'

'O Mammy,' Maud would murmur, giggling and plucking her cheeks to disguise her blush.

'And don't call me Mammy, it's so common, call me Mummy or Mother, but not Mammy. My God, you sound like one of the laners, mammay, mammay, mammay all day long, and half the night too.'

'Yes, Mammy,' Maud would answer and run from the room, laughing.

Now her mother suddenly opened the door and looked out on to the landing.

'She's a terrible girl, isn't she, Mr MacDonnell?' she said, shaking her jet wire head.

'Oh, terrible, terrible, we must do something about her,' responded MacDonnell. It was a litany.

Before Mrs Daly could continue, Donie arrived with the tray, his knees bending under the weight of it. Mrs Daly believed in having the whole works, as it had been in her mother-in-law's time. Then there had been scones and three kinds of tiny sandwiches, tarts and muffins, jam and slivers of toast, and fruit cake, and walnut cake, and coffee cake, and madeira cake. On rare occasions when an old friend came, one who had lived in the really great days of afternoon tea, there was even a small salad and a lightly boiled egg.

The present Mrs Daly had made some alterations in this snack. Only two kinds of sandwiches were served, madeira cake always, but only one other cake — walnut today, luckily old MacDonnell's favourite — and not even the resurrection of old Mrs Daly herself from the family plot in Cornamagh cemetery would have forced the present holder of the Daly title to provide lightly-boiled eggs and salads. Enough was enough, she was wont to say, as her eyes darted greedily over the simplified fare.

But the accoutrements, heraldic symbols and sacred vessels accompanying this *te deum* to the family pride, had not changed; the heavy tray, the kettle, spirit-lamp, teapot, milk jug and bowl, spoons, butter-knife, butter-plate and toast container, with its hot water compartment, were all Irish silver, old and rare and valuable.

'O God in heaven missus I'm terrible sorry for de delayin',' panted Donie as he set down the tray on the table, gasping like a swimmer who has just attempted to break a record. 'Id's dat Mr Slyne, 'e 'ad me in 'is rooam, axin' me de daftust questions y'ever heard in all yer nanny, o me o my, de Lor' deliver me from Englishmen!'

'What sort of questions?' said Mrs Daly sharply, while Maud went to fetch the kettle, which was always taken off the tray at the door and left down on a side table, supposedly to ease the burden for the carrier. This ritual dated from 1887, when an untrained maid had collapsed when carrying up tea for the parish priest of the day.

'Aboud de histry a' de place, he wus readin' some kind of rawmeesh of a guidebook. I tole 'im d'otel wus famous from pole ta pole wid — ' he was about to say 'the British officers', but desisted out of consideration for old MacDonnell's feelings — 'foreign visitors. Better known dan de Shelburnt in Dublin, I tole im. An' he knocked down a table an' broke id — ' Donie straightened his back and pursed his lips like a prune.

'Broke it!' Three voices exclaimed at once.

'Why?' said Mrs Daly, solo.

'Clumsiniss, caan'd walk from wan end a de rooam t'dother widout knockin' down sometin'.'

'It will have to go down on his bill,' said Mrs Daly firmly. 'The round-topped walnut table, was it?'

'Yes'm.'

Old MacDonnell looked at Mrs Daly with admiration. He knew, and he knew that she knew, that half the furniture in the public rooms of The Duke of Clarence was either swaying with dry rot, or coming apart for want of repairs: all except where they were sitting, which was kept shining and regularly examined by an expert from Dublin.

'That was a perfectly good table — perhaps a little glue — all the same he'll have to pay for repairs.'

'Yes'm.' Donie knew that Mrs Daly wouldn't dream of

putting the collapsed table on Slyne's bill, but appearances had
to be kept.

'What else did he say?'

'Nudden much, except about de meedin' tonight.'

'I see. Well, that's all, Donie.'

'It's awful the way Donie puts on his Irish act for strangers,'
she said when he was gone. 'And it's such an awful accent, all
does dose did dat dese and dose an' me fadder and me mudder
an' thikin' an' trut' for truth and fate for faith, I used to be
terrified that Maud would pick it up when she was a child.'

'Mr MacDonnell has his Senator O'Conor stick with him
today,' put in Maud, but her mother did not seem to hear her.

'He never acts up with me,' said MacDonnell, stirring his tea
and smiling into Maud's eyes. 'But, of course, the accent is
genuine local.'

'Oh, nobody does it with you,' said Mrs Daly, helping herself
to a slice of bread and butter so thin that one could see the light
through it. 'They wouldn't dare.'

MacDonnell smiled and chuckled. Although he had been in
the States for forty years he had never developed a Yankee
accent.

'What's that you said about Mr MacDonnell's stick, dear?'

Maud was prepared for this. Her mother often underheard
something that was said, but she always brought it up again.

'Oh, that. He has several silver-handled sticks, and they
were all given to him by U.S. senators.' Maud blushed again,
but not as violently as before. This time annoyance with her
mother kept her blood cooler. These switchings about of the
conversation were, she well knew, calculated to keep her in her
place.

'I never knew that,' said Mrs Daly with a great show of
surprise. 'Is it true?'

MacDonnell smiled and nodded and dutifully handed over
his cup for another round. He could see that his hostess was
pleased, and he himself was immensely gratified that Maud
had made the remark. A little progress made, perhaps.

Mrs Daly chatted about the sticks and the Senators who had
presented them, not one of whom was known to her even by
name. She knew it pleased her guest. But there was, after this
suitable prologue, more serious business to discuss.

'What is this Slyne man giving for the land?' she asked, after a level of silence was attained, a sort of plateau devoid of other vegetation that might divert their interest. Tea was being sipped, but slowly, and the load of eatables was beginning to curl at the edges.

'Sixty pounds an acre,' said MacDonnell promptly.

'I had only Donie's word of it, you know,' Mrs Daly nodded her head and looked at him knowingly.

'I don't think he's been offered even a small tip. It isn't necessary — his wife owns some land up there, you know.'

'Poor woman,' sighed Mrs Daly who paid Donie nothing, fed him as sparingly as she could — although here she had to contend with Mrs O'Flaherty Flynn, who believed in plenty for everyone — and expected him to live on tips, which, miraculously, he did. 'All those children. Still, God bless them.'

'I think it's awful,' said Maud suddenly. She had been sitting very quietly without movement, as was her custom when her mother was entertaining important visitors. Although the Sacred Heart nuns in Mount Anville had given her a well-disciplined education, she possessed a natural gift for stillness. This had always impressed MacDonnell in particular, accustomed as he was to the spinning tops of American womanhood. Maud was delicious, plump and sensuously coloured, yet curiously nun-like. He was bewitched by her, and he knew he would have to do something about it soon.

'This meeting tonight,' Mrs Daly was saying. MacDonnell did not expect her to ask his advice about the land she herself owned up the bogs. She always pretended she knew nothing about it, and she would continue to hold this position while getting the last penny she could out of Slyne through Donie. 'What's it going to be like?'

'A big meeting. All our people will come.' MacDonnell flicked his waistcoat with a silk handkerchief. 'I don't know about the others. The Free Staters never had monster meetings, they have nobody like Mr De Valera.' Here his voice was lowered, and Mrs Daly felt that if he were wearing his hat he would lift it. But he was smiling at her. 'Most of their supporters are like you, ma'am. And you don't attend political meetings.'

Mrs Daly smiled vaguely. MacDonnell transferred his gaze to Maud, looking at her with hot blue eyes and a smile at the corner of his mouth. Maud was staring into her lap, but she gave her admirer a quick glance from under her lashes that was far more effective than the friendliest word.

'Some of Mr Cosgrave's supporters are down in your bar already, Mrs Daly,' said MacDonnell in a teasing voice. 'Drowning their sorrows before the event, no doubt.' He chuckled, and Mrs Daly poured another half cup of tea, after holding up the pot and raising her eyebrows at her guest and at Maud, who appeared to have retreated into her own dream world again.

'I wish you'd agree to selling me one of those lovely plates you have,' said MacDonnell. He was looking about the walls at the collection of Lambeth Delft plates that Mrs Daly's father-in-law had got together. They filled the vacant places on the walls instead of pictures, and were very striking with their plain modern colourings; an anticipation of the abstracts, the Adams man had said, and MacDonnell had heard of it, but didn't know what abstracts were. But he had flair.

Mrs Daly didn't understand it either, but had had every item in the room valued by Adams of Dublin for insurance, and for her own information, so she knew the price of everything in the room. And the Delft, she had been told, was before 1700 and extremely rare.

'It's not really mine to decide,' she said with a sigh. 'It's family, you know, and a sacred trust. It'll be Maud's charge one day.'

MacDonnell paused before changing the subject. He was embarrassed by so direct a hit, expecially as he knew it was done to wake Maud up. But she looked so lovely, lost in her own world. Now she gave her mother a furious glance and looked at the window. She had been thinking of nothing in particular, just allowing herself to drift in the pleasant haze of lethargy. But she always heard the call to arms when it came, as it always did when her mother was near.

'Well, that was a wonderful tea, ma'am. It reminds me of a restaurant in New York, before the war, which was entirely French. They didn't serve tea, of course, I'm talking about the quality of the food, the presentation, the marvellous vessels and all that. They used to serve snails on Sèvres plates.'

'Good heavens!' said Maud, turning to MacDonnell and smiling. 'The nuns had a complete Sèvres dinner service, it belonged to the wife of Louis XVIII. We weren't allowed to touch it. But to gaze. We called it 'The Save Us Set.' Like, if the nuns ran out of money — '

'Oh no, Mr MacDonnell,' said Mrs Daly quietly, disregarding Maud, 'the French never eat disgusting snails. That is a widespread misconception, I don't know how it came to be accepted by so many people of good education and experience, although the name of what they do serve is so similar, somebody high up got confused, and it's gone on to this day.' She smiled pityingly at her guest, who seemed amazed, while Maud turned pale rather than red.

'No?' he said wonderingly. 'Of course I only picked up a knowledge of these things as I went along in New York. Far from them I was reared,' he went on disarmingly. He found this confession an immense help in all sorts of company.

'No, Mr MacDonnell, what the French serve and eat is not snails — it's nails.'

'Nails!'

'Nails. You know that rusty nails left in a jar produce a fluid that's full of iron. Well, the French, who really are geniuses when it comes to cooking, save up all their rusty nails — some buy hundreds of them and store them in a damp place — then they grind them up in a special machine, rather like a coffee mill, and then they mix the dust with a special sort of wine and mould it into the shape of a snail. It's amazing the number of people who really believe they're eating horrible snails, instead of delicious, good-for-you nails.' Mrs Daly smiled and cracked a finger or two.

MacDonnell was left speechless for a moment, an extremely rare occurrence for him. Could Mrs Daly be mad? He knew that in every other way she was so sane as to be intimidating. But, of course, he knew nothing, absolutely nothing about French cooking, and those so-called snails he had eaten — much against his gorge — in New York long ago did not taste like anything he had ever eaten before, or since.

'Is that a fact?' he said weakly.

'It is indeed.' MacDonnell got the message, and glanced at Maud, but she was again staring into her lap and this time did not look up.

'You'll be at the meeting tonight?'

'Yes, ma'am, I'm one of the platform party.'

'Of course. Will you be meeting Mr Slyne?'

'Perhaps. Of course I'll tell you — '

'You *are* kind. That Donie — I must have some protection —'

'Don't worry about that,' said MacDonnell, as he rose to go.

'See Mr MacDonnell downstairs, dear.'

'Yes, Mammy, of course.'

'Maud!'

MacDonnell who knew about the struggle and was all in favour of 'Mammy', smiled to himself, and followed the girl out on to the landing. There, the hum of the Free Staters in the bar rose like the distant rolling of waves. There rose also the rich, tangy smell of neat whiskey, stronger than the salty sea. MacDonnell who had made much of his money in bootlegging, sniffed the rich air and shook his head, as if cherishing fond memories.

'Tell me,' he said, putting his hand on her arm as they went down to the first landing. This was a good place for a quiet conversation. Here, on a stand, stood a potted plant, grey with years and insects, and beside it, an old leather armchair, sagging at every spring but still doing duty as a symbol. Stop here and rest weary traveller, it seemed to say, and you will have a bigger shock when you see your bedroom. 'Tell me. Was your mother in earnest about the snails?'

'Oh yes, absolutely. She was once up to Dublin in the train with Lady Longford — you know the one with the big fat husband, and they run a theatre?'

'Yes, yes, I've heard of them. Is she odd?'

'Well, she must be, because she told that story about the nails to Mammy, and ever since Mammy has believed it absolutely. Queer, isn't it?'

'If you ask me, this Lady Longford must have a dry sense of humour. What would you say?'

'I'd say she has. To have Mammy, of all people, on like that!'

'It's the title, you know, Maud my dear. All Free Staters are silly about the Brits and their titles. Pity.' And he squeezed her elbow before going off chuckling. An exquisite unresisting arm — what were politics even, to that?

At eight o'clock the main square of Bridgeford was almost deserted. The two lorries, with flaps open at the sides from which the candidates were to speak, had already been put into

position, but there was no one near them. The workmen who
had driven them there had joined the rest of the crowd in the
three principal pubs facing the square: The Palace Bar,
Butler's Select Grocery and Bar, and Finnerty's Select Grocery
and Bar. The sounds that could be heard from outside these
establishments were thick and deep, though muted. They were
packed, but it was unusual for manslaughter or homicide to
commence until after the meetings were over, and the speakers
departed. Otherwise they might be embarrassed, or even
compromised.

The square at Bridgeford was rather like the setting for a film
with a nineteenth century background. The great, grey castle,
which Slyne had been reading about earlier, took up most of
one side of the open space, and completely dominated the
western end of the bridge. It seemed squat and massively
pressed into the ground from the opposite side of the square;
but on either side of the great keep, the streets dropped down to
river level, and the side and back of the castle were high,
overbearing and blind to anyone looking up from Main Street,
or the docks. Tiny windows and a few sinister gun-slits, high up
on the walls, gave it a peculiarly short-sighted and press-eyed
look. It was a fortress that brooded inwardly, with deep dark
dungeons that few of the townspeople had ever visited.
Ponderous, covering ground that no one could imagine ever
having been open, it squatted like a giant hippopotamus
bogged down in the mud by the river's side.

Over the top bastion the tricolour flew, adding a note of
heraldic fantasy to the grim battlements. There were people
whose hearts swelled with pride whenever they saw the
national flag flying over this ancient bastion of foreign
domination, but there were those who were cynical.

'Y'ever hear the story of the Normans and the Irish?' a
customer had asked Fenny one day in his bar. 'Well, the
Normans built all those castles and thought they were a cut
above everybody else as a result. I don't know what it is about
castles that gets people.'

'Dough,' said Fenny promptly. 'You can't afford to build one
without the loot, and you can't afford to live in one without
more loot.'

'Well, that's the truth, I declare to God. But the Normans
said that while they were livin' in their stinkin' aul castles, the

Irish were in huts with rush roofs. And d'ye know what the Irish said? They said: "Oh, we prefer the song of the lark to the squeak of the mouse." That shut the Normans up, I can tell ye.'

Facing this great castle across the wide square was the high iron-stone wall of the military barracks: the historical and present reason for the existence of Bridgeford as an important centre. Up they reared, these arrogant barriers between the civil and the military might, and at the end of the wall, not quite in the square, but set back from it a little, was the huge, arched barrack gate, nailed and studded and brazen and bronze-faced; the most emotional centre in the whole of Bridgeford.

Behind these gates, the British had built one of the largest military settlements in the country, covering an area of over forty acres in the centre of the town: square and parade ground, rows of high stone offices, sleeping quarters, various messes, rigidly separated from one another, a major's house, a colonel's house, quarters for adjutants, quartermaster-generals, record keepers, signals and communications, and every other department necessary to the running of an army, ready at any time to defend both Connaught and Ulster against the unlikely event of anyone having the ambition to take them over. Indeed, it was generally accepted by military strategists that in any invasion of Ireland, in order to hold Ulster, it was first necessary to have Bridgeford. Hence the great open space of the barracks across the way from the bridge and the castle; an enormous concentration of military might to control the passage from east to west.

The barracks possessed a curious mystery for the locals, since few of them had ever been inside it, although soldiers were a natural feature of the scene in the streets, and had been for centuries; the long occupation by the redcoats, and in these later days, the Irish troops in their green bulls-wool uniform. And over the stone-plumed gate, itself a heraldic device of brutal design — a war-horse rearing up in opposition to the mud-grey hippo — beyond that remorseless gate, the tricolour flew also; brave and sprightly and new both to the world and to itself.

'Be the hokey,' a passerby would say, 'will ye look up at the green white, and is it orange? Have they d'Orangemen included?'

'Green white and gold, Harry. Not orange.'

'Well, what's the odds? They won't hold Ulster anymore.'

'Yes, they will, Harry, they will.'

'D'ye mean our lot? What would they want with Ulster?'

'All the same they made a brave sight, the British, with all that gold braid, and plumes and bearskins and red coats, and the horses, did ye ever see anything like the way they kept the horses? Glitterin'.'

'An' "Goodbye Dolly Grey" and "Tipperary". Ah well — '

At nine, a few stragglers drifted into the square, some coming round from the side of the castle, from the pubs in Main Street, others appearing as if by magic out of the side of The Palace Bar, which stood opposite the barrack gate. Those coming over the bridge paid no attention to that narrow street between the gate and the bar. It led to Connaught Street and the bogs: strangers took the sharp turn to the right at the bridge, and went along the new road between the barracks and the river, the road to the west and the stone-walls and the blue mountains. They retained the impression that the square of Bridgeford was rather like a theatre setting, with its line of tall eighteenth century houses, facing the bridge, its lowering keep, its armed camp and its striding soldiers.

At twenty past nine the lamps were all lighted. Micky Hatter, the stick-man, as well as the town crier, was given a cheer as he flicked up every lamp. Then, suddenly, a group of men got out of motors parked along the river side of the barrack wall, and walked quickly to the lorry, parked with its back to the houses. Chairs appeared from behind, followed by a long bench for the back. Men in dark suits, some wearing hats, and a few country tweeds, took up their places on the platform, while behind it two Civic Guards appeared, and stood looking in front of them, blank-eyed, dough-faced, seeing and hearing everything. This was the platform for the Free Staters, the Fine Gael party which had, until recently, been in power for ten years. A small crowd of quiet shuffling men gathered below the lorry, and a man on it stood up and began to introduce the main speakers.

'Fearless integrity . . . respected by friend and foe alike . . . brilliant academic career . . . a cornerstone of the new Ireland . . . our great privilege . . . first time in this ancient and honourable town . . . ladies and gentlemen. . . .'

Donie, who had a sixth sense, the devil's scent as it was

known, had advised Mr Slyne not to leave the hotel until the
meetings were well under way. At half-past nine he knocked at
his door, behind which Slyne was enjoying a quiet gin and tonic
to help him recover after his dinner of tepid Brown Windsor
soup, hot, tough mutton on a cold plate, and mortified ginger
pudding.

'Time to go, sir. De Dev min are comin' oud. I'll run over
firss an see ta de landowners, you juss folla, an' stan' ad de other
side a' de bridge, outside de Fadder Matthews Hall, de red
brick-brack buildin' wid ids groun' floor on de street, an' de rest
of id down in de river. Id's a cinemat, ye can't miss id. Tarzan
dis week.' And off he trotted.

Back in the square things were livening up. Men suddenly
burst out of the pubs, and appeared from the Barrack
Street-King Street entrance, came round the side of the castle,
swarmed across the bridge, and ran out from behind the
opposition lorry to form a great crowd in front of the De Valera
candidate's platform. Then the cheering began, the singing of
songs and the shouting of slogans. The lorry, which was parked
under the castle wall at right angles to the opposition, filled up
quickly with men in brown boots, caps, soft hats and various
coloured suits. The whole thing, the sudden arrival of the
crowd and its representatives, like a chorus from the wings,
made the square, with its great grey walls on which the gas
light flickered, throwing shadows like the ghosts of history,
appear very much like a stage setting of a Verdi opera. The
curtain was up, the footlights glaring, the cast waiting and
making a sound like a half-muttered chorus of conspirators,
setting the stage for the star tenor.

He came marching across the bridge, led by a cheering
crowd of men, all carrying lighted and flaring sods of turf on the
ends of pikes, held aloft and waving dangerously in the fine
evening twilight — that Irish twilight which lingers in June
until midnight. It was a barbaric entry, worthy of Attila, with
the pikes blazing, the men now roaring, the cheering and
screaming in the square, all making a tremendous noise, not
musical, like so many early Verdi choruses, but true, apt and
inevitable. The candidate was carried shoulder-high between
the flaring pikes, and thrust bodily onto the lorry. Cheer after
cheer rose and fell as he waved his hands, held them up and out
in front of him. He could have been singing a succession of

fierce top notes over an unruly band; and the time was not yet
ready for recitative. The crowd began to sing:

> De Valera lead us,
> Soldiers of the Legion of the Rearguard.

On they went in different pitches, roaring out different lines
from time to time, but making a huge noise of male triumph and
uneasy victory. The flaming pikes waved, the caps were thrown
into the air, the boots stamped upon the flinty ground, and the
din re-echoed from the castle walls and went faintly out over the
great river, lingering over the flat meadows on either side.

'A cairde gael!' A small man was standing in the middle of
the lorry, trying to make himself heard by the mob. 'Men and
women of Ireland. Descendants of the saints and scholars.' The
mob roared louder, until after a few minutes of rising hysteria, a
tall man, dressed in a brown suit with a broad green sash across
his breast, pushed the little man aside, planted his fists on his
hips, and glared down at the crowd.

'De Valera!' he roared. The noise increased. 'I'm here to
speak on behalf of The Chief,' he roared louder still, and
immediately the crowd in the front began to simmer down, and
after a further call in the leader's name for quiet, silence was
suddenly restored. The grim hush that follows the fall of a
hammer on a stone.

Donie arrived at Slyne's side just as the candidate — for it
was he — was introducing himself.

'My name is Kelly, Eamon Kelly, and I'm here to ask you to
vote for Eamon De Valera' — cheers broke upon cheers, waved
into silence by Kelly, who had now established complete
control of the mob. 'The greatest leader Ireland has had since
Cucuilan, Brian Boru and Parnell — ' the cheers were louder
and higher now, but shorter. The crowd was responding to
Kelly like an orchestra to a masterful conductor. 'Look at that
flag over there, high above our military barracks! How long was
the hated emblem of the oppressor flaunting itself there?'
'Seven hundred years,' roared back the crowd. 'Aye, and it'd be
seven hundred more, if De Valera didn't appear at Easter Week
— remember Bolands Mills! — and freed this proud country
from tyranny. Wolfe Tone couldn't do it, Grattan couldn't do
it, Lord Edward couldn't do it. But Dev did it!'

Roars, screams, jumpings up and down, caps flung into the

air, then a silence like the sudden switching off of an engine. Kelly knew how to punctuate his words, having established control of this chorus. 'That green, white and gold was put over that barracks, which now houses the green-clad and proud soldiers of the new Ireland, all this came about because Eamon De Valera was sent to free us from the yoke — '

'If we dodge in 'ere,' said Donie to Slyne, 'be d'edge o' de road, be de footpat', we'll get over ta d'odder side.'

'What did you say that man's name was?' Slyne whispered, as they made their way carefully round the outskirts of the mob.

'Kelly, Yamon Kelly, as big a hoor as ye'd meet from here ta Baltimore, he'd take de glass eye outova blind man's eye and sell id for a marble ta de kids, also de fillin' outs yer teet', an' de patch outa yer trowsers pocket, an' sell id to a tailor.' All behind Donie's hand.

'He knows how to control a crowd.'

'You said id. Willya lissen t'im.'

But by now they had moved into the orbit of the other platform, on which a well-dressed man with fair hair was talking, a sheaf of notes in his hands.

'The gross national product of this small agricultural country has fallen to eight and four-fifths of what it was in 1930, a year of dismal recession and unemployment in every country in the world. Unemployment is up by 12 per cent, and in the last years alone, the De Valera government have transported nearly a hundred thousand people to England, to work in the mines, toil on the roads, break their backs in the building trade, like hired coolies in China or Hong Kong.'

'And who is he?' whispered Slyne, halting to listen.

'Mr FitzClarence, sir, a gintleman.'

'Oh, so that's the way you vote,' said Slyne, laughing low.

'Christ, no. I'm fur Kelly an' de Man. Bud doan tell de missus dat, she's a mad Free Stater. All de Dalys wus.'

In front of them two men stood back and looked over to the other speaker.

'Aw God,' muttered one of them, 'figures. We might as well be back at school. I don't want to listen to this stuff.'

'And, anyway who is he to say we're a lot of Chinese hoolies, whatever they are. And breakin' our backs on the English roads, Jasus! That's a good one.'

'A Chinese coolie,' said a woman who had joined the two

men, 'is the lowest form of animal life in China. The nerve of him — '

And they drifted off followed by several others. Slyne had noticed that people on the rim of the Fine Gael crowd were edging towards the Kelly platform. Only the hard core, solid blue shirts, remained.

'A Gaelic Ireland for a Gaelic people,' thundered Kelly, 'Let Erin remember the days of old, when Malachy wore the collar of gold, and we were ruled by our own princes and kings, the oldest in Europe, next to the Greeks. Our own culture, the finest flower of Christendom. That's what we want, and that's what De Valera has pledged himself to restore.'

A great cheer went up and echoed back from the walls of the castle. Slyne could just hear by standing a little behind Donie, who had paused to listen to Kelly, and the faint voice of Mr FitzClarence.

'In two years' time, half the calves in this country will be slaughtered, and the farmers ruined. The dole queues will lengthen from every corner of Ireland to the mail boat in Dun Laoghaire. Incomes will fall, and the grass that is growing in some of the streets of this town will spread like a fungus, encouraged by the Government, over the whole ancient borough. And when all the hundreds of thousands have been exported to England, like cattle, De Valera will claim that unemployment is down.'

'God Almighty,' Slyne heard a voice behind him say, 'Wouldn't that aul Fitz put years on ye. Him and his cattle! What's the bugger Kelly sayin'? Come on Mickser.'

'But the dream will not come true until we have rubbed out the partition of this proud island off the face of the map. Down with partition! We want a United Ireland! What did the martyrs shed their blood for? Not for an Orange state where Catholics are treated like niggers, they the original princes of the province, their proud heritage denied them — '

'Down with Partition!'

'Soldiers of the Legion of the Rearguard. De Valera lead us —'

'Up the IRA!'

'Up the Republic!'

Donie began to move away sideways, and Slyne followed him.

'Id's hottin' up,' whispered Donie.

'Most interesting though,' said Slyne in his ear, 'the difference between the two styles of speaking.'

'Ah sure, dat Mr FitzClarence — he offen comes inta d'otel an' Mrs Daly tinks de world a' him, a gread auld famly, dey were out wid Parnell — an' he'd mow ye down wid misery. Bud a gintleman.'

They had now sidled their way round the edges of both crowds, and Slyne allowed Donie to take his arm to guide him to the back of the Fine Gael lorry, where in several deep shop doorways the landowners awaited him. Mrs Prendergast had insisted on bringing Miss McLurry and Hosannah into one doorway. When they protested, she rounded on them.

'What kinda fool are yez anyhow? Don't ye want to keep Coffey's doorway for ourselves, and not have every passing slut pressing herself in. An' supposin' it rains?'

So there they were, flanked on both sides with wax models, displaying the latest styles for men and women — men in the right window, women in the left. Donie made his introductions in a low voice but with some elaboration.

'Mr Hector Slyne. Mrs Marcella Prendergast, Miss Sarah Jane McLurry, and Miss Susannah Braiden, all extensible owners a' lan' in de beootifool area dat yer innerisked in.'

They all shook hands, and Mrs Prendergast was the first to speak.

'Is there any mistake about the price you're offerin'?' she said softly. Kelly was roaring away, but sound was muffled in the deep doorway, nearly four feet long, flanked on either side with large glass display windows to show off Messrs Coffey's drapery.

'I hope not,' said Slyne. He looked from one to another of the eager faces dappled with light and shade in the doorway. 'You've been told of the amount. It's — '

'Sssh,' hissed Mrs Pig. 'Everybody is listenin'.' Slyne glanced briefly at the wall of backs presented to him, he heard the fierce cries of the crowd, then turned to see Miss McLurry holding out a slip of paper to him.

'Just write it down please, so that we can be sure.'

Slyne took out his pocket diary, and holding it under the paper wrote down what they had been already told. But of course they wanted to make sure that he was offering the same price to all; that there were no secret deals.

'What's this "according to situation"?' Mrs Pig enquired. It was something they all deplored.

'Well, as you know, some sites are more suitable than others.' Slyne's voice was almost drowned by a section of the crowd who had begun to sing something which was unfamiliar to him, and also to them, he assumed, since no words beyond the first three could be made out. He looked at the ladies with raised eyebrows.

'It's de National Anthem,' explained Hosannah, putting her hand to the side of her mouth, and standing on her toes to inform him. Slyne was assailed by an extraordinary smell like dry rot and fungus — it was the only way he could describe it. 'None of them know de words of it, of course. Silly ole song anyways.'

'It is not,' said Miss McLurry firmly. 'It's the finest anthem in the world, everybody knows that, better even than the French one.'

'That's given up by all to it,' declared Mrs Pig.

'Given up?' said Slyne in amazement.

'Id's local fur bein' admittened be everywan,' whispered Donie in his ear. He was an old hand at translating the native idiom for strangers.

'Oh, I see.'

'It's the finest land this side of Mullingar,' said Mrs Pig. 'That's given up to it be all.'

'So it is,' said the other two in unison.

'I'm sure it is,' said Slyne. 'When can I see it?'

The ladies withdrew into the depths of the doorway and whispered together while the National Anthem, which signified that the Fine Gael meeting was over, went on and on and on.

'No time like the present,' said Mrs Pig coming out. 'Tomorrow?'

'Yes, indeed. What time will suit you?'

They withdrew, whispered, returned.

'Half past seven in the evening. You see, we're all businesswomen.' Miss McLurry was speaking now, 'and I don't close my shop, but as a special concession to a visiting guest, I'll do it tomorrow. My busiest time of the year too, especially after seven.'

'Good.' Slyne looked at Donie, who nodded in return. He could get away at any time.

But the De Valera supporters were not going to let the opposition get away with singing "The Soldiers' Song", the official National Anthem. They had their own.

Twas the twenty-eight day of November
Outside the town of Macroom
The Tans in their big Crossley tender
Were hurtling along to their doom
(Dere Do-oo-om, yodelled a lone tenor.)
The lads in the column were waiting
Their hand grenades primed, on the spot,
And the Irish Republican Army
Made balls of the whole fucking lot.

'Oh Mother a' God,' cried Hosannah, crossing herself three times.

'God, dat brings me back,' said Mrs Pig dreamily. 'Great days.'

'Shocking language. The patriots didn't talk like that,' said Miss McLurry severely, although she revered the sentiments, sometimes.

Suddenly the singers began to waver and then fall back, silent. Another voice rose above the crowd, weak, plaintive, hardly heard.

'Ladies and gentlemen, I must ask you not to sing songs of a controversial nature, ah.'

'Up the Rebels.' the singers replied lustily.

'Up the Republic!'

'Up the IRA!'

'Gintlemin, *a cairde gael* — '

'That's Baldy Sullivan, Kelly's hatchet man, nod wort' a dam wid de crowd,' said Donie. He and the ladies had observed that the Fine Gael crowd was now beginning to disperse, and some were lingering at the edge of the Fianna Fail crowd. The women exchanged glances, and Miss McLurry spoke up:

'I'm afraid we must be going now, Mr Slyne. It's late for us elderly ladies to be out — and all those men—' she broke off, and before Slyne's eyes the three disappeared — there was no other word for the swiftness of their whisking round the corner into Barrack Street. They were gone.

'Would anyone attack them?' said Slyne wonderingly.

Donie gave him a cynical look.

'Dem wimmen id be safe, locked up naked in Mountjoy, wid lickur smuggled in, an' de boys on de loose. A cure for concupissence is wha' dey are.'

And now Slyne noticed that shadows were moving quickly, backwards and forwards, on the window glass on each side of him. The gas was lit, the long twilight was deepening. Shades were reaching out over the square.

Then, quite abruptly, a high tenor, followed after a moment by a large chorus began to sing again:

St Patrick's Day we'll be merry and gay,
An' we'll kick de aul' Protestants out of our way.

'Oh,' said Slyne, beginning to feel uneasy. But just as Donie laid a hand on his arm, a new voice arose from the platform, over the heads of the crowd.

'You there, that's trying to sing, God help us, don't you know that this is a sovereign independent nation, with an army and a parliament of its own? And that all religions have equal rights here? Don't you know that Wolfe Tone, Grattan, Lord Edward, Robert Emmet, aye, and the greatest of them all until De Valera came to save us, Parnell himself, were Protestants? Sing, "The Soldier's song", that's our song, and doesn't belong to the opposition.'

'Marvellous,' said Slyne quickly. 'Who is he?'

'Ole MacDonnell, de ony man dat won't sell de land ta ye. Bud he's terrible rich, an' has a terrible effect on a crowd. He has ta do dis at ivery meetin', oh, he's a great man surely.'

'At every meeting?' said Slyne, beginning to understand. 'You mean it's a kind of ritual, like a church service?'

'No, I wooden say id wus religus, no, id's more like dem bull fights dey have in Spain, somewan tole me about dem. Shortly now we'll have a fight. Dat's why de land-owning ladies left so soon.'

'Hadn't we better get out of here?' said Slyne nervously, speaking into Donie's ear. Outside the haven of the dark glass doorway, the National Anthem rose and fell in a mighty if untuneful chorus.

For answer Donie rang the bell, which was set over the door to prevent children from swinging out of it, and running. It rang inside four times, the door opened silently, they slipped inside, and it was closed again behind them.

'Tank ye very much, Mr Coffey,' said Donie, 'Ye'r a gintleman.'

'Don't mention it,' said the draper politely. 'Perhaps you'll introduce me?'

Donie made the formal introductions and the two men bowed, while outside the singing stopped. There was a sudden lull, policemen appeared as suddenly as the women had disappeared, and in a few moments the square was filled with shouts, screams, yells — men in mortal agony, or so they believed as their hair was pulled back from their heads, and their shins neatly and effectively kicked. There was nothing quite as useful as that famous undercover kick. It had laid out mobs by the hundred since the Free State was founded.

The men in the shop moved to the window and watched the fun outside. But after a few minutes their host decided that they would have a better view from upstairs, and he led them out of the shop, into the hall-door passage, up thickly carpeted stairs and into a big room, where a woman was sitting on a red plush sofa, saying her rosary. This was Mrs Coffey, who put her beads down, and prepared to entertain the visitors.

Slyne found himself sitting beside her; a plump, middle-aged woman with a kind face.

'And how are you finding Bridgeford, Mr Slyne?' she asked in her best hostess manner.

Although the windows overlooking the square were heavily curtained, the blue repp had been pulled back for the summer, and Mr Coffey and Donie were peering out from behind the inner lace curtain.

'Bloody Blueshirts!'

'Who murdered Mick Collins?'

'You did, ye effer!!'

'Who licked Lloyd George's a—?'

'Beautiful weather we're having, Mr Slyne,' said Mrs Coffey, cutting in on that one. The shouts could be plainly heard in the room.

'Oh, ah, yes quite.' Slyne managed a smile, but he was furious at Donie for arranging it so that he missed the fight.

'Up the IRA!'

'Up Dev!'

'Up Cosgrave!'

'Who split Ireland?'

'Who signed the effin' Treaty?'

'Are you enjoying your stay among us, Mr Slyne?'

'Oh yes, indeed yes.'

'Kick him in de balls, bloody Blueshirt!'

'Who went in at de Dail wid guns? Gunmen, terrorists, murderers — '

'Be de cross a' Christ, I'll divide ye!'

Mrs Coffey got up and went to a bamboo cabinet beside the fireplace.

'A little drop of port?'

'Ah, no, Mrs Coffey, too kind of you.'

'Whiskey perhaps? You can't leave with the curse of a dry mouth on you.'

'The port, please. Too kind.' He was straining his ears to hear what was going on outside. But all he heard, while Mrs Coffey put back the port in the cabinet, was a whisper from Donie: 'Be the hokey de Gyards is movin in.'

'How many are stretched?' said Coffee excitedly.

'D'ye see dat big long leeb of a fella? Well — '

'Well, *slainte*, as we say in Ireland,' said Mrs Coffey, holding up her own glass of port.

'*Slainte*,' said Slyne, who was a quick study.

'Lave us alone, ye blue bastards, spawn of d'RIC. Hired killers.'

'Have respect for de law. Dey're our own, tanks ta Cosgrave.'

'Murderin' bastards, swipe de balls off thim!'

'Aow murder murder murder murder, hauld me back biys, or be de Cross I'll divide thim.'

'Up de Republic!'

'Up Dev!'

'Up de Irish Free State!'

'Have you a good book to read at night in the hotel?' enquired Mrs Coffey politely. 'There's nothing like a good book.'

'Ah,' said Donie, half turning from the window with a disgusted expression, 'dere ony shoutin' sloggins, while de peelers pick up de dead.'

'Dead!' exclaimed Slyne, putting down his glass of quite excellent port, and jumping up from the sofa. He was at the window in two strides and peered out between Donie and Mr Coffey. But the action seemed over. The Guards were helping men to their feet, while other members of the force linked arms on either side of the central area, where it would appear that most of the fighting had taken place. A man lying just outside the clearing seemed dead enough to Slyne, but he suddenly jumped up and disappeared into the crowd. The remnants of the mob began to sing "Faith of our Fathers."

'The real national anthem,' said Coffey with a smile. Then he turned away with the air of a connoisseur. 'I've seen worse.'

'I doan tink dat'll go down as wan a' de great meetins,' said Donie with a disgusted expression. 'Ony a few drops a teet' blood, an' nod a single bone broken.'

Below in the square, the 'few drops' from broken teeth and raw knuckles glistened under the yellow lamps. The Guards had, with perfect impartiality, marched off six men to the barracks in Excise Street behind the castle; three from the Cosgrave supporters, three from the opposing camp. There they would be given strong tea, and a teaspoonful of poteen to help sober them up. No charges would be brought. They were put to bed on blankets in the one cell the station boasted of, and unless a wife came along in a towering temper and demanded her man, they would be left to sleep peacefully until the morning.

Back in the square, everyone disappeared after the arrests were made. Many went home to tell a tale of derring-do and fiddle-de-faddle, raised by the telling into deeds of heroic proportions. The others melted into the bars, where they recommenced their interrupted drinking, and began the legend of the Blueshirts, which meeting by meeting during the next few years, assumed monstrous growth in folklore. They had been first named at that meeting in Bridgeford in June 1933.

But in Coffey's drawing room, it was as if nothing had happened. And it took Slyne rather more than his usual ten seconds to scent the social implications. Although she once or twice included him in her smile, Mrs Coffey never addressed Donie. Slyne finished his port and got up, thanked his hosts profusely and left with his 'guide', as Mrs Coffey thoughtfully called Donie.

They walked silently to the hotel.

And so the next evening, which was as mild and lightly coloured as the day before, Slyne and Donie had gone down to the water-meadows, by way of the docks on the Connaught side of the river, where canal boats loaded with flour, Guinness and other necessities of life were tied up. A large amount of Bridgeford's comestibles, drench and draughts were sent by barge, and delivered in the town by drays pulled by enormous Irish draught horses. Donie had a word with the keeper as they passed the lock gates, and slipped round the sewage pipes at the end of the convent wall, on to the meadows.

These fields, known as the Queen's Meadows, were a splendid sight, below the town by the river's edge, on a fine summer evening. But none of that enormous parcel of land was for sale. Fenny owned a few acres near the convent, a great stretch in the middle belonged to MacDonnell, while the rest, here, there and hidden, was owned by the Church. Fenny was already there, waiting for them.

No matter how often he came down here, in winter or summer, Fenny was always moved and delighted by the scene. It was not a conventional beauty spot. It was one in which a sense of limitless space was suggested by the flat land, flowing away to the south by the side of the river, an illusion heightened by the sky, which everywhere reflected this vastness, this glowing plain full of gentle colours, green, blue, brown fading into pink at the clearly drawn line of the horizon.

The land on either side of the river was flat, meadows blending into dark bog-land, and here the Shannon could be seen completing its great arc around the town; a half circle joined at the bottom of the horse-shoe by a canal, trim, neat, narrowly contained. But by the shore of the river, the stones sprinkled along the muddy edges had a temporary look as if they had been put there by children for the summer. For nothing contained the Shannon. Soft-rooted rushes were equally fugitive.

Simply by bending a little, Fenny could see trees, bushes and roofs sharply outlined against the sky. Once, dropping to his knees, Fenny had seen three men in single file walk across the rim of the world against a milk-blue summer sky. It was an image that always remained in his mind, like the first sight of a horse in early childhood, or the realization that someone — in his case, Ellen — walked in grace upon the face of a world grown suddenly brighter; or the first note of music heard by an ear with true pitch, or the earliest memory of the beating of wings. These images, familiar and quiet, had the same vivid wonder for him as the discovery of an unknown valley, startling in its colour and contour, might have for some old explorer in Tibet.

But it was the stillness above all that moved him most. Then, Slyne and Donie came up to him along a narrow path through the high, yellowing grass. Above them a lark thrilled; and Fenny held up a finger, and cocked his large head to one side. For a moment, which Slyne was to remember for the rest of his life, just for a few unsplit seconds, the song of the lark seemed to hover over a world that was perfectly still, and without even the echo of any kind of other sound.

The river gleamed and glinted in the sun, a few yards from where they were standing: it could be seen at the end of another footpath through the meadow grass; and it too was soundless. For a little while, which struck Donie as queer, the three of them stood motionless, while the lark hovered and thrilled above their heads. Then, mercifully as Donie thought, for he could not bear to be silent, the sound of chugging began to be heard. One of the big canal boats was coming up the river from Limerick. The spell was broken.

Nevertheless, Slyne remained in a receptive mood. He turned and looked back at the town. It rose above them, its spires, roofs and single tower, cleanly and darkly outlined against the evening sky. And a few windows here and there glittered in the shimmering light, while the river moved like a great serpent under the bridge, its ancient and only boundary.

'How lovely the skyline appears from here,' said Slyne softly.

Fenny looked at him sharply. He was surprised at the Englishman's tone. There was a note of genuine feeling in it.

'Like a Dutch landscape,' said Fenny with a smile.

'Yes, and no,' said Slyne holding out one forefinger, and tapping it with another. 'The flat land, of course, and the objects outlined against the sky. Also the sense of isolation.'

'But not of space?' He had a book about the artists of the Lowlands. 'I mean not in the Dutch painters.'

'No, it is domesticated. And space is a very rare quality in any painter. But I was thinking of something else — the colours here. The extraordinary shifting quality of the light. It is never hard, as the Suffolk light is, it is curiously radiant and soft. And then of course the subtle shades, the browns, blues and greens, all most delicate. It's exquisite country.'

'Ye mean roun' here?' said Donie, who had been listening impatiently to this nonsense, and had just stopped himself from adding, "up the bogs" to what he said.

'Yes, of course,' said Slyne. 'That's why I selected it for my holiday homes. It's relaxing, no garish colours, everything muted and quiet. The silence, the soft air, the sense of space. Yes, I think it's unique, certainly in the British Isles.'

'But nobody has ever painted it,' said Fenny after a pause, during which he shot a sharp look at Slyne's rapt profile. After all, the man was not a fool. Just what was he up to? How curious the English were.

'Haven't they? That surprises me. Although I went to the National Gallery in Dublin, and as you say, most of the landscapes were Connemara, Donegal, Kerry.'

Donie dug his toe into the clay of the path, well trodden for generations, and baked to a bread-like firmness by the heat of the sun. Soon, he would have to find an excuse to break up this conversation.

Donie found something to say which killed two eggs with the same fist.

'Oh, where's me manners, gintlemin, I never intraduced ye, Mr Slyne, dis is Mr O'Farrell.'

The two men shook hands and smiled.

'Here we've been rattling away for the past ten minutes, and never an introduction,' said Fenny. 'Very dreadful, Mr Slyne.'

'Well, I wasn't absolutely certain that you were Mr O'Farrell, but I assumed you were. And anyway, we haven't talked business, have we?'

'No, true.' Fenny thought that Slyne was no fool, not anyone's fool for even a minute. And he wondered the more at him. Curiouser and curiouser the English got, more like Alice in Wonderland, every minute you knew them.

'Ye weren't at de meetin' las' night,' said Donie accusingly. 'I tole Mr Slyne dat he'd meet all de land-owners dere. A course de tree ladies wur dere.'

'And there's only one other, apart from Mrs Daly. As a matter of fact, I couldn't get away from the bar, it was very busy.'

'Of course, of course, I understand,' murmured Slyne.

But Donie was not convinced. Naturally Fenny would hear of this evening's meeting here from the women. But why had he said he'd meet Slyne at the political meeting in the first place? All publicans knew that political shindigs meant heavy business.

'I hear old MacDonnell made his usual intervention,' said Fenny to Donie in particular. One had to be careful not to leave Donie out of a conversation. He could be difficult and treacherous.

'Yeh, de usual.'

'You mean the man who spoke about the Protestants?' said Slyne, looking at the barge chugging up the river. A line of swans veered towards the rushes to let it pass. Swans on the river and something in the air, the song of the lark, the ripple of the river water at the edge of the meadow as the barge passed on — how quickly it had come up stream — the dipping green-gold meadows flowing away, the silence that was returning like a cloud after the boat, or like a ghost displaced by a living man in an empty room, passing through, passing through.

'Protestant,' Slyne heard himself saying, 'you know, I never heard that word until I came to Ireland?'

'Ye mane ye have no Prodistands in Englan'?' said Donie, amazed.

'Well, you see, in England we have the Church of England, of which I am a member, and we are called Anglicans.'

'Bud y'are Prodistands?' insisted Donie, his curiosity getting the better of his deep-rooted native cunning.

'Well, no,' explained Slyne patiently, tapping his forefinger again, 'We're Catholics, Anglo-Catholics, you know. We merely went back to basic Catholicism a few hundred years ago, reformed ourselves you might say, that's all.'

'So dats wha' de call Catlicks in Englan',' said Donie thoughtfully. 'I never knew dat. An' I tinkin' ye were a Prod, imagine!' Donie gave the new convert a brilliant smile, a wide, gap-toothed grin that wrinkled up his eyes, and brought out two deep dimples, like belly buttons, in his plump cheeks.

'Well, actually, they're called Roman Catholics in England,' explained Slyne with a sort of playful patience. Fenny smiled to himself. The age-old Irish-English confrontation was in full debate; hatted and wigged, musketed and bannered, incomprehensible, mildly daft, and smokily dangerous, as it had so often been by the banks of the Shannon river.

'RC, is id?' declared Donie hotly. 'Id's nod right ta call a Catlick a Roman Catlick. De nunners tole us dat.'

'Did they?' Slyne smiled. 'Well, I daresay they did. But in England Roman Catholics describe themselves as such. It's accepted.'

Donie looked helplessly to Fenny, who nodded and winked. The effect on Donie was like a shot of raw whiskey. He jumped a little, opened his mouth and drew in air as if to cool his throat, and grinned again from belly button to belly button.

'Aw shue, shue, I know well, Mr Slyne. I wus ony havin' ye on. D'aul blarney, like ye know.'

'I rather thought you were,' said Slyne. And there the matter rested on a boggy basin of mutual misunderstanding, as so many other arguments of greater consequence had rested and rusted, for so many hundreds of years.

'Here come the ladies,' said Fenny, looking upstream above the high meadow grass. And through it the ladies came indeed, in single file on the narrow path, paddling their way along, with hands flapping on either side over the grass, as if they were wading through shallow waters. Mrs Pig came first, and if there had not been a considerable distance between the ladies, the other two would have been blanked out by the width of Mrs Pig's countenance and shoulders. As a tribute to the occasion she had left off her frieze coat and put on her old grey-brown showerproof, which she always wore unbuttoned, thus exposing a vast expanse of bosom decently covered by a blue overall. With her wild fuzzy hair, her large and piercing eyes, and firm jutting jaw, she was handsome in a barbaric way. A necklace of amber, a few dozen gold bracelets, and some great rings, and she could have been the great pirate queen herself in everyday attire, before or after visiting the court of Elizabeth I.

Fenny, who had seen Mrs Prendergast cleaned up a few times before, was not surprised. He remembered her as a young wife, vividly handsome, full-breasted and high-nosed, so that she looked like the prow of a ship — even then it would have been a pirate ship. There was nothing small about Mrs Prendergast.

'Good evenin', min,' she said graciously.

'Good evening, Mrs Prendergast,' said the men in unison. They repeated the salutation as the other two land-owners joined them, except that Hosannah and Miss McLurry were not on the same word.

'Thank you so much for coming here,' Slyne began with a courtly inclination of his head.

'Don't mention it,' said Miss McLurry, who was highly sensitive to elaborate manners. 'The pleasure is all ours, I assure you, and more than ours, if I may put it that way. Very kind of you to ask us, I'm sure.'

'Indeeden it was,' put in Hosannah, not to be out-mannered. 'It's a favourmost place for us all ta walk, and what could be nicer?'

Fenny stood back a little, his thick, slightly bandy legs planted wide apart, his splendid stomach stuck out, his chins resting on his chest, his eyes darting like tiny birds of a bright hue, from one to another of the motley group. The civilities were going to be long and well-plumed.

'An' a gorgeocious evenin' too,' said Mrs Pig with a smile.

'Best this summer by far, o far far,' said Miss McLurry warmly.

'Tanks be ta God,' said Hosannah. 'He looks down in favour upon us, like me poor mudder used ta say.'

'You are enjoying your stay?' said Sarah Jane McLurry, producing a pink parasol which she opened, not without some dust sprinkling the air, and thrust out straight into their faces, before resting it coquettishly on her large left shoulder. The two other ladies gazed at her in amazement, they having taken it for granted that Sarah Jane had brought an umbrella, faded to the colour of nothing on earth, in case of rain. She now twirled the parasol with a practised hand, as she often did in front of the glass at home.

'What a pretty parasol,' said Slyne as if he meant it. 'My mother always carried one in the summer. It *does* bring back memories.'

Mrs Pig and Hosannah said nothing. They were thinking that it was a bad case of aping up, and the way Sarah Jane was simpering was disgusting.

'Ah, summermsummermm,' cooed Sarah Jane, 'what is more beooitful than evening by the river, with a parasol to shade one's eyes from the heat and the glare?' And she shifted the pink parasol from one shoulder to another, as if she had been using it every summer of her life. It was too much for the other ladies.

'It makes yer face all red,' said Mrs Pig, looking at her distastefully and sniffing, as if the parasol had a bad smell, and indeed it was a bit fusty. 'Ye look like ye have de German measles or de scarletina fever. Very flushed y'are.'

'An' yer all blotchety too,' put in Hosannah, going round through the meadow grass to have a good look. She was up to her waist in potential hay and looked like some old, prehistoric bird with her beaked nose, always with a drop at the end, her small glinting eyes, and her incongruous flat mass-hat perched on the top of her thin hair.

And poor Sarah Jane did look blotched, for the parasol, like human skin, was spotted with dark yellow patches like liver spots. Damp. In spite of Mr Slyne's approving smile and kind words, Sarah Jane suddenly felt hurt and ridiculous, and her broad red face began to crumble. Fenny came to the rescue.

'I remember that parasol, or one like it, when I was a youngster. Of course you were only a kid then, Miss McLurry, so it must have belonged to your mother. But we all thought it was beautiful. A pink parasol on a summer's day, what could be nicer? Susannah, I'm surprised at you. You're jealous, that's what you are, and Mrs Prendergast, too.' And he folded his red-haired arms across his chest and frowned. Slyne and Donie, in their separate ways, looked startled. It was the first piece of straight talking that Slyne had heard since he came to Bridgeford.

'I am not,' said Mrs Pig firmly. But she said no more. Fenny O'Barrell had a way with him and was slightly feared by most of his neighbours in the street. He was a sort of arbiter of the place: a travelled man, he was instantly and instinctively recognized as non-provincial. Never put in words, it was known and felt. Also he was well read, had been taught Latin and Greek, and his parents had been educated before him. And he could write a good letter. All these factors added to his presence.

'And now,' he said blinking a little, 'isn't it about time we got down to this business of the land?'

'Indeeden id iss,' declared Donie loudly, so that his voice re-echoed faintly from the river.

'Is everybody — ?' began Slyne, looking about him.

'We are,' declared Mrs Pig firmly. 'It'll be de middle of de night soon if we don't foot dem lands. Not dat I wouldn't be able ta see da corners on a summer night like dis, but we all have to be up in de mornin' airly, or some of us do.'

Fenny smiled at her and she grinned back. Mrs Prendergast was not a woman who took affront at every word that was said by friends, and she liked Fenny. Fair play to him, if he stayed in bed until all hours in the morning; it did not worry her.

'Does everybody know what acreage they have?' said Fenny.

'I have id in me han' an' me head,' said Donie quickly. 'Mrs Prendergast five acres, two roods and fourteen perches; Miss Sarah Jane McLurry four acres, three roods, and six perches; me wife, Mrs Elizabeth Bridget Donnelly, nee Caulfield, five acres, two roods and eleven perches; Miss Braiden three acres, nine roods and sixteen perches; Mrs Katherine Anne Daly — ' and so he went on ticking off each measurement on a finger, while the others heard their property read out as if by a solicitor after a big funeral. They stood quite still under the slanting sun which turned the swaying meadows amber, the river to a dark brown, and lit up the faces of the trees, leaving the backs of them in a violet shadow. No one noticed the pair of plump rats plopping into the water a few yards away from them, nor the line of swans, pink and white in the glow, or the pony running along the edge of the earth at the end of the flat fields. They all assumed that each knew what they owned down to the last spadeful, so Donie's reading out of their acreage did not surprise them in the least. Nor did they think it odd that he could drop his lazy native dis-dat drawl and put on a fine stage accent for the enunciation of such important detail. They all listened attentively until he was finished. He was correct down to the last inch.

So was Mr Slyne. He had consulted the maps and records of the Ordnance Survey — made, he noted happily, in the British time — as well as the local county council charts, dating from the same period, and had his Dublin solicitor check them twice over.

'Thank you, Mr Donnelly,' he said with a little bow, which impressed everybody, except perhaps Fenny, who had however already agreed to sell a portion of his land near the town, and had nodded his head when Donie read it out. It was a smaller lot than the rest, and he had bought it years ago for his pony, but the pony was very old, and he had been thinking of acquiring a motor. Besides, there was something about this big deal of Slyne's that appealed to Fenny. It seemed so completely cock-eyed — and he wanted to find out if it was not.

'I'm sure you're absolutely correct in your measurements,' went on Slyne casually. 'We won't fall out over a perch or two, will we?"

They all laughed. They would cause someone to fall off a cliff, or hold his head under the river water over less than a perch, but of course the Englishman had to be humoured.

'Well, shall we be going along?' Slyne looked about him. All the pieces of land adjoined one another, which was why he had contacted those present in the first place. If he had wanted land further down river, or up river, he would have been dealing with different people. Naturally he expected each one of them to foot their property with him, in the time-splashed custom of buying and selling land. He was a little surprised when Hosannah and Miss McLurry stepped back and shook their heads.

'I'll waid 'ere for ye,' said Hosannah. She knew what she was going to get, and did not fancy the idea of trampling halfway over the bog, when she could get her money by simply standing still. Besides, her old shoes, the newest she had and eight years in wear, would not stand under the tramp.

'So will I,' declared Miss McLurry. No one, except Slyne, was surprised at this. She had never had any intention of footing her own land, otherwise she'd not have arrived for a tramp through soaky paths, and ditches bridged by slipper-slidy planks, in a pair of high-heeled shoes, and flaunting a parasol like a lady. She too knew her work would be done for her by others.

'Come on,' said Mrs Pig briskly, starting off with a look of disapproval at her over-dressed friend. Then she was off down the trail, and preparing for the first ditch, head up and body tensed and gathered, like a seasoned old show jumper.

'Off we go,' said Fenny, after some business with Slyne as to who should lead in the narrow way. Slyne was reluctant; after all, he did not know the place as well as they did. Eventually Donie, impatient to be off to count his wife's acres and money, trotted on ahead, and the others followed.

Almost immediately Miss McLurry plumped down on a stone, polished to a high gloss by the backsides of Connaught Street inhabitants, who had rested here, year after year, while on their walks by the river, among the whispering meadow grass.

Down went Sarah Jane, her full skirts billowing out, so as to cover the whole of the stone, which was able to hold two persons whose flesh was acquainted and gave off no aura of mistrust or aversion. Two greyhounds, brought up together from earliest puppyhood had been known to squat on this stone, but not Sarah Jane McLurry and Hosannah Braiden. The latter, with feet aching, back creaking and joints slowly stiffening up as a result of the water underfoot, gave her companion a look of pure, heightened and unambiguous hatred.

Miss McLurry was not prepared to forgive Hosannah's remarks about her parasol easily, so she spread her skirts still wider over the stone — very bad to sit on a stone: piles, — and gazed dreamily into the distance. Not a care in the world had she, twirling her parasol languidly and a sweet little smile playing about her pretty lips, like a fine lady in a play.

Hosannah stood, bent a little forward, her mouth open on her terrible teeth, her red-rimmed eyes glistening, and her wisps of hair hanging down like spiders' legs from under her mass-hat, the only one she possessed. Then she straightened up a little, licked her blue lips and prepared to lift the McLurry slut, with her airs and graces, off the face of the stone, if not the meadow.

'Are ye,' she began softly, 'are ye nod a bid worried ad bein' oud ad dis time a de evenin'?'

Miss McLurry whose instincts were as finely tuned as anyone in Bridgeford, brought back her gaze from the void, like the Queen of Spain who, she had read, focused her eyes well over the heads of her subjects in audience, so now she looked vaguely over the top of Hosannah's mass-hat.

'I am frequently out at this time of evening, at this time of year,' she said in a flat voice. Then just before Hosannah retaliated, she lowered her eyes and her parasol a little. But Hosannah, returning her unspoken cry as if it were an object beneath a pawn-broker's notice, prepared for a direct hit.

'Well, nod very offen,' Hosannah went on, 'nod two nites

runnin'. An' dere's ta be annudder evening' a' dis.' She paused, and craned her long unplumed neck to see the others' bobbing heads over the uncut hay, retreating into the orange-red, shot-eyed sunset with a pony moving back along the coal-fire edge of the world, as the party footed the sunken fields. 'Id'll take 'em two or tree nites more ta finish dis business.' She contracted herself and looked again at her victim who was staring at her with horror in her eyes. 'I mane dere's nowan ad 'ome. Aren'd ye worried, I mane, no wan ad all. . .'

It was never mentioned in Bridgeford, this fact of Miss McLurry's retarded brother. He was kept in a back room over the shop, and had never been seen by anyone since the handywoman delivered him on a bitter night in December, crossing herself when she had a free hand, and never breathing a word, even to her husband, of the child that had been born alive to poor, frightened, galloping-consumptive Mrs McLurry and her big, thick-mick husband with the hog-mouth, ear to ear like a split banana, a neck like a horse's flank, and feet as big as sacks of meal. Both of them, husband and wife, were dead within two years of the monster's birth. Sarah Jane was eighteen at the time and carrying an extra layer of trouble-fat since before she was ten.

Some said that the brother had only half a head, growing out of the stump of another; others, that he was all head and little else, hideous and slobbering, and given to loud wailing like the barking of a fox; still more, and especially the children claiming to have seen a head, half animal, pig-donkey-badger-cat, peering out of the upstairs window at the back of the house. No one knew for certain. Sarah Jane would not even allow the priests in to see him. She said he had already been baptized and that as far as sin went he was not responsible: which Canon Sharkey and Father Raft had to agree with. Sarah Jane McLurry had succeeded in burying her brother alive in the full gaze, narrow-eyed and piercing, of the whole of Connaught Street. It was so extraordinary an achievement that people were overawed by it and deferred to her arrangements. No one was ever brought behind the shop in McLurry's; no one mentioned the awful thing that was sometimes heard to bark in the night. In time no one wanted to know. And now, nearly forty years after her brother's birth, Miss McLurry was gazing into his reflection in the eyes of Susannah Braiden.

She reacted instinctively, the blood running down under her billowing summer frock, and gathering in a pile of mud about her ankles, and aimed straight for the most vulnerable part of her antagonist's visible skin and secret half-knowledge. She opened her handbag, took out her handkerchief and held it against her nose, looking at Hosannah steadily above it while the sinking sun set them both ahaze in a shimmering, lurid glow.

Hosannah knew that she was unclean, knew that her clothes were old, worn, soiled and smelly, that her feet and her teeth stank, that it would take a hospital bath to clean her and a fortune in new clothes to cover her decently. All this she knew. And knew also that it was worse than Sarah Jane's half-buried brother.

But Sarah Jane herself, having given Hosannah her answer, was left with a curiously empty feeling. Further discussion of the things they had indicated to each other was unthinkable. She must get away from this subject at once, and merely to walk away home was not enough. She would have made a mortal, unspeaking enemy, and that was always uncomfortable, especially since they had a common interest at present. And God only knows what Hosannah would say about her. She might even succeed in making poor Christy a subject of gossip, something she had for so long successfully avoided. Supposing she said he was getting better? That would start tongues wagging again.

Nevertheless, it was Hosannah who broke the silence. Something equally fundamental in her nature uncoiled itself from the mixed and raging elements of her iddy-biddy and the twisted guts of her mind. Besides, if she continued to share the monster with Sarah Jane, he would grow between them and drive both of them mad. All this Hosannah knew in her bones.

'Oo,' she moaned, swaying from side to side, 'I'm nudden bud a rodden ole bag a' bones in de sight a' de Lord God, Jesus help me, Mary pray, amn't I down on me knees half de nite imploratin' God an' 'is blessed sains ta overlook me humiliality an' rise me ub fur ony God knows how far down I am, ole an' shakin' an' harly able to breat' wid me cough an' ivry bone in me body achin' an wakin' an' queakin' like mice in de nite in a cage an' nudden bud worse ta look forward ta all de few days a' me life dat's left ta me, O Lord I'm pudden true me Purge-a-tory on dis 'eart', worse dan de leppers dat de Lord rus ub an' rubbed clean, bud id'll never happen ta me, me sight is goin' an' me chest is congregated wid pus, an' I can harly get down on me knockers ta implorade God ta help me, I have ta do id standin' ub ad de mercy a' every breeze dat blows, an' wheniver de church door does be open, a knife goes through me like id was rusted for de job, O woe, woe — '

.'Now Susannah, you mustn't let yourself think like that,' said Miss McLurry, much relieved at this turn of events, this rolling-over sideways of a soul. 'I'm sure there isn't another man, woman or child in the parish including the Canon who is nearer to God than you are. If I said a tenth of the prayers that you say I'd be flying by now. Now, now.'

'O woe woe woe woe,' moaned Hosannah, 'an' me standin' near de place where me ansistors wus driven ta Hell or ta Connaught be de English divil wid de name C, an' we wus always dacent people, ta tink dat I have ta sell me inheritance t'a stranger dat may be a low soljer's son for all I know.'

'We all want the money,' said Miss McLurry simply. She made no effort to make room for Hosannah on the stone: after what had passed between them it would have been impossible and unnecessary. They were far beyond small, civil gestures. There was a knowledge of murder, desired and wished for, between them.

'Egcep' for Mr O'Farrell,' said Hosannah, resuming her normal everyday manner, as Sarah Jane expected she would.

'And he doesn't need the money.'

'So far as we know.'

The two women looked at each other, probing for secret knowledge withheld, sensing rather than seeing. But it was not there. Fenny was solvent.

'I think he's just joined up for the fun of it, if you ask me,' said Miss McLurry, who knew Fenny better than he imagined.

'Fun!' Hosannah made it sound like the cry of a strangled cat.

'And of course he knows that the small parcel of land he's selling is the only outlet to the town, except for the bog road, which is a long way round.'

'Oh, yes, I forgot,' said Hosannah humbly, bowing low and coughing fustily into her fist. 'Oh. Oh.'

'So he'll get a bigger price than anyone. O, there's no flies on Benedict O'Farrell. Of course he didn't get it off the ground. His father was a very shrewd man, and even though the mother was stuck-up and grand — the bishop, you know — she didn't throw away any money either. And Fenny's married a good, working wife.'

'But ol' MacDonnell is de man dat holes de rale openin' — or de rale ting, as dey say in Kekrerry. He has all de land on a level wid de town. Ony de Canon has as much. Well, so dat's ony right.'

'A perch or two less in fact,' said Miss McLurry. Then, as it was growing quite chilly, she stood up, found herself swaying a little and had to support herself with the parasol. She looked out over the fields, to where the men and Mrs Pig were still bobbing about like corks in a twilight sea.

'They're — where?' Miss McLurry screwed up her eyes.

'Dere wan fiel' yet from de cross-river,' said Hosannah, who claimed to be going blind, but in fact had very long sight.

'And Mrs Daly has fields the other side, hasn't she? They'll hardly get over there this night.' Miss McLurry, having folded her parasol, was now firmly established on her feet and finding the support grateful.

'Yes, dey will,' said Hosannah quickly. 'Donie will see ta dat. An' besides an' before, ye can see a fiel' very well ad nite in de summer. Bud dey'll come agin, id'll take several days ta ged dis bisness starded.' She clasped her sunken chest and began to cough.

Miss McLurry waited patiently for this 'paradoxysm' — as Brother Ulick once called it — to cease. Hosannah clutched at the air, as if it were balm to apply to her cheating, crackling chest. Then, with a sudden, but characteristic spurt of life, she straightened up, brushed past her companion and sank down on the stone, which was still warm from the pressure of Sarah Jane's ample bottom.

'Oo oo ooh,' she groaned piteously, her head falling forward like a stricken goose. Hosannah had the longest and darkest and scrawniest neck in town, and on that there was no argument. Miss McLurry remembered as a girl having Miss Braiden pointed out to her as something quite extraordinary in the neck line. Which reminded her now that the creature must be seventy if she was a day.

'You should come home now, Susannah,' she said kindly. 'It's always very damp by the river at night, and you might catch your death.'

'Havven I caught id already?' panted Hosannah. 'I'm dyin' be degrees since I wus born, I'm ony haf-alive and whole mortificated'.

'Come now.' But Miss McLurry was very still and was listening. The reeds by the river swayed in the breeze, making a sound like the crackling of sweet bags, an oar was splashed on the water. Across the great meadows little sounds rose and fell in the dusky air, like fish surfacing for a moment; there was a running ripple of wind over the long grass; the sudden flurry of wings from a night bird; the distant chug of a barge down river; and from over the river, from the little park at the edge of the town, came the low gurgling sound of a woman laughing. It lingered in the air, now rising, now falling, a happy head-tilted chuckle, the signal of someone's happiness. Long years afterwards, Sarah Jane was to remember that night and recall beyond everything else that low, thrilling laugh, that vibrated across the great river. And above, the endless arc of the sky, never still even for a moment; all pulse, and flicker and gleam above the voices, the whisper, the tinkles and plops and the swish-swash of a summer's night.

'Oo, me feet,' moaned Hosannah, getting ready to hoist herself from the stone. But she paused half-way, and stood half crouched, listening. The woman's laugh floated again over the river. 'There's a trollop in Burgesses Park,' she said with a hoarse quiver in her voice.

'Oh no,' exclaimed Miss McLurry, who was feeling a rare sense of peace and happiness. Even poor Christy was forgotten for a few enchanting minutes. 'It's a lovely night.'

'Hmph,' snorted Hosannah, darting out into the path before Sarah Jane, and setting off back at a cracking pace.

The other woman, her worries and fears and the branded pain of her frustrated life all lost in the little scurrying noises of a warm night by the river, followed slowly, slowly, feeling the happiness drain out of her, like a glass of wine tilted over sand.

So she went, back to the gathering darkness of the town walls, trailing her ragged pink parasol behind her.

During the first five or six days of Mr Slyne's visit in June, Willie Wickham, who was so wetly to renew his acquaintance in November, was absent from the town. He was home on the farm, trying to sort out bills, cheques, wages, church dues, and to listen to the lengthy complaints of his old housekeeper, Belinda, and his foreman, Hughie Harney, neither of whom had good news for the young master.

'Dry rot in the dining-room floor, wet rot in the cellar, the beetle in d'upstairs beams, rats in the pantry and walking like lords round the chicken house, and the banshee screechin' every night over at Talbots. That child is goin' to die.'

This was the sort of recital that Willie had to put up with from Belinda every time he came home, and especially when he came home after a bender. The old lady was a fanatical teetotaller, having lost a husband early from falling while climbing a tree in pursuit of a bald cat with red eyes and a forked tail, that was spitting at him.

Hughie Harney's method was fundamentally the same, but the technique was different. He would knock on the front door dressed in his best Sunday suit, and no matter how often Willie tried to open it for him, he was always forestalled by Belinda, who was as fleet as a doped whippet, although she claimed she had corns as big as walnuts between every toe, ingrown nails that caused her agony every day and bad circulation which made her nights a 'mare', a cap of thorns, a fall from a high window into a pit of burning oil and an air that stank of a fat corpse unburied in the heat for a week. That was what *her* nights were like.

'It's that Harney fella at the front door,' she would say, closing her eyes and rubbing her thigh which was 'beyond all' according to herself.

'I told him, as I've told him ten hundred times and thirteen, that he's not to come to the front door, like the gintry, and the bank manager, but — ' she stopped and raised clenched fists like the roots of a little old tree, shaking them in front of her quivering jaw, 'but round the back *to me.*'

And round the back this father of fourteen children of his own name, known naturally as 'Horny' Harney, had to go, where Belinda kept him waiting, while she made a slow progress through the house in the opposite direction of the back door, to let him in. So measured were these stately progresses, that

Willie had once noticed that some of the china received its only
flick of the cloth, while Belinda was keeping 'Horny' Harney
cooling his heels on the stone outside her kitchen. Pathpavanes,
pathpavanes, thought Willie once, watching her ritual
procession.

A small man with very bandy legs, and the face of a fanatical
ascetic, the foreman's method was very different from
Belinda's. For one thing he was quick.

'Good day to ye, bosso,' he would say, flapping his cap
against his hip, and jerking his head up and down like Mr
Punch. 'Be de hokey, bud id's a gread ting to see ye again afther
yer buzness, shure ye can take it aisy now and doan worry
aboud a ting.'

After a stiff whiskey, which Willie sometimes shared with
him, if he was sufficiently steady or sufficiently unsteady, they
would sit down and discuss the state of the property.
Everything was fine, great, gone past the post, its skin had
grown again over the knuckles — and here Horny would look at
his clenched fist — after that scrape with the insurance
company, pigs were leaping to go to market, leppin' sky high, as
were the horses, and the fortune of a Vanderbilt or a Grosvenor
was standing around on the hoof for all to see.

'Tanks be ta God an' de Liddle Flour,' as Horny always said,
rolling his eyes up in the direction of the Kingdom of Heaven,
and dipping his crooked knees like a stage policeman. 'Bud ye
have all de luck a' de divil, an' he converted.'

A tour of the place afterward, or next morning more often, as
he was often too tired to set out with Horny at once, was a
chastening and bewildering experience. Everything seemed to
have gone wrong overnight, and Horny was amazed at what he
saw.

'Oh, that fence,' Willie once exclaimed, 'it was to be up,
wasn't it?'

'An' id wus ub, de finess fench in Westmade, standin' like de
Nelson monumemmon, bud a freak win' blew id down ony a
few hours after ye god home lass nite. De divil does be on full
pay in dis place betimes, sendin' 'is fairies be de squadroon ta
befuddle everyting, an' mordal man, even if he slaves noon an'
nite in two places ad de wan time, wid 'is tongue blisteraded,
an' his eyes blinded be de sweat, has ony de Liddle Flour an'
Blessed Oviler ta fall back on, an de divil disappearin' before

dey can take a shot ad 'im. Besides Blessed Oviler, isn'd even a rale saint yit.'

At other times the cattle had a murrain, or a couple of cows had aborted, or the sow had eaten half the bonhims, and was losing weight like a ship unloading lagan, or the red pony was hanging its head and sagging at the knees and before twenty-four hours was dead. And chickens which were Belinda's province, were according to Horny, the meek and willing prey of every fox in Westmeath.

'Dem chicks does be runnin' oud ta meed de fox, sir, givin' demselves up like. Ye aud ta take ta hutn, sur. Prayers is no good wid foxes, de holy saints doan reckanise dem, de're sent for a trial for us below, and for de makin' of a huntin' man.'

In the beginning Willie used to flee from these disasters, until a letter from his bank manager reminded him that he had an overdraft to pay. Willie sold some stock at a loss and paid it off, since he was too nervous to owe anything to anybody, even a bank manager. Now he still had the land, which was worth a lot of money, the house, a small Georgian building full of good furniture and silver, and a few good horses, which even Horny hesitated to give up to the powers of evil. A foreman might preside over the disappearance of a few hundred head of cattle, a college of pigs, a convent of ducks, and a congregation of sheep, but to lose more than one or two aged ponies was to suffer a serious loss of face. Horses were different, as every turtle and tinker knew. Willie kept his hunters and half-breds, which of course cost a great deal to maintain when he was not running a stud. Horny, so well blessed with abundance of offspring, seemed to be incapable of encouraging or supervising fertility in any other form.

Belinda had her own theory.

'Fourteen children go through a power of bacon, eggs and beef, if they're all as fat and snotty as them young Harneys,' she remarked one day, stroking the side of her long nose and looking at Willie with narrowed eyes.

'Oh, Belinda!' exclaimed Willie, deeply shocked.

'I know about the litany of the saints,' she went on relentlessly, 'and the power of the devil, but the devil doesn't have to raise a hand here. It's all done for him.'

Willie drove into Bridgeford after these encounters, much

depressed, and in need of loving care and sympathy. At the beginning — everything pleasant in Willie's life seemed to be associated with the beginning of things — he received it from Mrs Daly and her daughter. But after a few years the mother took to lecturing him, and even Maud began to express reservations.

Four or five days — it was not always possible to ascertain the exact day in Bridgeford — after Slyne had met the land-owners in the meadows, Willie, having spent a short time in the Trappist monastery in Roscrea, which had a great reputation for drying out drunks; and as he was young, and 'at the beginning' of his dealings with the monks, came back from the place glowing with health, strength and colour.

Mrs Daly who happened to be arranging flowers in the hall, looked around expecting to see a mere customer, and was startled.

'William!' she cried, using the name his mother always called him, and dropping an iris, which William picked up gracefully for her, handing it back with a brilliant smile. 'What have you done with yourself?'

'Nothing,' said Willie opening his splendid dark eyes innocently, and raising his beautiful dark head gracefully, 'unless it's my new shirt.' He looked down and plucked at the snappy check shirt he had bought in Tysons, before giving himself up to the monks. 'Do you like it?'

Mrs Daly ignored this remark as frivolous in the extreme, and subjected the young man to a scrutiny worthy of a medieval abbot inspecting a new novice. Hair, eyes, teeth — gleaming and strong when he smiled at her over the new shirt — hands, shoulders, legs and general bearing, were all assessed quickly and with all the swift decision of authority.

'William Wickham,' she declared, putting down the flower he had handed to her as too frivolous an object to hold, while engaged in a serious discussion, 'you have a splendid appearance, your hair is thick and glossy, you have all your own teeth — and a pity you wouldn't — and very good they are, your eyes are sparkling and those awful blue bags you had under them are gone. Your shoulders look as if you could lift a horse, your hands too, and you have a fine long straight pair of legs. A horse in your condition would fetch a pretty price, according to breeding, and remember, I knew your parents, and you have inherited your wind and limb from them. And you're very nearly as handsome as your daddy was.'

During this frank appraisal, Willie shuffled his feet, shod in hand-made leather from Callaghans of Dublin, and grew very red about the muzzle and cheek. If Mrs Daly could have seen his withers and stifle she would have noted with approval that they were shivering a little, as a thoroughbred's ought to do when under inspection. So were his barrel, gaskin and croup. He had never in his life received such a compliment as this, and his heart swelled with gratitude and affection.

But Mrs Daly did not linger long on Willie's physique or height in hands — he was six foot two in human measurements, and the object of fervent admiration from the female population of Bridgeford — all this meant little to Mrs Daly. But she was fond of the young man: he came from a good family, was quiet and well broken in, when sober; but she hated to think of all those rich acres and stock dwindling into cash for drink, even though she benefitted most from his custom. Mrs Daly's respect for money and property was such that she could not bear to see it abused, even for her own profit. She was a truly religious woman in this regard.

'Something has happened to you,' she said narrowly.

'I took a few days rest without the drink, that's all,' said Willie with perfect truth.

Before she had time to reply Slyne appeared from the dining-room, and hesitated for a moment.

'Oh, Mr Slyne, do let me introduce you to Mr Wickham.'

Slyne was surprised by this, as Mrs Daly never spoke to mere guests in her hotel and confined herself to floral arrangements. He was not even sure who she was, but he assumed she was someone well known in the hotel, so he bowed, exchanged a 'how do you do' with the well-dressed young man and passed on.

'I suppose you want to see Maud?' Mrs Daly said with a smile.

Willie smiled back, giving her every opportunity to see his healthy white teeth and the way his nose wrinkled up so beguilingly. He knew about this since a girl at the Dublin Horse Show had told him that the way his muzzle wrinkled up made her guts turn over, even when she was jumping to win.

'She's upstairs in the drawing-room.'

Willie went up the stairs two at a time and burst into the drawing-room without knocking, something he would never have done in ordinary circumstances.

Maud Daly, the secret passion of at least thirty local men and dozens of passing strangers, and well aware of it, was sitting on a high chair with her skirt drawn well above her knees, exposing a delicious pair of plump, silken thighs. She was looking down at her leg which had one hand poised with a needle and thread over a ladder that had just begun at the top of her stocking. She looked up and her rosy mouth fell open. For a dazzling moment, while Willie hung on to the door-knob, equally open mouthed, he knew he would never forget this moment if he lived to be a hundred.

'Willie Wickham, you dirty hound! How dare you burst into a lady's room like a mad ape. Were you born in a field, you big thick slob?' Maud drew down her skirt over her knees, held the needle pointed in her fingers, rose from her chair, and darkened her face with anger all at once and as quickly as a carefully rehearsed actress in a play.

'Oh Maud — ' was all that Willie could stammer, feeling slightly dizzy from the sight he had just seen. Pin-points of light ran through his mind. His knees were weak, and he wanted to fall upon them and express his share of joy at the vision he had glimpsed.

'Well, close the door, you fool, or get out,' Maud snapped, very cross indeed to be surprised in such an undignified position, especially as she had glimpsed him crossing the street, looking marvellous, and had been sure that what with her mother in the hall, she would have the damned ladder repaired before he knocked at the door. Even if she were not finished, he would merely find her with a needle and thread in her hand. Maud thought of everything, but she had not reckoned with Willie's splendid resurrection. He now stood in the doorway, gripping the handle, and gaping like a fish, but he looked healthy, well-groomed, glossy of hair and clear of eye. For the first time in her life, for Maud had known Willie since she was a small girl and he a growing boy, she realized that he was an extremely handsome man. Small wonder that silly girls giggled, nudged one another and squirmed when he passed by on the streets, or so she had been told by several acquaintances.

'O Maud, Maud, I've never felt so ashamed in my life,'

stammered Willie, whose confusion added to his newly acquired gloss.

'I should hope so,' said Maud coldly. 'I wouldn't like to think that you made a habit of bursting in on girls when they're dressing, or undressing. Not very nice.' She turned away and raised her dainty nose into the air, pointing straight at the elaborate frieze.

'I never — ' gasped Willie.

'Oh, well, I don't suppose you did,' Maud allowed, dying as she was to find out what had happened to this admirer. 'All the same, I'm very surprised, very surprised indeed, at the way you charged in, like a mad bull, without even the faintest scratch, even when you think a room is empty.'

'I know that,' said Willie, closing the door as quietly and silently as a ghost, and looking thoroughly chastened when he turned round again. 'I'm sorry.' He knew no sane person could possibly be sorry for seeing the vision that he had seen, but one had to play the game with women. They made you say things which you knew they knew were nonsense, but it was important to them that you said it just the same.

'What have you been doing with yourself?' said Maud, turning to him with so sweet a smile that he swayed a little and blinked. Maud Daly's sudden smiles, her spring-clear laughter, the lighting up of her thick-lashed eyes were famous in Bridgeford — and far beyond it. She had passed more than one stranger staying in the hotel, and given him one of her smiles, thus nailing many an unsuspecting male to the skin of his own vanity for weeks, and even years after.

The smile she bestowed on Willie was a special one, indicating that, although she had been imposed upon by him, she was not a bad-tempered girl who kept it in for others. She patted a chair at a reasonable distance from her and indicated that Willie might sit down. He did so humbly, but pulling the chair nearer than was intended. Maud had been too lazy to take a bath this morning; the weather was very hot, and she knew she was not smelling as fresh as she usually was. He *would* come in on a day like this! Little did she know that the slight smell of warm arm-pits and the sweat that gathered between her breasts in weather like this, was the scent that Willie — and many another man — loved best in all the world and found difficulty in restraining themselves when under its influence.

He made a low, slightly plaintive sound in his throat as he sat down and looked at her. Maud knew that it was really not plaintive, but the well-mannered growl of a male trying very hard to control himself. Circus lions, she thought, must be a bit like this.

'Well?' she enquired sweetly, taking up a newspaper from a table beside her and fanning herself with it.

Willie, somewhat incoherently, told her all. At the end of it she was left with two distinct impressions: that Willie Wickham, when sober, and as high spirited as he was now, was a very attractive man; and secondly, that he had a very valuable house and land which he was not managing rightly.

'That's wonderful, Willie,' she commented gravely. 'You must keep this way.'

'I've taken the pledge,' he swore. Maud knew how much this was worth.

'What did Belinda say?' she said unexpectedly.

'Belinda?' Willie blinked.

'Yes, Belinda Bain, your housekeeper.'

'She complained about Harney,' said Willie guilelessly. Little did he know that Belinda had made it her business to pay a call on Maud one day Willie had brought her into town to shop. Belinda had said little, but indicated a lot. She made it clear that she was prepared to sign a treaty with Maud should she become Mrs Wickham. And she made it clearer still that Harney must go.

'Well, naturally,' said Maud with no particular emphasis. 'Of course she would, as I'm told she's absolutely devoted to you. Whereas the whole town and country knows that Harney is robbing you right left and centre. You might be an absentee landlord the way he carries on.' She paused and gave Willie a small, slightly wistful smile. He shifted in his chair and felt his heart hammering in his chest. The same as the muscle in your arm, an elderly relation had once told him: it flexes and swells, and throbs. So people are really suffering from muscular distortion when they're in love. This had stuck in Willie's mind, and was apt to rise to the surface when he was sober and feeling swollen as a result of Maud.

'He's unlucky,' he said uneasily.

'He's very lucky to have a softy like you employing him.'

'I'm no softy,' said Willie, stung. He suddenly became aware of the light streaming through the windows, the gleaming plates on the wall, the soft and gently-blending colours; and for a moment Maud melted into them, as if it were her natural habitat. 'I've just gone through five days in Roscrea, I've kicked the liquor habit. I've taken the pledge. I'm a man who can make up his mind.'

'Then sack Harney.'

There was a long pause, during which the room and its contents assumed an even greater reality in Willie's conscious-ness than it had ever done before. He had the impression of being at one with these beautiful objects, of owning them and living for them at the same time. But after a few moments he shook his head sadly. Willie had certain knowledge of the workings of fate: it was the only highly developed sense he possessed.

'I can't, Maud.' He knotted his big brown hands and twisted the fingers to and fro. Then he drew them apart and slapped one hand with the other, as if he were punishing it for being restless and childish.

'You can't?' Maud forgot the ladder which she felt had now reached her knee, which she clutched with a firm hand.

'No, I can't.' Willie shook his head. 'You see, if I sacked him everybody would know it was for dishonesty. Where would he get a job after that, especially now in these hard times for farmers? And think of his wife and all those children. No sooner was he out of the gate than people would begin to blame me. God knows what would happen. Supposing they started land agitation?' He looked at her with a slight frown which made him appear decisive, strong, even wise in a male sort of a way. And Maud saw the point immediately.

'Yes, I know.' She thought for a few moments while the ladder ran, and Willie, leaning forward anxiously got another and even more potent indication of Maud's exquisitely sweating body, found it difficult to control himself. Love potions that cast spells were made of this.

'In that case the only thing left to you is to manage the place efficiently yourself. You must stay out there all day, give up all thought of coming into town the way you do, and drinking in the morning. You must take off your coat and watch Harney like a hawk. When he sees you doing this, the chickens will stop disappearing, and the stock will suddenly become as healthy as anyone else's. That's what you must do, Willie Wickham.'

'When do I see you?' Willie was still dazed under the spell of Maud's special scent.

'You can always come in in the evening. I can get a lift out to see you. Don't worry about that end of things. The main point is that neither I nor anyone else, unless she's a calculating slut, will marry you while you're letting the roof fall in over your head and the land to pick up its aftergrass and walk away with it.'

Willie listened to this pointed and practical advice intently. It struck him as absolutely right; just as anything that Maud might say just then would strike him in the same manner. O that sweet, milk-white body, those wide and beautiful eyes, the shining curls falling on her alabaster forehead.

'Well?' said Maud, who had remembered her ladder again and was clutching her knee tightly, another aspect of her that inflamed poor Willie. O that maddening, wonderful chastity of hers! She had not yet recovered from being seen in a state of only very slight undress. Sweet Maud.

'I'll do it,' he said in as firm a voice as he could command.

Maud was just about to reward him with one of her very special smiles when the door opened and Mrs Daly came in, bearing a silver bowl filled, through wire, with red and pink roses. She carried the bowl reverently to a table just under the pedigree scroll, and laid it down with great care on what might have been an altar. Then, after looking up in silent contemplation for a few moments, she turned to the waiting pair, Willie having got to his feet, and smiled at them both while patting the hair over her ear.

'Maud,' she said, killing two lame ducks with the one intent, 'you know my blue silk handkerchief? The one with the eau-de-cologne on it? Well, I have a bit of a headache. Will you be a lamb and run over to my room for it? I think it's on the dressing-table.'

Rarely had Maud obeyed her mother with such alacrity. She jumped up and ran from the room, leaving Willie slightly dazed by the sudden disappearance of his vision.

'Now, William,' said Mrs Daly, sitting down in the chair the blessed one had vacated, and assaulting his nose with a strong dose of expensive French scent. 'Oh, sit down, please. You've been calling on my Maud for quite some time now, and while I don't disapprove — after all, I know your family, almost as old as my own — I do not approve either, because you know, William dear, you are often such a naughty boy, I won't say how, but I'm sure the reason must be quite clear to you now.'

Willie nodded. She might have been speaking of a misuse of the most sacred aspects of life, a problem of an esoteric and unmentionable magnitude in Willie's past. An adulterer, gently admonished by a saint, could not have felt more scaly of soul than Willie did then, fresh as he was from the hushed atmosphere and the clear eyes of the monks in Roscrea. He felt as if his guts were hanging out and making an unholy stink, which Mrs Daly heroically ignored, like the saint he had read about who was lifted several feet into the air whenever a person in mortal sin came within ten feet of her.

Outside the big windows the sun was shining, dust hung and glinted in the air, carts and traps rolled and rattled by, followed by an occasional motor. People were talking and several were laughing; the whole town and all its people — so varied, so rich in incident, so warm, quick and responsive to the little events of every single day — there they all were, in the old narrow streets with the river running between them, the great serpent, but good people all; and there was Willie, miserable in the full knowledge that he was a worm with guts out.

'I've given up all that now,' he said humbly.

'Good,' said Mrs Daly briskly. Then snatching the blue satin cushion from behind her back, she punched it thoroughly, before settling it in its place comfortably again. 'What have you been saying to Maud?'

'Talking.' Willie shifted his seat and felt his thighs beginning to sweat. It was all right for the sweet-skinned Maud to sweat, but he knew it was disgusting for him to smell of perspiration. He shifted in his chair and looked very uneasy. Mrs Daly noted this, and brought her business out as quickly as a dagger-man using his blade in an emergency.

'Did you propose to Maud?'

Willie made so abrupt a movement that he nearly fell off his chair, sitting as he was on the very edge. He gripped both arms fiercely, and stared at Mrs Daly.

'I've asked Maud ten times to marry me.'

'No doubt. But you didn't ask me.' Mrs Daly patted the hair over her ears again and pursed her lips.

'Ask *you*!' For a moment Willie was confused and goggled at Mrs Daly in a most unflattering way.

'Don't be silly, William. Have you lost your wits? Although I must say, I've had many proposals of marriage, from men older — and I might say — more distinguished than you. One of them a man of title: I could have been the wife of a Baron, if I wished.' She paused to allow this to sink in, break, knock out or stagger. Willie, however, showed no surprise or interest, so she went on: 'I mean, you haven't asked me for permission to pay court to my daughter Maud.' She drew herself up, her hands lying along the arms of her chair, every ring flashing, perfectly composed as she imagined a real Baroness would be.

'Oh,' said Willie, much relieved. 'So that's it.' Then revived in spirit, he too drew himself up, tucked in the stomach he was acquiring and smiled winningly at his propective mother-in-law. 'Well, may I marry Maud, ma'am?'

Mrs Daly paused, frowned, appeared to give the matter much thought, clasped her hands as if in prayer, closed her eyes, then slowly opened them again.

'You may,' she intoned solemnly. 'You have my permission. But of course, she'll have to accept you.'

'Yes,' said Willie, a trifle downcast, for Maud had never given him a straight answer on this matter.

'And put it in writing,' added Mrs Daly.

While her mother was interviewing Willie, Maud had run to her bedroom and put a few stitches in her stocking, which had not run as far as she had feared. It would now do for every-day wear. So she took the pair off, and put on a new pair, gleaming and glistening in her hands like a couple of circus snakes, as she lifted them out of the drawer. She ran her fingers down their silken length, and then began slowly and ritualistically, as if she were performing in front of an audience, to put the sheer stockings on her white and shapely legs. She lifted one leg into the air, held it out, wriggled it, put her head on one side to admire it, ran her hand over her knee, looked at herself in the glass and giggled. Once connected with herself in the mirror, she paused and looked earnestly at herself. It was something she never tired of doing. She often spent an hour gazing at her image in the glass, turning her pretty head this way and that, stretching her neck, and slipping a dress over one shoulder so as to admire the smooth, marble whiteness of her upper arm, her plump and sloping shoulder and the shape of her perfectly rounded breasts.

These she never uncovered fully, being a modest girl, but she was aware of how well moulded they were, and how men reacted to them, staring like cows when she wore something a little lower than usual. Oh, dear, she sighed, what fools men are, going all gooey and fooey over two lumps of fat with pink tips that were as often as not a nuisance to a girl. She remembered that fat girl at school — nick-named the 'Lucan Dairy' — telling her in a flood of tears that her breasts always rolled under her arms at night, and that she longed for the courage to cut the damn things off. Maud was so shaken and frightened that she ran to the convent chapel and lit four candles to Our Blessed Lady, and said a decade of the rosary, a devotion that bored her to stupefaction.

But now she threw off these childish memories, since they were apt to descend to vulgarity. It was really awful what a girl had to listen to, especially when she knew in her heart that all these terrible things were true. Being a girl was no joke, no matter how beautiful, because men looked at you *in that way*, and you could guess what was in their minds, always the one thing; do-me-ray and rape and sliding their hands up. The whole thing was sickening. All Maud wanted was for everything and everybody to be nice. Pleasant and kind and considerate and *nice*. And people, especially men, hardly ever were, even when they were pretending to be tame, just to please.

Maud attended to herself in the mirror for a few more minutes, knowing that she, like most girls, was a great deal more virtuous than any man. She did not feel in the least better than they were — indeed she recognized that men were superior in many ways — but they were also dirtier, more lecherous, and a great deal more ruthless about what they wanted than girls could ever be. Maud had no doubt of this at all.

Suddenly she remembered her discomfort in the drawing-room. She bent down, like a bird about to tuck its head under its wings, and sniffed delicately under her arms. Not bad, not nearly as bad as she had thought, and for the rest, she knew from changing her stockings that she smelled quite sweet and not at all of warm, sweaty flesh. It must have been Willie bursting in like that, and looking at her with his nostrils quivering like a horse, that made her imagine she was not as well groomed as usual. But she made a resolution never to miss her daily bath again.

Then she stiffened, opened her eyes wide and, after a few seconds, looked round at the door. A little whistling sound, like the call of a bird, came from the key-hole. She jumped up, pulled down her dress, ran to the door and opened it, and there was Hamlet standing outside, holding a small blue shoehorn in his hand. His red hair was slicked with water, his vague mouth compressed like a piece of dough well thumbed out, his piercing little eyes were watery with determination, and the shoehorn lay in the palm of his huge hand, like the leaf of a flower on a piece of bark.

'Hamlet, love, where did you find that?' Maud recognized her own property, which always lay on a little shelf in the corner of her room, where she kept odds and ends. She had another silver-topped shoehorn on her dressing table.

He shook his head, muttered something like: 'Inunno Miz O'Flary Flynn ounded in detichen miz' — and held out the offering an inch further.

'Well, Hamlet, you're a very good boy to run up here with it for me.' Maud gave him an enchanting smile, one of her very best, which made the boy redden from the base of his throat to the thicket of his flaming hair.

Every few days a small object would suddenly disappear from Maud's room, a silver thimble, a comb with broken teeth kept from school days, a tiny carved box used for bits of ribbon and lace, a tract — Hell — which one of the priests had given her, a little black Italian lace fan, a small roll of silk thread. Hamlet's trading toys, as she thought of them, were all small and easily carried in his trouser pocket. How he got into her room, and how he knew when she was alone in it during the day, were mysteries she never found out, but this was the way he had hit upon to keep in touch with her. Maud played up, and rather enjoyed the whole thing. At least poor Hamlet did not have that lecherous look in his eyes, as yet. The moment she saw it she was determined to cut out this harmless little game. But for the moment it was pleasant to have her own dedicated little page.

'Are you sure you don't peep through the key-hole before you give that little whistle?' she asked, stepping back into the room, and allowing him to stand on the threshold.

Hamlet's expression was so stricken, so hurt and terrified at the same time, that she knew he was not guilty. She had warned him sternly of this the first time he had brought back one of her things, and she felt certain that he was telling the truth. If you couldn't believe Hamlet, who could you believe?

'O O nono nono miz.' He looked at her with real pain in his eyes, blue as fresh paint, yet curiously old, so deep-set and sunken were they under an arched forehead. They were like live things, little blue animals blinking out from the opening of a cave.

'What was that little whistle you gave today?' said Maud kindly.

'Blackcap, miz.'

'Wonderful, Hamlet, it really is.' Maud had to take his word for it when he explained the tiny bird calls he was able to give through the key-hole, even though one of the Brothers who had reared Hamlet had told her that he was always out in the woods and knew all the calls and sounds of every animal and bird. She was just about to bring him in for a minute — what a strange boy he was — for a bar of chocolate, or the handful of sweets she kept for him, when he glanced over his shoulder, gave a little squawk, and disappeared down the corridor like a puff of brown smoke.

As Maud anticipated, for she knew of Hamlet's extrordinary perception in these things, Donie appeared at the top of the front stairs — she came out of her room as instinctively as Hamlet had bolted down the back stairs — and was just turning the knob in the door when she turned to face Donie with a slightly surprised expression on her face.

Donie arrived at her side, puffing, and out of breath, a condition he was rarely in, since he was accustomed since boyhood to running up and down stairs, carrying glasses, trays and cases before Hamlet came, and running through the streets, delivering messages. But today he was obviously much agitated, and really, Maud thought, the plain truth was that poor old Donie was getting old.

'O miz,' he panted, 'de train is in. De train Mr Slyne wus ta 'have cum 'ere in an' id's twenny minnits I heard id crossin' de bridge so he'd be here iffen he wus on id, an' 'e's bin away tree whole days now, an' we spint four nites trampin' de bogs, measuradin' de lan' an' all, so dere should be no disbute, an' he brough' ivrythin outa 'is room and didden pay de bill aider. Where's dat Hamlet?'

'Hamlet?' said Maud with a vague look in her eye. 'Hamlet? How should I know? I thought you were talking about Mr Slyne.'

'So wus I, God help me, miz, bud supposin' e's gone on de run like, an' leff us high an' dry wid de lan', merciful God, whad'll happen ta me, an' me poor Lizzy Biddy an' de childer all a' dem an' de wan dat's haff here, O O O O I'm ruinaded, ruinaded, an' whad'll yer Mammy say?'

'I hardly think Mr Slyne is the sort of man who leaves without paying his bill, and he did say he was going to Dublin to instruct his solicitor, and that he'd have the contracts back with him. Well, you know what solicitors are like. They don't even die suddenly, they have such a fear of hurry. Don't worry, Donie, he'll be back. He told me he would.'

'An' did ye believe 'im, miz?' Donie was calming down under the balm of Maud's sweet composure.

'Yes, I did,' she said firmly. 'I'm sure he was telling the truth. He's absolutely serious about buying that land. Why, I can't imagine, because you know — '

'Doan say id miz, doan say id. Sweed Jasus, doan even tink of id, because ye know — ' he stopped with a gasp, and stared at Maud with bulging eyes. 'D'ye tink anywan has — I mane,' he broke off in a whisper, clasped his hands and rolled his eyes up. It was so sudden and sweeping a gesture that Maud almost expected him to take his eyes out and toss them up and down in his hand like bulls' eyes.

'Of course not,' she said soothingly.

'Dey have, dey have, I know id, I know id,' he moaned. 'Ony God can save us now. O wad did I ever do ta deserve dis? An' me poor Lizzy Biddy and the innersand childer, answer me dat.'

'Now, now Donie, don't let go. Everything will be all right.'

'Where's dat Hamlet? De lazy houn'.' Donie looked around, his fear as always turning into rage. 'I'll skin 'im alive when I git 'im.'

But Maud, who was thinking that Hamlet would never behave like this even in a real crisis, had a lucky stroke. There was an old lady in room 30, who was staying for a few days, but went out very little. She had returned to the town after forty years in Boston, and no one remembered her, nor did she recognize anyone. So she sat drinking whiskey all day in her room.

'Miss Fingal File sent Hamlet out with a letter, which she says has to have an answer.'

'Why didden 'e tell me, de tramp?'

'He hadn't time, she was all upset and wanted the thing done at once. You know what Americans are like.'

'Doan I bud?'

'So Hamlet asked me to tell you, Donie.'

Donie knew a conspiracy when he saw one, but there was nothing to be said about this one. Just wait for the little rat to get back. With many a mumbled complaint, and an occasional cry to heaven, he went off along the corridor and disappeared down the stairs.

Maud went on towards her mother's drawing-room, quite sure that she had forgotten what she had been sent for, but equally certain that it was not important, since her mother had made it plain that she merely wanted her out of the room. Maud was used to such tactics.

Just as she was half-way down the corridor, dark and covered with a worn brown carpet with holes in strategic spots to trip the unwary, the drawing-room door opened. Blinded as she was from the sudden flood of light, Maud was only able to make out a tall figure with broad shoulders. She knew it was Willie, but made no sign of recognition.

Willie, having completed his somewhat surprising business with Mrs Daly, was in a rigs and jeels mood, and if a piper had struck up somewhere in the street, he would have broken out in a rig-ajig-adee himself. But Maud's face froze him. Surely she must know him, the light full on her face, and gave no sign. She looked pensive, remote and gorgeous.

'You mean to say you didn't see me?' he said when she stood before him, looking up into his flushed face.

'Of course I saw you — ' she began, when suddenly, without warning, Donie came bounding up the stairs.

'A word wid ye miz,' he spluttered. 'Id's somethin' I discovered aboud Hamlet. No, miz nod here, id's privade. 'cuse me Mr Willie.' And he led the way back down the corridor until

Maud was at the door of her own room again.

'I wus so flusteraded when I wus speakin' ta ye jus' now dat I forgod ta tell ye on no accound ta tell Mister Willie aboud de lan'. He *knows*, like ye know. Ye know?'

Maud nodded gravely.

'Of course not. Neither Mammy nor I would dream of — '

'O tank God, tank God,' broke out Donie, rolling his eyes in that peculiar pop-out way he had.

Willie stood looking after the pair, and waited by the drawing-room door, now closed, as Maud came back. He moved to the top of the stairs and waited for her there — a sudden impulse. And he knew, from the way she still looked blankly at him, that he would have to work very hard indeed on the farm to win the heart and hand of Maud Daly. It was a sudden, piercing jab of self-knowledge that Willie was unaccustomed to, and it went into him like a rusty blade.

Nevertheless, and for the first time with Maud, he concealed his feelings.

'Why, Willie, I'm terribly sorry, I hardly saw you. Donie is so worried about his wife.' She was smiling at him now, but Willie had seen her face when he first looked at it, and she was looking straight at him and not seeing him, not until he moved to the top of the stairs and she couldn't miss him.

'Your ma's been lecturing me,' he said quietly, playing with his cap, his hands awkward like a road worker. 'I'm going home to work the place.'

'O Willie, I'm so glad. It's the only thing to do,' She was smiling at him now, the old sweet, intoxicating smile, and it too pierced him — a clean blade. But he could not escape it. One last clutch at the bank before the waters flowed over him.

'I don't know when I'll see you next.'

'This day week,' said Maud promptly. 'You can always get away for an evening if you run the place right. Keep Harney watched. Remember.'

'What day of the week is it?'

'I don't know. Look at a newspaper.'

'Right, I will.' And he turned abruptly and ran down the stairs. Maud, feeling slightly disappointed, went in to her mother.

Hamlet let himself into Slyne's room and with quick, steady hands conducted a thorough search of the drawers, wardrobe, the mattress, under the carpet, even the waste-paper basket. MacDonnell had been particularly insistent about the waste-paper basket, and every day that he had the opportunity Hamlet had gone through this, even when the room was vacant. He had already, just after Slyne left, found a few pieces of torn paper, an envelope addressed to Slyne at a Dublin hotel, and an Irish railway ticket.

It was not always easy for him to get out of the hotel, but he had judged it a good time when Donie, after his interview with Maud, had departed, telling Mrs O'Flaherty Flynn that he was going home to comfort his poor wife and their destitute little ones. Between comforting Lizzy Biddy and his ten ravenous offspring, he would be gone for at least an hour.

'Poor Bizzy Lizzy,' said Mrs O'Flaherty Flynn, as she told all this to Hamlet who was a pet of hers. There were times when the poor child looked pale as death, with his eyes gone back in his head like someone with galloping consumption. Although the good woman knew that Hamlet had come from the Brothers of Mercy with a certificate that he was not, and never had been suffering from consumption, she was not quite convinced. Yet she did not feel afraid of him. She did not think it necessary to make him drink his tea and eat his meat and potatoes out of his own cup and plate, and wash them himself afterwards. Indeed she often shared a cup of punch with him on a cold night, when the pair of them were sitting in front of the kitchen range, telling ghost stories, while Donie was behind the bar with the regulars. If they heard him coming down the passage, Hamlet would dodge into the back kitchen and out on to the back stairs, sometimes with a hunk of bread and jam, which Mrs O'Flaherty Flynn kept in a 'private' place for him.

Indeed, the imposing Mrs O'Flaherty Flynn, huge, red-faced, ham-fisted, was the real power behind The Duke of Clarence Hotel. Not only was she a first-class cook when in the mood — it was said she could make dead meat live again — but she was at the centre of the complicated system of the place. Donie received no official salary, except presents at Christmas, Easter and his wedding anniversary; but he had Lizzy Biddy and ten children to support: two chickens a day, a pound of bacon and two pounds of sausages were allotted to him by the cook. And he was never left short of milk, if one of the younger children was delicate.

The cook also saw to it that Hamlet had meat at least four times a week, a glass of milk a day and all the bread and jam he could eat. Mrs O'Flaherty Flynn was a truly splendid woman, and a mighty Christian. Even Mrs Daly thought twice about crossing her on any item of expense in the kitchen. The bar and the bed-and-breakfast trade kept the place with its foundations well above water.

So now, when Hamlet indicated that he had to run on a message for Mr MacDonnell, the cook smiled benignly and patted him on the shoulder. The boy was going the right way. To be running messages for old MacDonnell at Hamlet's age was an achievement. She knew that Donie passed on information that might be of use to the great man. But to be picked out, as the boy was, by the grand master of the many-pull, was a credit to the boy's intelligence.

'O a' course ye can go off, alannah,' smiled the cook. 'Donie'll be gone an hour an' tin minnits.' She chuckled to herself at some secret joke and helped herself to another slice of chocolate cake she made for herself, and which was too rich for Hamlet's stomach. 'An' wile yer ad id, doan forgit to axe Misther MacDonnell aboud dat job fur me neffphew, ye hear me? Doan forgit t'axe 'im.'

Miss McLurry's shop was a good place to meet. Mrs Pig in particular often went there when there was anything to discuss. She was recognized as a friend of the owner and might go into the shop without anyone noticing anything unusual about it.

It was a very small shop, and had once been the front room of the older McLurrys. After their deaths, with the pensions gone — her father had been an engine driver on the railway — and every second woman in the town dress-making, she had staked her all on a wooden counter and a few shelves put up for her by an old butty of her father. She then had the place blessed by Canon Sharkey and opened shop.

Her stock was small but it was nearly always fresh. Bulls' eyes, caramels with Devlin's Irish-made assortment in prominent display. 'Buy Irish and die a happy death,' a cynical customer had once remarked to her, and Miss McLurry, who was a strong Dev woman, tartly replied: 'Yes indeed, and the British Legion will bury you free.' Cadburys, Frys and Rowntrees chocolate — 'Quaker-takers' as Miss McLurry wittily described them: a name that stuck. It could be heard in America long years after.

She had a small (dear) selection of Nougat, and a nice little corner in acid drops and licorice allsorts: 'lick 'er yersel'. But it was her soft blackcurrant gums that made her name. She would put one hand on the blackcurrant jar, another on the acid drops and ask': 'Is it the soft ones or the hard ones that you want?' Since she had a quivery voice, rather like a singer with a wobble, this innocent question was repeated in juddering imitation all over the town by children, and later by their parents. Miss McLurry became an institution.

But during the three days that Slyne was absent from the town, she was still in the early stages of her business career. Her mad brother Christy was lying on a sofa in the back kitchen, with the door to the yard padlocked and the windows barred, in case he got out and took off. And then Christy had to be fed, and he had a huge appetite. There were times when Sarah Jane did not know where to turn, but something always turned up. Somebody bought a large box of chocolates, and she had money again. All due, she knew, to Canon Sharkey's blessing.

'There ye are now, Janie,' he had said with a smile, having drenched the stock and its owner in holy water, 'the divil himself won't steal a sweet out of your jars after that lashing. And there's good profit in sweets, 33 %. That's allowed by the Church, you know, as a reasonable profit, but over that you'd have to ask me in Confession, according to Theology and Canon Law, because of the fear of extortion. Like the Jews, you know,' he ended vaguely, looking around the tiny shop and wondering if 50% profit would allow Miss McLurry to live on the pathetic little stock she was starting with — and keep poor Christy as well.

In spite of the Canon's reservations, Miss McLurry did make enough to live on, but not enough to be able to afford to decline the money she was expecting from Slyne for her bit of land.

'What are we going to do?' she said to Mrs Pig on the afternoon of the third day. She supported herself with clenched fists on the little bit of counter between jars and cardboard boxes. This was a stance reserved only for occasions of extreme gravity. When chatting normally she crossed her arms over her chest and leaned them on the counter; a comfortable position which took the weight off her feet and allowed her sometimes to kick off her shoes when her ankles had swollen.

'If only someone had news of him,' said Mrs Pig, sitting up very straight on the wooden bench, which was placed for the convenience of customers against the wall facing the counter. When, as often happened, three or four country lads came in to buy sweets and smoke cigarettes, they took over the bench and stretched out their legs and big boots in careless abandon. Anyone wanting to get to the end of the counter would have had to negotiate these obstacles first. Others just stood at the door and indicated their preference for the soft or the hard as required. The lads never changed position, stared straight ahead while chewing or smoking and hardly exchanged a word. They were tired after washing themselves for town, shaving, changing into clean shirts and blue serge suits, and so they rested until the pubs called. Miss McLurry was a little afraid of them, but they were good customers and always paid cash, mostly in pennies. Mrs Pig was quite unawed by them, and had once ordered them out when she arrived later than usual with some important news for her friend.

But today she had the shop to herself.

'He might have said something to Donie Donnelly before he left,' said Miss McLurry crossly.

'He did. He told 'im he'd be back.'

'I know that. But he didn't say when.'

'He said he'd be back when he had de contracts made out be his solicitor in Dublin. He doesn't trust de locals an' I don't blame 'im.'

'It's not the lawyers here he doesn't trust, it's the clerks. Everyone knows they talk.'

'The girruls do, not de men, girruls should be barred from solicitors' offices. Dere was an awful case in Tralee, all Kerry noo it, of a slut of a girrul dat tole her boy frien' — '

Miss McLurry was not to hear that day of the solicitor's clerk from Tralee, or Tralalee, as Mrs Pig sometimes called it, sin city of the south west — for just then Hosannah walked in and stood inside the door, looking from one lady to another like a stray dog.

'Have ye hard anyting?' she croaked, thumping her chest.

The two ladies shook their heads, and Miss McLurry insultingly, did not even raise herself from her now comfortably slumped position on the counter. Hosannah gave both of them a look calculated to stop a cat lowering its head on to a saucer of milk, then turned and walked out as abruptly as she had arrived.

The friends shook their heads, then Mrs Pig buried her hands in the pockets of her butcher-blue apron and shook her head again.

'Gettin' dafter every day,' was her sad comment when Hosannah was out of earshot. Then she realized that she had offended Sarah Jane by her reference to insanity. Miss McLurry stood up straight and stiff from the counter, took out an account book from a ledge under the counter and consulted it with every appearance of deep concentration. In the kitchen, during the silence that followed, a faint whisper could be heard. Miss McLurry frowned even more as she pored over the book, and held it closer to her face, while Mrs Pig, after clearing her throat and grasping her neck as if she were in the strangle-hold of a person unseen, got up and stalked out. She knew whom she would consult.

So did Hosannah. After her humiliating experience in the twopenny-halfpenny sweetshop, she wouldn't patronize the place again for fear of poison, even if she had the money. Wasn't it said that the mad brother came out into the shop many a night, sucked bulls' eyes, and dug his dirty paws into every jar in the place? This fantasy was thought up by Hosannah herself, but by now she imagined someone had told her, and she had not as yet spread the news. It was ammunition to keep in store for a future ambush.

What made Hosannah feel even worse about her reception in McLurry's was the fact that she had never passed on this secret to a living soul. This was because she had consulted Father Raft, the Canon's curate, in Confession about it, telling him in perfect good faith that she had been told it by another, and was it not a matter of public concern and hygiene?

Father Raft told her it would be a terrible mortal sin if she spread the news. It would mean taking away another person's living, taking away another's character, and in general giving scandal of the worst conscription. Besides, if she heard it from a second party it might not be true.

But Hosannah did not think it might be any kind of sin if she discussed her Confession in a general way, giving no names: a theological subtlety which might have kept Roman clerics in debate for a year if they heard of it. But although she had hinted it to a few people the response was poor: no one was interested in Hosannah's Confession, good or bad.

So she made her way slowly up the curve of Connaught Street — a curve so slight that some people had lived all their lives there without noticing it — nodded automatically when someone spoke to her, and smiled at one or two others. In spite of these friendly contacts, almost the only ones she had most days, she arrived home feeling very depressed.

Hosannah lived in a curious house in a curious position at the back of the street. All the lanes off Connaught Street were inhabited by large families who lived in tiny dwellings. Some of the openings, between the houses facing the street, were more like courtyards, in which carts and traps were tied up on Fair days. Many of the larger businesses had their own yard, with an arched gate leading to it, and some had big orchards at the end of their yards. But Hosannah lived on the corner of an opening between two high premises, one a pub, the other a hardware shop, and hers was the first of what used to be a row of small houses, which faced on to a lane running parallel to the main street, until it ended at the wicket gate of the largest orchard in the town.

Braiden's was the only one in the row still occupied. Most of the others had fallen in, but enough remained to make it still a sort of row, even if the other four remaining cottages were blind and bald. The place was known as the Via Dolorosa, on account of Hosannah.

And she knew that the shop-keeper who owned the yard behind her dwelling was waiting for her to die so he could extend his premises, just as all the other merchants had taken over the decayed hovels when the inhabitants had obligingly died. She also knew, which was worst of all, that the owners of the yards behind the few remaining vacant dwellings were waiting for her to die on account of the neighbouring houses as well. Then a clean sweep would be made, and the shop-keepers involved would have acquired fine back entrances to their premises. Dying for the sake of her own home was bad enough, but to be expected to expire to make the dead neighbours also useful was almost more than Hosannah could bear.

She was the youngest daughter of a family of six sisters and three brothers. Only three, a brother and two sisters, had remained in the old home. The others were scattered to England, Australia and Boston. While they were alive, the trio at home were provided for fairly comfortably, but the exiles had all died in a sudden rush, to be followed a year later by the brother and sister who lived with Hosannah. It had been a terrible time for her, even though her brother and sister had both been incontinent and weak in the head long before they died.

It was these few lingering years that had given Hosannah and her little house its reputation for dirt and squalor. It was said that you had to hold your nose once you turned off the street, and get out a handkerchief as you approached the Braiden dwelling. Hosannah knew about this and knew also that she herself was unclean. But she could never understand why people said — o, she heard it all — that poor Bea Sarah, and harmless, stuttering Charlie, were also dirty. She thought she had cared for her brother and sister in warmth and comfort, and cleaned up regularly after them. She loved them; and even now, with the hovel empty and cold, she felt that the pair were still waiting for her, eager for news and attention.

But today she was tired. The two empty chairs on either side of the tiny range, were merely empty and in need of repair. Although she felt her brother and sister were near, of recent years she no longer spoke to them. She had mentioned that also to Canon Sharkey in Confession, and he had reprimanded her very sharply. The dead were not to be spoken to. Prayed for, yes; prayed to, perhaps. But to hold conversations with them in their old chairs was sinful and led fast to insanity. She was to stop it at once, and say her rosary whenever she felt tempted.

She sat down on the kitchen chair facing the low fire of sticks and a few lumps of coal in the range. She did not even put a kettle on for tea. She took her rosary out of her apron pocket, wrapped her coat around her knees and let the worn beads slip through her fingers. She no longer saw the walls, with their green-purple patches of damp, the holes in the linoleum, the dirt of the once-green curtains, which she had sewn up herself and which now slumped from their rail like weary women at the end of the day. She did not notice the bits and pieces of broken china and crusts of bread, half-cleared plates, and the empty blue mug on the table; nor the litter of years stuffed under the table — papers and old bits of cloth and wool, the remains of her sister's clothes, covered with a flour sack; nor the smell that came from the slops pail that stood at the end of the table, and that she was no longer able to carry out to the yard — she kept it from overflowing by dipping a mug into it every day or so and throwing *that* out; nor the queer light that came from one of the doors at the side of the range, the one that was locked, but opened onto a room that had collapsed years before, and caught the glare of the gas-light at the top of the lane — it was not on now, but the light remained the same in Susannah's mind. Nor did she look at the alarm clock that stood on the mantel over the range and had not worked for years; it was always nine o'clock in the Braiden kitchen, and, besides, Susannah kept her own time and knew her own version of the years.

She noticed none of these things, because she had lived with them for so long, and because she was tired and ill. Whenever she felt the first stab of the pain in her chest, which had been troubling her for some years now, her immediate reaction was to start up, to get on her feet at any cost. This she did now and managed to get as far as the window, where she peered through the curtains and looked out sideways at the small green wicket gate in the brick wall at the other end of the court. This was the garden of the people who also owned Cox's orchard at the far end of her lane, a family called Brennock, rich and long established and always a source of great interest to Hosannah. She often saw the small boy, the only son of the house, pass along the lane towards the big orchard, beyond which his grandmother and aunt lived, in a big house facing King Street.

But today Hosannah hardly noticed the trim little gate, as she waited for the pain to grow more insistent, with hunched shoulders and clenched fists. This time she was only aware that the first little stab was not followed by another. Very slowly, dragging her feet like heavy stones attached to her ankles, she made her way back to her chair and sank into it, clutching her rosary in her damp fingers.

'Oh, Sacred Heart of Jesus,' she prayed, 'I give Thee thanks for sparing me the big pain this time. And grant me, through the intercession of Our Blessed Lady, a bit of a cure from it from now on.'

Hosannah paused and looked up at the oleograph of the Sacred Heart, which hung over the mantelpiece and with which she had several chats during the day and half the night as well. Not knowing that she had mastered the technique of the rosary, one of the most difficult of all religious exercises, Hosannah often followed the stories of the Mysteries of the Catholic faith in her mind, while the words of the rosary were said by her lips. But more often, she let one bead after another slip through her fingers, while she talked to the image of her God. In a voice like Father Raft's.

'And O Lord, I wouldn't ask it if I wasn't in dire need of it, but please send a holy angel to whisper into the Englishman's ear to make up his mind to buy my land. O Lord, all I want out of the money is a bit of heat in the winter. One of them oil stoves that I hear the women talk about, that I could keep here instead of the range that I'm not able to keep any more, and I could fry an egg on top of the oil stove, and even boil the kettle, they say. And I want a couple of new blankets for my bed in the deep winter, the old ones are worn as thin as my skin, and I'm famished every night. Lord, save me from a stiffening death. And I want a few pence to pay a man to clean out the place, for You know I'm not able to do it myself now, and the money will come in useful for the O'Briens in O'Farrell's lane, there's one boy that's honest, and I can let him in here while I'm watching. O Lord grant that I get the money before Christmas, for apart from the O'Brien's, God help them, I give a few pence to the real poor as well. And — ' she paused and held up her clasped hands with the rosary twisted about them, like the swollen veins she already had — 'I promise You, O Lord, that I'll never again even think about poor Sarah Jane McLurry's unfortunate brother, who may be very dear to You. And if I swear honestly never to mention him even to myself, maybe You'll let me off the chest pains now and again. Because it isn't true about him and the sweet jars. Everybody knows that Sarah Jane locks the shop door, and bars it every night when she closes up, and he never got into it even once. Maybe the poor unfortunate can't move. The shadow some people saw that night was Sarah Jane herself, going back into the shop, because she forgot her beads, she told me the next morning at mass. O Lord, accept my prayer and hear me, and for Your Holy Mother's sake make that Slyne decide the right way for me.'

The whispering went on and on, for Hosannah had the idea that God was very busy (who could deny thāt?) and had to be asked again and again for the same thing. And in perfectly accented English too, as she imagined.

And all the time the fire in the range burned lower and lower and the lane outside darkened and voices were heard faintly from the street and a cat jumped up on the window-sill and the wind blew a paper across the door and the little old house creaked and nothing apart from the torn old newspaper came to the door nor had anything else or anybody for many a long year now.

Although Hosannah lived in a kind of perpetual shade in her little house, since it got hardly any light, it was still the height of the day when Hamlet darted through the streets on his way to MacDonnell's. He had his own way of going. Out the back door of the hotel, into a semi-circular lane that led from Church Street to Northgate Street, near the bridge. It was a small, slightly isolated little community although just off the main street, narrow and old-fashioned in character, rows of small, two-storey houses, a few larger ones and a few larger still behind high grey walls.

Hamlet's hard-heeled boots, a present from Maud, rang uncomfortably loud on the stone pavement. He did not notice the houses, nor the various ornaments, religious and lay, in the windows, nor the tiny forecourts in front of a row of houses set back a few yards from the others; nor the narrow, twisting lanes that linked every street, backwards and forwards all over Bridgeford, like the circulatory system of the body.

These things did not appeal to Hamlet. It was people he watched. A glimpse of a grey face and dark eyes behind a twitched lace curtain, on the lanes behind the hotel; a drunk, leaning nerveless against a wall and slowly crumpling to the ground like a discarded topcoat; a yellow hand with many rings framed in a window-pane, gleaming for an instant, then disappearing; a stocky, serge-clothed proprietor, standing at the door of his shop, blowing through his moustache, resting an eye for business on Hamlet for a moment, then gliding on, expressionless, to seek the familiar face, the well-lined pocket; a pair of nuns, black and white, yellow-faced with shuttered eyes, making their way across a street where all traffic stopped to let them pass; a brown-habited Franciscan, laughing with shaking belly; a line of tinkers in single file, brown-shawled women and tight-ragged men walking in the gutter, making their own silence, broken occasionally by a harsh barking sound; a couple of old ladies in black, touched with purple cloth flowers in their hats, neat white hair, gloved hands, long narrow shoes with buttoned straps, nodding to each other as they murmured along, casting side glances at shop windows; a pretty girl with a flower-like face, a bright summer frock, delicate well-covered breasts, gleaming dark hair, walking with straight, proud shoulders and slightly heavy feet.

Hamlet had noticed that there were many such girls in Bridgeford, and was not at all surprised to overhear men in the hotel proclaiming that the town was famous for its pretty girls. Delicate consumptive beauties with lambent eyes sometimes harshly aglow, small, finely-moulded noses, cherry red lips that parted over small, pearl teeth, blue veins on long slender necks, sloping shoulders, a slight roundness in the back, and a haunting dim glow about their feet. Girls whose sweetness and unearthly beauty would haunt many a memory down the years. A race destined for extinction, and one never to rise again.

And the healthy ones, not quite as exquisite as their doomed sisters, but tense with braced vitality, bubbling with suppressed laughter, with long black hair braided into neat buns, plaits and heavy folded coils, every hair flickering with electricity; happily advancing into life and husbands and children and illness and trouble, but caught for an instant in Hamlet's gaze, remembered by him, but overlaid in his mind by the all-embracing image of Maud.

But, crossing the street and onto the bridge, even with his lack of interest in things, he always looked upstream towards the gleaming three-arched railway bridge, brilliantly white over the summer river, spanning the northern sky. Hamlet, being an outsider, always looked north first, while the natives instinctively glanced south. After all, the railway bridge in its deceptively frail and lacy wrought iron, had not been there even a hundred years, while the Vikings had always sailed upriver from the Shannon estuary. It was a curious trait, and not much remarked upon.

But the railway bridge remained, a magnificent set piece, spanning the widest reach of water in the country. There it reared, on Hamlet's brief summer and sunshine day, for one swift dazzling moment. And then he was off, head down, shoulders up, across the square, under the high stone military walls, into the narrow, half-hidden path of Barrack Street, up the steep slope of King Street and round the corner into Connaught Street.

Few knew him. Those who vaguely recognized the hurrying boy did not bother to talk to him, and he kept his eyes on the ground, until he reached the top of the street where MacDonnell lived in a high stone house at the opening of Blackberry Lane, which itself ran downhill, for Connaught Street ran along the top of a steep hill overlooking the great barrack square on one side; on the other, the canal, straight as a ruler, the wide curve of the Shannon, the water-meadows and the great brown bog.

All Hamlet knew for certain was that he must pause at a shop window near MacDonnell's, watch those coming and going and then slip round the corner of Blackberry Lane. There were no small teeming hovels in this lane. MacDonnell had bought them all up and razed them to the ground. He had built a row of clean, trim dwellings, half-way down the lane near the canal banks, and the occupiers never ceased to bemoan their exiled state, claiming that although they paid only sixpence a week rent, they had been evicted from their former and proper homes, which stank to high planets and cost two shillings a week. And they had been moved at least twenty yards further away from the street; an awful act of landlordism.

And of course they bemoaned the blackberries also. There were none on this lane anymore. MacDonnell had turned his long strip of orchard, the second finest in the street, into a terraced garden, with clipped hedges, lines of poplars, and a row of beech trees, imported from Dublin half-grown to come between him and the new concrete cottages. If a foreigner had done all this on ground sacred to poverty, charity and the loose garment topped by a shawl, he would have been murdered. But old MacDonnell got away with everything. America, Tammany and the old man himself, were too much for them. The tenants of Our Lady's Place, as Canon Sharkey insisted upon naming it, began to settle down, and the youngsters began to forget the shared pot and the earthen floor, the shawl across the mouth and the garments made from old flour sacks.

A fine brick wall had been raised to shelter MacDonnell, and along by this Hamlet walked quickly and sure-footedly. He had disappeared round the corner of the street from the gaze of a passing stranger, like a puff of smoke, a grey squirrel round the bole of a tree.

He let himself in through the small, green wicket gate, which was open night and day for those friends and pensioners who did not want to pass through the front door for all the world to see, and for the not inconsiderable number who did not care to pass the scrutiny of Macroom, MacDonnell's 'man', secretary, valet, cook, housekeeper, and bodyguard from the good old bootlegging days.

From the corner of his eye as he sped, noiseless as a barefooted child on a springing turf, he caught a glimpse of the blackcoated familiar, stabbing a finger at the gardener, who was looking at him with round eyes and a collapsed mouth.

'Holy,' said Hamlet to himself, 'but Mickser is bein' rightly macroomed.'

MacDonnell opened the kitchen door himself, and Hamlet slipped in.

'Come on up,' said MacDonnell, leading the way through the breakfast room, into the hall of the big nineteenth-century house, and across to a room at the back of the front drawing-room, which he used as a study.

MacDonnell was in his shirt sleeves, his powerful belly kept in place by a wide leather belt with an elaborate Mexican buckle. He sat down behind his big, wide desk which was topped with green leather and loaded with many objects; boxes, a file, a green marble and gold inkstand, and a signed photograph of President Roosevelt, which had haunted Hamlet's dreams ever since MacDonnell showed it to him. The President was in power less than a year; but the photograph had arrived less than a month after his inauguration, a marvellous gesture to an old supporter. Bridgeford had been stunned into silence by the arrival of the sacred *ex-voto*, a living testimonial of the friendship of the most powerful prince on earth, and a confirmation of the greatness, success and potency of MacDonnell.

Hamlet gazed at the side of the heavy silver frame bearing the ikon, and felt his heart thumping within him. MacDonnell lit a cigar and leaned back against his massive swivel chair, also in green tooled leather, his broad shoulders blocking out the light of the window behind him, hung with weighty green velvet curtains.

'Well, sonny, what have you for me this time?'

Hamlet felt in his trousers, under the buttons of his braces, to the little pocket he had sewn on himself when he had been inducted into MacDonnell's secret service. He had been instructed to collect every scrap of paper that Slyne threw into the waste-paper basket in his hotel room, and this Hamlet had scrupulously done. He had also memorized and jotted down various numbers and columns of figures, which Slyne had left on newspapers and the backs of envelopes, and had carefully gone through the pockets of his second suit when Slyne was out of the hotel. Everything was committed to the bits and pieces of paper he now dug up from their warm kangaroo pouch, and handed across the vast desk with its shining and terrifying silver frame.

MacDonnell looked through them, not pausing even at the number he had hoped to find, put them down carelessly on the desk and looked at the eager, bone-white face that was staring at him with a mixture of awe and worship. The old man smiled.

'You're a good boy, Hamlet,' he said, pushing the scraps from him as if they were quite useless. 'I think I can make you useful.' He puffed on his cigar and smiled. 'I hope you've been looking after Miss Maud too?'

Hamlet blushed to the top of his forehead, and his sunken eyes glistened. MacDonnell realized that, if he had a mind to it, he could make this sprouting manikin very unhappy. Of course he was in love with Maud. It would be very odd if he were not. He got up from his chair, came round to the front of the desk, patted Hamlet's shoulders, and walked slowly from the room.

'Sir — ' Hamlet began to call after him. He was suddenly overcome with a mixture of fear and elation. To be left alone in this room was, he knew, a most significant thing and one he knew instinctively few others had experienced. It was a compliment of the easiest and subtlest kind; for he never believed for a moment that the old man would do him any harm. He was completely devoted, was Hamlet, to this tremendous patron.

Suddenly MacDonnell was in the open doorway. Hamlet sprang rigidly to attention.

'That's all right, boy, everything's OK. I'll be back in a few minutes.' And he walked across the hall leaving the door half-closed behind him.

Little by little Hamlet began to look around the walls of the room, turning his eyes farther than his head. Since he was first allowed in this room he had wanted to inspect the photographs that hung on the walls. Would he ever be able to tell anyone that he had seen and knew what these photographs meant? According to local legend, they were all signed mementoes of American political giants of the nineties and early part of the present century. Some said — having heard it from the man who was called in to fix the window which leaked at one time — that they were all signed photographs of former Presidents; but the local wits, having discovered that there were more than twenty of these representations, these ghostly lineaments of far off and probably departed souls, were quick to point out that so many US presidents just did not exist, now or in the past.

In fact, with the exception of one New England Congressman, who was in mortal debt to MacDonnell, the likenesses that now looked down on the awe-struck Hamlet were mostly those of battered, tired ward-dealers and wheelers, Tammany officials, and a few minor names in the Democratic Party. The boy did not know it, but Roosevelt did not send his signed portrait until he knew that MacDonnell was well out of the country, and Tammany well on its way to liquidation. And the famous silver-framed photograph was not dedicated to MacDonnell, but merely bore the President's signature.

In spite of the attraction of the President's gift and the crowded photographs of old politicos, who were lavish with their dedications, it was the great office file that most fascinated Hamlet. It was American, and said to be the last word in efficiency. Those business houses in Bridgeford who had files kept them between flat boards, secured by steel points, onto which receipts and bills fitted, having been punched so to do, and the file was held in place by a spring coil which fastened the back board over the points with curved steel holders. Hearing the sound of this had a nostalgic appeal for those who worked in offices in their youth, and had the luck to escape later in life.

Hamlet raised himself on his toes, craned his neck forward and tried to get a view of the open drawer of the file, which MacDonnell had left pulled out. He could see line after line of stiff brown cardboard holders, all marked with letters of the alphabet. What mysterious treasures of policy information did these folders contain? What human secrets? For, like most people in Bridgeford, and many beyond it, Hamlet firmly believed that MacDonnell knew everything about everybody everywhere. The boy trembled with excitement, and his toes also began to wobble from the strain of standing upon them. Regretfully he lowered himself to the flat and the floor, and merely gazed at the celebrated cabinet. He was still standing, like someone who had seen a vision and was struck rigid by it, when MacDonnell came back. He returned so silently that Hamlet jumped when a large but benevolent hand was laid on his shoulder.

'Oh God! Oh, sir!'

'That's a good boy,' said MacDonnell, going to his desk and sitting down in his splendid chair. He was carrying a small square box wrapped in gold paper in his hand. 'You didn't move while I was out.'

'No, sir, I dinint,' Hamlet's natural wariness was returning to him.

'I can see that.' He waved a hand in the direction of the filing cabinet. 'I left it open. I saw you looking at it the last time you were here. I thought you might take a peek while I was in the john.'

'Oh, no, sir, I wudden dream —'

'Well, you might dream, but you didn't move. Notice the scrap of paper between you and the cabinet? Well, you might have walked on it, and then again you might not. It doesn't matter, I'd still know.' He tapped the little gold box as he placed it on the desk, then stopped abruptly and rubbed it gently with his finger.

'Yes sir, I know.'

'How would I have known?' said MacDonnell, smiling.

'Be lookin' at me.'

MacDonnell smiled and nodded, took his wallet — a magnificent Mexican one of barbaric design — extracted a ten-shilling note from it, folded it under the box, and held both up to Hamlet.

'Put this box in Miss Maud's dressing room, will you?'

MacDonnell was interested in the boy's reaction. He turned very pale, shook his head as if he had a tic and made no immediate effort to take either the box or the note. A tall, skinny boy, with carrot hair and a thin peaked face, he did not look the sort that would refuse ten shillings for an errand that called for no effort. He raised his sunken eyes, blue and sharp and burning within his skull, and looked at MacDonnell almost like a grown man. There was a glint of aggressive masculinity in that brief stare, which MacDonnell recognized and appreciated. A boy with spirit was a good henchman.

'I'm not allowed into Miss Maud's room, sir.'

The voice was thin, forced, and sounded like a stale crust of bread rubbed against a grater. MacDonnell looked down at the box, opened a drawer and put it inside. There was a time when he could have used this young man, brave in spite of raw-edged nerves, intelligent and possessing a sense of honour — of that MacDonnell was sure. Sure, also, that men who succeed always start with some sort of code, otherwise they were useless: monkeys with guns. But the day was long past when he could make the career of a protege by a word here, a nod there, a favour bestowed at the right moment.

'Of course,' he said, nodding his head and smiling up at the boy. 'And very proper too. I've gotten too used to American manners.' But he had not lost his cunning. He would present a very bad face to the youngster if he admitted defeat on so trivial an issue. And he was well aware of the indignity an elderly man — hell no, he was old — can be made to suffer, if he finds himself in love with a young girl. 'It's just that Miss Maud's mother gave me a brooch to be fixed — I know a man in Tullamore who's a genius — he'd have made a fortune in the States — and I thought if you were going back to the hotel you might deliver it for me, to Mrs Daly.'

MacDonnell looked down at his freckled and splotched hands, as they rested clasped and reassuring on the leather-topped desk. He was waiting. The reaction came in a second, and it told MacDonnell everything.

'Oh yes, sir, a' course sir, I'll give it to Miz Daly herself, thank ye, sir.'

'Then, wait a minute. I'll write a few lines.' MacDonnell drew a sheet of thick blue paper from a holder on the desk, wrote a few lines as he had said, folded it into a small square, took out the gold-wrapped box, and attached the note enclosed in an envelope with a piece of adhesive tape, pulled out and cut off from a little machine by the side of the paper-holder. Hamlet was by now much more interested in this 'sticking machine', the like of which he had never seen before. Shopkeepers in Bridgeford still tied up their parcels with twine, and possessed the fine art of breaking it with a twist of the fingers.

MacDonnell handed over the box and the ten-shilling note. Hamlet accepted both with a bob of his red head; then glanced at the adhesive tape again. MacDonnell smiled. He knew now what he would give the boy as a present, if the information he had brought with him today on one of the scraps of paper turned out to be what MacDonnell thought it was.

'If you go out now by the front door, sonny, you'll escape Macroom. He's still in the garden, fairly dug into poor Mattie.'

'Macroomed,' said Hamlet, who was feeling light-headed and ready for anything. The things you could buy for ten whole shillings!

MacDonnell chuckled. He was far from displeased with Hamlet's remark. After all Macroom was part of Tammany history, and had left his own legend behind him in New York.

'He put his name into the American language. So it's got over here now? Well, well, well. Tell me something. Do people use it like that because they heard it from the States, or did it start up on its own here too?'

'I don't know, sir,' said Hamlet with honest wonder. Since he was sent to the Duke of Clarence he had heard the locals joking about 'being macroomed', 'I gave him a macroom' or 'doing a macroom', it was used in all sorts of connotations. And he had learned that it was MacDonnell's man who had put the word into the language.

'I'd like to find out,' said MacDonnell. 'Let me know if you hear anything.' He had already asked several people, but he liked to check his references.

'Oh yes sir, indeeden I will.' Hamlet walked sideways to the door, not liking to turn his back on so great a personage. But when he got there he disappeared round the end of it, open as it was, with a speed which resembled a conjuring trick. MacDonnell had noticed Hamlet's ability to appear and disappear like a rabbit in a hat, and he approved of it. Nearly all of the successful hoodlums, business operators and really well-heeled politicians he had known had possessed the same ability.

He listened carefully for the click of the front door. He almost did not catch it. He smiled again and nodded his head. Hamlet had the priceless gifts of secrecy and discretion, the absolute essentials, in MacDonnell's experience, for success. The boy would not even commit himself to entering Maud's room. The notion that he would not commit himself to putting the brooch on Maud's dressing-table pleased him. What if someone nabbed it? The possibility was remote, but it could happen, and Hamlet had foreseen this.

But MacDonnell had other work to do, important work. He took a few scraps of papers from his hip wallet and spread them out carefully on the desk. One made a complete number with which he was acquainted; it was repeated on three torn scraps of paper when put together. He was surprised that an experienced man like Slyne should show such carelessness. But then, of course, the number was a very private one, known only to a dozen or so people. This did not excuse the man's imprudence, even if it was a very lucky break for MacDonnell.

He took up the telephone receiver from its high brass cradle at the side of his desk, and waited for the exchange to answer. MacDonnell had one of the nine telephones which the street boasted, but it was the only desk model: all the others were wall phones and used only by business houses.

'Hello, Philomena, agraw macree, 'tis bright and silvery ye sound — ' MacDonnell beamed as he welcomed an old friend known to him not only for her clear voice on the telephone, but also as the niece of two very helpful members of New York's Finest. 'It isn't! You mean you're not Philomena? Is there anything wrong? Is she ill?' A note of deep, operatic emotion entered his voice. 'No? Oh, good, thanks be to God. So you're the new girl? Well, well, I hope we'll be friends, of course we will. And your name is? Assumpta Shine, well that's a fine old local name. And where are you from, Assumpta? Buggawn? Timmy Shine's daughter? Ah, sure, I should have known, for I knew your grandfather before he went to Chicago. One of the best, the very best. I was at his funeral, Assumpta. You know! Well, if that isn't something that makes life worth living.'

MacDonnell and Assumpta then went into a long conversation, tracing relatives alive and dead, finding the different graveyards that all the Shines were buried in, and discussing them in detail, great family occasions — 'your uncle Pat had the biggest funeral the Bowery ever saw in 1904' — the marriages of her six aunts spread across the United States like settlements, their children, their careers and the two who had gone on to make a real name for themselves in local politics. MacDonnell could have kept this up — and with pleasure — for hours, but after about twenty minutes, Philomena herself came on the line and reminded MacDonnell that she was his best girl, and was he being unfaithful to her, and Assumpta was still learning, and they were very busy — over a dozen calls that morning alone, and the tally for the afternoon was far from over yet.

Presently MacDonnell and Assumpta got down to business.

'Well, Assumpta, agraw, you'll have to try and get this Dublin number for me. No problem? Of course not.' Nevertheless, MacDonnell's thick histrionic eyebrows went up as Assumpta made this reckless assumption. But whether by good luck or good management — the Post Office had cleared the line for him more than once before — he got through to his contact in less than five minutes. Then, lowering his head he launched into code. For, of course, both Assumpta and Philomena would be listening to every word he said.

'Is that Frank? How are ye, Frank? And the little woman? And the children, God bless them. Now — oh it's lovely down here, warm and bright and sunny — you know my cousin Ned? Well, I've heard that one of his boys, the eldest one, is not too well. I heard it was a touch of polio, God save us, and I know Ned will be distracted. Now, it's very hard to get through from here to Ned's, living in the country as he does, although the telephone exchange here is wonderful, a model for the nation, that's what it is, and the two operators could give the Bell staff a tip or two for efficiency and courtesy. Well now, about poor Ned. Will you get in touch with him, and try to find out — very tactfully now, Frank — just what the situation is? Has Shamus, that's the boy's name, got polio, or is it only a rumour? Then I'll know what to write to him. Well, I won't keep you now, Frank.

I know you're busy. Just give me a ring and let me know whether it is or it isn't.'

The old women were waiting. Sarah Jane McLurry would have been horrified to hear herself described as old, but that was the way the street, and the town in general, thought of them as a trio. They should have been used to waiting by now, for all three of them had had long and varied experience of it. Waiting for a husband to come home in Mrs Pig's case; waiting for her brother to show signs of some improvement, watching out anxiously for customers in a slack period, in Miss McLurry's case. In Hosannah's case waiting had become a way of life. She had, like many others, waited for something to happen all her life; a husband, a legacy from the American cousins, a cure for her ailing brother and sister in their last, lingering illness, an answer to the many candles she had lit in front of the statues of the Blessed Virgin, St Joseph, and the Sacred Heart Himself. She had grown old with waiting, yet the curious thing was that she never thought of it as that. She was always occupied, sewing, baking, decorating cakes, running errands for the nuns when she was younger, shopping when the family was still alive. 'I'm killed, dat's wad I am,' she used to say with a moan, 'I haven't a minute to sid down an' rest me feet, I'm goin' night an' day, id's only de Lord an' our Blessed Lady keeps me going, nudden else could do id. And me chest —'

Mrs Prendergast, on the other hand, often complained that she had nothing to do since her husband died. After his death she had continued to run the shop, which had never been more than a side-line in Prendergast's day. And there was always a plentiful supply of pigs' feet in those days: her husband knew all the dealers, all the small farmers who kept a few pigs for sale. During her years in Connaught Street, Mrs Prendergast had built up quite a reputation for pigs' crubeens, and people came from other towns to buy this great delicacy from her. She even had customers from Dublin, who called on their way to Galway for the summer holidays.

But these days were gone. She hardly bothered now to open the shop, and although a few local farmers still brought her a few pigs' feet, which she displayed in the windows, they could hardly be seen lying on the big cracked earthenware dish, so thick was the dust and grime on the glass of the shop.

It smelt, even to Mrs Prendergast, whose nose was a good deal keener than she was given credit for, a bit like a piggery unused, but not cleaned out, when the last pig had died. She did not find it an unpleasant smell, this aura of ghostly bonhims, and their adult brothers and sisters. Swine was not a pejorative word in Mrs Prendergast's language. After all, their feet were so dainty and well-shaped, and melted on the tongue when properly cooked.

This was what she felt now as she let herself into her shop after leaving Sarah Jane. The whiff of salt bacon, sour though it now was, gave her a tremendous appetite: she longed with all her soul for a dish of crubeens which had sustained her family down the centuries, but which she could no longer enjoy in this strange midland town, flat as a straight road through a bog, open to every blast of wind and rain that blew, and every scorching ray of sun that burned down upon it. Nothing but black, lonesome bog all the way to the very rim of the earth, so that it made Mrs Prendergast dizzy when she thought of it — and in her early days in the town she had often thought about it. Supposing she were to creep to the edge of it and peer over and see, as she had dreamed several times, the sea below at the bottom of a cliff so high that a stone thrown down would never reach the water. And the sky: it was everywhere here, pressing down on the roofs of the houses, and slipping over the horizon like glossy blue satin. Nowhere to hide from the sun here, or the moon or the stars — you could see them from your own kitchen window, coming out in the pale twilight and disappearing in the rising dawn, a glimmer of light at the edge of the flat land — she had seen it herself.

She settled herself in her sagging old cane chair beside the range in her kitchen, folded her hands in the lap of the loose blue bib that she wore, summer and winter, over a black blouse and a long dark grey skirt. Her kitchen was white-washed, and she renewed it every two years. She liked the healthy smell of lime, clean and bitter and blue-white, and she never forgot to appreciate the difference between her closed shop and her kitchen.

Slyne's miraculous offer of £60 an acre for her five acres, two roods and fourteen perches would leave her with well over three hundred pounds; a fortune in Mrs Prendergast's eyes, beyond the waking visions of avarice. With it she would be able to buy a few new chairs for her kitchen, a new mattress for her bed, and put a few new slates on the roof where it was leaking. After that, there were so many things she might do, and still keep two hundred for a rainy day.

The kettle was beginning to sing on the range, and she took down the canister from its ledge above her shoulder, tipped the kettle into the teapot, warmed it in a gentle circular motion between her palms, threw the water out into the bucket under the table beside her, scooped a handful of tea from the canister and threw it into the pot. That was the way to make tea, by the handful. Spoons, her grandmother always told her, spoiled the flavour of tea.

She looked around her kitchen and thought it was no wonder that people thought she was a miser, hoarding up all her husband's enormous fortune in flour sacks under the bed. O'Farrell's calendar hung over the mantel, the head of a red setter looking out sideways; a blob of colour against the white-wash, her grandmother's sugawn chair that she had brought all the way from Kerry, and now kept for the priest or the doctor or anyone else of superior powers that might call.

She took in the old deal dresser with the remains of her mother-in-law's willow pattern plates, and the flagged floor, worn under the step from the shop, and the bin under the window, empty now, (for what did a lone woman want with a bag of meal with nobody to bake for?), and her big frieze coat hung on a nail in the door with her cap on top like a figure on a gibbet, and the small looking glass on the window sill where she combed her hair, and the blue rack lying beside ('what's a rack?' Sarah Jane had once asked, and Mrs Prendergast had enriched her ignorance by explaining that it was a comb, that's what it was), and the smell of the good red carbolic soap that she kept on a ledge under the window where she washed herself, with the curtains drawn upon the glass and the outer world, every day, stripping down to the waist, as her mother had done. Mrs Prendergast was a clean woman in spite of her wild hair, big winter boots and the coat that she had worn now for twelve winters.

That was another thing she would buy with the English-man's money: a coat and a good woollen scarf and knitted gloves like the gentry, for she was getting no younger, and a few new blouses, and maybe a new skirt.

How many knew, she wondered to herself, as she poured out a new mug of scalding tea, that she had been left penniless, that her husband had gambled his last shilling away, and that for the last few years she had survived only by selling the few cattle she had left on the bit of land she was now also selling. Benedict O'Farrell knew. Otherwise, why should she find a pound note hidden in the few groceries she bought from him once a week? The first time she had brought it back he had clearly been embarrassed, since his wife was in the shop, but a glance at Ellen's face told her that whatever Benedict did in his dealings with other people was all right with his wife. The subject was not mentioned again.

Canon Sharkey gave her a pound a week, after making very close enquiries, which Mrs Prendergast in no way resented. And the parish priest had instructed his curate, Father Raft, to give her five shillings, these transactions to be made every month in the form of two postal orders. Her sister in Bristol, who was matron of a big hospital there, sent her money fairly regularly too. Mrs Prendergast was able to live — it did not, as she knew, cost very much just to live — but unless she got this windfall from Slyne, or whatever his name was, she would never see her native Kerry again, and never put her arms into a brand new coat. A second-hand one from the nuns she could expect, but Mrs Prendergast did not like nuns, and that was that.

She looked up at a sound from the window. The big black cat from next door was touching the glass gently with her paw. This was Mrs Prendergast's own, particular friend; all the more so since Roseen Dubd, Mrs Prendergast's name for her, belonged to the Gleesons next door, who were so stuck up that they went to Dublin to buy their tea, and pretended they did not see their neighbour if she happened to be out in her back yard when they were in theirs. Neighbours develop a sixth sense about this. Not for over three years had the Gleesons chanced to be in their yard at the same time as Mrs Pig was in hers. But Mrs Prendergast did not regret anything: she had won the undying affection of Roseen Dubd, who was known to the Gleesons by the uncatlike and thoroughly insensitive name of Kitty. Rose, one of the hidden Ireland's most mysterious titles, suited this cat from her whiskers to the end of her tail. Most every day, not regularly, since this would be common and undignified, she tapped gently on Mrs Prendergast's window, and was immediately admitted by the back door. She came in, loose-limbed, lovely, with her brilliant green eyes playful and gleaming, and sprang up on the sugawn chair, where she curled her tail gracefully round her loins, and listened attentively as Mrs Prendergast began to talk to her in a low, crooning voice.

'What would you like for a present, Roseen Dudb, when I come into me kingdom? Ah, now, don't say anything, I began too soon, I'm dat excited about it, but here's your milk, agradh machree. Look at de blue shining through it, isn't it lovely?'

The whispered conversation went on, to which Roseen contributed a few purring comments, and the evening flowed by. The sun turned to yellow on the white-washed wall, and the alarm clock on the mantel began to change voice from the brittle tick of daylight to the hoarser tock of the darkening hours. Roseen Dudb had to go, and Mrs Prendergast, suddenly, without any reason that she could explain, began to think of Benedict O'Farrell and how it was that she must go over and see him that very evening. She even knew the time, for it was not yet too dark, even in her shadowed kitchen, for her not to be able to see the time, and at half-past that hour she knew she would go over to O'Farrell's, for there was news for her there and a welcome.

The thought of going over to Fenny's occurred to the three women almost at the same time, about half-past eight. Miss McLurry was closing her shop, which she sometimes did after the picture crowd had passed, trooping into her to buy sweets and chocolates to bring with them to the cinema in the Father Matthew Hall, by the turn of the bridge, set in between a great arched passageway to the docks, and bounded on the other side by the promenade, green and tree-shaded and sloping and beseated, with a boat club and low narrow boats like greyhounds coursing on the water. It was the best situated picture-house in Ireland, someone had said, but Miss McLurry thought it was a shame to waste it on all that American cowboy trash and film stars that got divorced. It should be made into a library, was what she said. And still calling it the Father Matthew Hall — the man that very nearly drove the Guinnesses out of Ireland — and showing silly coarse pictures!

And then she thought, I can't stick this any longer, I'll go up to O'Farrell's. Fenny is sure to know.

But not until ten at least, Hosannah thought, for she made up her mind to do the same thing. Mr O'Farrell would know, and she couldn't stick it in the house any longer. Summer darkness was the worst of all, and her little house seemed danker and damper and deader than ever when she knew that over the walls of the garden, yard and orchard, the sun was shining low and mellow and sudden in the eye. Anyway, she argued to herself, everybody goes to O'Farrell's when they want to know anything. But not until ten, he'll be busy until ten, maybe later. I'll see.

Mrs Prendergast had been down to the church to say her rosary and do the Stations, as was her habit every evening. This time she went to the parish church, a penal chapel with galleries grouped round an altar set on ten steps, so that everyone could see. It smelled of peppermint, wax, snuff, incense, dust and old men, and it was the only place in the whole of Bridgeford where Mrs Prendergast felt completely and easily at home. (She loved the Friary too, if not quite as passionately as she loved this dusty old church, but only the Friars had seven o'clock mass in the morning, every morning.) Here she brought her first baby to be baptized, and her second, both dead in infancy. Johnny had begun to decline from then on. Her Johnny, a good, kind husband in spite of his addiction to gambling, had had his Requiem Mass here, and Mrs Prendergast remembered with pride the size of the funeral. Not only the locals, but every pig dealer stood in the crowded little porch of the church, with its table — one leg wobbly — for the Sunday collection. Johnny was remembered by his memorial card, framed and hung up there with all the worthies of the town, so that the good people who prayed for the dead should remember him before the altar.

Her Stations followed to the end, and her rosary said, Mrs Prendergast went out into the porch and touched Johnny's memorial with fingertips that trembled only slightly. Then she spoke to him softly, here where he seemed so much nearer to her than anywhere else, maybe because he always stood with the rest of the men outside in the porch, and even in the churchyard during mass. Canon Sharkey might thunder against it — 'are we a nation of gypsies?' — but it made no difference. The men stayed outside and got down on one knee for the Consecration. It all came back to Mrs Prendergast, and she never stayed long in the porch, although she loved it dearly, for fear she might be caught crying.

So she hurried out through the chapel yard, up the steep hill of Chapel Street and O'Connell Street to come out on the level top of Connaught Street. By the clock in Lennon's window it showed half-past nine. Just time for another cup of tea before she went over to O'Farrell's.

While the three women were going about their business of praying, closing shop, and in Hosannah's case, washing her face — the third time she had done it that week — Fenny was being interviewed at MacDonnell's front door by Macroom.

'Who are you?' Macroom opened the door a few inches and peered out, rattling the chain as he did so. His sharp little eyes, the colour of dog piss, as one local wit described them, were narrowed and hostile, and his pointed nose, as sharp and grey as a cobbler's awl, were all that were immediately visible.

'I'm Ben O'Farrell. I have an appointment with Mr MacDonnell.' Ben was prepared for a fairly lengthy siege, but it was too complicated going round to the back door. At this time of the evening, with no gardener to torment, Macroom would pounce on him there too.

'No, you haven't. If you had I'd know.'

'Maybe Mr MacDonnell forgot to tell you.'

'Don't get fresh with me, bud. I don't take that kind of pig-cheek from no one, ye hear me?' Macroom had returned from New York with a Yankee accent that would perforate a solid silver tray. But it had gradually disappeared on MacDonnell's orders, and now Macroom spoke his native Cork patois, one of the more obscure Anglo-Irish dialects, more or less as he used it before he emigrated sixty years before. But occasionally he reverted to the lingo he had picked up as MacDonnell's personal security man.

'I think Mr MacDonnell is standing in the hall behind you,' said Fenny, taking a chance. Visitors to MacDonnell's fine town house were carefully scrutinized through curtains by the street, and he could feel the eyes turned on him like the rays of a hot, slanting summer sun.

'Drunk too, eh? Go away.' Macroom's nose wrinkled with disgust, and he managed through the slender opening of the door to inspect Fenny from the top of his head to the position of his boots.

'Are you sure you haven't one over the eight yourself?'

'Insults will get you no place, buster. Skidaddle, ye hear me?'

'I hear you, and so does Mr MacDonnell. He's just behind you.'

'I know where he is,' retorted Macroom in his best Macroom manner, 'And he isn't here.' He opened the door half-way, and there standing at the back of the hall, grinning broadly, was the great man himself. 'Ye see?' went on Macroom. 'He ain't here. But what am I wasting me valuable time on a drunk like you for? Get off me steps. You're gettin' between me and the sun.'

'I made my appointment over the telephone,' said Fenny, who was beginning to doubt the evidence of his senses, like so many people who found themselves confronted with Macroom. Since MacDonnell had retired and come back home to live, everybody knew that Macroom had to be humoured, and why not? It was a harmless enough game, but Fenny resented it. He usually discussed his business with MacDonnell in his own house, when the Tammany man dropped in for a drink, as he sometimes did. Then he was ceremoniously shown up to the drawing-room, and his drink carried upstairs.

'No, you didn't,' retorted Macroom. 'There's no telephone in this house. And anyway what would you know about it? Like as not ye'd speak into the wrong end of it, like some of the galoots hereabouts.'

'We're a long way from Cork,' said Fenny quietly, feeling the eyes behind him literally burning the back of his neck.

'What did ye say yer name was?' enquired Macroom in an equally soft and ironic voice. It was difficult to get the better of him, and Fenny knew that MacDonnell often stood listening to one of these conversations for quite a while, to see if the old bodyguard had lost his touch.

'I'd give you a card if you could read.'

'Listen you,' croaked Macroom, 'If I have any more greasy pole out of you, I tell Mr MacDonnell about you, every single word, if not more, and then you'd better walk careful, because if you were to hide yourself up a ferret he'll catch ye when yer comin' out. Now git.' And he slammed the door in Fenny's face.

While the heat on the back of his neck had now extended to his shoulders and threatened to roast his back, Fenny knew — as one knew everything in that street — that if MacDonnell showed himself during the dialogue with Macroom at the door, he would, after a decent interval, come and open the door himself.

So Fenny turned round quickly, and as he did so at least eight lace curtains fell back into place, and several wavering faces disappeared into the gloom behind them. He named them over silently to himself as he waited, and had time to rediscover the real meaning of macrooming: it meant telling an outrageous untruth straight in the face of the evidence, and getting away with it.

The door opened behind him, and MacDonnell himself stood there, with a welcoming smile on his handsome red face. He even came out and stood on the top step to shake hands with Fenny, his way of telling the neighbours that, in spite of Macroom's act, this was a visitor he was glad to see. The curtains twitched again, and this time remained back.

MacDonnell's house was under constant scrutiny, for it was rumoured in the town that since his accession to power, De Valera himself was very likely to visit his old American ally. Had not the two men already met on the platform in the square, when Dev came to town last year? Preceded by every band in town, a mile long procession of motors, and a huge crowd of men, roaring and holding aloft burning sods of turf on pikes; and the pikes blazed and the motors honked and the men screamed as the tall, black figure of The Chief rose above the others on the platform, and seared his image into the minds of the children who had been taken along by their parents for a glimpse of the great man.

After a few moments talk about the weather, MacDonnell put his hand on Fenny's shoulder and said: 'Come in, come in.'

When they were inside Fenny looked around for Macroom, but the large hall was empty, polished, picture-hung, freshly painted and half-covered by a magnificent worn Persian carpet; one of MacDonnell's better 'per cents' for services rendered. So too were the pair of Sèvres vases on a side table, objects that Fenny had always regarded with admiration and envy.

They went into the study and MacDonnell poured out a

couple of whiskeys for his guest and himself. When he was seated and had taken a reasonable mouthful of the kind of whiskey that should be savoured slowly, Fenny could no longer repress a question which he had meant to ask his host before.

'Does Macroom really not know me when I come to the door? You know he meets me in the street now and again, and always knows my name.'

'That's different. Outside the house he's not on duty.' MacDonnell was looking down at his glass, and Fenny noticed that his colour had heightened.

'But surely he wouldn't treat me the way he does at the door, unless you had told him to,' Fenny insisted.

There was a slight pause. MacDonnell's lips tightened and a folded line appeared between his bushy eyebrows.

'I give him no instructions,' said MacDonnell sharply, and looked up suddenly, giving Fenny an almost hostile look.

'But —' Fenny was about to insist and press his question, when he suddenly realized that MacDonnell knew all about Macroom's activities down to the smallest detail, and approved of them. Another thought flashed across Fenny's mind: the old man had been used for many years to the kind of protection Macroom gave him, if protection it could be called, and did not relish the idea of giving it up, even though it was a slightly dotty piece of ham-acting. Macroom, one of the best known characters in the New York of his day, had been preserved in aspic and could not be expected to change.

Fenny changed his tactics. There was no point in challenging the feelings of two old men.

'Oh, I see. He treats everybody the same way, so that if someone really undesirable turns up at the door he's able to cope.'

'That's more or less the idea. I have many enemies, Mr O'Farrell.' MacDonnell always addressed Fenny formally when he was in a particularly pompous mood; and he seemed pleased by Fenny's explanation of Macroom's antics. Fenny realized that Macroom was of immense importance to MacDonnell, now that he was retired and respectable.

'Surely not,' said Fenny lightly, for our understanding does not always run abreast with our intuitions. Besides, the remark was intended to flatter.

'Surely yes,' snapped MacDonnell with a return of his surly

manner, and a deep, vexed frown. 'There are many people in this country today who would like to see the end of me. Naturally you wouldn't know anything about that, but so it is.'

'Well,' said Fenny, now sure of his line, 'they'll have their work cut out. I wouldn't like to try it, I can tell you.'

MacDonnell relaxed, and became his old genial self again.

'You said on the telephone —' he began, but then changed his mind, held up his hand and leaned forward on the desk, looking at Fenny with steady, unblinking eyes, the picture of a highly experienced professional about to give a client or a patient a piece of bad news.

'There are certain men, extremists, that I helped in the fight for independence. Now that we have our own government, at least in the South, we have no further need of extremists, especially since that great man God has seen fit to send us into power. You understand me?'

'Of course.'

MacDonnell leaned back in his leather chair and joined the tips of his fleshy fingers together.

'So Macroom keeps guard. Overdoing it a bit, I admit, but erring in the right direction, I think. What are you going to do about Slyne?'

The conversation was changed so abruptly and with so little alteration of tone that Fenny was left suspended, mouth half open, for a few seconds. But he adjusted himself quickly, and looked at MacDonnell with a most serious expression. His instinct was now fully alert: he would make no more fox passes.

'I don't know. What would you advise?'

MacDonnell paused, then he opened a drawer and took out a box of cigars, held it out to Fenny who took one with considerable respect, for the old man's cigars were justly famous.

'Do you mind if I smoke this later? I have to get back to the shop.' He put the cigar in the breast pocket of his light summer jacket, and patted it gently.

'Of course not. I'd advise you to sell your land to him.' MacDonnell ran his cigar under his nose, then took up a small, ivory-handled knife from his desk.

'He hasn't made a definite offer yet.'

'He will.' MacDonnell cut his cigar, and took up a box of long matches.

'You mean he's going ahead with the deal?'

MacDonnell nodded and lit up.

'Does he know —' Fenny did not mean to complete this question, and MacDonnell acknowledged his tact and understanding by pausing in the ceremony of lighting a perfect cigar, and allowing the match to go out, his hand bringing the unlighted cigar to rest on the desk.

'He is going ahead with the deal,' he repeated softly. 'All the land from the others — the old ladies in this street. And Mrs Daly of course — and your bit. He's anxious to buy that also.'

'I'll think about it.' Fenny smiled. 'I'm glad for the old ladies' sake — I mean the three neighbours here — Mrs Daly is hardly in need of the money.'

'Hardly.'

'Have you changed your mind about selling your land?' said Fenny, cheered by the news that the old women were not going to be let down.

MacDonnell smiled, and this time went through the slow, hieratic, slightly obscene ceremony of lighting his cigar. The room was filled with a rich, autumnal scent; dried leaves and gum, and something black and mysterious like truffles that make up the aroma of a good cigar. MacDonnell smacked his damp lips, and watched the smoke coil slowly over the desk and float above Fenny's head. It was a long, scented and slightly dead moment. Fenny felt no sense of irritation or menace or displeasure. He merely felt that he had never asked the question, and that MacDonnell had never heard it. This he thought is what a stillborn baby must be like; there and not there, a memory untouched by events, a moment killed by consent.

For a decent interval, they chatted about a photograph of Mrs Prendergast that had surprisingly appeared in the Westmeath Independent during the week. It seemed that her nephew was a famous actor in New York, and he was making his first film with Joan Crawford.

After MacDonnell had made a courteous enquiry about Ellen, whom he admired and genuinely respected, they rose and went into the hall. On a chair inside the door, sitting with his hands placed on his knees, like a Russian moujik of pre-revolutionary days, was Macroom. He stood up and gave

Fenny a grin which transformed his face into that of a Chinese
petty lawbreaker of about ninety.

'Tis welcome you are, Mister O'Farrell.'

'And the froth of the day to you too, Macroom,' replied
Fenny in the same idiom. He was feeling rather cross with this
old buffoon — who may of course also be quite a dangerous one
— but surely all that drama at the door was unnecessary. Of
course, if it was something he kept up because he could not face
the emptiness of his days, then it was an annoying and
essentially pathetic little theatre; but Fenny was not in the
mood to indulge the old man just now. And he had, after all,
received very good news from MacDonnell.

Macroom, still grinning, opened the door, and MacDonnell,
holding his cigar in his hand with a slightly bloated air, came
out on to the steps to see him off.

'How on earth do you know all these things, about the land, I
mean?' said Fenny in a low voice, which MacDonnell took as a
compliment. He smiled, waved his cigar carelessly and put his
free hand on his departing guest's shoulder.

'I keep in touch. And it's perfectly true. You need have no
qualms about telling the women. And think about your own
bit, won't you?'

'Thank you, thank you,' murmured Fenny, taking MacDonnell's outstretched hand. The old man always shook hands.
Even if he met the same person five times in one day he shook
hands. It meant nothing, and everything.

The three women converged on O'Farrell's while Fenny was
still closeted with MacDonnell. They gave him about half an
hour more, and as usual their instinct was right.

Hosannah was the first, and she stood at the grocery counter
until Ellen, who was pulling beer at the bar, had served
whatever pints had to be served and came across the shop,
lifting the flap of the grocery counter so that Hosannah might
appear to be buying something. Ellen was learning to be what
Fenny called a 'street woman'.

'Is de boss back yet?' whispered Hosannah, tapping the
counter with the edge of a halfpenny, so as to give the
impression to the four or five male backs at the bar that she was
doing mighty purchasing in the grocery line.

'Not yet. Would you like to wait inside? Or upstairs?' she added hastily. For inside meant Gummy Hayes, who was out at the moment, as Hosannah had anticipated, but who might return any minute. And sitting upstairs would give her a certain immunity. Besides, she expected that Sarah Jane and Mrs Pig would drop in later and join her. They would be a certain protection, especially Mrs Pig for whom Gummy had some respect. 'Dem Kerry women is nod Irish, ye know, we doan know dere ways, an' some o' thim have de powers.' This did not prevent Gummy from getting a few sly sideways digs through Mrs Pig's ribs, a remark Fenny had once passed. 'Don't be diggen her ribs, Gumsheen, she sells them, you know.'

'Would you be needin' a pound o' tay in de house?' whispered Hosannah.

Ellen nodded, almost a complete Bridgeford woman by now, and Hosannah went through the private door holding a pound of Musgrave's best tea outstretched in her hand. With Ellen busy at the bar, she was demonstrating to the men's shoulders that she was looking after the house for Mrs O'Farrell, and Hosannah knew that just then the fearful Gummy Hayes was out doing the Stations in the church. Moreover, Ellen had told her to go upstairs to the drawing-room, so even if Gummy had been in the kitchen Hosannah would have been able to slip upstairs, and Gummy would not hear her. When it came to flitting softly from one place to another Hosannah was an angel.

Miss McLurry was the next to arrive. She too walked determinedly to the grocery counter, causing Ellen to come across from the bar again, lifting the two counter flaps — a means of entrance and exit which used to delight and fascinate Sarah Jane before she had a shop of her own — to meet her new 'customer'.

'I've come about the Black Babies,' said Miss McLurry in a loud voice. 'I'd 've come sooner, only there's my own shop, you know, and anyway the nuns didn't leave the collection box until just before I was closing. Not the nuns themselves of course — they wouldn't be out at this time of night. God looks down upon them in their hard little beds — but they sent one of the orphan girls they keep — O a real half-wit. Sure, she didn't know what she was sent to deliver. O I see,' she hurried on before

Ellen had time to say more than a few words, indicating that she'd contribute of course. 'Your husband keeps the Mission money upstairs, for fear it would get mixed up with the shop cash. Well, I do think that's a good sensible idea, and you and he are always so generous. Would you like me to wait until he comes back? This box is for you, by the way, it's empty, and Sister Fechin wrote me a little note, asking me to ask you if you'd keep one on your own counter. So I'd better wait until himself comes back.'

Never were so many birds knocked sideways by the same volley of consonants: the original excuse of delivering the box late, the Mission money upstairs meant that she would have to be brought in, and finally, and most important of all, she knew that Ellen knew that no respectable girl like Miss McLurry would remain in a shop where men were drinking. She could of course have been put into the snug inside the door, a small enclosure rather like an oversized confession box with a grill for serving drinks, where elderly women, who had reached the canonical age, were accommodated with port and mulled stout on market days. But Miss McLurry reckoned it would be unthinkable to be put there alone, where she could hear the men talk: moreover, she was carrying the nuns' box, and in any case did not drink. It all amounted to a weighty argument, with many side-sections and sub-sections, and innumerable precedents for appeal. Miss McLurry was shown upstairs.

Where of course she met Hosannah. Neither of them expressed surprise at seeing the other.

'I wonder if Mrs Prendergast will come,' said Hosannah, who was perched on the very edge and at the very end of an enormously wide, deep and long sofa covered with chintz; one of Ellen's first innovations when she came as Mrs O'Farrell.

'Of course she'll come,' snapped Miss McLurry who was rather displeased to find Susannah Braiden cocked up in the O'Farrell's drawing-room; surely the little dining-room behind the shop would have been more than good enough for the likes of her. And on the sofa too, almost as if she expected someone to share it with her.

Miss McLurry marched straight to the window, and began a complicated series of movements, twitching her body backwards and forwards, from side to side, and craning her neck in between the curtains and the wall.

'Can you see id?' said Hosannah mildly.

'See what?' Miss McLurry was too far gone in her contortions to unbend and untie herself in order to give Hosannah the answer she deserved.

'Wrigleys, a' course.' Hosannah's tone was still flat; the voice of a woman who would do exactly the same thing as Miss McLurry was doing now, if she were in her place. 'And dey're giving extra gums, an' even a curreny bun for all buyers over sixpence.'

'I know, I know. It's not fair, that's what it is. Not fair.' Sarah Jane could not conceal her indignation, even in front of Hosannah Braiden. The Wrigleys were her great rivals for the sweet trade of the street.

Hosannah was not paying much attention to Sarah Jane. She was still basking in the luxury of sitting in O'Farrell's upstairs drawing-room: not simply in the ornaments that loaded every table, or the heavily framed coloured photographs of Fenny's father and mother, nor the silver, nor anything indeed except the *idea* of it all. To have a huge room running the whole length of the shop, with private stairs and enormous windows looking down on the street, commanding a view which she could indulge every hour of the day and night, was intoxicating. Nevertheless she had to try and keep in touch with Miss McLurry, since they were on the same errand, and a split in the camp now would be a disaster.

'De Brannigans are doin' id too,' she said in a low voice, putting her hands out and feeling the weight and depth, the length and sheer roominess of the sofa she was perched upon. One could sleep in a yoke like this, even live in it altogether.

'Yes, I know,' said Miss McLurry with one last lingering look at Wrigleys.

'Times is hard in Bridgeford,' said Hosannah simply. 'Bisness poor, an' money terrible scarce.'

This stark truth silenced both of them, and they were sitting in gloomy, if roomy, silence, when in marched Mrs Prendergast in her blue bib, and cotton gloves on her big hands to show that she knew how to behave in a drawing-room.

'Marcella!' exclaimed Sarah Jane, who was the only person in the town to call her by her christian name, and one of the few who knew it.

'Good evenin', Mrs Pig,' said Hosannah coldly. She had not forgotten the incident in the sweet shop.

'How did you get up here?' said Sarah Jane, who was interested in excuses.

'I just came over, axed for Mr O'Farrell, although of course I know he's not back yet, and de wife told me to come straight up.' She sat down on the other end of the sofa from Hosannah, and looked about her with simple wonder. 'Isn't this a gorgeous room,' she remarked in a low mass voice.

'Did you tell Mrs O'Farrell anything? I mean about coming over. There's a crowd of men at the bar with ears like blind rabbits.'

'I just axed for himself.' Mrs Pig shrugged her shoulders in that peculiar see-saw motion common to Irish country women, and townee corner-boys. 'What do I care what the min say? I just read de cards before I came out.'

Sarah Jane and Hosannah became rigid with interest and curiosity. It was well known that Mrs Pig had the powers, which made her a slightly awesome figure to many. Kerry women all had the powers, according to Hosannah, whose American cousin had once spent a holiday in Ballybunion, where she had been told by a pious witch, who made a fortune designing woollen suits for foreigners, and read the tea leaves in her spare time, that although unmarried she was going to be the mother of twins. Four years later, she was married to one of New York's Finest, and the twins arrived in time for Christmas.

'As ye know, I don't look at de cards much since poor Pig died. I got an awful shock when I read dem on his annivercity, and found that he was in Purgatory; the four of spades and the ten of diamonds on either side of himself, the king of clubs.'

'God Almighty save us,' said Hosannah in a trembling voice. 'If id was the ace —' she broke off, and clapped her hand against her open mouth.

'No, he's not dere,' said Mrs Pig complacently, 'and he's all right in Purgatory, plenty o' company dere. But what I wanted to tell ye was dat I read the cards just before I came out, de nine o' clubs and d'ace of diamonds. Money on de way. So what did I care for the min in the bar?'

'You mean you're sure he's buying the land?' said Sarah Jane fretfully.

'Certainly he is. The cards never lie'.

The two others were silent, although their hearts were beating hard with excitement at the news, which they did not doubt for a moment. The day was won. But Canon Sharkey was terribly hard on fortune telling, and had run several tinker women out of town for making a trade of it. So they were silent. Never treat the cards carelessly; never discount the tea leaves; never build on a fairy path, or a mass path; never touch a rag on an enchanted tree; never leave the dead alone for one single moment; go back home if you meet a red-haired woman first thing in the morning; have nothing to do with a whistling woman or a crowing hen; don't do anything on the sixth day, or in the sixth month, or six times running, for that's the devil's number; never bring a wart to a doctor, for if he cures it, it will break out in your guts, or your bowels and turn to cancer; never mention the word 'cancer', or 'consumption', or mention a half-wit in front of a pregnant woman; and every one knew that by holding up the ace of hearts during the Consecration at mass, and invoking the devil, you could win a fortune at gambling, but those who did it died rich and roaring; and never fight with a blacksmith, for he will curse you by name on his anvil. Above all, and this passed through the minds of the three childless women as they sat there waiting for their fortune, never tell a man how the sex of a child can be known at least four months before birth.

It was a secret every woman knew — but no man.

Miss McLurry who considered herself the most sophisticated woman of the three, if not in all Bridgeford, was just about to start up the conversation again on some nice neutral subject, for of course they must not pretend, by even the flicker of a mutual eyelash, that they knew already what Fenny was going to tell them. And it was much safer to talk of other things, for then their minds would be at least partially diverted from the great good news Mrs Pig had told them.

A diversion was not however necessary for them, since before Miss McLurry could say a word the door opened, and in walked Gummy Hayes. Instinctively the three women braced themselves, not catching one another's eyes, but by sitting up and squaring their shoulders.

'Well, well, well, id's a long time since we had tree bona fide ladies in our drawin'-room.'

This was bad enough, but she accompanied her remark by

dropping what she imagined was a deep curtsey: she went down on one knee in holy genuflection, which her muscles were well trained to do, and spread out her hands wide on either side, dropping her head until her chin touched her chest. Then she rose, not without a slight effort, and looked at the guests with a sarcastic smile, which was worse than anything. Hosannah huddled against the arm of the sofa, and Mrs Pig tugged at her soiled white cotton gloves.

'I thought you were crippled with the pains,' said Miss McLurry, who still felt that she was the first person there.

'And so I am, me lady, bud for de likes o' you, and yer lady friends, I hole me rumouratics as less dan a puddle on a wet Friday. And nod any ladies of high degree, but big lan'owners as well. I am onerated, de house is onerated —'

'We are honoured to see you also, Gummy,' said Miss McLurry recklessly. 'Are you having tea with us?'

The insult was calculated and dangerous, for Gummy was no ordinary object of fun, ridicule or fear. She was a woman whose tongue was known and dreaded from Summerhill to Bonavally Bridge, which was the entire length of the town, west to east.

Now she looked at Miss McLurry with a small, sweet smile, crossed her hands over her chest and bowed her head.

'Ah, sure dat's how all can see when de breedin' comes out. I declare to me God dat if I stuck a needle into yer neck dis very minnit, it'd bleed blue of the pewrist quality. No, milady, I won't be takin' tay wid ye, for I have yet to hear dat anywan of us was axed.'

'Is it very warm out, Miss Hayes?' said Hosannah, making a feeble effort to change the direction of the prevailing wind.

'Yes, Miss Braiden, id iss, warm enough for ye ta wear one o' dem summer frocks we all know ye get made in Lunnon. Be appointment to de Queen, ye might say.' For some reason this remark amused Gummy hugely, for she went off into a sudden explosion of disjointed cackles, like distant fireworks.

Mrs Pig was just about to make a remark, but Gummy saw her open her mouth and shut off the fireworks abruptly.

'And you, Mrs Prendergast, dat comes from de Kingdom o' Kerry, maybe you doan realize d'oner ye have in takin' tea wid two a' de bess bred lan'owners in de whole a' Bridgeford.' Gummy's tone was not aggressive; she gave the impression of sharing a joke with the Kerry woman, for whom she felt a certain awe, having heard that she had the powers, and could curse a pregnant sow so that she produced maggots.

Mrs Prendergast understood and took the opportunity of heading off the bickering.

'Before I come out I saw in de cards an event dat's goin' to take place in this house,' Mrs Pig said in a low, mysterious voice which she put on for these occasions, and it seemed to her that the only way to prevent mayhem between Gummy and the other two women was to frighten the moonshine out of them. 'Not now, but later. And de cards did not say what it was, but whenever three of them come together like dat, and I'm not going to tall you what three, it means dat only de three deepest things, a birth, death or marriage, are goin' to happen there. Are you thinkin' of gettin' married, Miss Hayes?' Sure of her position, Mrs Pig could not resist this little one-sided joke, for really Gummy had behaved very badly to her guests, thus breaking a law sacred in Kerry in her young days.

'Den id's a deat' for sure,' said Gummy, leaping onto her favourite hobby-horse. 'De Lord delibber us an' defen' us.' And she rolled her eyes ceiling-ward and blessed herself three times.

'Not for sure,' said Mrs Prendergast. 'Is Mrs O'Farrell expecting?'

'Ah, no, it's deat' for sure. Does it apply to people in de house now, but nod livin' in id, like de min below in de bar?'

Mrs Prendergast thought for a moment, and was pleased at the transformation she had brought about by thinking up something that had never happened. The cards had told her no such thing, but it seemed a bright idea to say so.

'Yes,' she said slowly, 'it could mean dat.'

'Ah aw,' said Gummy, sighing with relief. 'I noticed it de momend I came in an' for some liddle time now I've bin noticin' id — I doan't tink dat Miss McLurry looks well ad all, a terrible bad colour. Like ye know.' She gave the two visitors a meaningful glance they understood perfectly. That was one of the words that could not be mentioned. And everyone knew that there was consumption in the McLurry family. Two sisters of Sarah Jane had died of it, and then there was poor Christy, surely the product of the disease also, since they knew it attacked its victims in various ways. But 'a terrible bad colour' meant the Other Thing, which some people believed came from unhealed lesions that turned. . .

Then Ellen walked calmly into the room with a smile for everyone. It faded a little when she realized that Gummy was in one of her rages and Miss McLurry seemed to be the object of it.

'I'm very sorry for leaving you alone all this time,' she said softly, aware that the best thing to do was not to notice anything. 'But Benedict isn't back yet, and I couldn't get away. However, you know Pinky Egan? Well he's just come in, so I could leave him in charge of the bar, and come up. No one is expected at the grocery counter at this hour, but just in case there is one, would you ever mind going down and having a look, Miss Hayes? If it's someone you know, give them whatever they want, and let me know after. If it's a stranger, let me know.' She looked about the circle of ruffled women with another, still warmer smile, and Gummy slowly unhooked her claws from her hips, straightened herself up, and marched out of the room with one last, killing glance at Miss McLurry. There was nothing in the world that Gummy liked better than minding the shop, in spite of the fact that she could not read or write. But she could remember every single item she sold, even if the list of ounces, pounds and stones was the length of three chalk slates.

'You must be all stiff sitting here waiting,' Ellen went on, 'And no one to get you even a cup of tea. I'm ashamed of myself, really I am. Would you care for a little drop of port or sherry, or that little tot of whiskey that cures everything?' She went over to the big mahogany painted cabinet in the 'Gothic' style, which was one of the wonders of the street, so heavy, so lavishly, even recklessly, carved was it. She opened one of the panels and began to sort about the large supply of bottles kept there.

But they all accepted the drinks. Port for Mrs Pig, sherry for Hosannah, whiskey for Miss McLurry, 'It's good for my heart, the doctor says.' But she really needed it to steady her nerves, after what she had been through. Ellen took a small glass of mineral water and, having served the guests, was just about to seat herself on the sofa when Gummy burst into the room, marched across and fumbled in the cushions of the chair she had been sitting in. Then she straightened up and glared at the three visitors.

'Me teet', me teet', I put dem in de pocket a' me apron, and now where are dey? Is dere a witch in dis room dat has taken de teet' outa me pocket?' She turned to Ellen. 'And by de way ma'am, Mrs Pig is no witch, I didden mane her, so I didden, she's a wise woman wid powers, bud no witch.' She turned towards Miss McLurry again. 'Have dem teet' fur me before ye go, or I'll go straight down to de Peelers.' And wheeling round, flapping her arms, her loose apron flying, she hurried out of the room like a pantomime bird of prey.

'She puts them on a shelf in the shop, she always loses them when she's in charge of the grocery, it goes to her head,' said Ellen soothingly.

This conversation was abruptly brought to an end by the sound of shuffling and muttering outside the door. Ellen looked at her guests and got up to go to the door immediately.

Gummy was outside, swaying from side to side with her mouth covered by her hand.

'Me teet', me teet', somewan in dere has me teet',' she wailed.

'But Miss Hayes, who would want to steal your teeth?' said Ellen in a soothing voice.

'Dere's dem dat does. How can I look afther the shop wid me teet' in anodder woman's purse or somewhere? I'll have to drown dem for a week in sulpher, in case dere condamunated.'

'Now, now, Miss Hayes, don't fret. I'll look for them for you. Wait a moment.' Ellen closed the door, held up a finger in front of her pursed mouth, and began to turn up cushions, carpets and chair covers, looked into vases and flower pots, and every other silly place that one looks at, when looking for something one knows is not really lost.

The guests helped her with more than one fretful glance at the door. Nothing was found, but Miss McLurry had an idea.

'Does she do what *you* tell her?' she whispered to Ellen.

'Oh, yes.'

'Then send her down to the kitchen for something, and when she comes back, send her down for something else. You can't have her standing outside the door like that all evening.'

'I wonder,' said Ellen. But she went out to Gummy and asked her to look behind the grocery counter, in the till, or the shelves under the counter, for a bank book she thought she had left there. This sent off Gummy in a good humour.

The women chatted away, and Ellen filled their glasses twice, and twice Gummy came back with nothing to report. Ellen thought of various places she might have left the bank book, which was quite safe in Ben's locked box in the bedroom; and three times Gummy went down to look for it. Sarah Jane developed a grin which made her look like the cat who has not only got the cream, but named it also. Ellen noticed this: noticed the glee which both Miss McLurry and Hosannah showed when poor old Gummy was sent off scurrying downstairs, her 'rumouratics' making noises like the cracking of biscuits. When she heard Gummy slowly and puffily coming upstairs again — and noticed that the other women fell silent as if they were listening — she determined to do something about it. Gummy got to the top of the stairs and was obviously standing outside on the landing. Ellen could hear her wheezing and muttering to herself. If the famous teet' had been found, the old woman would not have come upstairs again.

Ellen heard a heavy, quick step on the stairs, and knew that her husband had returned. Her heart, which had been troubled, lightened, and her whole body seemed suddenly to relax from a sort of rigid pose.

The door was flung open, but Fenny did not come in. With one hand on the knob he was talking to Gummy.

'Well, Gumboil, what are you doing up here, all on your ownio?'

'I losh me teet',' quavered Gummy, who wouldn't have dreamed of telling a tall sorty to her adored Mr Benny. The idea of Miss McLurry stealing her teeth, or even of Gummy herself losing them in the drawing-room, and running up and down the stairs as a result, would not have impressed him for one moment.

'They're not in there, are they?' he asked Ellen softly.

'I don't think so.'

Fenny sensed at once that something had happened between the visitors and his old nurse; the fact of Hosannah and Miss McLurry locked up in his mother's drawing-room, was not an event calculated to appeal to Gummy's sense of humour. Without a word he turned, ran downstairs, and out into the shop.

'Where did Gummy leave her teeth?' he asked the men at the bar.

'Behind d'Arrowroot biscuits,' said three voices speaking in unison.

Fenny retrieved them at once, and went back upstairs. The

landing was a large one, and was lit by a high window overlooking the orchard yard. Several heavy mahogany chairs were placed around the wall on which no one had ever sat, except during the waking of his parents, when people queued up to pay their respects to the corpses. These leather-seated chairs, and the vast rubber plant, which was sited in a brass tub in the corner, always reminded Fenny of home, the old age of his grandparents, the decline of his father and mother, and the chasing Gummy had often had to do to pull him out from behind one of the chairs, or more frequently the rubber plant, to give him his bath. This arid square, with its worn green carpet and the delicate Beleek vase, encrusted with a riot of porcelain roses, that had withstood the years, standing on a small table in the centre of the space, was home to him in a way none of the other rooms in the house were, although he loved every one of them.

And the sight of Gummy, half-hiding herself between the wall and the rubber plant, her wire-framed spectacles askew on her reddened nose, every angular inch of her body expressing guilt, embarrassment, and even a suggestion of fear, made his heart stop with pity and affection, in much the same way as Ellen's had leaped when she heard his steps on the stairs.

Gummy was impossible, of course; she could be both vindictive and vicious-tongued, but she was also old, frail and passionately loyal. He remembered her affection and care when he was young and frightened; her brave lies to his mother in defence of some misbehaviour in the orchard; the story his mother had told him about the baby she had had by a married soldier, which Mrs O'Farrell had had adopted through an order of nuns she knew in Cork; the maternal, fierce protection that Gummy had lavished on him when he was a bachelor, and had been drinking for three or four days and had to take to his bed.

He went over to her corner, put the teeth, wrapped in tissue paper, in her hands, and patted her arm affectionately. It was as thin and hard as a broomstick. Tears filled her eyes and she dodged past him and hurried downstairs.

He kept his news until he had gone into the drawing-room and seen the women. Yes, something had happened. There had been a row of some kind; Ellen would tell him. But what chiefly struck him was the expression of fear on the faces of Sarah Jane and Hosannah. It was a look he had often observed on the features of old people. And he suddenly was aware that these women, like Gummy, were old and frightened, and had even less purchase on the future than the old nurse-housekeeper: she at least would always have his roof over her head, and he would see that she was well looked after if she became ill. But Hosannah? Sarah Jane?

As usual Mrs Pig was her own woman. She obviously was not involved in the row, and she sat upright in her faded blue bib, and looked him mildly, but steadily in the eye. With Ellen, the beloved presence by his side, the slightly bewildered expression now vanished from her eyes, he was in high, good humour and felt a sort of responsibility, something akin to protection for these old neighbours of his. And the fact that he had the best news in the world for them, made him forget everything but the moment that seemed to linger, pulling time along with it, like a strap-holder on a tram.

'He's buying,' he announced with a broad smile. 'The contracts will be ready tomorrow, or the next. You'll get your deposits, and the whole deal should be completed inside a month, if not sooner.'

They all rose to their feet with the exception of Miss McLurry who was convinced that a lady should never rise in the presence of a gentleman, unless he gave her his hand and asked her to dance, or took his arm for dinner downstairs, or was taken by him to be introduced to another member of the party whom she did not know. All this she had culled from a book of etiquette, which was her favourite reading. She had once given it to Mrs Pig, who had returned it with the opinion that it was certainly the funniest book she had ever read in her life. Miss McLurry put this down to crass ignorance.

'Oh, Mr O'Farrell!' she exclaimed, clasping her hands under her chin in her 'little girl' gesture.

'Tanks be ta God!' said Hosannah, joining her hands in front of her chin, bowing to Fenny, and rolling her eyes heavenwards.

'Dat's what Mr MacDonnell said?' put in Mrs Pig sensibly.

'He says it's in the bag.'

'Den it is. Well, I'm glad it's over, I was gettin' worried.'

'Another drink for all,' declared Fenny expansively. But they all refused, and Fenny understood why. They wanted to walk out of his house with an expression of success, if not triumph, on their faces, and pass slowly to their own houses for all the street to witness. To stay drinking in O'Farrell's would be a false touch, and this the man of the house also understood. So he went round and took each of the ladies' hands in his own and pressed them. All of them, even Mrs Prendergast, flushed with pleasure. Then, one by one, they left, each murmuring a word of admiration for the Beleek vase, which still stood on the table where it had first been placed more than fifty years ago. Pale porcelain roses festooned the large ornament, combining the careful craftsmanship of the nineteenth century with a curious, almost oriental delicacy of style.

When Slyne arrived back at The Duke of Clarence, the first person he asked to see was Benedict O'Farrell.

'Fenny O'Barrell, is id?' said Donie, who had carried his overnight case up to his room for him, leaving the heavier luggage for Hamlet to toil up with later.

'That's neat,' commented Slyne with a thin smile. He had what Donie once described as a kind of a 'starved' mouth; starved by nature so that all the sap had gone out of his lips, and paralyzed by an acute sense of form, so that he sometimes gave the impression of being half-way out of an injection from the dentist.

'I hope all yer biznus went well for ye, sir,' said Donie, putting down the case with a wince, as if the carrying of it had given him acute neuritis. Although he knew that the performance did not convince this cool customer, he had grown so used to giving it that it had now become second nature. Indeed, there were times Donie really believed that he was crippled with rheumatism and hard work.

'I suppose ye'll be wantin' de rest of de lugidge up now, sir?' Slyne had arrived with two items of luggage more than he had taken away with him. Both of them, one a box from a well-known Dublin drapers, were heavy.

'If it's convenient,' said Slyne with a slight smile that indicated that the injection was wearing off. It also meant in plain language, as Donie knew from experience, that Slyne wanted his stuff up at once.

'Yer welcome back, sir,' said Donie with a brave smile, while contriving to sigh and rub his arm tenderly at the same time.

'Very glad to be back myself. And I see you've kept the same room for me.' He looked pointedly at the space where the table had once been before it collapsed out of sight. No new one had replaced it.

'No sooner said dan done,' said Donie, retreating to the door with unexpected haste. Long experience had given him the insight to know when an issue more urgent than the one he had been debating came up. 'Would ye like tay or anating? Would ye like me to bring id up for ye? Sangwitches, soda bread, iced fancies?'

Slyne looked at Donie in the bemused way he sometimes did. It was exactly ten minutes past one, and he had been looking forward to his lunch. This he now said, with the hope that the admirable Mrs O'Flaherty Flynn was in good shape.

'Begod, dere's nothin' wrong wid her shape, sir,' said Donie glad of a moment of light relief. After all, an immense amount depended on the good will of this Englishman, and none of them had any real feeling of certainty where he was concerned. The very thought of him, much less the actual sight, filled all of the sellers, with the exception of Fenny, with a terrible dread. 'She'd fill a playhouse for de want of an audience.'

Slyne laughed his usual laugh whenever Donie made one of his sallies, and then looked at him silently. He had arrived without Donie's knowledge, and had by chance met the cook in the hall. After a profuse welcome, she had rolled off to the kitchen to prepare his lunch. While this momentous arrival was taking place, Donie had been seated in the lavatory, taking his ease with the aid of a baby Power, which was well known to be a powerful cure for constipation, even while seated on the bowl. He had been vexed to discover Slyne already in conversation with Hamlet, when he had at last finished his business, and thrown away the empty bottle out of the window. The earth-work surrounding the back of The Duke of Clarence was full of strange blooms of a surrealist nature. Near the last resting place of the bottle Donie had just got rid of, lay another full-sized bottle, which over the years had filled up with clay, and out of which a yellow-grey weed now grew.

'I'll fix up everything for ye, sir,' said Donie, backing to the door, and getting out of the room as fast as he could. And imagine not even a shilling, not even a sixpenny, or a threepenny bit for all his labour in carrying that case upstairs.

The first person he met when he came down into the hall was Hamlet, lurking in the shadow on the huge bannisters, half-way to his own dug-out. Donie took him by the arm and dragged him along the corridor to the cupboard where the boy lived.

'Where de hell were you when dat man arrived?' he demanded.

'Is it Mister Slyne you mean?' replied Hamlet with his usual maddening evasion. Donie gave him a clip over the ear, and swore a long oath at him.

'Wha's dat lugidge doin' sitting' dere in de hall, waitin' ta be transportated be us so?'

'You told me to leave any doin's for Mr Slyne for yourself,' said Hamlet truthfully. He had indeed behaved with the utmost propriety and correctness, according to his instructions, when Slyne arrived unexpectedly in a taxi from the mid-morning train, which more often than not got in in time for lunch.

'Why didden ye call me ye sly little runk?'

'I didden know where you —'

'Yes, ye did. Yer tryin' ta destroy me politics wid Mister Slyne, dats what yer trin' to do, ye bugabuganassit. Now go and carry de rest of dat luggage upstairs to de room, imedjit if nod sooner.'

So Hamlet toiled up the stairs with the extra luggage, and was rewarded with a sixpence by Slyne, who liked the boy. The Englishman was standing by his window, looking out at the Protestant church of St Mary, the front door of which faced the side of the hotel. Surrounded by tombs, vaults and headstones, it seemed more part of a street than any other churchyard that Slyne had ever seen. Children passing the low wall which built up the graves, trailed careless, sticky fingers along the grass over some long-dead and worthy landowner or burgher. A dog sniffed at the railed entrance to a vault — a few steps down and one could, he imagined, see the velvet covered coffins on their shelves. A few motor-cars chugged by, carts rattled, footsteps beat a kind of irregular tattoo, the sound of time passing, running, dawdling and tripping by. At the top of the lane a tall, lean Franciscan made a playful swipe with his cord at a couple of youngsters passing by. They screamed with mock fear and scampered off. The friar looked across the road at the graves of the opposition and blinked thoughtfully, before turning back down his lane to the Friary.

Slyne went over to the water basin, found it full, much to his surprise, and a cake of new soap laid on the marble top beside it. But no towel. He got out one of his own, washed his hands, threw some water on his face, brushed his hair, and had another session at his window watching the people amble by, or stop for a chat with their shoulders against some friendly doorway. For a moment everything and everybody stopped, as a piebald pony, mane and tail flying, went galloping up the street, followed by a tinker man with a swarm of red-haired children, bare-footed and in sober rags, all racing after it.

Slyne waited to see if any further sights were on offer from his window, but apart from the dust, and the people who stopped to stare after the pony, until he was long out of sight, nothing further happened. Then, after opening his briefcase, looking at some documents for a while, he locked them away again and went slowly downstairs. Mrs O'Flaherty Flynn, superb cook though she was, always needed time, like most artists, to extend herself on a special creation. So Slyne went into the lounge and knocked on the service hatch. He waited for some more time among the potted plants and the sagging horsehair, breathing the smell of whiskey and cigarettes, and the thick blue curtains, stiff with age and the dust that went with it — curtained corpses, one wit had dubbed them — until he got his whiskey from one of the girls in the office. For so important a client she came round with the drink on a small, heavy silver tray with the arms of The Duke of Clarence engraved upon it, but with no soda. When she discovered her omission, she banged the silver tray in mock anger at herself against one of the chairs, which toppled over. But so eager was she to please Mr Slyne that he himself had to raise the chair gingerly to its legs, while he waited for his soda water.

When Hamlet came downstairs, Donie was waiting for him, and beckoned to him to follow along the corridor outside Hamlet's habitation.

'Did he give ye anyting?' demanded Donie, giving the boy a look which, he claimed, could read the soul of a bookmaker in an instant. It did not read Hamlet's, for that close young man had hidden his sixpence under the carpet in one of the disused bedrooms, where he would retrieve it later.

'Not even talk. He seemed terrible serious and in on himself.'

'Mmmnn,' said Donie, who did not like this piece of information. However, he had other business on hand. He had no intention in the world of running across the town to tell Benny O'Farrell that Slyne wanted him to come to the hotel for a meeting. It sounded too much like a summons. Besides, not wanting to be the bearer of bad news, it was utterly beneath Donie's position to run errands across the whole length of the town, into the wilds of Connaught. There were special circumstances which might make him do so: his own immediate interest, or the passing of a ten bob note, but not otherwise.

'Now dat ye have, ad last, brough' up all Mr Slyne's lugidge, ye lazy houn', you're ta go over to O'Farrell's in Connaught Street, an' tell Mr O'Farrell dat Mr Slyne wants ta speak t'im. Hurry up now, an' stop dawdlin'.'

'But Mr Slyne is ony juss goin't to have his lunch —' protested Hamlet, before Donie got in with another clip on the glue.

'Ye dirty eejit,' he shouted. 'There's raisins for everything an' currants for a cake. What would you know about tings? Get off wid ye at once.' As Hamlet moved away, Donie gripped his arm and pulled him back, bringing his eyes as close to the boy's as he could. 'Are ye sure Mr Slyne gave ye nuttin'? Tell me de trut' or I'll have yer liver for dawgs.'

'Money, is it?' squealed Hamlet, keeping his eyes as steady as marbles, 'That fella is so mane that he wouldn't give you a pinch in a salt mine.'

Donie slowly released him, although he was sorely troubled in his mind. Was this young clip getting to be an expert in deception, something Donie hated, abused, condemned and abominated? That was bad enough, but there was also the worry of Slyne's summons to Benny O'Farrell. It was Donie's experience that when one party to a deal summoned the other to meet him, it was usually more profitable for the man who issued the invitation than for the man who was asked to call. He let Hamlet go on his way, and retired to his cosy lavatory with a copy of an English newspaper, which featured a big divorce case; and a full packet of Players to ease his mind and pass the time. The hotel was full of Americans, all travelling in a bus; obviously Irish-Americans, who had saved up for the last forty years to make this last sentimental journey to the aul sod. Donie could see that they were bad marks for money, even though he and Hamlet had toiled all yesterday morning, bringing their innumerable bags up to their rooms. They were now in the dining-room eating bacon and cabbage, while Mrs O'Flaherty Flynn prepared a delicious lunch of roast duck, followed by brandy balls, for the estimable Mr Slyne.

On his way over to O'Farrell's, Hamlet took his time, since he had come to the same conclusion as Donie. Fenny was being summoned to appear at the hotel, because Slyne had something to tell him which was not to Fenny's advantage. Hamlet leaned on the wooden part of the bridge — he could never remember what it was called, but it could be opened up to let large vessels through. It was years since that had happened, for the great era of the canals and river navigation was on the decline, and most of the raw material for the town came by rail, or in a few private lorries. Flour and porter still came by canal.

It was a radiant summer's day, and down below him the promenade, with its trees, walks, grassy knolls, where at night the soldiers were supposed to sit with the bolder girls of the town, was alive with bright summer dresses and one or two parasols. A few men leaned over the rail, watching the boats pass back and forward under the bridge, but the lunchtime population of the prom was almost always exclusively feminine.

Fenny usually sat down to his lunch at about ten past one, giving his wife time to have hers at half past twelve, since she got up earlier than he did in the morning. So at half past one, when Hamlet reached O'Farrell's, there was no one in the shop at all. Ellen had stayed at the table chatting with Fenny longer than usual, and had then gone upstairs to 'wash her hands'. Gummy, who was in the passage off the shop, always hoping that some benighted customer would drop in during the lunch hour, heard the bell on the front door and popped into the shop.

'Who are ye when yer away from home?' she demanded when she saw that Hamlet was a mere menial, and wore some kind of dirty uniform. Maybe he was an orphanage boy escaped

from the Brothers, and bent on robbing shops while their
owners were eating their lawful luncheons.

'I have a message for Mr O'Farrell from Mr Slyne, who is
stayin' at The Duke of Clarence Hotel.' Hamlet, who could
speak quite distinctly when he wanted to, rolled out the names
as importantly as a major-domo, and was clearly a man-of-
parts in the making.

'Wha' does 'e wand?' Gummy asked in a less aggressive
manner.

'It's a private message,' declared Hamlet loftily, 'and only
for Mr O'Farrell himself. Are you his wife?'

'Well, you impuddin' little runt, I wooden wash yer face if ye
wus laid out as a corpse, and corpses is all supposed to be the
same in the sight o' God, bud dere's some in the wind an' water
o' their health — and you doan look all dat healthy to me, wid
yer yalla face and them purpile circles under yer eyes — abusin'
yerself, I suppose, like all the young now, wid filthy, dirty
scutterin' fags, when ye should be out in God's open air, diggin'
de turf up de bog for next year's firin'. What's goin' to happen
to de poor if de likes o' you is idlyin' roun' like bare-backed
porkupinnies, ruinin' yer healt' wid bad habits, an' whistlin'
after girls, and some o' them no betther dan yerself —'

While she paused for breath, Hamlet was about to reply in
his most impertinent voice — a register he rarely used — when
he was saved from further inquisition by the arrival of Ellen,
who told Gummy that the boss wanted another cup of tea; a
message which caused the old lady to disappear as fast as she
could. She had nothing further to say to Hamlet anyway, so it
was just as well to go out on a full tide.

Ellen knew the boy, having often seen him around the hotel
when she was coming back from mass, or passing by in Church
Street. He looked peaked and famished to her, but perhaps it
was the heat. However, having heard his message, she asked
him if he would like a glass of lemonade. Hamlet would love
one. He drank it in one gulp, and Ellen, who liked the
unfortunate boy, filled him up another, and offered him a slice
of fruit cake, which she always kept in a tin on the grocery shelf,
in case one of the many ancient female customers came into
town to do their shopping, and dropped into O'Farrell's for a
glass of port or mulled stout in the snug inside the door.

'I hope Mrs O'Flynn keeps you well fed, boy,' she said

kindly.

'O yes, ma'am, she does indeed. Plenty of leftovers; I'm never hungry.'

Leftovers, thought Ellen sadly, and remembered hearing that Mrs Daly and her daughter lived of the best, and ate off silver trays. In spite of this young man's defence of Mrs O'Flaherty Flynn, he looked white and delicate to Ellen, whose heart went out to him.

'What is your name?' she said.

'Hamlet, ma'am,' said he, doing his best to keep down the wind which his sudden large consumption of lemonade had stirred up in his stomach.

'That's a nice name,' said Ellen, thinking how odd it was. 'I'll go and tell my husband that you want to see him.'

When she was gone Hamlet belched to his heart's content, and he made a note that Mrs O'Farrell was a lady and no mistake. He had just recovered from his attack of gas when Fenny appeared in the shop.

'Hullo, Hamlet,' said Fenny, 'has the wife been doing you well?'

'O Lord, I'm stuffed, Mr O'Farrell.'

'What does Slyne want me for?' Fenny looked at the boy keenly.

'O I wouldn't know, Mr O'Farrell,' said Hamlet, reverting to type. Don't get involved. Ever. Not ever. That was his motto. 'He wouldn't tell the likes of me.'

'A close man,' conceded Fenny.

There seemed little doubt that Slyne still intended to buy the land. If not MacDonnell would have got the word to Fenny before now. Or would he? Something was in the air; something which would benefit Slyne.

'Well, as you can see,' he said to Hamlet, 'I've no one here to mind the shop at the moment, my wife has work to do in the house, and I can't get away just now. Will you be a good boy, go back and tell that to Mr Slyne, and ask him what time it would be convenient for him for me to call late this afternoon? I think I can get someone to stay in the shop while I'm away then.'

'Right ho, sir,' said Hamlet smartly, and turned sharply, but not fast enough not to turn back at the first word of further communication.

'Here's a sixpence for you, Hamlet, that's a good fellow. By the way, what do you think of this Slyne?' Fenny's question was casual, but it produced an unexpected effect on Hamlet, who had never been consulted in this adult and intimate way before.

'I think —' he began, scratching his head — 'I think he knows more than he pretends.'

This answer was loaded with meaning, as Fenny knew Hamlet must realize.

'You mean he knows what the rest of us do?' Fenny went on softly.

Hamlet retreated. A blurred look came into his eyes, and his whole body, which had been stiff with interest as he spoke to Fenny and Ellen, went slack again; a table with a touch of the worm.

'I wooden no wha' de rest do be tinkin' ' he muttered.

Then Fenny remembered something. This boy was one of MacDonnell's contacts: he had been seen getting into the house without being macroomed.

'Well, Hamlet, would you be so good as to deliver this message to Mr MacDonnell's at the top of this street, and wait for an answer.' Fenny took up a writing pad and envelope he kept under the counter, and scribbled a few words to the old Tammany boss. When he looked up, prepared to give the note to Hamlet, he was struck to see that the boy's face had taken on an expression of horror. He looked sick, frightened and speechless.

'What is it?' said Fenny, fishing in his waistcoat pocket for another sixpence, or perhaps a shilling would have to be paid for this service.

'I'd be afeared, mister, I'd be macroomed and murdered.' Hamlet was a fine actor, for MacDonnell had told him never to speak to anyone of the visits to the house. The fact that most of the street already knew about it did not matter to MacDonnell. He knew that a thing denied hotly and often enough acquires a meaning of its own, and besides, if people realized that he wanted this transaction to be private, they would pretend not to notice. They all knew the rules of the game.

'All you have to do is get this note to Mr MacDonnell, a close friend of mine. I can't get away myself, but he will quite understand that I asked you to deliver the message. Nothing could be more rational.'

But Hamlet would have none of this sensible talk. He would

not mix up MacDonnell with any other business. So he backed to the door slowly.

'I'm in dread o' me life of that auld fella, he'd macroom me flat, like a steamroller. No, Mr O'Farrell, besides I haven de time, I'm ony let outa d'otel for a few minnits.'

Fenny recognized defeat when he saw it. The shilling went back to his pocket, and he smiled at the boy. There was no doubt about it but MacDonnell inspired loyalty, even if it was a fearful loyalty. But already Fenny had thought of something else.

'Do you know where Mrs Prendergast lives?'

Hamlet nodded. He did not know this side of the town well, but he had noticed the pigs' feet in the window once.

Fenny took down a half bottle of whiskey from the shelf behind him, and wrapped a paper round it in such a way that no person of sound mind could fail to recognize what it was. This, with the shilling retrieved again, he gave to Hamlet and told him to leave it at Mrs Prendergast's, and ask the woman of the house to come across the road to see him at once.

In a short while, sticking the bottle under her arm, now visible for all to see as she had removed the paper for tonight's reading, Mrs Pig went over to O'Farrell's.

Fenny got down from his bum-boat when she came in and held up his hand in salute.

'What —?' she began, but Fenny let it go no further. Someone might come into the shop, and they had business to do in the meantime.

'So as to confuse,' he explained. 'People know he's the boots at the hotel, so if he ran over with one hand as long as the other, they'd know he was being sent on a message.' Fenny had got off his bum-boat, and was leaning very earnestly on the counter, at the side of his beautiful china pint-puller.

'Oh, I see.' Mrs Pig handed back the bottle, but Fenny did not touch it.

'Slyne sent word that he wanted to see me.'

'Oh.' Mrs Pig looked stricken and was silent for a moment. Were all her dreams of what she was going to do with her new-found riches to disappear? Something in her soul, tempered by the fires of hardship and poverty, told her that no one ever had luck like that. So it was all over. 'I see'.

'I don't think it's that,' said Fenny with assurance. 'But I want to find out what's in the wind from old MacDonnell. After all, he was sure that the deal was on. But I want you to go and ask him.'

'Me?'

'Yes, you. You're the only one that Macroom is afraid of. Everybody knows that. So all you have to do is bring the bottle up the street, and no one will know what we're up to. The bottle will throw them off the scent, you see?'

'I do,' said Mrs Pig shortly, taking up the bottle again.

'Have ye a message for me to give him?'

Fenny produced another sealed envelope and handed it to Mrs Pig, who, being a woman of action when required, marched out and up the street to MacDonnell's door. Macroom opened it.

'Oh,' he muttered. 'You.'

'Yes, me,' declared Mrs Pig firmly. Macroom had shown a marked preference for large women with broad beams, and since Mrs Pig was larger and broader than almost anyone in town, Macroom for a time had taken to walking up and down the street past her shop, and had even gone in and bought some pigs' feet from her, when she had them in stock. Mrs Pig was quite aware of the feelings she inspired in Macroom, and thought the whole thing ridiculous, but obviously it could be put to good use.

'Will you hand in this to Mr MacDonnell?' she went on, thrusting the bottle of whiskey into Macroom's hands. He looked at it as if it contained dynamite, which was the way he thought about most parcels, having done some bomb-planting in his time.

'I will not,' he said, recoiling from her and almost shutting the door in her face. 'Besides, he's not in.'

'Don't be daft,' said Mrs Pig, wedging her boot firmly in the doorway. 'If you're afraid to carry de parcel, I'm not.' She looked past Macroom's shoulder and saw MacDonnell, who enjoyed these encounters, at the back of the hall. 'O hullo, Mr MacDonnell. I have a message here for ye from Mr O'Farrell.'

'He isn't in, I tell you,' insisted Macroom. He did not, however, attempt to push the door against her foot. It was a moment of weakness, and like many a man in love, Macroom was the loser.

'I forgot to tell you,' said MacDonnell, coming forward with his hand out, so that Macroom had to open the door. 'I was expecting Mrs Prendergast. How are you, Mrs P?'

MacDonnell and his visitor shook hands cordially, for old MacDonnell also admired the tall, straight-backed Kerry woman, though not in the way Macroom did. He stepped back and, taking his opportunity, flashed a broad smile at her.

'Indeed you are welcome, Mrs Prendergast. How was I to know you were invited? You must tell me yourself the next time, huh?'

Mrs Prendergast ignored him and followed MacDonnell into his study. There he held a chair for her to sit down, before opening the note that accompanied the whiskey. He looked up with a smile.

'I suppose you're worried about the land deal?' he said.

'Very worried. What's d'Englishman up to?'

MacDonnell put the tips of his fingers together and looked wise and solemn.

'He wants O'Farrell to sell him the whole of his land near the town. Otherwise, he says that the whole scheme will fall through.'

'You mean he won't go on wid buyin' our land?' Mrs Prendergast, that valiant woman, paled and clasped her fist against her heart.

'Yes, he means that.'

'What will Mr O'Farrell do?'

'If I know him he'll sell it, if he thinks the rest of the deal is threatened. He doesn't really want the land, but he's sentimental about it, and then of course, he has already agreed to sell part of it to Slyne. So, if he sells the rest, he'll insist on a hefty figure for it.'

'And I hope to God he gets it,' declared Mrs Pig fervently. She had rarely felt so terrified in her life. If this deal did not go through, nothing remained except the County Home.

'I figure he will,' said MacDonnell slowly. Then he held up the bottle of whiskey. 'What are you going to say about this? I'll keep it, by the way, and pay Fenny for it later, if he wishes, or I'll give it back to him.'

Mrs Prendergast had lost none of her native Kerry cunning. She knew exactly what she was going to say about that. And now that the whole question of all the lands and their sale was in doubt again, it was more than ever necessary to keep the neighbours guessing.

'I'll tell dem dat Slyne sent de whiskey as a present to you. That de boots of d'otel did not rightly know where you lived, and called into O'Farrell's to ask. Well, Mr O'Farrell was busy at the moment, de boots was in a terrible hurry back or Donie Donnelly would murder him, so Mr O'Farrell told de young fella to leave it into me, because it was no good tellin' him where your house was, the boots would never get in on account of Macroom. Whereas nobody would keep me out.'

MacDonnell smiled and rubbed his mouth with his forefingers. A tortuous tale like this was very much to his liking. Had he not been inventing them himself for years?

'There's one thing,' he said in the level, assured tone of the perfectionist. 'That boots, young Hamlet, has been to this house before and got past Macroom.'

'How was Mr O'Farrell to know dat?' answered Mrs Prendergast. 'Besides, de boy was in a terrible hurry.'

'Yes, I think that'll pass. At least it'll throw them off the real scent for a while.'

'And you were sent de present because you won't even listen to an offer for your own land, which lies next to O'Farrell's.'

MacDonnell looked at Mrs Prendergast gravely for a moment; then nodded his head.

'It all adds up,' he said, giving nothing away.

Mrs Prendergast stood up, and so did her host.

'How am I to get past Macroom?' she demanded, plucking at the sides of her bib like a hugely overgrown schoolgirl.

'I'll see you to the door,' said old MacDonnell, taking her by the elbow and ushering her into the hall. But Macroom was there at the front door with a gleam in his eye.

'You're welcome at any time, Mrs P,' he said huskily as he opened the door for her. But in doing so he also contrived to give her broad bottom the most stupendous pinch. She swung round, and gave Macroom such a slap in the mouth that he fell back against the wall.

Getting more slowly to his feet than he would have done some few years before, Macroom looked at Mrs Prendergast with the expression of a man completely enslaved by passion. He stared at her with dog-like devotion as she sailed out the front door with a hurried goodbye to MacDonnell.

'O what a wummun, what a wummun,' panted Macroom,

who had just lived through one of the vivid and recurring fantasies of his life; a big, ample woman, with a strong arm, who would beat the living daylights, and half his last meal, out of him.

MacDonnell chuckled and shook his head wisely.

'It comes to us all sometime or other, later or sooner, Macroom.'

'Jeez,' muttered the bodyguard hoarsely. 'Jeez!' Then he trotted off to the back of the house to set a stiff one up for himself.

When Hamlet got back to the hotel it was nearly three o'clock, a time, he surmised, Mr Slyne would have finished his gorgeous, crisp and meltingly stuffed duckling, and be in a mellow mood. But he had been delayed by the sight of Miss Maud walking along the other side of the bridge, on her way, no doubt, to the promenade.

The sight of Maud Daly walking out on a summer's day was enough to stop a high proportion of the male population of Bridgeford. But on a day of particular sunshiny glory, with small white clouds drifting over the railway bridge like swans, and real swans floating down the river beyond the weir wall, she was a vision that remained so vivid that forty years after elderly men were saying to one another: 'Do you remember the day in '33, or was it '34? no, definitely '33, the year after the Congress, that Maud walked across the town in a sheer white silk frock, with high-heeled shoes. And a parasol.'

It was the parasol that temporarily blinded Hamlet. Never had he seen his only love, his passion, his madness and hope of salvation, walking out under a parasol of exactly that shade. It was generally pink, a colour Hamlet, like most men, did not like. But this pink was different: it was very pale, just touched with the colour, like the edge of an early dawn, or the inside of an oyster. And the effect of this unearthly light shining on his loved one's face, filtering the sun to a shade of sweet and blessed gentleness, nailed his soul as effectively as if Maud had shut her parasol with a snap, and run the ferrule through his breast. He stood and gaped.

Maud sauntered along, nodding her head from side to side, like royalty at a garden party, stopping to speak to no one. Even old Mrs Duncan, a great figure in local society and a member of the old ascendancy, was left with a smile and a wave and a tinkle of toy-bell laughter.

'I must be outside the barrack gate before half-three,' she trilled, 'Otherwise I might lose my man.'

'Oh, ho!' laughed Mrs Duncan, who had an earthy sense of humour, and stumped off. But Hamlet, who had heard the exchange with the super-sensitive ear of love, was ashamed for his darling, and felt himself blush hot and cold all over. How could Miss Maud say such things! Even when he knew that all she was going to do was sit on the promenade for half an hour, and allow herself to be admired. He burned even deeper over the thought of the young fellows, who would pass up and down the lower path of the prom, just over the water, while Maud sat on a seat higher up, with her knees modestly held together, a book in her hand — she was carrying a white bag on her arm — and a dreamy, lost look in her eyes whenever she looked up, as if her author had transported her to strange lands and curious customs, known only to himself and, of course, to Maud.

Hamlet watched her out of sight as she rounded the bridge, having crossed over to his side to get onto the road that ran straight along under the high barrack wall, and was edged by the promenade, the boat club, and the Father Matthew Hall on the other side. Hamlet felt a furious hatred for the big thugs of the boating club, who would soon put on their blazers, oil their hair and begin to walk up and down under the pink-white goddess. He followed her progress all the way when she came into sight again, chose her seat carefully, spread a handkerchief, which she took from her bag, on it, sat down with a graceful curving movement and gave herself up to the admiration of the passers-by.

Hamlet could never make up his mind if Maud was teasing all these youths and men who followed her about with dazed eyes, and shook their heads with admiration whenever her name was mentioned. All those books she read must have given her a horrid insight into human nature. Surely she was aware of all that male foolishness, and was always laughing inside herself at the sight of it.

When Hamlet got back he reported to Mr Slyne, who was

waiting in the commercial room. This was a small, poky cell behind the dining-room, where Mrs Daly allowed the travellers, who made up the greater proportiion of her customers since the British garrison was withdrawn, to write their letters and fill in their order forms after the day's business. She never knew one of them by name.

'Well?' said Slyne, who was standing at the narrow window that looked out on a tiny inner yard of the hotel, and was known by all, except, Mrs Daly, as Cats' Corner. She called it 'the inner courtyard', and claimed that the Duke of Clarence himself had once sat in it for half an hour to keep out of the sun.

'Mr O'Farrell is terrible busy sir, and he kep me a gradeal o' time waitin'.'

'Yes, I can understand that. What did he say when he met you?' Slyne turned away from the window, and his voice rather than his face, which was in shadow in the gloomy room, told Hamlet that he was in a bad humour. Hamlet was a great expert on tones of voice.

'He said he'd be over as soon as he could get away,' muttered the boy.

'Did he indicate what time that might be?'

'No sir.'

'Well, go back again and tell him that this is an important matter, not only for himself but for the others — will you remember that, the others?'

Hamlet nodded. He was beginning to detect a slightly false note in Slyne's voice. If it were possible to believe it in the circumstances — and Hamlet knew them all — he would be inclined to think that Mr Slyne was more anxious to meet Mr O'Farrell than the other way around.

'Yessir. I'll run over at wanst.'

The boy was about to disappear, after giving a fine military salute, when Slyne called him back. To Hamlet's surprise it was another sixpence.

'You're a good boy. Now see that he makes some sort of appointment for this evening, will you?'

Hamlet gave an even more elaborate salute, and was now certain that Slyne was uneasy. He had been hoping he would be able to nip upstairs, and hide his extra sixpence under the carpet with the rest of the loot, but he had hardly left the room when Donie was upon him, dragging him round the front hall

by the ear, to the amazement of a small party of summer visitors
from New Jersey, who had just arrived and were filling the hall
with shrill, bird-like calls, like exotic creatures in a private
aviary, transported whole from country to country.

Donie did not heed them as they crowded round the bemused
girl in the office. She in her turn was making frantic signs to
Donie to come to her aid, while Hamlet was rolling his eyes in a
fine representation of frantic terror, so as to inflame the visiting
ladies further. But Donie dragged him round the corner and
into Hamlet's hole under the stairs.

'Now gimme dat sixpence he gave ye, ye thievin' liddle —'
and he shook the boy's shoulders violently, when at last he was
free after a particularly vicious clip over the glue. 'Ye sneakin'
liddle snake suckin' up to dat Englishman who's so mean dat
he'd rob de glass eye outa of a stuffed dog. And nod a hayport
for me dat's slavin' and runnin' for him day and night and
beyond id. What did he say about Fenny? Now tell me de trutt
or I'll disemball ye.'

Hamlet repeated word for word what he had already said to
Slyne, and what instructions Slyne had given to him. Since
Donie had been listening at the door, there was not much point
in telling anything else, although it went much against
Hamlet's nature to tell the truth to Donie, especially as he
considered himself to be the past master of door listening and
throwing his eye through keyholes. It was disgraceful and
totally unjust that Donie should, at his time of life, suddenly
display an equal mastery with his young pupil. Hamlet
resolved to kill him.

'Well, off ye go so,' said Donie grudgingly, and was just
about to push him out of the cupboard, when they both heard
the shrill chatter of voices outside. 'Jasus,' whispered Donie,
'de Yanks have follied us. Quick, lie down an' foam at de mout,
quick, quick.' Then he opened the door.

'What are you doing to that poor boy, you awful man?' said
one particularly gorgeously plumed woman, with a purple and
red feather attached to a small green pin cushion at the side of
her head. Her face was painted in vivid streaks of red, black
round the eyes, and scarlet on the lips, while the rest of her skin
was powdered as if with flour.

But before Donie could answer, and he had a particularly
good answer in mind, a voice from the stairs cut in on the

conversation. It was Mrs Daly. With one hand resting lightly on the banister, the other resting on her hip, she was looking very regal and very angry indeed.

'What is all this?' she demanded, looking at the painted woman, who seemed to her like something out of a circus. Paint, except on the most discreet terms, like a touch of powder on the nose, a dab of pink on the cheek, and some good scent behind the ear, was not yet worn by respectable women in Bridgeford. 'Who are you?'

There was a moment's pause. It might safely be said that no one had ever addressed the New Jersey spokeswoman in such a tone before in her entire life.

'We,' she said slowly, as if speaking to a mentally retarded person, 'are the Noo Joisee cultooral group.'

'And does your culture consist of bullying my old and trusted and very experienced porter, Mr Donnelly, as if he were a common boot-boy?'

The parrot-painted woman was again at a loss for an immediate answer, but a male voice spoke up from the rear of the group.

'It was he that was torturing the boy. We all saw it. He had him by the ear, and o boy it was like Halloween in Noo Orleans, crazy.'

'Donie, where is Hamlet?' said Mrs Daly.

Everyone watched silently as Donie opened the door of the cupboard, took Hamlet by the shoulders and dragged him head first out into the corridor, where he lay twitching and bubbling at the mouth.

'My God!' exclaimed Mrs Daly, coming down to the last step of the stairs to view this awesome spectacle. To descend to the same floor level as the Americans would, she sensed, have put her on an equal footing with them, and Mrs Daly, high-handed though she was, knew a tough customer when she saw one. 'Not content with bullying Mr Donnelly, you have also sent poor little Hamlet, as willing, honest and hard-working a boy as ever lived, into a fit. Donie, bring Hamlet into the kitchen — no, not you —' she commanded, as one of the men stepped forward to help with removing the invalid, whose mouth Donie had thoughtfully filled with a cork, which he always carried about with him; one never knew in an hotel when a gentleman might throw a real fit — 'I'll call Mrs O'Flaherty Flynn.' Which she did, in a voice which would have carried on a barrack square in a February storm.

Out from the kitchen lumbered the large lady, expecting a fire at the very least, or one of the Sinn Fein gunmen, only to be confronted with as grim a sight as ever she saw, she afterwards declared, in all her nanny — a local version of anno domini.

'Jesus, Mary and Blessed Saint Joseph,' she panted, after delivering herself of a screech which unnerved some of the New Jersey group, who fled out of the front door of the hotel to the comparative safety of the street. 'O me poor liddle orphant bulliud an' set on and throawn inta a fearful, fearsome fit be de power o' de Divil, o mercy me. Here Donsheen, take him be de shoulders and I'll lift 'is feet. Aw God, de creeture, O O O O. Keep well away yoo.'

And the New Jersey party did step back as the little cortege moved off, leaving the cultural group to face Mrs Daly, who stood quite still on her step, looking coldly at them.

'Well?' she asked in a soft, menacing voice.

'Is this the hotel where the famous Dook of Clarence, elder son and sometime heir of the Prince of Wales and the Princess of Wales, afterwards King Edward the Seventh of England and Queen Alexandra, was once?' The voice was suing for peace, still a little aggressive, but the posture, which surprised some of the party, was an ingratiating one. Nevertheless there was a small silence. The leader of the group thought it just as well for the peace of all concerned; and she had four coronaries in her group, and one recovered stroke, as well as numerous high-blood pressures running to hyper-tension. It was all down on their cards, kept in her large holdall, which she now held peacefully by her thigh.

'If you mean Prince Eddy,' began Mrs Daly with cutting politeness, 'he often stayed near here when in Ireland with the Handcock family, Lord Castlemaine, you know. Prince Eddy and they, with some of his fellow officers, often came in here for a drink or a meal. There is a small courtyard, in the inner part of the hotel, where he used to sit on a plain deck chair, just to be on his own for a while. That, naturally, was a great luxury for him.'

A voice from the rear, this time a female one, or nearly so, so deep was its tone, spoke out plaintively.

'But this courtyard is not on our cultooral itinery, Miss Van Dongen.'

There was a murmur of dissent, almost the first far sound of rebellion from the group, and Miss Van Dongen pulled herself together.

'Of course it's not on our itinerary, which is a literary one. We are here to visit the birthplace of the English-Irish poet, and well-known essayist, Oliver Goldsmith.'

'Yes, of course,' said Mrs Daly lightly, as if she were dealing with children, 'He's on school courses here too. And a half-brother of his used to be minister of the church outside, while one of the bank managers in the town is a descendant of his. I remember cousins of his, the Turkingtons, still living in the town when I was a child. And now, I must go and see if my staff have recovered yet.'

She stepped down and walked through the party, which divided like the Red Sea, and left behind her a rising murmur of displeasure against Miss Van Dongen, especially as that lady had bullied them unmercifully since they left their native shores, showing off her literary knowledge, and making sarcastic remarks when they proved ignorant of a particularly well-known name. Now the spirit of American independence began to assert itself, even in the face of culture. Mrs Daly went on her way, pleased to know that the disgracefully painted Miss Van Dongen was in for — what did the cowboys say? — a rough ride.

When Mrs Daly got to the kitchen much had been accomplished. Hamlet had been dragged in, the door closed and bolted, and Mrs O'Flaherty Flynn was clearly disappointed when the boy stood up at once, wiped the foam from his mouth and winked at her. She had been looking forward to a nice long nursing session, with Hamlet swaying on the edge of death, and she attending upon his every movement, and telling him exactly what to do.

But when Donie grabbed Hamlet's arm and demanded the sixpence from him, she understood all. 'An' hauld yer whist, lad,' hissed Donie.

'Merciful God, an' I thinkin' ye were dyin'. Ye stinkin' liddle bully ye, Donie Donnelly, takin' a sixpence from a hard-workin' lad like our Hamlet.'

'It's *my* money, Mrs FF. How am I supposed to live on what I get here, or don't get is nearer to de trutt? Now off wid ye,' he said to Hamlet, giving him a shove in the back that hurled him out the open back door, staggering on his legs and moaning. Mrs O'Flaherty Flynn took up her rolling pin and delivered a ─ sharp, short blow to Donie's elbow, which made him howl and hop around the kitchen on one foot, clutching his elbow.

'Dat'll teach ye nod to call me Mrs FF, like as if I had no name, an' I know what FF stands for too, ye dirty liddle squirt. Get outa me kitchen, or I'll make dog mate outa yer guts.'

Then she remembered the bolted door, and had a suspicion that Mrs Daly would shortly make her appearance. And she had hardly unlocked the door, when that lady did arrive, looking slightly flushed but triumphant.

'Where is Hamlet?' she said looking about her. Donie was on two legs again, but still clutching his elbow.

'He's gone over on a message to Mr O'Farrell from Mr Slyne,' moaned Donie.

'What sort of message?' said Mrs Daly, who was after all an interested party.

'Nod a word did he say except dat he wanted Mr O'Farrell ta call on him here. Ooo, me arm!'

'Don't be silly, Donie,' snapped Mrs Daly. 'Carrying a boy like Hamlet from the stairs to here is child's play.'

'Course id is,' put in Mrs O'Flaherty Flynn. 'I'd 'ave carried him mesel' if I wus let.' She glared at Donie. One squeak out of him and goodbye to his rations for wife and family for a week.

'Tell Hamlet I want to see him when he gets back,' said Mrs Daly, sweeping from the kitchen, a place she seldom visited. She was disturbed by the news she had heard; but of course one must never show discomfiture in front of staff.

Hamlet got back half an hour later, having lingered on the bridge to watch Maud having a conversation with a tall young man of about eighteen, or less, that he knew was the son of a lord. There was no danger there; Maud was a strong Catholic, and would never marry a title in a Protestant Church. All the same it was a stab in the heart. Mrs Daly was at the top of the stairs, and beckoned him up to whisper that he was to come to her when he finished with Mr Slyne.

Slyne had been waiting in the commercial room for well over two hours while negotiations for the meeting were going on between O'Farrell and himself, with Hamlet as plenipotentiary. Well, not that, said Slyne severely to himself, just a messenger invested with no powers. But he also reflected that life among the natives over here did lead one to exaggeration of speech. It never occurred to him for a moment to suspect Hamlet of malingering: it was clearly this O'Farrell fellow playing hard to get. Well, he would take him down a peg when at last they met.

'I see,' said Slyne, nodding his head gravely, when Hamlet told him that Mr O'Farrell could not give the exact time that he would be able to get away, but he would be over to the hotel that evening for sure. 'Thank you,' he said smiling at Hamlet, a curious boy he rather liked, suspecting him of having brains, unlike that awful Donnelly man.

'Is that all, sir?'

'Yes, there's no point in going again. Here, boy, a few pence for all your trouble.' And he handed over a threepenny bit. Hamlet grinned, saluted, and made for the bedroom as fast as a whippet, pulled back the carpet, discovered that his earlier treasure was still there, sighed with content, and made for Mrs Daly's room at the speed of a sedate old greyhound.

Mrs Daly could not quite make up her mind at the turn of events. She thought of sending for Mr MacDonnell, but that might expose her as too anxious to sell, and Mrs Daly's attitude from the beginning had been that she could not care less whether or not she sold these few bog acres that were a part of a property she hardly knew. 'A sort of oddment, an end of a rather big estate once, that was separated from the rest, God knows how, rent due perhaps in the old days, I've never really enquired,' she explained to Mr Slyne, when he approached her about it at the beginning.

Slyne himself was, by now, convinced that O'Farrell intended to keep him waiting for the rest of the day, and this horrid little room, with its smell of stale tobacco and dust that had begun to breed, was a dispiriting place.

So he decided to meet O'Farrell and if possible beat him at his game, in his own time and place.

His departure from the hotel did not go unnoticed. Donie told Hamlet, who by now was feeling exhausted, to run over and tell Mr O'Farrell that the Englishman had left the hotel.

'And he's not goin' to Connaud either,' said Donie, as he watched the tall figure cross the street, and disappear down the Friary Lane. 'Unless he's goin' de long way round juss ta keep yer man waidin'. I'll run down home an' see what way he passes.' And Donie set off at a brisk pace down another lane, which led to the Strand by the river, toward the little house where his wife and family lived.

Hamlet felt curiously tired, and longed only to creep back into his little cupboard under the stairs. He went along the passage as quietly as he could, slipped into the dark cabin, lay down and fell asleep almost instantly.

Donie did not have to go far to see that, if Slyne was making his way in the general direction of Connaught, he was tacking a bit. He had just got into the shelter of his own little alleyway when Slyne passed, went up the lane towards Church Street and across the road and under the archway to the semi-circular court, which Hamlet had traversed on his first journey that morning. Donie decided to give up the chase for the moment, for he was too tired out with waiting and watching. He marched into his tiny house, held his head and groaned when he saw his skinny little wife and half at least of their ten children, and went upstairs with dragging feet, where he fell on the bed with his boots on, and very shortly was snoring loudly.

Mrs Donnelly, a slight, fey creature, put her finger to her lips to hush her family, and tiptoed upstairs where she drew a sheet over her recumbent husband, splashed holy water over him, looked up with an imploring glance at the statue of the Child of Prague, suitably broken according to custom, habit and superstition, and went quietly downstairs into the tiny kitchen, where the five were still waiting, huddled together near the door.

Four daughters: Maud Gonne Donnelly, Constance Markievitch Donnelly, Sarah Curren Donnelly, and Patricia H. Pearse Donnelly; all had been given names in honour of great Irishwomen who had taken part in rebellions, or, as in the case of Sarah, had been associated with men who had. Maud was the eldest, and the only one Mrs Daly had enquired after when she was born. Told that she had been named Maud, she nodded and gave her approval. As one daughter followed another in that family, broken here and there by a male, she heard of the births, but took no further interest. It might lead, all this fertility, to granting Donie some kind of regular salary, and since she abhorred the idea of this, the spread of the Donnellys, like an invading army infiltrating territory behind the lines, she cut them out of her thoughts. Whenever a visitor was indelicate enough to mention the upkeep of Donie's expanding brood, Mrs Daly murmured something about 'self-control being entirely absent among the poorer families'.

'I know of course of Donie's terrible load, but even though I disapprove of his utter lack of control, I can't very well discuss the matter with him, can I? And of course he has a huge income from the hotel. Perhaps if I cut it, he might be more continent.' And that was that.

Little Mrs Donnelly looked at her half portion, with Charles Stewart standing a few inches apart, as befitted a boy that everyone said was cut out for a Roman collar, or a monk's cord and hood. Her priesteen, she called him proudly and was unaware that he was known to all his schoolmates as 'stewie-phewie', for it was well known, even to small boys, that Parnell had been a terrible sinner in England, that land where paganism abounded.

'If you only knew all de tings your poor father has to do, nigh' n' day to pud bread in our mouts, and clothe ye all —' she began with a deep sigh, her tiny head held sideways, and her small, red-wrinkled hands joined together in an attitude of prayer: a maidenly posture she always adopted, whenever she attempted to explain the ways of their father to his children.

'All he has to do,' she repeated in good ritualistic order, 'you wouldn't believe. O, all he has to do, nigh' n' day.'

Stewie, the priesteen, waited until his mother had finished her sermon. Then, he thrust his face forward a little, and looked at her with cold, steady, accusing eyes.

'We know,' he said quietly.

The lanes of Bridgeford all tumbled down to the river on one side of the two main streets: Connaught Street and Church Street. These thoroughfares ran narrowly but stubbornly stuck-up, while the poor huddled in their tiny cabins, aware only from their doors — no one ever looked through the windows in these dwellings, clean glass, unbroken and gleaming was for the street dwellers — of the backsides of these towering premises, devoted to cleaning, and washing, and the cultivation of hardy rose trees here and there, and the great apple orchards that lay behind some of the street houses between the lanes.

Fenny was on good terms with his neighbours in Pipe Lane, and often walked down that way for a stroll, which took him to the banks of the canal, and on a little further to the delectable water-meadows themselves, where few of the laners ever walked. They preferred to squat by the banks of the canal, unused for many years, and stare into the brackish water with its spots of green slime, its occasional floating cat much enlarged by its immersion in this particular Styx. No dog, cat or rodent sank, without suffering a profound mud change into something strange and out of mould, like grotesques encountered in a dream. It was a faintly sinister place, with its high banks paved with rubble, and a coke-like substance that came from years of dumped ashes from the hearths of the cottages. It fascinated Fenny, but he seldom lingered there because of the smell.

The people of the lane also smelled of various human ailments, and the sweat of ordinary human activity. Fenny never ceased to ponder as well as wonder at the way some of them kept themselves so clean and tidy, since none of the hovels had running water. But no matter how much washing they did of their hands, faces and feet, they all stank to the middle sky of turf smoke. It clung to their clothes like opium on a Chinese smock, and like the pipe of heavenly peace, it was not unpleasant; a bit like the scent of smoked ham.

Somebody from each house was at the door to salute Fenny as he walked down in his slow, rolling way. The names ran through his mind like a litany heard outside a church door: Kellys and O'Briens, Loobys, Hogans, Dowleys and Glaveys, and the few that told of the days of the British occupation, west country soldier names like Edgeworthy, Dando, Bartlett and Weeks. Fenny knew the few rascals that flourished in the three lanes that ran down from his side of the street, and did not consider them very wicked. Who would not, living in dwellings not much bigger than hound kennels, and smaller in some ways than horse boxes, drink himself into the Irish Nearawanna on a Saturday night, and come to blows in the pubs as a form of entertainment: they had no other in their lives, for the fathering and mothering of children was not regarded as a pleasure, but as a force of nature, like eating when one could, and resting when one was flaccid of limb — indeed most of the children of the lanes had come into the world as a result of deadly tired mothers rather than fathers.

They tumbled now about Fenny's feet, some obeying calls from their mothers to salute him, which they did with smart military pride, for that breeding was in them, and if not, copied. Others just stared, and a few ran into the kitchens and grabbed their mothers' aprons. Life, he felt, as he went on his way with a salute of his own for all, was shaking the earth all about him; a raggedy, rowdy, raw-boned vitality kept bursting through in the close, sticky humanity of Pipe Lane. It always made him sad in a way he did not acknowledge. But no one, except the old wise woman Betty Rattigan, who sat in the gloom inside her door most of the day, smoking a small dudeen clay pipe, guessed this.

'Good morrow, good morrow, Betty Bid,' called Fenny as he passed.

'Saints on ye, Mister Benny,' she croaked, taking the pipe out of her little round mouth —'like a duck's arse' as Gummy, who was terrified of her, once described it — 'yer business'll thrive de year, an' I doan mane uppa da shop. Saints agin.' And she bowed her nearly bald skull as he saluted her respectfully. He went on pondering more than ever. The sophisticates of Church Street and beyond pretended that she was a complete fraud, but Fenny knew better. The land had its own wisdom, and Betty-Bid embodied all of it. Mrs Pig, he reminded himself, often consulted her and was sometimes seen leaning on the jamb of Rattigan's door talking quickly and softly in Irish to the old woman.

But Fenny had other things on his mind today, and while he stored Betty-Bid's words at the back of his mind, his squirrel's nest of memory, he was not walking down Pipe Lane entirely for the good of his circulation.

'Good morrow, Mrs Hogan,' he called out to a big, high-shouldered woman, hung about with babies like carobs on an evergreen tree. 'How many today?'

'Fifteen, and de shtandin' nine an' a half a' me own.' Mrs Hogan was the local minding woman. Not content with her own brood, and another on the way eternally, she looked after all the children of mothers who were sick or had a part-time job. Mrs Hogan stank of the goat, which she kept half-way in the kitchen, and half-way in the tiny back patch, and like goat's milk she was rich and rare and blessedly beneficial.

'May they increase,' said Fenny with a smile.

'God's will,' intoned Mrs Hogan with a huge, split grin, hugging her adopted carobs to her great breasts.

And so on to that little house which stood apart from the line of cottages, at the end of Pipe Lane, almost on the canal bank. Many of the cabins in the lane had collapsed as people died out, and were left, like their late occupants, to sink into the ground. On one of these ruins a small two-roomed miniature bungalow had been built ten years ago, of cement — a new concept in Bridgeford — and roofed with expensive blue slates. No one had ever been inside it, but it was rumoured to have running water from a rain tank at the back of the roof, and to be fitted out with an abandon of chairs, carpets and a special bed unknown to the laners, except in the pictures, when a few of them had the money to spend on the four-penny seats. They did not like this house, and walked past it with eyes averted; for it was occupied by a man of curious habits, and a mysterious past. His name was Flynn, and he was a cripple, having only one leg, nor none at all, as some said.

The lane had watched the building of the houseen with ossified curiosity, their eyes fixed upon it like a blind statue. And one morning it was finished, and Mr Flynn was installed without any of them, even Betty-Bid, knowing it. His magic was not the same as hers, that was evident; and when reproached with not foreseeing his advent, she opened her gaping mouth and mumbled a few words before pulling herself up, and speaking, but speaking low.

'A mystery man,' she laid down, 'wid nuttin' good in 'im exept goalden sovereens, and no Flynn was ever born here in my time, nor in me mudders nor me fadders time. No Flynn at anny time ad all. Keep away from him wimmen, unless ye see the priest callin'.'

The priest never called, and Mr Flynn was left alone to the solitude he apparently wanted. All kinds of stories and myths about him shuddered their way from door to door in the lane and beyond it. He had two humps and one eye. He was black.

He was suspected of offering money to maidens of the lane, some of them virtuous, even at twenty. He was a 'hateyist' who did not believe in God. He was forbidden.

'Is it true that a haunchback with one leg has settled in that house at the bottom of the lane?' Miss McLurry had asked her friend Mrs Pig one day after the stranger's arrival.

'Arrah, have sense girrel,' said her informant, 'De laners was always full of marvels and wonders and general rawmesh. Accorin' to them he has two heads and a tail. He's one of old MacDonnell's men, who was shot up in a gang row in Chicago — where he had no cause to be, his plot bein' New York. Lost one leg and a little finger, dat's all the matter with him. Macroom brings him down his food every night, he's able to cook it himself out of an American wheelchair dat's like a bus, and what with dat and de whiskey bottle — one and a half a day, comin' up to two — he's as happy as a jockey that has just won the Derby back to front.'

'And where did you hear all this?' said Sarah Jane softly, giving her friend a sideways glance.

'From Macroom of course,' declared honest Mrs Pig.

'Oh, I see,' said Miss McLurry with great inner-and-between meaning.

'No, you don't, ye eejit,' snapped Mrs Pig. 'He comes into de shop for a crubeen or two, and how can I stop him? He's an aul fool and deserves to be leathered. But when he does come, I might as well get some news outa him, mightn't I?'

'Well, indeed you might. All the same —' Miss McLurry's voice trailed away into suggestion of the most diaphanous kind.

'That's enough of that, Sarah Jane, ye hear me,' boomed Mrs Pig. 'Or I'll never pass on a spit of information to you agin.'

Fenny was soon informed about Flynn by old MacDonnell himself. And he also learned that although retired from active service, Flynn still had his uses in the MacDonnell organization. His neat little house served as a sort of unofficial post office. Fenny himself had seen men unknown to him enter and leave the tiny place in the middle of the night, appearing and disappearing along the dark canal banks. MacDonnell was a man of many interests, all of them silent, far-flung, and mysterious.

Betty-Bid's interdict did not of course apply to Fenny, who was recognized by all in Pipe Lane as a man of the world, unafraid of almost anything. Besides, a man of property like him would have means to defend himself against the powers of darkness, unlike the people of the lane, who had to rely on their own wits, and the general good will of God Almighty and Betty-Bid.

Since Flynn arrived, Fenny had always gone to his door, if it was open, and bade him good day. Sometimes he was answered in a deep hoarse voice touched with the Yankee twang, and at other times only a grunt. But once before he had stood at the door, and Flynn had delivered a message to him from MacDonnell in a matter of mutual interest, which neither of them wanted the neighbours to know about. It occurred to Fenny that Flynn might well have some message for him today: one which he had not put in straight language even to Mrs Pig. There were, after all, large stakes to be played for, and the utmost discretion imperative.

'Good day Mr Flynn,' said Fenny, approaching the door.

Flynn was seated inside in a huge wheelchair much beknobbed and belevered, with his one leg propped on a rubber-covered platform. Behind him unknown objects glimmered in the dark of the room: Fenny had heard that he had a notable collection of crystal paperweights, a curious interest for one of his profession. It gave the dwelling an even greater air of danger for the laners who swore, on hearing it from someone who had it from Gummy Hayes, that it was surely the evil one himself appearing in sparkles, like he did while flying low over the bog. One glance at one of these lights, and you were blinded for life, if not longer.

'Don't sell, promise only,' said Flynn in a low voice. He was smoking a cigar which he took out of his mouth for a moment, gave his message and then took up the tumbler of whiskey, which was placed on a table by his elbow. A triple movement, beautifully executed, Fenny thought.

'Thank you, Mr Flynn,' he murmured and passed on. Something very big indeed was in the air, a spirit not yet materialized.

It was the very end of the long afternoon, tea-time in Bridgeford, and just as the twilight began Fenny emerged from his rambling among the lanes and side streets of the Connaught side, and made his way slowly across the bridge. The light would linger over the water on either side for hours yet, slow trailing shadows sweeping over the surface like great trawling nets. Sounds would separate themselves from the business of the day, like a crowd breaking up and going singly home; the dipping of an oar, the plop of a water rat, the cry of a widgeon, the tinkling of a girl's laugh, the distant hum of an outboard engine, the slow merging roar of the weir, which mysteriously could still be heard on stretched summer nights, when one could walk across its dry tip. Sounds that were all mingled in Fenny's head as he walked slowly along, sauntering like the easy-going man he was, and gravely saluting the ladies he knew, like the prosperous merchant that he also was; a solid outward expansion that gave little hint of the quick murmurings of his heart and mind.

Just beyond the bridge, at the corner of the post office, a few paces down Northgate Street, there was a small and dingy little shop with no name over the window, which itself was thick with dust and grime. Only a small hole at the side, which was rubbed out every morning to give the proprietress, Mrs Spencer, her share of the light, and her views of the world. She sold rabbits, game in season, postcards of almost every town in Ireland except Bridgeford, and a few hand-made souvenirs, which she claimed were the remains of her family heirlooms. She was, according to herself, a cousin of Earl Spencer and was the only person in Bridgeford to sell flowers.

Fenny bought a bunch of splendid blue iris from the pigtailed small girl who was in charge of the shop. Mrs Spencer sometimes disappeared for days, retiring to bed with depression or diarrhoea, her two favourite complaints. Naturally the bottle went to bed with her.

'Whisper,' said the girl as she handed him his change, 'is herself —' she jerked her head sideways and up, in the general direction of her employer — 'is the auld wan reely related to dat big English lord? Me mudder says it all rawmeesh.'

Fenny had a soft spot for Mrs Spencer, and had known her husband.

'Her husband was,' he said softly. 'He was a major in the British army, stationed here. One of the other officers told me first, not Spencer himself. O no, there's no doubt about that.'

The girl seemed astonished and also resentful. She looked over her shoulder at Mrs Spencer's premises. Narrow in front, it stretched back a long way, and was rather like a bowling alley. It had fallen into disrepair, for part of the floor had caved in, exposing a terrifying-looking cellar. One had to walk carefully on the remaining boards to get to Mrs Spencer's apartments at the end. It was like walking a plank over a deep ditch. How the old lady managed it was more than Fenny or anyone else understood.

'Well, if that's so, you'd think he'd send her a few happences to tie her auld floor together,' said the girl scornfully. 'And pay me a shilling a week more.'

'You meet very nice people coming in here,' said Fenny, defending an old friend who was also one of the town's great eccentrics, 'Mrs Spencer has a great way with customers.'

'She has wha —?'

'She has a good business manner,' went on Fenny carefully.

'She calls dem, even some women be their names, sur or sometin, like "Murphy" and "how are ye today, Mulligan?" Well, I mane to say, the nuns never taught me to speak to people like dat.'

'Ah, but the nuns had no hand in educating Mrs Spencer,' said Fenny, making his escape with a broad grin. The girl had something in her, but old Ma Spencer was not the person to bring it out.

He paused outside the shop holding his big bunch of flowers, wrapped in newspaper already soaked with water, well away from his chest, and gazed across the narrow street at the little Methodist church. It was one of the few architectural gems in Bridgeford: a small, Victorian chapel, perfectly proportioned, with exquisitely carved stone-work and tiny, diamond-like windows. A scale model of a great cathedral, it was, in its way in better taste, and admirable in its modesty.

But Fenny also wanted as many people as possible to see him going into the Duke of Clarence with a huge bunch of flowers in his arms. And as he turned the corner and walked slowly along Church Street, he was glad that more than two dozen neighbours and acquaintances spoke to him, and looked hard at the flowers. What on earth, they would say to themselves and their families, was Fenny O'Barrell doing, going into the hotel with a bunch of iris? Surely he's not gone on Maud, is he?

Fenny arrived in the hotel in good order, and in high spirits that he had succeeded in confusing so many people. Not all of them, of course, but enough to make his visit ambiguous. He would hardly be going to do business with the Englishman with a bunch of flowers in his hands. What *was* he up to?

In the hall he met Miss Mutton, whose real name for the moment escaped him, so he gave her a wide smile, and put the flowers into her arms.

'I wish they were for you, Miss M,' he chuckled. 'You deserve them, but I'm afraid they're for the Friary. I have to see someone here, and I'd never have time to go down to the door with them. Would you ever give them in from my wife?'

'Of course I will, Mr O'Farrell, and welcome,' said Miss Mutton, a large, square-shouldered big girl, with a beautiful clear voice that tinkled like tapped silver when she laughed.

'Oh, aren't they beootiful? I'll give them to Father Aiden. He's gorgeous, and a real saint.'

'So I hear.'

'Oh, he is,' declared Miss Mutton, rolling her eyes upwards, and sighing.

'Like Ivor Novello,' went on Fenny wickedly.

'No. Like Valentino used to be. But a saint.'

'Of course. Is Mr Slyne in?'

'Well, he's only just after coming in the door a few minutes before you. I think he's in the commercial room. Will I —?'

'Not at all Miss M. I'll find my own way. Besides he's expecting me, I think. Now don't forget the flowers for Father Aiden.'

'And for St Francis,' said Miss Mutton tactfully.

Slyne had brought along a large whiskey to the commercial room, and was settling down to read *The Irish Independent* when Fenny arrived at the door. Slyne folded the paper carefully, taking his time, then stood up to receive his visitor.

'Ah, good evening, Mr O'Farrell. How kind of you to come. Do sit down.' This gracious reception was rather qualified by the fact that there was hardly a chair in the room fit to carry Fenny's girth comfortably. He therefore acknowledged his host's greeting by a small bow, a smile and a murmur of thanks, but did not come into the room.

'Will you excuse me for a moment, Mr Slyne?' he said, and disappeared.

O how tiresome they are no appointments kept no sense of time they're like those mercury boxes you tip the thing and you think you have the blob and then it's gone again I don't think all the smiles and the beautiful manners and the quick wit really make up for it lucky I don't keep a diary or I would know by now just exactly how many hours I have spent here waiting around and they won't give me a straight answer and they all know what's going on in one another's mind and there's this elaborate game of doing things on the sly is it just another kind of smokescreen they send up to give them time to think to disappear to knife you in the back careful careful keep to the text it's written down in your mind don't for a moment allow them to draw your attention away from it of course they know the law backwards but it's one of the things that makes them uneasy and when they're uneasy one can sometimes deal with them. . .

Fenny came back to the room carrying a large armchair lined with faded red plush, which Slyne remembered having seen in the bar. He set it down opposite Slyne's own chair: on either side of the famous courtyard, they now both had seats, and a table of sorts by their elbow to give them the feeling of a proper business discussion. Slyne opened his mouth to say something, but Fenny disappeared again, and came back a few minutes later with a large tumbler of whiskey for himself.

It's very formal that's the way they like it well I can be too and of course he thinks that sticking to the point and backing it up with what he thinks is strict and legal will always win why do they go on thinking like this when they're every bit as devious as we are and a great deal more because of that outer skin of honest broker that they've grown and of course he'll try the element of surprise too and catch me off guard if he can they really do believe they're right and no other country can equal them in anything except opera singing which is frivolous when the English become a nation of singers and actors it'll mean they're finished or will they will they ever really be finished in anything one thing given up another acquired Ireland gone they have us breaking our backs to get over to work in England and it'll get worse it's a good thing I have nothing to lose in this and then of course he has a master plan that even old MacDonnell won't reveal could it be that they're both in on something of course that's it I should have thought of that after all that's always the way they've worked divide and conquer have an Irish ally for the loot and conquer they will God I'm an eejit not to have thought of this sooner no wonder the Irish don't trust one another what the hell is he going to say for an opening.

'Time is beginning to press, Mr O'Farrell, and I haven't all the rest of the month to complete my business here, so do you mind if we skip the preliminaries and get down to business?'

Slyne looked at his visitor with grave, slightly hurt eyes, and a twiddling of the knot of his tie with one hand, to demonstrate that he was just a bit on edge with all these dealings.

'Not at all,' said Fenny politely. He smiled and looked at his glass with the interest of a connoisseur. The room was stuffy, and dust floated on the light coming from the dirty window.

'I'm particularly anxious to see you before I go any further in this business.' Slyne paused long enough for Fenny to reply, but since he did not, he was forced to go on.

'You see, I doubt if I'll be able to make any deal with the other principals in this business without your help.' Another pause, and still Fenny did not respond. He gave Slyne a slight smile and took up his glass: it had left a neat circle in the fine dust on the table.

'This would be a matter of regret for me, but unavoidable, I'm afraid.' Slyne paused again. Fenny coughed slightly, put down his glass after a minute sip, placing it very carefully and accurately in his own rim of dust.

'You are prepared to sell the parcel of land we have already agreed upon?' went on Slyne without the slightest hint of irritation. That showed in the toe of one shoe, which he tapped twice on the floor, and then stopped as if he had made an error; or was it done to indicate that his patience was running out?

'Of course,' replied Fenny quietly. 'I thought that was settled.'

'I'm afraid it's not.' Slyne crossed his legs and took up his glass. The room was now beginning to smell faintly of whiskey, a welcome change from the dust and damp.

'What someone should invent is a whiskey spray,' said Fenny suddenly with a grin. 'It would do a power of good in a room like this.'

'Would it?' said Slyne shortly. He tapped his own glass with a pen he had taken out of his inner pocket. The tiny sound was vastly enlarged in the warm, still room. Both men looked at the pen, held in a large, steady hand.

'You see,' Slyne went on in a low, flat voice, 'the rest of the land will really be no good to me, unless you sell me all of yours.'

This was the first surprise, and Fenny marked it by taking another, rather deeper sip of whiskey. He replaced the glass very carefully in its ring.

'I was under the impression that you wanted an opening near the town, and what you have bought — '

'Not quite that yet,' put in Slyne quickly. Perhaps a little too swiftly.

'Of course. What you have made an offer for is the opening you wanted.'

'I find now that it would be insufficient. To make the project workable I would need the rest of your land.' Slyne's tone did not change: it indicated neither eagerness nor regret.

'That leaves us in an interesting situation,' said Fenny with another grin. He shifted his bulk, plucked at the top of his trousers, and patted his belly. A long incarceration in this grimy commercial hole would bring on a lot of sweat, which Fenny dreaded because it made him sticky, uncomfortable, and uneasily aware that he probably stank in other people's nostrils. He edged his armchair backwards a little, but it would not budge. So he got slowly to his feet and lifted it back. The first thing he noted when he reseated himself was his glass. It was now a little too far to reach without stretching his arm, but he comforted himself with the thought that he might be able to leave a little trail of tumbler rings on the table before he was finished.

Slyne watched him with slightly baffled curiosity. Really one never knew what way these people were going to behave.

Smokescreens in the old times they used to set them up by putting branches of trees on fire and of course the soldiers faced this to find themselves attacked from the back and wasn't it they after all who perfected guerrilla warfare the Boers claim it but the Irish were at it in the eighteenth century and that Collins man brought it to a fine art less than twenty years ago the slightest move is calculated to distract even this ridiculous whiskey glass business has some evasive purpose if only one had even a tiny dry piece of common territory to start off from but no one is simply left sloshing around in one of their awful bogs full of dark holes and sudden steep slopes they are as treacherous as wild mushrooms on a desert island.

Slyne waited grimly for Fenny to add to his last remark. What does he mean by 'an interesting situation?'

'It never entered my mind to sell that piece of land, even a part of it, as I have done.' Fenny paused to sip in slow motion, 'A slow potion' he murmured to himself when he put down his glass on yet another plane of dust.

'What's that?' said Slyne with a frown. If there was one thing he couldn't abide it was muttering. 'I didn't hear you.'

'I was about to say,' went on Fenny, raising his voice and speaking with careful precision, 'that although everybody is buying motors nowadays, and I had planned to get one maybe next year, I still want to keep a bit of grass for my old pony. Traps are going to be as dead as unicorns in another few years, but I'll keep mine. It's a beautiful, hand-made job. Then of course no Irishman is really happy unless he has a bit of grass of his own to stand on.'

'You can always buy yourself another field,' said Slyne shortly. This rambling on was extremely tedious, and no doubt served as a smokescreen. What was he really getting at behind all those words?

'True.' Fenny inclined his head, stroked one eye with a finger and ran his tongue around the inside of his mouth. 'But where would I get a place so convenient? Not to mention the place being very nicely situated. You have bought all the rest of the land up to the cross-river, and old MacDonnell won't sell his plot, so I'd have to go — '

'I have not bought all the rest of the land as you put it,' Slyne put in quickly. 'Nothing has been signed. I have merely indicated that I would buy it at a certain price. But of course I can always change my mind.'

'Why didn't you tell me this at the beginning, before you went on to deal with the old ladies?' Fenny raised his massive head and looked at Slyne accusingly. He might have been on the point of rebuking a man who had got himself just that one glass too many in O'Farrell's own bar. Fenny was a good-natured man, as was known by all, but he had a fierce temper and a very strong will. Few people ever dared to cross him.

'Naturally I wanted to make sure that they would sell first —'

'And my refusal would be a good get-out if they proved difficult?'

'Not at all. It's simply that one cannot do everything at the same time. I approached the women first, then you almost at once, and as you know, you agreed to sell part of the land you own. What I was not aware of at the time was the extent of the opening I wanted at the town end.' Slyne was firm, clear and steady, conveying conviction in the rightness of his position.

'I see.' Fenny rubbed his belly thoughtfully, but held his whist.

'If you don't sell the rest of your land,' went on Slyne, speaking slowly and flatly, 'it means I won't be able to go through with the rest of the sale.'

'You mean you won't go on with the purchases from the old ladies? I don't mean Mrs Daly, of course, although she's hardly a girl, but she is not relying on the deal, whereas the others are.' In this important moment he did not take up his glass as he wanted to, but remained perfectly still, as Slyne was doing.

Slyne's big fair face interested Fenny as he gazed at it. He looked at his visitor as if he were a man with a gun in his pocket, which at any moment he might produce. Try as he might, embarrassment was written into every line of his face, and distrust between every other line.

This is where the going gets really tricky walking carefully over a bog that might give way under me any minute it's when they make a sort of plea for compassion or pretend to be in need and you're the only one that can help them that's the worst time of all and this fat slob who's such a gentleman among them I suppose he's descended from kings too like the rest of them they're all really too tiresome but one must be patient patient patient they have none of that and it always wins in the end

'Yes, I suppose that's what I do mean,' said Slyne shaking his head, as if he were deeply saddened by the whole business. 'Of course I know they're more or less expecting the money, as none of them is working the land — '

He broke off as Fenny suddenly giggled. But he stopped almost at once and reached for his glass, from which he took a good swallow.

What an amazing thing to do what's behind it that frivolity which breaks out in them so unexpectedly one never knows what's behind it I bet they laughed into some of Cromwell's men's faces I'm perfectly sure they did what an awful bloody race

'Did you expect them to be working it?' said Fenny, suddenly regaining his gravity.

'Well, no. But that's not the point.'

'You have a perfectly good opening on the town side as it is,' went on Fenny earnestly, 'twice the width of a good road.'

'Perhaps you'd like to think it over, Mr O'Farrell?' said Slyne in an exhausted voice. He suddenly felt very tired.

'I'll think it over all right, but I won't change my mind.'

'I hope you will. However, that's the position. Perhaps you wouldn't mind my asking you not to mention any of this conversation to the old ladies?'

'And make four enemies for life? Not to mention their relations, friends and neighbours. You can be quite sure I'll keep my mouth shut.' He took up his glass and drained it. 'I think you should have ensured the opening you wanted was available before you approached the women.'

Slyne's ruddy complexion paled a little, his steady eyes hardened, and he uncrossed his legs and placed them firmly on the dusty carpet. But he smiled.

'I wasn't sure that they were prepared to sell at all, or how much, if any, they would part with.'

Fenny smiled and looked down at Slyne's well-polished shoes. Even after a walk through the dusty lanes and streets, they were still shining. The man must keep a chamois in his kit, and dash up to his room to clean his shoes the moment he comes in. Well, you have to hand it to them for tidiness. But there's something wrong about his excuse. I'm not quite sure what it is, but it only sounds well. It's like an invisible crack in good china: it rings hollow when you tap it, but still you can't see the crack.

'And of course,' Fenny went on smoothly, 'I wouldn't consider letting go even the piece I have offered to you, if you do not go on with the deal with the old ladies.' He picked up his empty glass, pursed up his lips and ran a finger along the rim of the glass.

'But I wouldn't need it if—' Slyne broke off. There was more in this than meets the eye, he said to himself. It can't mean just exactly what it says.

This is where they stab you in the back they lead you into a thick fog on a bog and while you're sloshing around they come in behind you it happened to one of Elizabeth's armies that's why Cromwell wouldn't treat with them at all he knew his mark this Farrell fellow has something up his sleeve now what does he mean by saying that it's perfectly obvious that I won't want his land or wouldn't want it if I didn't buy the bog from the old hags they're all witches too I saw that little old one the one they call Hallelujah or something looking at me in a very queer way she's just the type to make a little doll of me and put a pin in my heart and that's morbid but you get these notions when you're here a while it must be the air or something — and what do they know?

'I see,' said Slyne with the utmost composure. 'Well, it's interesting of you to say that. I'll bear it in mind.' He paused and licked his lips. 'And if I do go ahead, would you consider parting with the rest of your property down there?'

Fenny remembered Flynn's message, 'promise'.

'I would certainly consider it, yes,' he said, looking at Slyne with a friendly little smile.

'Good.' Slyne felt in his inside pocket and took out his wallet, from which he extracted a card.

'That's my card, as you can see. If you want to get in touch with me just give me a ring.'

Fenny looked at the card. It gave Slyne's name, and an address in London W1. And the telephone number. He flicked the card against his knuckle and looked up at Slyne.

'I suppose one could through the operator. But I really don't know. You can from Dublin.'

'It's eighty miles from here to Dublin,' said Fenny mildly.

'Of course, of course. But at least you know where to contact me. You could write.'

'Of course,' said Fenny taking out his own wallet, putting Slyne's card in carefully, and taking out another one. 'This is my card,' he said cheerfully. 'I don't know about the telephone to there either, but you can certainly write.'

Slyne who was a trifle long-sighted and did not like to hold the card at arm's length, glanced at it and nodded.

'Thank you so much. Very kind.' He put it into his wallet, and when he had put that back in his inside breast pocket, he looked up to see that Fenny had got up from his chair, and was making for the door.

'I have to get back, Mr Slyne. My wife gets nervous when left too long on her own. I hope everything goes well with you.'

Slyne rose and inclined his head one tenth of an inch.

'Thank you, Mr O'Farrell, you've been very helpful, very kind.'

When Fenny was gone, and he felt he was alone for a few moments, Slyne took out the card, put on his reading glasses and read it, then he put it down carefully in one of the circles Fenny had made with his glass, smiled his own little smile — a slight flexing of the muscles at the corner of the mouth — and walked slowly out of the room.

The card Fenny had given him, read, under a telephone number:

Mme. Tilly Renard
14 Rue de la Louisiane,
Palais Royale,
Paris 1

'Where did ye get dis?'

'In de commercial room, Mrs O'Flaherty, after I —'

'Flynn.'

'After I came back, Mrs O'Flaherty Flynn, from visitin' me poor liddle wife and the brood of hungry mouths the Lord has sent us.'

'Am I not givin' ye enough, Donseen Donnelly? A cut offa de best af everyting ye get, doan' ye?'

'Oh, indeeden, I'm not complainin' Mrs O'Flaherty Flynn, and as for prayer, me wife an' —'

'Well, dis card is far from a prayer. A wummin in Paris. Angels a the Lord protect us all. A course id's d'Englishman.'

'Ya tink so?'

'I knew de minnit I saw 'im, he diddn fool me for wan single, solitry, bald minnit.'

'Bud Fenny O'Barrell wus in dere wid 'im.'

'No, Donie. De same Fenny is a gamy aul pie, and as juicy as a pigeon, bud he'd niver descend ta dis. Anyways how would he get ta Paris?'

'He wus widely travelled man in his day. He wus in Rome an saw de Pope.'

'In the name of de Fadder and de Son and de Holy Ghost.'

'Amen.'

'Rome is a long ways from Paris, and nod de same ting at all. Besides dis card is a new wan, not thumbed nor nudden, so how could Fenny keep a ting like dat so clean all dese years? Answer me dat.'

'Ye're right dere.'

'A course I am. Besides I was never taken in be dat Englishman, nod for wan, single, solitry, flyin' minnit. He has dat kinda heat comin' off him, like a wickedy pony or a pot-oven.'

'Has he?'

'Anny married wummin'l tell ye. I got it de furst time I went into de dinin'-room to butther him up. O I know he's all smooth an' simule like an aul' tom-cat, an' I don't mind ad all standin' beside him, and I'll cook de brains of a dead nigger if dat's what he wants fur 'im, bud I wouldn't care to be washin' up after 'im.'

'Why, Mrs O'Flaherty Flynn?'

'Because a de disease they get from wummin like dat, ye can get paralitis and go stark, ravin' mad an' lose all yer hair 'n yer teet', and have to be corked like a corpse because ye have no control a yoursel' ad all in the wide wurruld.'

'Jez, Mary and Joseph, I never heard a de stuffin'.'

'An' it's contagin' too. Remember, I have a sister a nurse in England, an' all de rich Englishmen is mad, outa dere minds over filthy French wummin.'

'Catchin' is it? Well, I know dat, but I tought — '

'Men doan' know de half of id. Anytin' dat comes next to his skin is dangerous. It's nod so bad washin's his plates on account of de hot water, an' anyways id's Maureen Pox dat does dat, an' she's indoculated on account of Polly 'er sister.'

'But surely Polly hasn't de French disease.'

'She has every known disease, Donie Donnelly, Afrigan an' all, from de British soljers, ye see. Now poor Maureen is a harmless poor craythur, and ye know we couldn't refuse de nuns when dey axed for a job for her on account of bein' in d'Orphantidge — O God, I clean forgot, she's makin' de beds too some days, when dat lazy slut Maisie Hound is oud sick. All the same in de name of whoomanity, I'll have ta tell 'er to get a pair of cotton gloves ta wear when she's makin' up his bed, an' especially when she's foldin' his piejammers, because dere terrible dangerous for de pox.'

'Ye're a saint, Mrs O'Flaherty Flynn. Bud, havin' taken all due care and precautions, tanks ta you, we muss remember dat he hasn't finished his business yet. We can't let 'im know wad we know — '

'A course nod. I'll go out an' take his order especial tonite — I have a gorgeous Lough Ree trout laid oud special for 'im. And you juss watch me dealing with 'im. I'll stand a good foot away from 'im, an' I'll give 'im as many smiles, nods an' shouldershakes as a whole chorus a' whores!'

'O Mrs O'Flaherty Flynn, bud you're a wonder.'

'Sorry for knocking on the hall door, Herbie, but — '

'Come in, Benny, come in.'

'Is the shop closed? I wasn't quite sure.'

'Well, I closed the door, I got kinda bored, and besides the wife is havin' a bath.'

'She is?'

'Well, I have to be nearby in case she god scalded or something. I don't trust them new tanks. One exploded last week in Kilkenny. I saw it in *The Independent*.'

'Was anyone killed, Herbie?'

'No, just concussed. And Crissie stays an awful long time in the bath. I mean, she doesn't take it to clean herself, or anything like that, because she's like a new pin — but she says she loves soaking in it. Queer isn't it?'

'Twenty years time, and everybody will be soaking in them.'

'I suppose so.'

'I'm looking for a couple of sleeping pills, Herbie.'

'What kind do you want, medium or extra strong?'

'Oh, the strong ones. I'm having a terrible time with the sale of the bog. Well, it's not that so much, it's the old women. They'd give a pain to a headstone.'

'I know. Do you think he's in earnest?'

'I think he is.'

'Jasus.'

'Oh, well, the English always have a reason.'

'Too true, Ben, too true. How many pills do you want?'

'Two or three, I suppose. If I got a couple of nights sleep, I'd be all right.'

'I'll give you half a dozen of the yellow ones. They'd knock out a race horse.'

'How much, Herbie?'

'Arrah, nothing at all. I get them as samples. O God, is that the wife I hear? It is. She wants me to dry her.'

'I hear the nuns are taking baths now, twice a year, in long white shifts. How do they dry themselves, shifts and all?'

'You're joking, Benny. The nuns don't take baths. I have two sisters in convents: they'd faint if you mentioned the idea.'

'It must be American nuns I read about.'

'Nothing would surprise me about them. O God, there's Crissie again. So long Ben. Sleep tight.'

It was a warm evening, and as Fenny came away from Herbie Hoban's Medical Hall, summer lay heavy upon Connaught Street. Dust had settled on the road, and was not at the moment disturbed by any passing vehicle. Two dogs lay in the middle of the tarred surface, a red and white sheepdog and a setter who had once been the same colour, but was now a sort of dirty pink all over. Both might have been dead.

The sky over the uneven roofs was blurred, and glimmered faintly as layers of pale clouds passed before the sun. Shadows were grey, streaked with brown. A few dark-coloured cats almost blended into the shade, except that they were more active than the dogs. They lay with their tails flicking idly, and a few were on the move, walking softly, heavily, even awkwardly, like pregnant women known to be beautiful. No humans livened the scene. It was one of those blank periods when silence falls on a street, a square, even an entire village in the same way as it cuts through the chatter of a dinner party.

Fenny, who was attuned to the slightest mood of the street, had experienced moments like this all his life. But as he made his way along the path from Hoban's, he became conscious of something else. This summer lethargy was not altogether the result of the season, and the wilting end of a long hot day. But he gave no sign. He continued his slow, slightly ponderous way, his massive head set quite straight on his shoulders, his small neat feet carrying him with well-paced, mandarin dignity. No one searching Fenny's sweat-streaked face would have been able to deduce any kind of information from it, good or bad.

He understood at once the reason for the deserted appearance of the place. He had had a meeting with Slyne, who must have had fresh proposals to make. Their instinct told them that a turning point had been reached. No one wanted to be the first to ask Fenny if he had failed to win the Englishman over. Some tribal instinct was at work: huddled together, under no outside eye, keeping quiet as they had done so often down the years, they avoided a direct confrontation. The messenger was on his way, certainly, but what had he to tell? We don't want to hear. Not yet. Not yet.

It had happened a few times before in Fenny's lifetime. That time when young Mrs Moore was dying of consumption, with six children to mourn her: for three nights running the street had been like it was now. And before the first candle was lit, before the blinds were drawn, they knew and were preparing to go over to the dazed husband, the quietly hysterical children, and the poor wasted corpse of the prettiest woman in the street.

It had happened also, Fenny's father told him, on the day that news of Parnell's death had come through, uncertainly at first, then with no doubt. A terrible pall of silence had descended upon the entire town; the grief was too deep even for weeping.

When Fenny turned into his shop he was not a bit surprised to find it empty, except for Ellen. She was sitting in his bum-boat, placidly knitting a blue scarf.

'Well, well, well,' he said gently as he came in. 'I hope you're not drinking too. That stool was designed for it, you can sell with it too, but only incidentally.'

'Oh, Benedict, I am glad you're back,' said Ellen with a wonderful smile of happiness that made his heart turn over and over, and alter its rhythm entirely. 'Would you believe it, but not a single person has darkened the door this two hours. I've never seen anything like it.'

'You seem to be thriving on it.'

'Maybe I am.' She rolled up her knitting and slipped down from the bum-boat.

It happens like this and we're lucky if we understand the moment how many moments are there like this in life plenty I think but we're too taken up with other things to notice them they've withdrawn all the watchers the others that press around and may not be watching at all but are there there there all the time and I never guessed that maybe that's what's wrong with my Ellen she's never really got used to the pressure of the locals she gets up in the morning prepared to meet them and it's a strain from the moment of waiting to go out all day long and she's still tensed up when it's time to go to bed how often have I come up after her to find her asleep but I can see it now her hands clasped tightly over the sheet her body never slack so it's no wonder and now I know that we've been given one of those gifts in life that only a whole community can offer and a particularly tight-knit one at that my Ellen and me are alone tonight in a way we've never been before you can't understand the removal of pressure unless you've lived with it night and day it must be like a cage bird when the green cloth is taken off in the morning and the door is opened my poor little Ellen has been caged in like that and of course I've known it or sensed it for a long time those pills it was in my mind all day I suppose we anticipate the future over and over again and don't know that either but the gods the saints the angels the

cabelli I've always believed in them somehow men who exist in their
thoughts and imagine they still have bodies they all know and maybe we
know too in a queer kind of way that makes us —

He looked at Ellen, and she smiled back at him. For a
moment both were silent, and, as if to emphasize the total
absence of noise, they both started at the faint sound of tapping
somewhere outside on the path. Or so Fenny thought. He went
to the door and peered out.

The old man with the twisted leg who stayed in Janey
Horan's lodging house down the street was crossing the road to
it. They were listening to the drag of his heels and the tap-tap of
his big blackthorn stick.

Fenny smiled to himself and looked up at the roofs for a
moment. Moss was growing on many of them, yellow summer
moss, and dirty white withered grass in the gutters, while a long
dim streak down some of the houses told the tale of downpipes
missing. Yet as he gazed, in a half-sleepy way, like those who
are secretly happy, he could feel a great surge of love for the old
street in his heart, which at that moment he did not distinguish
from the love, deep-rooted, constant and clear-eyed which he
felt for his wife.

He closed the door of the shop and turned to meet Ellen's
smiling glance.

'I'm tired,' lied Fenny. He had never felt less so in his life.

'It's a strange evening,' Ellen was saying when he had
fastened the lock on the front door, and she was taking a few
pounds out of the grocery till. She tapped the purse. 'I have the
bar takings here.'

'It's a wonderful evening, Nell. Have you ever felt anything
like it before?'

'No, truly.' Her eyes were shining, and it seemed to her
husband that he had never seen her so happy, carefree and
relaxed before. She had always been shy and nervous, and had
not grown less so after their marriage.

Years later Fenny thought idly, and then with concentration,
of that night and the consequences of it. Perhaps, he thought,
this is the way primitive tribes behave when two young people
are given to each other, and the future of the tribe is uncertain.
Did the older ones, the long-wedded, draw back and leave the
young people to themselves, so that no prying eye might trouble
the bride? Not on the first night, perhaps, but when the

festivities were over? Was it some obscure, tribal instinct, that, mixed with their anxiety about his meeting with Slyne, worked upon them so that for a while they seemed to withdraw? The fact that Ellen felt some sort of release made the whole thing seem absolutely real; because Ellen did not understand these people — or did she? And how much a part of the old street, the old community by the river was he himself? Was their little boy conceived that night in mid-summer with a haze about the moon?

'Really and truly?' he said, teasing her a little.

'Rahlee and trowly,' she laughed, imitating an affected woman they both knew, and holding out her hand for Fenny to take.

Clouds moved in during the night and the morning dawned heavy and pall-faced. Everyone was late that morning, although only Fenny seemed to remember it afterwards. For one thing Ellen missed seven o'clock mass for the seventh time in twelve years. 'Seven is a good number, one of the best,' he had reassured her, when she came back from mass at ten in a great flurry, because she had seen Slyne passing the church as she came out, and was only a few paces behind him — for he was walking slowly and deliberately — when she reached her own door. He had passed by, and she did not want to stand at the entrance and watch him.

Others did it for her. She was hardly inside her own shop, and was just taking off her light summer hat — blond straw with a thin blue ribbon — when Mrs Pig came charging in from across the road, and thumped on the bar with her fist.

'He's gone into MacDonnell's,' she said shortly when Ellen turned back from the uneven patch of mirror behind the bar. When on her own, she often played a sort of game of hide and seek, dodging from bottle to bottle as they stood ranged against the glass like guardsmen with lank necks and needle-heads.

'Who — ?' began Ellen whose mind was on other things.

'Who!' exclaimed Mrs Pig with an expression of shock, as if in touching the top of the bar she had touched one of those electric wires which she had read about, and which people with more money than sense were getting into their houses, risking their lives to be better than their neighbours.

'Oh, yes of course, Mr MacDonnell,' said Ellen recovering herself, but not instantly. 'Mr Slyne.'

'And who else, in de name of de dead generations of Irishmen — ' began Mrs Pig, who when moved, often fell back on rhetoric and could quote extensive passages from the Irish patriots.

'Emmet,' said Fenny, bundling in the door from the hall. He had slept late, but awakened with every sense alert when the street suddenly came alive with the passing of Slyne. Fenny, acutely aware of such things, had rolled out of bed, fingered and toed his way into his clothes, and was coming down the last few steps of the stairs when he heard Mrs Pig orating — he called it oprating — in the shop.

'No,' she replied firmly, 'Easter Proclamation, 1916.'

'Can it be possible that I'm not fully awake?' said Fenny, hitching up his belly with one hand and running his fingers through his hair with the other. He had washed his eyes, but badly needed a shave.

'It can be possible that you're wrong — sometimes,' said Mrs Pig with a smile. 'Slyne is gone up the street to MacDonnells.'

'Ah, so that's what's up,' said Fenny, pulling at his unshaven chin as if he sported a beard. It was a gesture many men of his age made; they were all sons of fathers who had beards in which to ruminate, prate, oprate, or mutter. 'Me-m-m-me-me-me,' shan-songed Fenny, as his father used to do, to remind his listeners that he sang in the choir. Solo, too. Shanvanvoct in the mouth of an old man, and why not? Old men, and young men too, often sang the song of the Old Woman.

Mrs Pig recognized it and smiled, but she did not forget the purpose of her visit.

'What does he want with old MacDonnell?'

Fenny had had time to think, but he continued his beardless bearding until a tiny sound from Ellen, the echo of a chuckle, made it plain that he was passing from a philosopher into a clown, a transformation he was prepared to defend on other occasions.

'Well, it must be a last offer to buy his land, mustn't it?' He looked out at the street. Dust filled the air as youngsters ran to and fro, frenetic but strangely silent. 'Otherwise he wouldn't walk up the street in broad daylight, would he?'

'Englishmen'd do anything, night or day,' commented Mrs Pig grimly.

'True for you. But I think all the same if yer man was reneging his offer, he'd do it through a solicitor. Besides, he's not going to do that.'

Mrs Pig did not dispute this. Benedict O'Farrell would never say such an awful thing if he was not sure of it.

But just then Ellen gave a gasp, and clutched her husband's shirt sleeve. Mrs Pig turned to the window instinctively just as Slyne was passing the door, walking quickly with a set look on his face. For a moment they were all silent, giving him time to pass into the medley of footsteps that still sounded at the end of the street into which he was heading. They stopped abruptly, but Slyne made no other sound. He was a tall man with long strides, and by now, they judged, he had turned into King Street, which ran downhill steeply from Connaught Street into the castle square.

'Merciful God and Holy St Joseph,' breathed Mrs Pig, 'Finished already. Oh ho, but the Easter Proclamation wasn't bloody well read in vain — I always said —'

What she had always said was not heard again on that occasion, for just as she was about to launch into a speech, Susannah Braiden tottered into the shop, ash on her hat and soot on her face, as if she had just rushed out from stooping over her summer fire, always more grey-black than red, and run out into the street to face the Last Trump.

'Hauld me up, hauld me up,' she quavered, stretching out her hands weakly in front of her like a blind woman.

'Take it aisy,' commanded Mrs Pig, giving her arm such a jerk as she grabbed her that Ellen winced and closed her eyes, half expecting to see Miss Braiden's arm break off from her trunk. But before she could recover herself properly and come to the old lady's aid, Mrs Pig and Fenny had already taken her between them, and were leading her into the snug. Fenny looked over his shoulder, mouthed 'brandy', and Ellen hurried behind the counter to pour a sustaining few drops.

The snug in O'Farrell's was very much like all the other compartments set up in bars to provide wordahs for the women who never, *of course*, drank with the men in the public area. These tiny cloisters were usually situated at the end of the bar counter, so that a hatch could be opened conveniently, and the ladies given their drinks, uncontaminated by the lustful eyes of the men, who would also, so the theory went, not know how much the womenfolk were spending on fire-water. In reality everyone knew exactly what any particular lady drank at any particular time, and how often she drank it; but at least she was spared the embarrassment of being seen to do so. Young women were not served in respectable bars, even in snugs, and O'Farrell's dimbo had never been occupied by any female less than fifty.

But O'Farrell's snug had a distinction which made it unique among the cloisters of Bridgeford. Like all the others it had a bench running along the wall, a table and two or three chairs. But Fenny's mother had an aunt, who claimed to have been taken by her husband to the Cafe Royal in London, long before Oscar Wilde made it notorious. Her description of this famous and exclusive place had fired old Mrs O'Farrell's imagination. She had her snug bench covered with red plush, and had a fake pillar of rounded wood put in at the end of the bar and painted with gold leaf. Over the bench she hung a coloured photograph of Piccadilly Circus as it was in 1900, and obviously taken from the first floor of Swan and Edgars. The old lady would point to this scene with some pride, for it had been given to her by her rich English-based aunt, and run her finger along the picture until she came to the frame. Then she would indicate a spot on the wall about two inches from the photograph. 'There,' she would say proudly, 'just about there, in Regent Street, you know, is the Cafe Royal, where my aunt used to dine, oh long before it got a bad name.' On this spot Fenny in his youth had painted a large, gold leaf X to mark the site of the celebrated cafe, and of course the snug was known locally, especially to older women as The Cafe Royal. And many a story of a slightly bawdy nature was told about it.

But that morning, with Miss Braiden in a fainting condition, there was no time for gad-flies. Ellen arrived back with a glass of brandy so large that her husband tried to catch her eye, and failing, caught Mrs Pig's instead. That quick-witted lady made a grab for the glass, about to declare her own interest in shocks of the large and sudden variety, but Hosannah was too quick for her. She shot forward like an uncoiled spring from the red plush back against which she had been slumped, grabbed the glass from Ellen's hand, and drank it off like water taken in a gulp with a pill.

Then she collapsed against the wall and closed her eyes, while Fenny succeeded in catching Ellen's eye. Ellen was careful enough with drinks while using the measuring cup, but never having taken any sort of alcohol herself, she was inclined to pour out whiskey and brandy for visitors as if it were lemonade.

'Macroomed by God!' said Hosannah, opening her eyes abruptly, like a torn sheet hung out and stretched by the wind.

'Susannah!' exclaimed Mrs Pig, shocked by such strong language on the lips of Miss Braiden.

'Well, macroomed anyway. I cudden believe me own wan eye, for ye all know I'm nearly stone blind in wan, and have to hauld id back when I'm using the good wan, well anyway —'

'You don't mean to tell me that that little monkey Macroom wouldn't let the Englishman in?' said Mrs Pig in a shocked voice.

'He would not,' said Hosannah, looking at her empty glass wistfully. 'He opened de door and banged id again straight inta 'is face. Did ye ever hear de like a' dat?'

'What does dis mean?' Mrs Pig said to Fenny.

'Well, obviously it means that MacDonnell won't even discuss the sale of his land.'

'Bud wha' aboud de rest of us?' said Hosannah shrilly, sitting up stark and poised like a suicide on the edge of a roof. She clutched the red plush beside her and leaned forward with a wild, hexed look in her eye. 'What's goin' ta happen t'our land?' She came dangerously near the edge of the seat, and Mrs Pig pushed her back with a quick but fairly gentle hand.

'Yes,' Mrs Pig repeated, 'What's going to happen to us? I always said and I say it again, dat where Englishmen are concerned —'

They were not to know what Slyne might do, for at that moment Hamlet stuck his head into the snug, having come into the shop noiselessly as was his way. He was very pale and was rasping for breath.

'Hamlet, boy, what's up?' said Fenny. He took the lad by the shoulder, and put him down on one of the chairs.

'Would you like a cup of tea, child?' said Ellen whose heart was touched by the young fellow's exhausted appearance; there was something strange but appealing in the depths of his blue eyes. She had often seen him scrubbing the steps of the hotel, or polishing the windows in his orphanage suit. His freckled face, blurred mouth and chin running into his long neck — features which made others look past him — awakened a strange mixture of sadness and pity in Ellen.

'Yes, mm, please,' panted Hamlet. They let him recover his breath, while Ellen went out to get tea; silent all and still for a long moment, while they waited for Hamlet to speak.

'Mr Donnelly sent me out after Mr Slyne to see where he was goin', and after bein' turned away from Mr MacDonnell's he went back down King Street and into Mr Fair the solicitor.'

'Fair!' said Fenny stroking his nose.

'Fair,' growled Mrs Pig, 'a Free State solicitor.'

'Fair,' croaked Hosannah, 'Merciful Lord, we're all done fur!'

Hamlet cleared his throat and sat up very straight, some slight colour coming back into his wan face.

'Mr Slyne wrote a letter to Mr Fair two days ago,' he said in a low voice, which was so much older than his face. They leaned towards him, the three of them and he paused for a moment savouring the importance of the moment. 'And then tore it up again.'

'Aw, for God's sake,' said Mrs Pig disgustedly.

'Did you put it together again?' said Fenny, who thought Hamlet was quicker than most.

'I did,' said Hamlet with a show of humility, 'and I didden.'

'What did he say?' said Fenny, who knew his man.

'He said dat he would call this morning at d' office, and dat he expected Mr Fair to have the contracts ready for to sign, and dat he was goin' away today as well.'

'Did you tell this to Donie?' urged Fenny.

'No, sir, I didden.'

'Well you deserve something for this. I don't know exactly what, but I'll get it for you.' Fenny went out and got behind the bar to reach the till. Ten shillings he thought would be enough, but not in front of the ladies. 'Hamlet,' he called, and the boy came out of the snug, his hands hanging by his sides, a look of suspicion on his white face, and something about his whole general appearance that indicated a sense of shame. A curious boy, Fenny thought, as he handed him the note, put a finger to his lips, and then told him to go back into the snug to wait for his tea.

'Well, maybe you're as well to go in that door over there, Hamlet, and my wife will give it to you in the room.'

Hamlet hesitated for a moment, and Fenny knew why.

'The moment any news comes through you'll know,' he said with a smile. 'If you're left with Miss Hayes, our housekeeper, just say you're deaf and dumb. Point to your mouth and ears.' Fenny made the gesture, and winked. Hamlet smiled and nodded. It was a part he well knew how to play.

'Just now,' went on Fenny, hitching his belly with two hands, a mannerism he had when there was serious work to be done, 'I'm going to MacDonnell's to find out what's up. Don't worry, son, you'll be the first to hear.'

Hamlet flushed and smiled — was it the first time anyone had called him 'son'? — and went obediently to the door leading to the dining-room, where he met Ellen on her way out with a tray of tea and biscuits.

'Mr O'Farrell tole me to come in here,' he whispered, holding a hand against the side of his mouth.

'Oh,' said Ellen in a puzzled voice. Then she smiled. 'I expect he thinks you're too old to be with the ladies in the snug.'

Hamlet blushed again and screwed up his mouth to strangle a grin.

'The boss also tole me if I meet Miss Hayes I'm to be deaf and dumb,' he whispered, stretching out his neck and tapping his ears and mouth.

Ellen began to chuckle like a young girl, a sort of conspirator's giggle, and Hamlet had taken another idol to his sad, undernourished heart.

'Come back into the room with me, and don't say a word,' she whispered.

Back in the snug with the ladies, Fenny hitched up his belly again, and prepared himself for action.

'I'm off to MacDonnell's now,' he announced, 'and I'll be back as soon as I can.'

'We were thinkin' a Parnell Keegan,' said Mrs Pig.

'Yes, we were, ad least id wus me dat mentioned him, a rale aul frien', an' dussen everybody know he does all de rale work in Mr Fair's office?' croaked Hosannah, who had two bright spots on the bones of her cheeks, and was blowing little bubbles as she spoke.

'I'll get MacDonnell to give Parnell a ring,' said Fenny.

'And if dat little ape Macroom tries to hold ye up, kick him in the balls,' advised Mrs Pig.

'Mrs Prendergast,' squealed Hosannah, 'Mrs Prendergast, remember where y'are.' She pointed a slightly wavering finger at the photograph behind her. 'In the Caff Royal. A place for ladies, please.'

'Shut up, you,' said Mrs Pig, snatching the brandy glass from the table in front of Hosannah, a real coup, for the other had taken one hand away, while she was indicating the general direction of Regent Street behind her, and kept the other grasped around her precious empty glass.

'Gimme back dat,' cried Hosannah, 'I haven finish' — ' she drew herself up, and stuck her chin out, 'I'm still partakin', isn't dat right, Mr O'Farrell?'

'When I come back with good news, there'll be another,' said Fenny, backing out of the snug with Hosannah's blessing hot upon the back of his neck.

He went out his own front door, and walked quickly up towards MacDonnell's at the top of the street. Although Fenny had a belly fit for an abbot, he had a pair of thick, strong legs, and was still able to walk at a brisk rate and without a suggestion of a waddle. Everyone saw him on his way, and he was well aware of it. But there was work to be done, and this time there must be no secrecy. He was on his way to find out just what was the position regarding the Englishman.

The door was opened by MacDonnell himself, much to the surprise of the neighbours opposite who had never seen him do this before. Did it mean a high regard for Fenny? Or was Macroom in disgrace for turning away the Englishman?

Fenny stepped inside, and there, sitting on his little stool was the great Macroom himself, reading a magazine over which he gave Fenny a look like the flicker of a wasp's wings.

'I was expecting you,' said old MacDonnell, leading the way to his study. The silver frame of the Roosevelt picture gleamed in the dull light, as it was specially polished to do. The massive file, ominous and heavy with suggestion, competed with the old man himself for dominance in the room. Fenny suspected that it was half empty, and the old man's real secrets were kept in a locked strongbox in the bank.

'You'll want to know about Slyne,' said MacDonnell, sitting down behind the wide open space of his desk, 'Take a seat, have a drink, smoke.'

Fenny did not respond to all this professional ease; he sat down, but accepted nothing else. MacDonnell looked at him levelly with his curious multi-coloured eyes — grey, light brown, green-blue — to various people they seemed all these colours at different times. But that straight honest gaze was too much for Fenny. There was something that MacDonnell was not going to tell him.

'He's in Fair's at the moment.'

'Yes, I know. I heard about the appointment.' MacDonnell leaned back and allowed his, head to drop forward, his heavy jowls sinking into the thick neck. He spread his small, youthful hands on the desk, and looked at them as if they were detachable, and he was wondering if he ought to take them off and change them.

'From Hamlet,' said Fenny with no question in his voice. For some reason he did not want it to be the boy.

'No. A boy like that is of only limited use. Lawyers and such might be above him, although of course he's cleverer than he admits. Curious kid.' MacDonnell paused and smiled to himself. He was thinking of the boy's ridiculous infatuation for Maud. 'No, Parnell is keeping me posted.'

'I see. Might I ask why you refused to see Slyne this morning?'

'I suppose the old women are anxious,' chuckled MacDonnell. 'Well, they needn't be. The contracts — deposits of course — are already drawn up. He has a meeting with old Fair this morning. For signing.'

'You seem very sure that he's going to go through with the whole business, to the end.'

'Have you heard that he isn't?' rapped back MacDonnell quickly. But Fenny noticed there was no real alarm in his multi-coloured eyes. Eyes, lies and goodbyes, as the saying went, that was a definition of a love story. Love, dove, and hand-in-glove. The silly, half-remembered words, like loosely strung beads, rattled through Fenny's mind. He was not really communicating with this devious old man.

'No,' said Fenny with a sigh.

There was silence for a minute during which MacDonnell looked straight at his visitor with his steady eyes, then a little above his shoulder, to wander away like jelly-fish in a pond. No, he thought, jelly-fish didn't 'wander', but they moved and swayed. And that was what he saw behind the professional straight-from-the-holster expression in MacDonnell's eyes.

Strange that a gaze, a regard, could be so apparently sincere, and yet give the impression of being unfocused and shifty. Sleight of eye, like sleight of hand, a conjuror's eye. What a loaded word that was, Fenny thought: con-man, con-the-jury, eyelid and eyeball. That was what MacDonnell was, a conjunctiviar, or maybe conjunctor; that would do. Whenever he looked at MacDonnell again, he would see the eyes of a conjunctor. And that would not do either. Did not 'conjunct' mean joined, associated? Yet, in a way, that could be part of the meaning also. After all, the old man was a fixer.

Fenny's musings, to which he was subject during idle moments — and he thought he was wasting his time with this old crook — were interrupted by the ringing of the telephone on the desk. He lifted it from its cradle and gave a number, which Fenny knew was not his own, or indeed anybody else's in that town. Old fox. Con, con conjewor? Was that number a pass word?

'I see. Thanks,' said MacDonnell briefly and laid the receiver gently to rest again. He gave Fenny a piercing look and a wide political smile. 'Well, that's it. He's signed the contracts. They're going out this evening. That was Parnell Keegan, a sound man. I don't know what Fair would do without him, he knows as much law as anyone I've ever met.'

'And anti-law,' said Fenny quietly. He did not approve of this network of informers, all paid by MacDonnell.

'What's that you said?' MacDonnell, who was reputed to hear a sigh falling against a stone in outer Mongolia, cupped a hand behind his ear: the very second pea-in-a-pod of a successful ward-healer, who has just performed a miracle.

Consurer, that's a little better.

'Nothing. Well, that seems to be that. I see now why you were able to turn him away this morning. But it gave the old women a bad time, all the same.' Fenny stood up.

'And now their relief will be all the greater,' smiled MacDonnell in his best pontifical tones.

Confurher, no, conjuraree. Yes, that's it, that's what he is, a conjuraree, the Irish diminutive would be conjurareen. A bit of a mouthful. I think conjuraree is it.

'What's that?' said Fenny, who was responding on a slightly gutteral level.

'You'll be very popular with the old women now,' said MacDonnell, an old hand at this sort of thing. 'Give them all my love, best little women in the world.'

Back in O'Farrell's breakfast-dining-knitting room, Hamlet was having a time with Gummy Hayes. Stunned for some minutes when she returned to the kitchen, after hanging out some washing, to find the mistress about to bring out a tray of tea and biscuits to the under-boots at the Duke of Clarence Hotel, she had waited for the sound of Ellen's voice to disappear before making her assault.

'Whad are you doin' here, ye liddle scut?' she hissed, sticking her neck out like a broody hen, and pointing a red finger at the boy, who was just swallowing his second swig of tea to wash down the small biscuit, which he had crammed whole into his mouth. When he was able to compose his lips in a more suitable form, he opened them, looked at her with blank, dummy eyes, and pointed with his crooked finger to his mouth and ears.

Gummy stared at him for a few moments, until the blood began to run to her head and set it wagging like a shop sign in a high wind.

'Well, of all d'impurance dat ever I seen in me mordal dis takes de biskit, ye liddle tramp I wudden be a bid surprised if ye didden learn dem signs from de soljers dirty jesters, as de Canon says, dirty jesters is right, an' if de mistress issen took in be her good nature id's a wonder she didden give ye a plate o' binyanas like one of de monkets in de zuer, gimme dat plate.' She made a furious grab at the tray, but Hamlet suddenly stood up and hissed at her like a gander. It was the most frightening noise that Gummy had ever heard, and for a moment she was stunned — the second stunning she had received that morning.

'God bless us,' she muttered, stepping back, 'Are ye enchanted or wh'an all? Is id de divil dat's in ye? O dat hotel an' de drinkin' an gamin' an' worse dat goes on in id, id's no wonder dat ye're turned queer — '

Hamlet sat down and began to pour himself another cup of tea. Generous Ellen had provided a pot, not just a full cup. Gummy watched him for a few moments, trying to make up her mind what to do or say, but the sight of a little menial calmly eating his way through tea and biscuits, which the mistress had served with her own hands, was too much for her.

'Hurry up wid that tay, it's well accustomated y'are to takin' tay sittin' down, and ye on yer knees all night polishin' boots be the light o' yer own shine. A nice ting — '

Hamlet swallowed hard again, and with great emphasis pointed to his mouth and ears.

'Stop makin' dem dirty signs ad me, ye liddle cannat yet, or is it dat yer tryin' ta tell me yer ateing, I can see dat, stuffin' yerself, greedy pig, an' I suppose yer pointin' to yer dirty ears to let me know dat yer listenin' t'everytin, ha ha, well used ye are to listenin' — be de keyholes a doors, ye dirty liddle bonham, I can see be yer face dat yer mind is full a' cess — '

Hamlet grabbed a piece of paper that was lying on the table beside his tray, and taking a stub of pencil from his pocket began to write a message in a large round hand. He held it up to her, waving it in front of her face.

'I'm deaf and dumb' it proclaimed, but since Gummy could neither read nor write — a fact she never admitted to anyone, even though it was generally known — she peered at it with narrowed eyes. Then she started back and covered her cheeks with her hands.

'I can't read widoud me glasses, bud I promise ye, ye liddle hound, dat if yer scribbling dirty words ad me, I'll wring yer dirty liddle neck and squeeze de washin' a years outa it.' And with a sudden turn, as swift and well balanced as a professional dancer, she was gone into the kitchen.

Hamlet sat on, poured himself another cup of tea — it was lovely and strong — crammed another biscuit into his mouth, and was rolling the sweetness round on his tongue when Gummy arrived back. She had no spectacles with her, but she had put in her teeth, the better to cope with this prob-lem of linguistics the brat from The Duke of Clarence had set her.

'I'm ragin',' she muttered to herself, shaking her head and

chomping her teeth, 'dat's whad I am.' Then, arriving at the table with her hands on her hips and her head lowered for battle, she watched the misbegotten young man lift a biscuit to his nose and sniff it, before popping it into his mouth and, raising the cup in a most aggravating manner, look straight over her head as he swallowed a whole half cupful of tea in one gulp.

Then, without even glancing in her direction, he picked up the piece of paper and held it out to her.

'I can't find me glasses,' Gummy muttered. The false teeth did not help her articulation much; but they gave her confidence. And this young fellow was clearly a smock-alley of the worst description. 'Ha,' she crowed suddenly, the Lord having sent her a bright idea with which she might confound her enemies. To give Him His due He was always doing things like that for Gummy Hayes. 'Ha-ha — ha, ye liddle twister, sure I knew it even before I cudden fin' me glasses. Sure, I nearly forgot. Isn't id well known in town and country dat the likes a' you can't read and write. There ye'are,' she croaked, throwing the paper across the table at him, 'take yer dirty stinkin' daubs a' dirt, rodden scrawls fit ony for soljers and ye have de nerve, de nerve, I say, to pass dat to me. As writing'! Ha ha, me buckeen, me liddle underboots, yer dealin' wid an ejicatered wummen now, so y'are, and ye know whad ye can do wid yer piece a paper — stick it up yer nose for a hanky. Ha ha, me boyo, yer rightly caught now.'

During this harangue Hamlet had finished his tea and carefully transferred two uneaten biscuits to his pocket, all the while acting as if he really were deaf; but as Gummy went on the blood slowly rose to his face until his very eyes were suffused with it. He jumped to his feet, leaned across the table, and shaking his fist in her face, roared:

'I'm deaf and dumb, y'eejit. Didden I tell ye! And that's my writin'. I learned it from the Brothers so I did, yes I did.' Then he came out from behind the table, and stood looking at Gummy with such an expression of ferocity in his sunken eyes, that she stepped back, and feeling that the time for words was not now, crossed herself and rolled up her eyes towards the floor above.

Fortunately at that moment Ellen called Hamlet from the

shop, and, with one final, fiery glance at the old woman, he turned and ran from the room.

When he had given him the news, Fenny, Ellen and even the two women in the snug, had urged Hamlet to stay and have a glass of lemonade before he went away, but he refused and backed towards the street door.

'I know, I know,' said Fenny good-humouredly. 'Off you go now, and be first with the news.' He felt it was safe to give the lad this satisfaction. Unless, of course, MacDonnell had telephoned Mrs Daly and told her in a roundabout way that the deal was on. But he doubted this. MacDonnell would not care to give the impression over the telephone to the people he was convinced listened to every word of his, that he had any message, vague or otherwise, to give Mrs Daly. And it was also well known that she maintained a lofty attitude towards the bog acres she had inherited. On the whole Fenny thought Hamlet would be first with the news.

Hamlet certainly acted as if he wanted to be first with everything, and it was all for Miss Maud. He flew along Connaught Street, down the steep hill of King Street like a wheel on fire, past the great grey wall and massive gate in Barrack Street, across the square and over the bridge in a series of flashes, his red hair streaming under the dun sky, up Church Street and into the lane beyond the archway, which led to the back of the hotel. Here Hamlet slowed down and suddenly stopped, leaning against a wall and panting. He closed his eyes and remained quite still until his breathing had returned to something like normal. Then he opened his eyes and began to think.

Donie would be all over the hotel, waiting for him. There was only one way to get in without his seeing, and that was through the little lavatory beyond the scullery, which Mrs Daly had put in with great boasting of her regard for her staff, a few years before. Privately she admitted to Maud and a few others, that it was to keep them from using the lavatory behind the dining-room, which was reserved for diners and men from the bar.

To this tiny lean-to, covered with corrugated iron, Hamlet

stole across the low wall from the lane, through a wilderness of unkempt shrubs, broken bottles and catmint, sown there years before by Mrs Daly's mother-in-law who loved cats. Hiding behind the last bush which smelled of dog, cat and man, Hamlet had a good view of the famous staff bathroom, as Mrs Daly put it. There was a small window at the back which he knew he was able to get through, so agile and bony was he. He sped, light as a whistle, across the few feet of open ground and reached up to open the window.

There was someone inside. Hamlet was looking at the back of her head for some moments before she realized that she was being observed. It was Maureen Pox, the kitchen maid, and as usual she had been sitting on the bowl reading the pictures in an old magazine. Maureen, whose real name was Cox, was a great reader and looker-at-pictures, but Mrs O'Flaherty Flynn had declared that she had the makings of a first-class cook, and would be well able to take over her job when she, the mistress of the art, retired in the long distant future.

'Mauryeen,' said Hamlet softly, and the girl jumped up with a cry which wasn't loud enough to bring attention from the kitchen. 'Where is Donie, Maureen?'

'Oh, Hamlet,' said the girl, closing her eyes and clutching her flat chest, 'you nearly frightened de life outa me. Suppose I was doin' someting.'

'I'd have waited until you were finished.'

'I'm terrible constipated,' sighed Maureen, a serious girl. She was a half-sister of Polly Pox, the most famous whore in the town during the British occupation, who was not yet retired officially. But Maureen was determined to succeed in her art. Already, she was able to cook some dishes just as well as the cook herself. 'There's pills advertissed in dis magazine and I keep looking at them, but it doesn't make a bit of difference. Do you want to go up the back stairs?'

'Yes, without Donie seeing me.'

'Come in and lock the door behind me,' said Maureen who was a good sport and liked by all. 'When I come back and knock twice it'll mean dat the coast is clear.'

She opened the door and went out. Hamlet wriggled through the tiny window and got in, where he stood brushing the whitewash and mortar from his sleeves and trousers. Then he sat down on the bowl and waited. It was some time before

Maureen returned, but when she did it was with good news.
Donie had been collared by a commercial traveller, who had
him by the end of his sleeve, and would keep him there for a
good few minutes yet.

'Come out,' whispered Maureen.

Hamlet unlocked the door and slid past her, down the
passage that ran alongside the kitchen from the back door, out
into the back hall, and up the stairs three at a time. He arrived
outside Miss Maud's room panting, so that he had to wait
awhile to recover his breath, and wipe the sweat from his
forehead with the cuff of his sleeve.

Inside, his faery, his inspiration, his love and his life was
singing softly to herself one of those tunes she knew, which was
both vague and off-key, but which sounded like the wings of
angels to Hamlet. He pressed his hot cheek against the cool
door for a moment, and then, throwing back his bony shoulders
and squaring himself, he knocked gently. Maud opened it
herself.

'Why Hamlet, come in. What do you want?' She was dressed
in a pale pink frock which took the sight of Hamlet's eyes for a
moment. He closed them and turned even paler. Like a saint
conferring a benediction, Maud gently touched his arm,
sending electric shocks through his entire body. He shivered
and put his back against the door.

'You poor boy,' said Maud kindly, 'I bet that Donie
Donnelly has you run off your feet all morning. Come here,
Hamlet, and sit down.' And taking him by the arm, she led him
to a small canebacked chair in the middle of her room, and sat
him down on it. Hamlet opened his eyes, but the sight of such
heavenly beauty and concern forced him to close them again.
He was sick, pale and trembling from love.

'Hamlet, you don't look at all well,' said Maud, bending over
him and sending waves of delicate scent up his nostrils. She
smelled like a rose garden in a slight breeze.

'Oh,' said Hamlet, biting his lip and swallowing. 'Oh.'

'Now, now, don't stir and I'll give you something that'll
bring you to yourself.' She went over to her dressing-table, a
bower of loveliness shimmering with silver, pink and gold in
Hamlet's eyes, opened a drawer and came back holding a small
bottle in her hand. 'Now, just sniff this,' she said softly, holding
it to his nose. Hamlet was assailed by the strongest dose of

smelling salts that he had ever experienced. He had already sampled the one Maud kept on her dressing-table, a quick sniff and away; but this was overpowering. With difficulty he kept hold of his senses, but could not keep himself from slumping in the chair, his head falling forward and his mouth dropping open. He knew he was a sight, and wanted to fall on his knees and crawl under the bed like a sick but faithful dog. Then, in a moment, he began to feel better, and with his recovery came the reward of Maud's most dazzling smile. His heart, guts and bowels melted within him, and for a moment the memory of Maureen's locked sanctuary flashed across his mind.

'And now, this is for a very good boy,' said Maud, coming back in a rustle of paper and silk, and holding out a box of chocolates surely made only for a princess. 'Take as many as you like, Hamlet, and then go down the back stairs, for Donie is looking for you. I heard him knocking at Mammy's door — complaining as usual — only a few minutes before you came. Take another one, two, go on, put them in your pocket.'

Hamlet held the chocolates, in their beautiful coloured wrappers, in the cup of his hands as if they were sacred. Then, with the mention of Donie's name still echoing in his mind he forced himself to attend to business.

'Oh, thank you, Miss Maud, you're awful good. Oh, I don't know what — I came up here to tell you the news about Mr Slyne first, even before Donie.' He paused and looked at her with sick and soulful eyes, but Maud was adjusting the shoulder strap of her new frock and frowning into the mirror.

'Slyne,' she murmured abstractedly, 'Such a boring man. What has he done now?'

'He's signed the contract, miss, that's what he's done.'

Maud sighed over a small bow at the base of the neckline. It would have to go. Too common.

'Does that mean Mammy has sold the land to him?' Maud touched a black gleaming curl delicately. Unlike bows on breasts, one could never have enough of curls like hers.

'Yes, and all the people in Connaught Street are — ' he tried to suppress a belch, but only partly succeeded — 'are celebrating.'

'They would, those Connaughts. No style,' Maud murmured.

She turned to Hamlet with a sweet smile and held her dark, gleaming head to one side.

'I'm afraid you'll have to go down to Donie, Hamlet, or he'll kill you.'

'I know, he'll give me a clip on the glue — ' Hamlet stopped short: he had never given so much information in his life before.

'He'll give what?' Maud's eyes had opened wide again, the sun shining forth from a clear sky.

'A bit of a clip,' muttered Hamlet, standing up, 'But he doesn't do it anymore. I'm too grown up now.'

'Of course you are,' murmured Maud soothingly. She was itching to get back to the contemplation of her dress. 'Take another chocolate.'

But Hamlet had already retreated to the door. It was impossible for him even to begin to thank Miss Maud for the way she treated him — like a queen with a beggar, like that Queen of Hungary who opened her cloak to the poor and a shower of roses fell out. The Brothers had talked a lot about her, but they did not know Maud Daly.

'Thanks, miss,' he mumbled, his sunken eyes moist with love, his face rigid with devotion. 'I muss go I muss go I — '

'Of course, Hamlet,' sighed Maud, 'That Donie — I suppose he'll tell Mammy about the sale.'

'O yes, miss, indeeden he will. I muss go — '

Maud turned away from the glass briefly and bestowed a smile of such heavenly perfection upon him that he had to grip the handle of the door to steady his nerves. His *nurves*, her *nurves*, as Mrs Daly and a few affected women in the town pronounced it. He was half-kilt with his *nurves*.

He got himself out of the room somehow, and Maud returned gratefully to the glass where the only truth, beauty and love, were to be found. She lifted one shoulder, then the other, plucked at the collar of the frock, smoothed it over her hips, turned and examined herself sideways, one side, then the other. She peeked at herself over her shoulder and giggled, then grew serious again as she stood holding her arms out, studying every detail of the fall of the garment. She felt she was getting at the centre of gravity, the place where Molly Mittens had failed to locate, and so had thrown the whole pink adventure most subtly out of joint.

Donie was waiting for Hamlet as he came in the front door at a fast trot, having gone down the back stairs, out the back door, through the shrubbery, over the wall, down the lane, under the archway, into the street and made for the hotel. He was panting like a dog.

With a quick glance about him to see if they were unobserved, Donie grabbed him by the collar and hauled him down the passage to his own dwelling-place under the stairs.

'Wha were ye doin' all dis time?' said Donie, with a face as grim as a slashed stomach.

'Nodden,' muttered Hamlet.

'Nudden,' squeaked Donie, 'be de holy — ' he restrained himself with a great show of discipline, throwing up his eyes and clasping his hands like a martyr in prayer. 'Well, did ye hear or see anyting?'

'I did.'

'Well?'

'Id's dun.'

Donie drew in his breath and half-raised one fist. A few short months ago he would have given Hamlet the biggest clip on the glue that he had ever received; but somehow Hamlet had changed.

Something, he did not know what, prevented Donie from hitting him. When he thought about it afterwards, he put it down to the increasing influence of the cook on Hamlet's behalf. And yet, Donie felt, it wasn't altogether that. Any blow he planted on the boy could always be denied, but what if Mrs O'Flaherty Flynn began to cut down on his rations? Would she ever do that? He knew too much about her. And too little about this budding youth with his sullen eyes and mouth.

'How is id done, ye eejit?'

'I was waidin' in Farrells while Mr Slyne was in MacDonnells — Den I was waidin' in Farrells while Mr Farrell went upta MacDonnells — '

Donie's arm shot out and grabbed Hamlet by the elbow.

'Has Slyne bought de land or hassen 'e?'

'I dunno.'

'I'll murder ye so help me.'

'Lemme go. He signed, so he did.'

'Who did, Slyne?'

'Mmmmnn,' Hamlet nodded with a malicious glint in the

depths of his sunken eyes. He paused for yet another moment, watching the expression of compressed pain and uncertainty on Donie's fat face. It was a moment to savour. 'Dat's whad dey tole me.'

'Who tole you, for Christ's sake?'

'Mr O'Farrell. He tole me Mr Slyne had gone into Fair's office to sign de contracts —'

'Deposits?' Donie swayed from one foot to another, his face glistening with sweat. He was panting and his little coated tongue could be seen curled over his lower teeth. Hot waves of peppermint came from him.

'Mmmn, I tink so.'

'Did Mr O'Farrell tell you so, Hamlet?' said Donie slowly and dangerously, and Hamlet was acute enough to realize that there comes a time when it is unsafe to tease any Irishman, even Donie, for whom he now felt utter contempt, over the sale of land.

'Miss Maud knows all about it,' he said quietly and distinctly. 'Mr O'Farrell told me that. He said Fair was the first to tell her — yesterday. She knows it's sold, and the deposits signed today.' Hamlet was really enjoying himself now. The idea had come to him like an angel from heaven, swift and clear and dazzling, and equally confusing. It certainly was heavenly to watch the workings of Donie's face. He did not follow the red herring of Maud's so-called involvement in the affair. All he wanted to hear was that the contract was signed.

'I can ask her, can I?' he whispered in a holy voice.

'I suppose so,' said Hamlet solemnly, 'She knows it all.'

At another time Donie would have grabbed him and demanded how he knew about Maud, but not now. Hamlet had the triumph of coupling the whole thing with the name of his beloved, and confusing Donie without fear of attack at the same time. It was a sweet moment: the first flush of Hamlet's manhood.

'Id wus God dat done id,' whispered Donie, crossing himself and closing his eyes. 'Himself went outa His way ta help us all. Glory be!'

'So it wasn't you after all,' said Hamlet making for the kitchen.

'Id wus God done it,' said Hosannah, clasping her hands and throwing her head back with eyes ecstatically closed.

'God helps him who helps himself,' said Mrs Pig more sensibly.

'All the same, God was on our side,' put in Sarah Jane McLurry who had joined the ladies in the snug, having closed her shop early that evening, leaving the picture-going crowd and her brother to the further indulgence of the Almighty. 'He's looking after my little shop this evening,' she added recklessly. She was on her second glass of port, and outside the cloistered snug the place was beginning to fill up. With men only.

'Who's lookin' after yer caboosh dis evenin'?' said Hosannah, coming out of her trance like a swimmer suddenly popping up for air.

'My shop,' said Miss McLurry, who did not care to have her premises described in such belittling terms; what exactly 'caboosh' meant none of them knew, but it was always used to describe something that was not first class. 'My premises are this evening under the care of Our Blessed Lord. Before I came out to join you two — who have, I believe been drinking all day — I went down on my knees to thank the Sacred Heart and place everything I had under His care and protection. It's a thing that could be copied by some.'

'Maybe,' said Mrs Pig cheerfully, 'when you get back you'll find the bulls' eyes have multified like de loaves and fishes. Dat'd be de right kind of business by God.'

'Marcella Prendergast, I'm surprised at you, so I am! You get a few pounds into your hands and start making little of the Lord!'

'Very unlucky,' murmured Hosannah, putting her fingers lovingly about the stem of her glass. Not long ago Fenny had taken it out and refilled it with a small portion of brandy and a large dash of water. He did not want to have Hosannah pass out, but neither did he want to have her taken home on this day of her triumph. Mrs Pig had, with one exchanged look, seen what he was doing. Several brandies ago she had taken up the first of Hosannah's watered glasses and sniffed it.

'This is strong stuff, Mr O'Farrell,' she said gravely.

'Nothing but the best here,' he had replied in the same tone.

'I know good brandy when I see id,' said Hosannah, proudly taking up her glass, 'Me fadder never drank anyting else.'

Ellen had provided sandwiches early on for the ladies in the snug, and what with chicken, ham and egg inside her, providing far more bulk than she was used to, Hosannah had been kept reasonably sober. She herself believed that she was sober as a prospective judge, and capable of giving opinions of the greatest weight and wisdom on all and every subject, but especially on God.

So when Miss McLurry, who was not her favourite person, started making loose statements about the Almighty, she felt it her duty and her special mandate from heaven to defend Him.

'De miracle of de loaves an' fishes, Miss McSlurry, in case ye doan know,' she said, wagging a finger before her, an exercise which caused her eyes to cross slightly, 'is something dat happened as surely as dat pair a' silk stockin' yer wearin' — '

'I don't see what my stockings have to do with it,' snapped Miss McLurry. 'And anyway, I didn't make any remark about the loaves and fishes — I wouldn't dream of saying any such thing. It was — ' she hesitated, since after all Mrs Pig was her friend.

'It was me,' put in Mrs Pig loyally.

'Miss McSlurry,' began Hosannah, ignoring the interruption.

'McLurry, please.'

'Ye tuk de name of de Lord in vain, all for a few dirty pounds, god from an Englishman who nidder believes in God nor man.'

'Well, of all the — Miss Braiden —' Sarah Jane drew herself up, squeezed her lips as if she had swallowed a banana skin, puffed out her cheeks and opened her mouth slowly to speak. 'You are — '

At that moment, whether inspired by God or not, Ellen put her head round the snug door and asked the ladies if they wanted to wash their hands.

'Like Pilate,' chuckled Mrs Pig to herself. She had already crossed the road, as steady as a sound door, even with all the whiskies she had knocked back, to make use of her own convenience in her own house. This was a wedding present from Aunt Kate, who had spent fifty years in the service of the Taft family in America. 'Up the Republicans!' Aunt Kate would cry: and the neighbours wondered greatly that the IRA had got on so well and were so rich in America. 'Say what you like girrel,' she had said to Marcella, when handing over her gift, 'no matter what they say about husbands, kids and all the rest of it, it all comes back to this in the end. Even corpses have to be drawn off before they can be laid out proper.' This magnificent chamber pot was painted in gold leaf, and had metallic green shamrocks overlaid, while in the middle of the white expanse inside, another splendid four-leafed shamrock was painted with a loving hand.

The whole street knew about Mrs Pig's jerry, and several of the women had used it, much moved by the idea that a President of the US had sat on it.

Hosannah had nothing but a cracked article at home, which often cut her when she used it too hastily at night in the dark. She was then very grateful for kind Mrs O'Farrell's offer and rose unsteadily to her feet, supported by Mrs Pig to the door, and by Ellen on their way through the crowd of men that was gathering to celebrate as the news got round.

Ellen had a fine commode placed in a large cupboard, just inside the door leading to the kitchen and the breakfast room, where Hamlet had had his encounter earlier with Gummy Hayes. Hosannah had never used anything so comfortable in her life, and vowed that the first thing she would buy when she got the money from Slyne was a good solid jerry, with a stout little stool on which to place it for her comfort.

'The blessings a' God an' all de saints af Ireland be mixed over ye, an' come down on top of ye like a shower o' hail in de night,' she said when the door was opened, and she saw the wonderful mahogany contraption that she had heard about.

'Just give me a call when you're finished washing,' said Ellen, who was helping her husband at the bar. She foresaw a long busy night ahead of them.

Back in the snug, Miss McLurry sat sipping her drink, immovable. She was one of those women who can sit drinking tea for hours and never feel the need for washing her hands. Mrs Pig had often wondered about it.

'Are yer kidneys all right?' she asked now, a little loosened up by drink.

'I don't know,' replied Sarah Jane loftily. 'It's something I never think of. My doctor looks after all that business for me.'

'First time I ever met anyone who left her liver and lights behind her at the doctor's,' Mrs Pig was moved to reply. There were times when Sarah Jane made her want to puke.

Her friend made no reply. She allowed a silent minute to drop like a heavy cloud between them, and did not speak until she was quite sure that Marcella had taken the hint about the vulgarity of her remarks.

'Poor Miss Braiden,' she began in a far-away voice, coming indeed as if divinely from a cloud, 'she really is getting quite shaky. Is that brandy she's consuming?'

'It is,' said Mrs Pig grimly. 'She has a great head. Be careful with dat port Sarah, you're one of these people who go on for a long time and den — ' she cracked her fingers, the sound of a gun in a distant hill — 'over you go like de Titanic.'

'The place is filling up,' remarked Miss McLurry, after another pause to indicate her further displeasure at being compared to a ship that was made, crewed and sunk by Freemasons.

Mrs Pig sipped her whiskey and rolled it round on her tongue. She was used to Miss McLurry's technique. It did not prevent her from speaking her mind; but there were times when she knew it was necessary to meet silence with a little infuriating humming. Now she looked into the distance, through the wooden partition of the snug, held her whiskey idly in her lap with a gentle but knowledgeable hand, as if she were handling a well-bred horse, and presently began to hum tonelessly to herself.

Sarah Jane put up with this as long as she could, especially as she expected Miss Braiden to appear any moment. But she did not know that such was the depth, height and breadth of the experience which Hosannah was having on her *chaise percée*, that she was happily extending the experience as long as she decently could.

Outside in the shop the clans were gathering. All the old street names were represented, for such a famous victory over an Englishman had no equal in the annals of the town, famed as it was for deeds of war and military defence. O'Connell, Fitzgerald, Kenny, Lennon, Keogh, Shine, Keane, O'Meara, Burke, Kirby, Moore, Walsh, Hannon, Byrne, Harkins, Bigley, Egan, McManus, Murray, Galvin, Grey and Grenham — the butcher, the baker, and Paddy Mullally who was a candle-stick maker's son: all were there, and except for Ellen and the ladies collected in the snug, not one woman among them.

As the silence grew a few ripe remarks were beginning to float over the top of the partition like a whiff of fresh air, in Mrs Pig's opinion, although she was not given to telling dirty stories herself. But they were clearly as welcome as a bad smell to her friend.

'Did ye hear what Maggie Murphy said to her little chiseller, aged ten? Well he came home one day and asked if it was true that his daddy had died of diarrhoea, and she was ragin', "begonorrhoea is what he had, son, not diarrhoea. Your daddy was a sport, not a shit."'

'I wonder if Hosannah is sick, or something,' said Miss McLurry hastily as a loud laugh went up after this sally-bargain. 'I mean to say, she'd looked awful before she went out, and all that brandy she's drinking —'

'Pass no heed on her,' said Mrs Pig with a shrug. 'You're good at that.'

'It's the only way to deal with ignorant drunks.'

'Hosannah isn't a drunk. She's just overcome with relief, and tinks she's drunk. As for dealin' with her, I think Mrs O'Farrell has shown how to do it perfectly.'

'It's her house, she has the ways and means. She doesn't have to sit here listening to Hosannah, and being insulted, like me.'

'Ye don't have to sit dere bein' insulted, Sarah Jane. All you have to do is get up and go home.'

'Why is she attacking me for something that you said?'

'Because she tinks that's the way drunks behave.' Mrs Pig smiled wisely and maddeningly and took another sip of whiskey. She was enjoying this argument with her best friend, since no one can have a more enjoyable row than people who know each other well.

'So there's a difference between being drunk and thinking you're drunk?'

Mrs Pig nodded. She wished Sarah Jane would go away and wash her hands, or powder her nose or whatever she called going to the jacks.

'You seem to be a real expert on drunks and their habits,' said her friend sarcastically.

'I owned a pub, I've studied people. I know for instance dat if ye take one more glass of port and mix it with just one teaspoonful of whiskey, you'll be out there takin' your skirt off

and dancin' for de man.' And Mrs Pig chuckled at her own
idea.

'Well of all the — ' Miss McLurry drew herself up again, and
was about to make a spirited reply when Mrs Pig interrupted.

'If ye keep on drawin' yerself up like dat you'll stretch a gut,
and get a conniption, or a bowel conscription, as me aul Aunt
Kate used to say.'

Miss McLurry did not reply. She closed her eyes and lifted
her chin out of its fleshy bed, like a parrot untucking its beak
from a wing. Outside the noise grew, raw laughter swept
against the snug like Shannon waves in a storm, and one man
rattled the entire Cafe Royal by bumping against the wall. Miss
McLurry began to look alarmed. Supposing the men invaded
the place and began to behave indecently.

'No such luck, Sarah,' said Mrs Pig reading her thoughts.
'Besides I'm here to protect ye. I haven't met a man yet dat I
haven't been able to flatten. It's a trick I learned from
Prendergast, de ony useful thing I ever did get out of him.'

'I was thinking of no such thing. Men are a matter of
complete indifference to me.'

'Doan be too sure. When dey're nicely dey go for anyting,
and when dey're beyond nicely a hole in de wall isn't safe from
them. It's a pity they can't put all dat stuff to some good use.
They could mix cement say, six or eight of dem, and if enough of
dem were really harnessed, when they're in that condition, dey
could do as much work creatin' power as a windmill, instead of
which it all goes to waste, on women for de most part. Isn't dat a
good idea?'

'I don't know what you're talking about,' said Miss
McLurry, drawing herself up again in spite of the danger of a
bowel conscription.

'I could explain it to ye in more detail,' said Mrs Pig with a
wicked smile.

'No, no, no,' burst out her friend, giving the game away, as
Mrs Pig confidently expected she would.

Before anything more could be said Ellen reappeared,
leading Hosannah gently but firmly, and putting her down
carefully on the red plush bench. Ellen had just entered one of
those periods of life when she could do no wrong — something
that often follows a long run of disappointments — and

fixed up in dat way, Mrs Prendergast, tank ye all de same.
Wha'

what she said now changed the tone, colour and temperament
of the whole night.

After Hosannah had called down the blessings of most of the
saints in the calendar and had taken up her half-filled glass
again, Ellen smiled at the three of them and said:

'What are you going to do with all the money that's coming
to you?'

The three women in the snug joined ranks, their expressions
changed from guarded antagonism to one of deep interest.
They looked at Ellen with immense gravity, and then
unfastened their gaze to let it wander within limits like birds on
strings.

'Ellen!' Fenny's voice came through the hatch, which he had
slid back a few inches. 'Come back for a minute. We're terribly
busy.' And with a flashing smile Ellen was gone.

'Well,' said Hosannah, settling herself comfortably on the
red plush, 'It's not every day you get the chance of indulging
yersel' in the Caff Royal, Miss McLurry. Dis is a very explusive
place, ony de quality get maggoty here, tanks to God an' His
Blessed Mother.'

'Well, what are you going to do with the money, Miss
Braiden, apart from the commody like O'Farrell's that you're
going to install?' said Mrs Pig the peacemaker.

'Id's a wonderful contription to be sure, but I'm very well
fixed up in dat way, Mrs Prendergast, tank ye all de same.
Wha' are you goin' to do, Miss McLurry?'

'The same as you,' that lady snapped back.

'I'll tell you what I'm going to do,' said Mrs Pig, sticking her
elbows out and working her shoulders up and down, a habit she
had when sitting in the one place for some time, and the ladies
had now been in the Cafe Royal for more hours than she could
count. Time had been rolled up in a ball, like a gathering of
string held behind the back. 'I'm goin' to hire a car to drive me
down to Tralee, which is a centre of high an' wide fashion, and
dere I'm goin' to outfit mesel' from top to bottom an' from
inside out, and I'm goin' to drive up to Lyracrumpawn in me
new eleganties, and knock the eyesight outa every one o' me
lousy mane relations. Dat's what I'm goin' to do.'

The splendour of Mrs Pig's intentions was enough to

separate the other two, and turn their thoughts to the same subject. The Kerrywoman could not be let away with all this on her own.

'I'm goin' ta take de train ta Dublin,' said Hosannah in a holy voice, 'an' I'm goin' ta do a roun' of de churches, startin' wid de pro-Cathadral an' endin' wid Adam and Eve's, an' I'm goin' to light six large candles in each place for de sins o' de world, and for me salvation, dat's what I'm goin' to do, so I am.'

'Are ye going to stop at Dublin?' put in Mrs Pig.

'A course not.' Hosannah put her glass to her lips and drank deeply before replying. 'I'm goin' to Mullingar, Tullamore, Roscommon, Ballinasloe and mebbe Galway to do de same. I'm goin' ta surround dis pagan town wid holy lights, bunin' at de foot of God for all de sins I see committed, permitted and provoted in dis dangerous town o' Bridgeford.'

'Promoted, I suppose you mean,' murmured Miss McLurry under her tooth, but it was the last echo of antagonism between the ladies. The notion of the money, its power and greatness had descended upon them like a tongue of fire.

'What are you goin' to do, Sarah Jane?' said Mrs Pig.

'I'll get the roof fixed. One has to be practical.'

'To be sure, to be sure,' urged her friend with a wonderful look.

Miss McLurry made full use of her pregnant pause, as she gazed up at the famous photograph of Piccadilly over the fascinated stares of the other two.

'And then,' she said slowly, 'I'm goin' to Pawris, for the autumn modes, you see.' She threw one leg daringly over the other, and passed a finger over her eyebrows, raising them high and closing her eyes.

'Paris?' said Mrs Pig, who was a little taken aback.

'Sin city,' commented Hosannah. 'When d'end of de wurruld comes, id's goin' ta start in Paris on account of id's sins, I heard a missioner say, and he said he read it in a book of profits.'

'Pawris is the most elegant and civilized city in the whole world. All the best people go there sometime or other, and it has all other centres, even Hollywood, beaten into the ground with the weight of its fashions. I'll probably buy myself a modelle unikew.'

'A what?' said Mrs Pig, much displeased by this speech.

'O, just a bit of French,' said Sarah Jane, airily touching the side of her hair with her fingers.

'A very dirty language I always heard say,' put in Hosannah. But before anything dangerous could arise between the ladies, Fenny opened the hatch and looked in, his face red and glistening with sweat. He had given the first round free to all who came; but at the rate people were drinking since, he'd still have a good profit at the end of the day.

'What, as they say, is your pleasure, ladies?'

Mrs Pig stood up, taking Hosannah's glass with her. She put them down on the hatch ledge with a nod that meant 'same again' and then looked over her shoulder at Miss McLurry.

'A teeny drop of port, please,' said that lady in a very affected tone, 'a tinny drup of purt,' was what it sounded like.

'Like nothin' on earth,' said Mrs Pig, giving Fenny a knowing look as she turned back with Miss McLurry's glass. He chuckled and winked.

'You mean the port of course,' he laughed, looking down at Sarah Jane.

'Nudden bud de best in de Caff Royal,' put in Hosannah, 'and well used to id some people are.'

'How many times have you been in here?' said Miss McLurry sweetly.

'Never before in me life, Miss McSlurry. I wudden dream a' comin' alone, bud dis is a special occasion, and after all de Caff Royal issen a bubbelick house, de men without — ' and she waved a floppy hand in the direction of the outer bar, 'are all respectable, an' wudden dream a comin' in ere.'

'Not while you're here certainly,' said Miss McLurry to herself.

But after they had taken delivery of the fresh round of drinks, the door opened a few inches and Donie stuck his nose in.

'How are things in the hotel?' said Mrs Pig, the first as always to cope with any situation.

'Flyin', I axed Mr Slyne himself when he got back, den I tole Mrs Daly, an' den I just took de' evenin' off. Are ye all set up we' drinks an' tings?' He had taken a good look at their well-filled glasses.

'We're Mrs O'Farrell's guests,' said Miss McLurry with a high air, 'and we'd be in the drawing-room upstairs, only she's so busy with all the men boozing out there.'

Donie saw there was no future in being kind to these old faggots, so he gave them a flashing smile and withdrew his nose.

'Common little man,' said Miss McLurry.

'No class,' said Hosannah, 'Soljers, ye know, bud his wife, God help her, is from de land and can trace herself.'

'She owns de bit of land Donie is selling, doesn't she?' said Mrs Pig.

She did not expect an answer to this, as they all knew it already; she was merely saying something to keep the party going, but it was increasingly difficult to keep awake as the snug had become intolerably hot with no door open, no window to open, and the great crush of men outside. Sweat, Guinness, John Jameson and the occasional whiff of feet wafted over the partition. The ladies, after the initial excitement of finding themselves heiresses, were beginning to tilt.

But before they could begin to gather themselves together for the long ceremony of goodnights with Fenny, Ellen, and all the rest of the people outside who would want to congratulate them, they were visited by an apparition. One moment she was not there, the next she was; and none of them, not even Mrs Pig, who was facing the door, had seen it open to reveal Mrs O'Brien from the lane.

'Treasures from heaven on ye, ladies and — ' she stopped, cast up her eyes, drawing her black shawl closely over her forehead, and allowed her mouth to fall open and her tongue to loll with the thirst.

'Here,' said Mrs Pig who had not touched her last whiskey yet, 'take a sup of this.'

Mrs O'Brien grabbed the glass with her small, yellow, stiff-veined hand, and knocked it back without as much as a slight tremor. Then, before Mrs Pig or Sarah Jane could do anything about her, she began to sing. Everyone in the street had at some time or another heard Mrs O'Brien's voice raised in song, whether she was mourning or, less often, rejoicing. Tonight she was in celebration, but the voice remained the same, it sounded like a railway whistle, bent sideways and peppered with shot. Nor did her songs make much sense.

> O me wind is in the weather
> And me heart is flyin' high
> For I'll give ye hell for leather
> Before we say goodbye.

She was about to launch into a second verse, shrugging her knife-edged shoulders and wiping her mouth with the back of her hand, but she had not gone beyond a deep breath when Fenny came in and, standing in the doorway, pressed a shilling into the old woman's hand, took her by the arm and spirited her away.

'Where do you think he's brought her?' asked Miss McLurry.

'Out de back way into de lane,' said Mrs Pig. 'She'd have gone for a threepenny bit, but it was right of Mr O'Farrell to give her a bob.'

'I don't see why,' said Miss McLurry.

'Dirty old faggot,' muttered Hosannah, 'She has poor Canon Sharkey pesterated, offen gives 'er ten bob, poor-man-he's-a-saint.'

'Would you think so?' murmured Mrs Pig. But Hosannah was not listening. She had grabbed her stomach and was pressing her hand against it and moaning. 'O me stomick me stomick.'

A few minutes later the crowd of men outside were astonished to see Mrs Marcella Prendergast and Miss Sarah Jane McLurry, supporting the sagging figure of Miss Susannah Braiden out of the Cafe Royal to the street door. Without looking at any of them Mrs Pig opened the half-door with her shoulder, Sarah Jane opened the other half, and between them they went out into the night, dragging their burden with them.

'I never knew she drank like dat,' said Donie.

'She doesn't. That's what's wrong with her. But she loves it if it's going, like you know.'

'Candles and booze aren't everyone's diet,' said another man in the slow, slurred Bridgeford accent. Overheard, it always gave the impression that the speaker was leaning against a wall, lazily lifting an arm to make a point with no great conviction.

'All the same aren't they three great auls wans to pull off a deal like that, Janey!' another man said.

'Of course I — ' Donie began to say that it was himself who did most of the dealing for them, but another voice moved over him like a lawn-roller.

'It was Fenny who engineered the whole business. He's a divil that way.'

Donie was about to speak, but he suddenly realized that he was in enemy territory. Historically it was all there in his stance, in the eyes of the Connaught men.

'Fit for anything.'

'Yes, indeed.'

'That Slyne fella didn't have a chance with Fenny in the field.'

'What kind of a gom was he?' This question was directed to Donie.

'Oh, very polite, very gentlemanly, a brilliant man I hear in business —'

This effort to make his own dealings with Slyne appear like a great feat against someone of immense experience and talent, was not successful. A general laugh went up from the men and it sounded very like a jeer.

'What's your wife goin' to do with the money, Donie?' said another voice.

'Still it's a great bit of business, Donie, and you ought to be thankful you had Fenny in the deal.'

'O I am. Mr O'Farrell is a rale gintleman.'

'You may say that. How is Mrs Daly? Is she still adding to her pedigree? At the far end, back towards Adam and Eve, you add as much as you like.'

'And Maud. Ah Donie, aren't you a lucky man to be under the same roof as Maud Daly? I saw her the other day walking along the Prom under a pink parasol and, if I was a poet, I'd have words to describe it.'

'She walks in beauty like the night, no that won't do, like the dawn, just think of all the poems about the dawn.'

> I have many a sight in mind
> That would last if I were blind;
> Many verses I could write
> That would bring me many a sight.
> Now I only see but one,
> See you running in the sun —

'I forget the rest of it, It's Gogarty, I think.'

'Good man yourself, Dessie. You have a great ear for poetry.'

'But Maud Daly doesn't run,' said a grumbling voice.

'She'd run for money.'

'Who's she going to marry, Donie, Wee Willie Wicky or Boss MacDonnell?'

Donie, who was thinking of something which would get him back into the conversation as the true architect of the water-meadows plan, tried again.

'Mr MacDonnell wus approached be Mr Slyne also, ye know?' he began.

'We know,' said several voices. 'He has his own scheme up his sleeve.'

There was a general guffaw at this, but soon the lazy but probing eyes were turned towards Donie again.

'I doan think she'll marry either,' he said slowly, falling back on experience: when in doubt say neither yes nor no, but neither or either.

'Very likely,' said another voice in a yawning tone.

'What would you do with the money if you had it?' someone asked generally.

'Buy a car like Fenny is goin' ta do.'

'Go to the Galway Races and flog it all.'

'Me too,' said several.

'I wonder what the old ladies are going to do with it?' someone else said.

'Put it under the bed you may be sure, and it'll be found when they're laid out.'

'Mr Slyne axed me quite a lot of questions about the deal,' put in Donie in another bid for attention. But although he could feel the mood of the men turn towards him again, he was never to have the opportunity of telling them, for at that moment Gummy Hayes made an appearance at the door leading to the kitchen, with an empty tray in her hands.

Immediately a deadly silence fell: a few voices were heard for some moments, but they dribbled away like a stream going underground.

Gummy, who had been on the watch upstairs, had seen the three ladies leave, and had arrived on the scene at the proper time — not too soon after departure, not too late — to take up the glasses in the Cafe Royal, which was sacred to the memory of her old mistress, Mrs O'Farrell the elder, and must always be tidied the moment it was vacated. She had brought a small private bottle of Jeyes Fluid in her apron pocket to sprinkle the place where Hosannah had sat.

She opened the door of the snug with one hand and marched in, closing it behind her. A few men muttered among themselves, but a curious change had come over the company when she appeared. Men who were staring at Donie with no friendly expression, and others who were smiling at him as if he were a comic turn, and a few who had their backs to him, all fell back into the ranks, as it were, and became just a crowd of men drinking in a bar. Nothing remained of their former high spirits and antagonism. Mild, quiet and well-behaved, they began to drift towards the door, finishing their glasses and leaving them on the bar counter with a little bob of the head to Ellen. Their progress was one of perfect timing and age-old good manners. Ellen thanked them all individually, and felt her heart warm towards them as it had never done before. There had been times that evening, when she had been distinctly uneasy as they questioned poor old Donie, but now they had changed so completely, and were so casually well-mannered, that she felt she had known them all her life. Yet for twelve years in Bridgeford she had thought of them as strangers.

In the snug, Gummy put down the tray on the table and sat down on the red velvet bench. She could smell Susannah, but that did not greatly trouble her, nor did the lingering aura of Mrs O'Brien. Gummy Hayes did not have big occasions in her life, and this gave her a pleasant feeling of power, which she greatly relished.

She knew that if she did not reappear immediately with the empty glasses on her tray, that the men in the bar would slowly begin to file out. It was part of a custom which had begun in Fenny's mother's time. If she thought the customers were lingering too long in the bar, she would send Gummy with her tray, and full freedom to pass any comment she liked on the men who might be in her way. It took three or four excursions of this kind to get the message accepted, for Gummy knew the family history of the entire street by heart, especially the passages which living members might not like to have called out in the presence of others.

'Hullo, Willie, did your sister get that child christened yet?' was the remark which finally won the night for Gummy Hayes and her late mistress. To address Willie Ryan, who was chairman of the urban council, in such a manner was unheard of, even in Connaught Street. Ryan never darkened the door again, but his friends and neighbours were delighted, and the story spread like a fleeing monkey swinging from tree to tree.

But, greatly though the men enjoyed Mr Ryan's discomfiture, they did not want to draw Gummy's tongue down on them. When therefore she appeared in the bar at the end of a crowded evening and made for the snug, they scattered. For it was from the door of the Cafe Royal that she had made the famous remark to old Willie. The thought of her lurking in there, listening to everything they had to say, and likely at any moment to pop out and say something awful to any one of them, was too dreadful to contemplate. She was the dangerous female fury which all of them feared; Alecto, Megaera and Tisiphone all rolled into one.

They did not blame Fenny in the least for it. Better Gummy whom they knew, than the presence of some unknown female, listening behind the thin partition. If a strange lady had in fact walked in and ordered a double whiskey in the Cafe Royal, it would have emptied the place even quicker.

Later, after they had washed up, helped by Gummy, Ellen and Fenny slowly made their way upstairs.

'Are they really as afraid of Gummy as all that?' said Ellen, sitting on the arm of one of the big padded chairs in the drawing-room.

'Well, no one wants to draw her out. But no, it isn't that. It's a sort of ritual established by my mother.' He looked up at the large coloured photograph of the handsome woman in dark, rich-looking clothes, her long neck encased in a high-boned lace blouse. 'She really did not want people drinking after hours, which my old Dad was only too ready to allow. Telling people to get out would have mortally offended them. So she thought up this devious way of using poor old Gummy. Clever of her.'

'Yes, but wasn't it bad for business?'

'No. Gummy was established as a "character", so she had a lot of freedom. If my mother had said anything indiscreet to old Willie Ryan, it would have been a terrible insult. No, they got the message, and, as the years passed, it became a sort of ritual — and once that's established here, it goes on for ever. Besides, we get the sort of customer who doesn't want to drink all night

— you can do that in most of the other pubs in Connaught Street — and Gummy is a good excuse to get them out on a night when there's a big crowd.'

'All the same, your mother must have had a lot of influence with the men. They got the message and they respected it.' She looked up at the pale, thin-boned face, so very unlike her son's.

'Well, as you know, she had a brother a bishop, and that in Ireland carries a lot of weight. I think it's hilarious. All that elaborate act and everybody playing up. Of course Gummy is by now convinced that they really do leave on account of her. And I think poor old Donie got the land of his life.'

'They didn't treat him very well, I thought.'

'Connaught and Leinster,' said Fenny yawning. 'It's as old as the hills. The old Irish provinces were all independent and they were always fighting.'

'Ah, but that's all over now, isn't it?' said Ellen softly as her husband came to her with his hand outstretched.

'Yes, love, of course it is. All over, all over — '

Part Three

NOVEMBER 1933

Fenny did not have to call on old MacDonnell for advice after all. That affable personage, dressed in a dark blue winter overcoat, with pigskin gloves and a yellow silk scarf, dropped into O'Farrell's in the late afternoon of the day that Slyne returned to the town.

'Would you like to come upstairs?' said Fenny who was reading the local paper, sitting in his bum-boat and puffing his pipe contentedly. He came down, pulled his pants clear on the inside where they were a bit tight at the groin, folded up *The Westmeath Independent*, laid his pipe on the ledge behind him, and gave his full, ceremonial attention to his important visitor.

'No, thanks, Benedict, I don't want to put Mrs O'Farrell to any trouble. How is she today?' MacDonnell smiled and allowed a benign twinkle to animate his eyes. He loved the advent of children: new voters. Although he could not hope to benefit from Ellen's unborn baby, long habit made his reaction almost automatic.

'Keeping very well. Gummy, of course, is fussing like an old hen, and the house is hardly ever without some woman offering advice.'

'Women,' remarked old MacDonnell weightily, 'are curious creatures. The snug will do. The Cafe Royal, isn't it?'

Fenny chuckled and lifted the counter flap to follow his visitor into the red plush interior, which had had little use in the five months since the three old ladies had sat in it on the night of Slyne's visit to Fair, the solicitor.

MacDonnell sat down carefully on the bench, then relaxed and smiled. It was really very comfortable. He took off his soft hat, his gloves, and loosened his scarf to reveal a heavy silk tie, grey with a quiet design of squares. He looked ruddy, glowing,

well washed and polished, and altogether mightily handsome
and sleek.

'Nice hat,' said Fenny, who had an eye for things.

'I got it in Locks,' said MacDonnell with a smile. 'Of course,
I've never been to London, and don't ordinarily wear English
clothes. But I have a friend who gets all his things in London,
and he got my hat measurements and gave me this as a present.
Ordered it by telegraph, and it's a perfect fit.'

'My father used to get his hats in Locks, his shirts in a shop
round the corner in Jermyn Street, Turnbull and Something,
and his suits in Savile Row. No wonder there was nothing in the
till when he died.' Fenny looked down at his own baggy
trousers. He had put on a clean shirt, bought in Tysons in
Dublin, and he always had a fine pair of shoes, but he felt sadly
frayed compared to old MacDonnell.

'The English were always terrible thieves. I'm not surprised
your father, Lord have mercy on his soul, was done in by them.'

'It wasn't the English outfitters who done for my father, it
was slow Irish horses.'

'On English courses,' murmured MacDonnell. 'Well, I
suppose you've heard about Slyne's return?'

'Of course. The whole town is agog. Listen, would you care
for a drop of something?'

'I know the hospitality of this house is as fine as anything in
Ireland, Benedict, but no, I never take anything now before
evening, and then only a sup of whiskey before retiring. But if
you like, give a drink in my name to someone you like.'
MacDonnell smiled benignly and patted his soft, white hands
gently, like a baker moulding a fine dough.

'That's a very good idea,' said Fenny, impressed in spite of
himself. The old fox knew how to behave. No wonder he was
such a success in America. O'Farrell hated his politics, but the
old man impressed him in spite of himself.

MacDonnell nodded and drummed his fingers on his gloves,
neatly laid on top of each other on the table. Very well polished
this table was, not once had the ladies, even those who drank
mulled wine, left a stain upon it. The few accidents that did
occur were quickly put to rights by Gummy, who rushed into
the snug the moment anyone left it.

'About this Slyne,' began MacDonnell, giving Fenny a quick
look. 'He arrived last night, and although he's been out and

about this morning, he's had lunch already, and not mentioned a word about the land.'

'He must have seen the floods.' Neither of them had to look out of their back windows to see the land, purchased by Slyne in June as a development site, now completely inundated by the overflowing waters of the river Shannon; something which happened to a greater or lesser degree every winter. And whenever it did, the same pictures of tin-roofed cowsheds and thatched cottages with water half-way up their walls, and the inhabitants in gumboots, appeared in all the papers under the headline:

FIVE HUNDRED ACRES SOUTH OF BRIDGEFORD
FLOODED BY SHANNON

And in smaller print: Shannon-side farmers walk the plank to their houses; hearths raised above the water in the kitchen; get from one room to another by plank; get out of bed in the morning to find the river Shannon lapping underneath; Wellington boots kept by bedsides.

All that, with about as much sense, had seeped into the minds of the reading public every winter, when they read once again about the breaking of the Shannon banks below Bridgeford. People of the district would not leave their houses, going about their work on planks raised above the water filling their houses, so that the beds had to be raised on wedges, and the fire on a pile of bricks and stone. It was an extraordinary story, but long years of reading about it had made people accept it as one of the facts of life. 'Old lady drowned under her bed' made the headlines one year, and it was quite true. So Mr Slyne could not fail to have heard of the flooding of his land when he got into Dublin and took up his *Irish Times*.

'And read about them. I'm going over to the hotel now,' said MacDonnell lightly, with a smile in his eye, the like of which must have fascinated many a Democratic voter in America in the heyday of Tammany.

'Not to see Mr Slyne, of course,' he said, retaining his smile. 'But if I meet him, naturally I'll have a little chat with him.'

'I suppose you don't know what he's going to say to you,' Fenny began. Somehow one felt that MacDonnell always knew about everything before he tackled it. All those contacts, all those men paid to hand on information, all the secrets —

'Of course not. I always play these things by ear. Experience counts, you know. Of course, you have nothing to worry about, the land you sold him is above the flood.'

'Yes, but he may not want to proceed now.' Fenny tapped his stomach idly. He was feeling the need of a drink, but as his visitor was not, it would be impolite to drink alone.

'He has signed the contract, he will have to buy it. Not, I suppose, that you're worried either way.'

'No indeed. I need a near field to put out Lizabelle, my old pony, now that I'm getting a motor.'

'Of course, but you retained part, didn't you? Or did you withdraw it at the last minute?' MacDonnell frowned, pretending to think, pretending that he had forgotten the whole affair.

'Yes,' said Fenny quickly, which could mean anything. MacDonnell did not give him even a cursory glance, he merely tightened his well-shaped mouth, and reached for his gloves. He left with many assurances of his regard for Ellen, a final smile and a little bow, and he was off, plucking at his scarf before he faced the cold November evening. Then, laying his gloved hand lightly upon his stick, he was gone.

'What did he say?' said Ellen some time later.

'Nothing. He never does.'

It was Donie who had the first encounter with Slyne.

The Englishman had breakfast at his usual time of nine, and came into the dining-room with his *Irish Times* under his arm, half expecting to see the strange man who had burst into the bathroom early that morning. He was the only person there when Mrs O'Flaherty Flynn made her appearance at the door.

She looked at him with amazement, her eyes seeming to grow as big as her mouth, which fell comfortably onto one of her chins. She might have been looking at a two-headed man in an exhibition. It was a great performance.

'Well, be the holy, Mr Slyne is it yersel' an' nod somewan else dat's innit? To be sure 'tis, for I wus dreamin' about ye all last night, gallopin' away ye were on a big white horse up a mountain.' Then she lowered her voice, which fell, like her chin, into the lower regions and became a husky contralto.

'And a white horse is the sign of death, so it is, the Lord save us all. Bud yer all right, aren't ye?'

Slyne smiled dimly over his paper, where he had been reading a report of the flooded areas in which he had invested so much money.

'What'll ye have for yer breakfast, Mr Slyne? The Duke of Clarence used to have cutlets, bud dat was before my time, all de same annyting ye want; steak, liver, kidneys, porridge, a wing a'duck or chicken, loads of bacon smoked and unsmoked —' and she went on to sing out a list of eatables, which if kept in stock, would have needed a cold room in the cellar as big as a ballroom, and lined with salt and ice. But it gave her time to study his face — he knew all and was not pleased — and prepare her own defence. She, of course, had nothing whatever to do with it, and knew nothing.

He settled for porridge and bacon and eggs, which was brought to him by Maureen Cox, who blushed beyond her ears when he looked at her.

'Good morning, Maureen,' he said with a small smile. This poor creature, he knew, was innocent at least. Strange, when one heard tales of her sister.

What a bore that it should attack me at this time of day and with all I have to do but from the first this little girl what age is she seventeen eighteen maybe less has got me like this it must be the sense of power that one has with her she's so pliant and timid and hardly ever speaking above a whisper maybe she has some of her sister's talents but really one shouldn't be thinking in this way a slip of a girl with hardly a decent stitch on her under that awful black frock undernourished like so many of them here and pitifully meek and humble ooo dear me what a thing to assail me first thing in the morning no not quite there was that drunk in the bathroom first how very odd one never really gets used to them will-o-the-wisp that's what they're like bog-fire I think they call it how very appropriate that's what this little girl is like I must be very careful goodness knows what they're up to they might have spotted me looking at her in the summer they miss nothing it's weird sometimes. . .

His breakfast finished and acknowledging a heart-breaking timid smile from Maureen, he made his way to the commercial room to read his paper, and wait until it was time to see Fair.

Donie was in the dank place, trying to light a fire in the grate, which had not been used for over a year, since the American bishop insisted on having it to write his letters. Imagine needing a fire to write with, Donie had gaily remarked at the time. And Miss Mutton had unexpectedly replied with 'burning words, Donie, take heed of them!' He wished now that that stern prelate had returned, and not the fearsome Slyne, who was standing in the doorway, looking down at him with a grim expression.

'Mornin' sir,' said Donie as brightly as he could. Faggots fell from his fingers, and he prayed to God his fingers would not tremble when he started lighting the match. 'Cold.'

Slyne sat down without a reply, and Donie could hear the rustling of the fatal newspaper. But he managed to get the fire lighted, and when he did, got to his feet by clinging to the ledge of the mantel. When he turned, Slyne was looking at him over the lowered paper.

'Good morning, sir,' he faltered, feeling for his dickie bow, which he did not put on until mid-morning. So he had to let his hand fall, like a shot bird hanging by his side.

'I'm reading all about the flood in the paper,' said Slyne, tapping it with his fingers as it lay on his knee. 'Don't you think you should have told me about it last summer?'

'I don't know anything about it, sir,' he said, and having said it almost instinctively, he knew that that was what his line was going to be. His defence.

'You seemed to know all about it last summer, you were what one might call a go-between, weren't you?'

'Yes, sir, dat's wad I wus, ye've said it yersel'. Ony a go-between, I wassen tole anyting.' Donie began to feel better, sensing that he was 'growing' into a part which he would play from now on, adding the little convincing touches later.

'Of course,' went on Slyne, folding the *Irish Times* and tapping it on his knee, 'I can't go through with the deal now.' He looked at Donie with an eye steady enough for any automatic, and frowned.

Donie wiped the palms of his hands on his backside.

'Is dat so?' he murmured, feigning innocence.

'It most certainly is so,' snapped Slyne. 'I've never heard of anything so disgraceful and dishonest in my life. I shall sue the people who tricked me for misappropriation and false pretences, and of course they'll have to pay the money back at once. I'm instructing Fair immediately.'

'Are ye, sir?' Donie's voice cracked, his shoulders sagged, his head began to sink into his shoulders and his kneees trembled.

'Of course I am, you little blackguard,' boomed Slyne, whose whole face had become swollen with righteous indignation. His voice had also altered; the smooth, quiet tones had given way to something louder and coarser. Donie had heard it before, long ago, passing the military barracks. It had come hurtling over the wall: the sergeant-major was knocking straight backs, stiff necks and wooden-like arms into the Irish recruits. 'I may even prosecute. I have every right to.'

'Ah sure I know dat, sir, you have de right ta be sure to do wad ye like.' Then, from the low estate of his stooping back, he looked up suddenly with an embryo glint in his eye. 'I hope de lawyers are givin' ye de right advice.'

'What do you mean by that?' said Slyne leaning forward, his face seeming to swell more.

'Nuttin', sir, nuttin', ' muttered Donie, turning to pick up his coal bucket. The fire was doing nicely, and it seemed to be a good moment to make an escape. He tip-toed towards the door, his shoulders raised as if to protect himself from the piercing glare of Slyne's eyes, and having got as far as the passage, he turned towards the kitchen and ran.

Slyne looked after him for a moment. Then his face resumed its normal impassive look. He stood up, and moving his chair nearer to the fire, sat down and began to read the financial page.

The whole place seemed to have felt the tremor of Slyne's advent. In the kitchen pandemonium had exploded like a burst kettle. Maisie, coming down from Maud's room, had bumped into Maureen Cox inside the door, and the impact had caused her to drop her tray and lose her head at the same time.

'You dirty, clumsy little slut, look what you've done! Ooooh!' cried Maisie with a note of hysteria in her voice.

'I'm sorry,' whispered Maureen, getting down on her knees, and picking up the broken china as quickly and quietly as she could. Maisie looked down scornfully at the thin shoulders of the frightened girl, and anger welled up in her like bile after an 'off' pudding.

'Well, surely it can be said today what the Lord said to the Jews long ago: "Behold, I frame evil against you, and devise a device against you: return ye now every one from his evil way, and amend your ways and your doings." '

This sermon would have passed over Maureen's head, for she was a quiet, harmless girl, but unfortunately for Maisie, Mrs O'Flaherty Flynn arrived in the kitchen from the back lavatory just as Maisie was launched on her Old Testament admonishment.

'Maisie Houn'!' she roared, planting her fists on her massive hips, 'Maisie Houn'! Did I or did I nod tell ye aboud spoutin' yer bloody aul bible nonsense in *my* kitchen. I woan have id, ye hear? Wad have ye bin sayin' to my Maureen, a quiet girleen dat says her prayers proper?'

But Maisie, who was always elated when she had had a really good chat with Maud, was feeling reckless, and said some of the things she had been making up in her mind, should the cook speak disrespectful again about the Holy Book. The woman was nothing but an ignorant pagan.

' "They have ears, but they hear not; noses have they, but they smell not —" ' she began in a particularly unfortunate passage from the Psalms.

'Jasus Christ!' bawled Mrs O'Flaherty Flynn, doubly outraged at what she thought was a reflection on her cooking. 'Where do ye get all dat bloody Protestant puke, yer a Catlick arrnen ye? In spite of yer fadder, yer mudder brought ye up a Catlick, didden she?'

'She brought me up as an educated Christian —' began Maisie loftily. But that was too much for the cook. She grasped a huge wooden spoon, and banged it so hard on the table that a cup near the edge flew off, and landed within a few inches of the broken china Maureen was already hurrying to pick up. The girl blessed herself and drew the newly-broken in among the old, her hands trembling with fear.

'She let odders I won't name bring ye up like a low-down street preacher dat's condemned ta hell before dey even open dere bloody mouts, dat's what she did. I was brought up an' me mudder and fadder an' all dere mudders and fadders back t'Adam and Eve in de Holy Catlick Church, an' we wur always tole be de best autorites dat de Bible wus forbidden te be read be anywan excep' godless herickles. No edjikated Catlick would be heard dead readin' de Bible. Doan set yersel' up as a Catlick before me, ye dirty pagan. O yer well named ye pagan houn'. Maureen machree, get up offa yer knees and let de lady preacher pick up wha' she dropped, like her religun.'

Before Maisie could think of making any answer to this assault, Donie rushed into the kitchen, pale as a dishcloth and sank into the old cane armchair which, covered with cushions of various colours and consistency, had always been sacred to the person of Mrs O'Flaherty Flynn. For Donie to drop into it, in full view of two of the menial staff, was a token of his agitation. It had never happened before.

The cook however handled the situation with admirable presence of mind. She turned to the girls who were both staring at Donie; Maureen still on her knees, with her head twisted and her mouth open, and Maisie simply and vulgarly looking. Mrs O'Flaherty Flynn composed her features. All trace of the violent anger, which she had just been displaying, was smoothed out as if her features had been wiped by a wet cloth. She now addressed herself to the girls in a low, composed manner, worthy of a great general in an hour of decision.

'Maureen, pick up dem few bits, dat's ride now. Lave dem oon de shelf, dat's ride, an' now off wid you two girruls. Shoo, off wid ye, shoo! shoo!'

Full though she was with the Holy Spirit, and stuffed to the eyeballs with quotations for all and every occasion, Maisie had nothing to say to the commander of the kitchen. Both she and Maureen were united in the bond of the disenfranchised, and began to speak in low voices the moment they left the door.

'Oh, Mrs O', oh, oh,' moaned Donie, holding his head in his hands. 'Mrs O', oh, oh.'

'Dere now, Donie agradh,' she said soothingly, going at once to the bin in the corner opposite the range, where she kept her own particular goodies: boxes of chocolates given to her or left in bedrooms, which were hers by right of an ancient treaty, silk handkerchiefs and scarves, various pairs of shoes, all too big for her, several jars of boiled sweets bought by herself at half price because of her influence as a buyer, an enormous quantity of pills and nostrums, which she concocted herself for every ailment from consumption to sudden heart failure — an elderly man, who had dropped down and was apparently dead in the dining-room, was once brought back to life by Mrs O'Flaherty Flynn's dashing the full contents of one of her bottles straight into his face — sherry, port, whiskey and brandy of the choicest

year or distiller, and most potent of all, the small cache she kept
of the finest Galway- and Mayo-brewed poteen. Eleven bottles
of it she kept, never more nor less, and it was one of these that
she now drew up from this almost bottomless well to succour
Donie and herself in their trouble.

'Oh, Mrs 'O', Oh, We're all ridely macroomed now,' said
Donie as she came back to him with the bottle in one hand, and
two glasses cunningly and deftly carried between the fingers of
her other hand.

'Dere, now, Donie. Dis'll put hair on ye where ye never had it
before. For orney setbacks, deats and tings, 60% is sometimes
all ride, bud when ye're in rale trouble, ye have ta have the
unner per cent. Dis is a blend o' de best Galway and Mayo
moonlight, made be generations a' de same famblys, and
it'd raise de dead a week after. Here now, take dis an' tell me
all.'

Donie took a gulp, and his head shook as if with an electric
shock that spread in slightly diminishing waves down to his
boots, which turned in at the toes. Mrs O'Flaherty Flynn took
the merest and daintiest sip: she had to keep her head. After
another gulp of the same, Donie sank back in the depths of the
chair, warmed and scented by the frequent enfolding of the
cook's ample presence and, closing his eyes, gave himself up for
a brief unconscious moment to the rich comforting odours of
this splendid kitchen. Fresh bread in a griddle at the side of the
range, tea of the most expensive blend from an open caddy on
the table beside him, the rich aroma of a great fruit cake baking
to a point of perfection in the oven, and the warm potato smell
of Mrs O'Flaherty Flynn herself, richest and most abandoned
of all. From all this accustomed abundance, which he had taken
for granted for so long, he now drew strength in this hour of
need.

'He's goin' to sue, Mrs O', and axe for his money back, so he
is, may de Blessed Virgin and all de saints protect us. He'll ruin
de whole lot of us, dat's certain. Oh, Mrs O', oh oh.'

Mrs O'Flaherty Flynn had pulled up a bare bentwood chair
and, with great condescension, sat down beside the table,
where she laid her strong right arm, ripely red and floury along
the top, her glass cradled in her lap, the very picture of
compassionate interest, out of her own rightful chair and all.

'He bought de lan' wid his eyes open, didden he?' she said

gravely, her handsome eyes supporting Donie like those electric beams, which as yet people had only read about.

'Yes, bud he bought id when id wus dry, nod under six foot a' flood water.'

'Well, den it was his own fault, he paid for wad he got, didden he?' Mrs O'Flaherty Flynn tried to put the utmost conviction into her voice, for she was a woman of sensibility, but she did not manage to do so very successfully. She had a natural aptitude for the law, and she knew already that Donie and all the others were on the top end of a noose, like acrobats in a circus. One tug from Slyne and they were all down in a heap, with the circus lion bounding out to attack them.

'He can sue for misrep — misreprehension — '

'Misagenation is de legal word,' Mrs O'Flaherty Flynn assured him.

'Dey sold id under false pretences, an' now he's goin' ta demand his money back, de deposit, ye know, oh, oh. . . .'

The cook smiled as she met Donie's imploring glance when he lifted his head, light as moonglow, to look at her. She took a tiny sip from the clear liquid and smacked her lips. They curled even more in a smile of utter conviction, while she shook her head slowly.

'An' where, Donie Donnelly, an' from who is he to get it back? Will ye tell me dat now? Apard from de missus here, nod wan o ye has a hump-backed bob to pawn off on a tinker. Back indeed, ha ha, ha ha.'

Since he had been dragged from his hole at the nightmare hour of the early morning, Hamlet had been avoiding Donie all day. Not that he was afraid of another clip over the glue; that had been an angry reversal to times past. But he did not want to let Donie see that his misery and fright were obvious, even to poor little Maureen Cox, much less his own assistant. Hamlet had a shrewd natural sense of how far he could go with anyone, and never overstepped the mark.

So he was posted at the bottom of the main stairs, in full view of the door and the street, where Donie could not attack him again, if he took to the bottle; and where it was possible also for Hamlet himself to appear preoccupied with the coming and going of people into the hotel, or passing by on the street.

Donie had not been very long in the kitchen, and Hamlet was at a general ease, when he was startled to see his boss, limp and floppy-necked, being half carried on Mrs O'Flaherty Flynn's arm in the direction of the Lock Hospital. Mr Slyne had kept to his room, spent some time out, and some more time in the commercial room with Donie, and was now, so far as Hamlet knew, back in his own room again.

Mrs O'Flaherty Flynn winked at him as she passed, and Hamlet smiled to himself. She was going to put Donie to bed with a bottle — there was nothing to worry about. He felt his heart beat with a sudden little tattoo of excitement at this show of his former overseer and tormentor, humiliated and brought to the twist. Never was a man more absolutely macroomed.

'Hamlet.'

He was shaken out of his pleasant fancy by the sound of a low and lovely voice above him, like an angel messenger. He turned round and saw Maud standing on the bend of the stairs. With a quick look around him — something he never forgot, even when his divinity called him — he went upstairs two at a time. Maud was standing in the shadow of a big potted palm, and as Hamlet drew near she stepped back still further. The warmth of her presence, the delicious scent which always floated about her, and the sweet odour of her breath always overcame Hamlet. He could have wished to stay here in the shadow of this mouldy plant, in the little space hallowed by her waiting there, forever.

'Yes, miss?' he panted, for added to his excitement now he had had a strenuous morning and afternoon, skipping here, there and backwards, avoiding Donie.

Before saying anything Maud smiled at him, and Hamlet could feel his stomach turn over, and his heart thumping in his breast like a steam engine. *Thump thump thump love love love*: everything has a beat.

'Are you killed Hamlet, with all the fuss of the day?' she enquired gently, and now he could feel himself beginning to sweat. Nothing of worth in life is ever dry.

'No, no, miss,' he replied stoutly, in case she wanted him to perform some special commission. He was game for any high blank walls that might rear up before him.

'Poor Donie,' she murmured, as if that institution had just closed after the death of the owner.

Hamlet said nothing, but his nostrils flicked and quivered with the warm scent of her. His eyes were fixed with tension, and he rubbed his hands together to try and get rid of the sweat on his palms. They were standing very close together, and for the first time in his life the boy wondered if he smelled unpleasantly. He was so rarely able to wash himself. At the back of his mind a resolution formed: he would have a full adult bath, up to his elbows in water in the Lock Hospital, whenever Donie took an hour off to go home. Mrs O' would give him soap, and when next Miss Maud stood close to him he would smell as clean as fresh bread.

'Hamlet,' the low beguiling voice whispered in his ear — oh, was there wax in it? — 'listen here to me, whisper. Will you go down to the school in the bar, and get Mr Wickham out of it, will you, Hamlet?'

Rarely was such an unpleasant request voiced in such tempting tones. When Hamlet had seen Willie Wickham take the place of old Colonel Hightatch, who had had a mild stroke yesterday, after playing at the same table for thirty-five years, he had rejoiced. Except for the Colonel, who made his living from it, no one had ever stood up from the poker school in The Duke of Clarence solvent. Hamlet would have given Willie about a year to eighteen months to get through the entire property he had inherited: several hundred acres — Hamlet was not sure how many — a big house packed with valuable furniture, a herd of cattle, six half-bred horses, one thorough-bred and some money in the bank as well. Already, since joining the school that morning he had lost forty-two pounds. The news of it had made it possible for Hamlet to endure Donie's uncertain temper.

And now the very queen of his heart, the goddess removed from all human sweat, stink and clips over the glue, had asked him to rescue a man who was well known to be in love with her. Hamlet turned very pale, and his sunken eyes appeared to recede further into his skull.

'You don't mind doing it, for me, do you Hamlet?' she whispered very close to his ear. Hamlet shook his head, and started like an untrained pony when she left her hand lightly on his arm. He began to tremble all over, and it was to conceal this that he turned away so quickly, and ran clumsily downstairs in the direction of the bar.

The poker school in the bar of The Duke of Clarence had been in existence since 1882, and was generally recognized as the oldest in Ireland. It was started at a time when that particular card game was unknown in the country, by an officer of the 7th Hertfordshire Regiment, whose sister had married a man attached to the court of the Queen. Queen Victoria was interested in poker, and under her patronage it spread rapidly to the upper classes in England, and thus arrived in Bridgeford in an army uniform. In the beginning straight poker was played, and the Duke of Clarence himself had taken a hand during his famous visit. The gentlemen he played with saw to it that he won four hundred pounds, which delighted him and led to an invitation to call on him at Marlborough House. When the young prince was dying in Sandringham, it was said that in his delirium he called out 'litttle dog' once, and repeated 'big cat' several times. His mother, though not his father, thought he was raving about a big game hunt; but in the regiment, and throughout the British army, it was always believed that he had been re-playing his poker game in Bridgeford.

The school played every day, and occasionally through the night as well. The old hands, whose lives had long been governed by gaming, often began at ten in the morning and played until six or seven in the evening. If the stakes were high, and a man's house, wife and children, not to mention horses, sheep and cattle were at stake, the same players would often go on for two or three nights, sustained by whiskey and sandwiches supplied by Donie.

It was a remarkably well-conducted school. Indeed, it was famous for its silence. Although at least three men had been driven to suicide by it, no screaming relations ever descended on the hotel, or rebuked any of the other players. There was something religious about this school, which imposed its own time-honoured rituals.

When a big land-owner in County Westmeath lost his last blade of grass after a marathon game in 1912, he stood up, took off his trousers, his shoes and socks, and walked out into the street at three in the afternoon in his hard hat, his shirt and tie, still carrying his ivory-handled cane. But nobody talked about it.

'It's the Irish version of bull-fighting,' Benny O'Farrell used to explain to his intimates. 'Risks are taken which bring a man as close to extinction as the horns of a bull. If he is killed he is killed. Great players are discussed and admired, when they bring off a grand slam it is remembered for a long time, and the money they make or lose is much discussed. But when they fail as bull-fighters do, no account is taken of their families, and, of course, nothing is said about the edge of anxiety that wives and families live on during a man's sporting life. It is a flirtation with ruin, and it has its own rules and ethics, just like the bull-ring.'

Only once had the school been cheated. In 1920 when the Tans were roaring up and down the street outside in their Crossley tenders, an American reporter called Jack Husband was allowed to join in. In two months he had won fourteen hundred pounds. After three days Colonel Hightatch discovered that Husband was cheating. The other players now began to watch him with an intensity worthy of the best bull in Spain. He was never uncovered, and departed with nearly two thousand pounds swiped under the very noses of some of the toughest and shrewdest players in the United Kingdom.

'Husband to Lady Luck,' a tactless man at the bar had remarked one evening after the reporter's departure. The four men at the card table looked up at the same time; four pairs of hard, killers' eyes were levelled at the unfortunate one, who quickly swallowed his drink and left, never to return. No one laughed. But between themselves the school remembered Husband on the anniversary of his first being discovered as a cheat. How he did it was never found out, although the school discussed and sometimes played every dirty trick they had ever heard of. Husband became a legend. And when in 1930 he was shot dead in Chicago, the Duke of Clarence poker school stood, and silently toasted his memory. He had been a better man than they were in his fashion.

Although at night five or six men played, and often a circular table was brought in from the commercial room, during the day the game was carried on usually by four players. The Colonel having been carried out, his three old comrades, fellows in many a close scrape from the horns, allowed Willie Wickham to take his place. Then they played on in grim silence; for the Colonel's sudden stroke had affected their deepest feelings, and they were playing as if for their very lives. No one looked up as Hamlet approached. Willie, having already lost more than forty pounds, was holding his cards close to his chin and biting his lip. The others were frozen-faced.

Hamlet bent down and in a voice low enough to make it quite clear that the message was private and for Wickham only, yet loud enough for the other players to hear, he whispered, 'there's a lady outside wants to see you.'

Willie started and looked up, and his hands began to tremble. The other men laid down their hands, and looked at one another with a very great sadness in their eyes. Never once in the history of the poker school had the men been interrupted by such a request. It was like allowing a female Spanish dancer to flounce into the ring, while Juan Belmonte was executing a perfect paso de pecho. An obscenity.

Hamlet of course realized this by not giving the lady's name. But Willie acted as if he had turned from the bull, and given his attention to the swinging skirt and the swaying hips on the bloodied sand. He put down his cards, got up hastily and left the bar. Hamlet, who had gone behind the bar, where Miss Cutlet was presiding that evening, took up a glass and began to polish it, much to the lady's surprise.

'Well,' she said in a low voice, 'it's worth a king's ransom to see you in here. Are you still dodging Donie?'

'Them days is gone,' mumbled Hamlet. 'I know nuttin' about aul Donie.'

'Auld Donie,' exclaimed Miss Cutlet, much surprised. 'Well, we *are* growing up to be sure. Are you sure you're able to walk in your boots?'

Hamlet ignored this offensive remark, and kept his silence, as he so often did. But he let Miss Cutlet chatter on, for the men of the school were holding a post-mortem on Willie Wickham, and, although Hamlet could not hear what they were saying, he had a fair general notion of the flick of it.

'He was never fit to be let in, not the right stuff at all, we all knew it.'

'Well, there was a possibility. He could have made it.'

'Not on the rebound,' the reply was scornful. 'Maud turned him down.'

'Oh, I didn't know that. He could never have made it in that way.'

'Of course not. However, he filled in the time after poor Hightee, not well at all today. I suppose we were caught off-balance.'

'Send out for Micky Foy. He's been waiting to get taken on for nearly a year. He's the right stuff.'

'By God, he is. We should have thought of him first. He has the makings of a great player. Here Hamlet, come here.'

Hamlet was summoned from behind the bar to the alcove on the right of the door where the school flourished, seated at a fine and remarkably well-preserved card table of George III. Stud poker had been introduced in the twenties, but the inner school, which had always consisted of four men, had long gone back to straight poker, the play of the real *torero*.

So Hamlet was sent to fetch the young man who was to become one of the greatest names in Bridgeford, and he did so with mixed feelings. Young Foy had extreme, dark good looks, the figure of a Spanish dancer, and wore his well-cut clothes with an air. Hamlet had always envied him: born to money, success with the women, and a natural gift for the cue and the cards. And, as the boy passed under the stairs, he looked up. Maud and Willie had disappeared. And it was with a troubled heart that he went slowly across the street to fetch the favoured young man.

In fact Maud and Willie had not gone very far: just to the top of the stairs, where they were standing in the long, narrow corridor, which had been covered with a second-hand carpet in 1900, and always smelt of dust and falling plaster.

'That's a place I'll never play again,' Willie was saying bitterly, as he realized from Maud's manner that she had not sent for him to tell him that she was going to marry him.

'And a good thing too,' Maud replied sharply. 'You wouldn't have a penny for the church plate if you stayed in there. I don't want you ruined, you know.'

'A lot you care about it,' said Willie bitterly. 'Sending the young boots in to tell me I was wanted, making a holy show of me in front of the men.'

'I've already told you this morning that you have to go home.'

'Why do you think I joined the poker school? What interest have I left? And now you've destroyed that too.' He pressed his lips together with angry pride, and frowned heavily at his beloved.

'Has it not occurred to you that I'm acting in your best

interests?' Maud's voice took on its old seductive quality. At
another time it would have rendered Willie's bone down to a
jelly. But he could imagine the scornful looks of the poker
school as he got up and ran from them, because Maud had sent
for him. Just like a spineless poodle. He twisted his fingers
through the curls that fell over his forehead and shook his head
with horror.

'Very well then,' Maud's voice changed again, and she
half-turned away from him. 'Go back, join the school and ruin
yourself.'

'How can I? They wouldn't have me,' said Willie piteously.
In spite of being able to feast his eyes on his beloved and inhale
her blessed scent, he found that all he wanted now was a long
stiff drink.

'I never heard such nonsense in my life. Of course they'll
have you.'

'No, they won't. Not ever. But I'm not going home as you
ordered me to this morning, that's final.'

'You don't seriously expect me, or any other girl — '

'I'm not interested in any other girl,' said Willie with a pout.

'To look at you seriously, while you're drinking and
gambling the way you are?'

'Not gambling.' Willie raised his eyes defiantly.

Maud paused and looked at him, catching his angry glare.
She had never seen Willie this way before, and she found it
interesting.

'No, not gambling,' she said softly.

'Maud —' his manner changed, and his eyes took on that
spaniel look which irritated her so much.

'No, Willie,' she put in quickly. 'You'll have to pull yourself
together.'

'How can I if you give me no encouragement?' he said very
sensibly.

The place where they stood at the head of the stairs, with
the long corridor weaving away from them, was always a
chilly spot. Winds blew down the passage, but so lank was the
carpet that it stuck to the uneven boards, like damp hair on a
piece of flotsam. The faded curtains on the small windows
lining the corridor, overlooking the street and the Church of
Ireland across the way, were always in a flutter like flags on a
processional route. And many a guest, making his way along

this stretch in search of a bathroom in the dead of night, had wondered if he had in fact wandered out into the open air.

So Maud sniffed the breeze, and decided that it was best to bring this particular interview to an end.

'All right,' she said soothingly. 'Don't drink anymore today, go home, spend a few days there and then come and see me. I can't talk reasonably when you've been drinking, and as for gambling — ' she closed her eyes and shuddered in the draught.

'But when you see me stone cold sober, after spending all that time at home, working my fingers to the bone, you won't give me a straight answer. So what am I to do?'

'Well, I'm not going to discuss anything with you today, that's final.'

'Or any other day, it seems to me, drunk or sober.'

'If that's what you think — ' Maud shrugged her plump shoulders and turned away.

Willie ran down the stairs, meeting in the hall Michael Foy on his way into his kingdom; young, flat-bellied, long-legged, crackling with vitality. Willie who knew at once what had happened, gave him a quick nod and hurried out. It was the bitterest day of his life, and young Foy's flashing and eager smile seemed to make it even more so. As he went out the door, Willie reflected that he still had money in his pocket, that there were over seventy pubs in Bridgeford, and that he was welcome in all of them. He would start in the club down the lane opposite, where men went when they wanted to do some real, hard drinking. There one could drown one's sorrows day and night, and follow the billiards from under the table for all anyone cared. That was the place for him.

Maud went into her mother's front drawing-room, Willie passed Micky Foy in the hall, and almost immediately after, old MacDonnell came in from the street to meet Mr Slyne, who was just descending the stairs, having heard from his room some of the conversation which had taken place between Maud and her distressed young man.

'Good afternoon, Mr MacDonnell,' he said when he reached the hall.

'Hullo there.'

Without any further discussion they both turned in the

direction of the commercial room, where a fairly lively fire was burning, and no traveller lurked to disrupt their meeting.

Slyne sat down in a chair which he drew close to the fire, and MacDonnell, taking off his hat and gloves and putting them on a side table, took the old walnut crinoline chair, which was close to collapse, but which for the moment afforded a delicious ease to men of weight in the hind-quarters.

'Well,' he said, when he had wedged his girth into the padded space, once occupied by the massive skirts and hoops of the Victorian ladies of the sixties, who had used it before it was auctioned to the elder Mrs Daly. She had kept it in her own sitting-room for some years among the good things, but it had been strained by the bottom of a large friar, and afterwards sent down to the commercial room.

'Is it true that you're suing the old ladies?' said MacDonnell coming straight to the point. Blunt word, sharpened steel, winged arrow from behind.

Slyne nodded. He also knew the value of silence.

'You won't get the deposit back from them, you know,' muttered old Mac Donnell, usually so articulate; but there were times when he longed for a private language that one could use for all the unspoken reservations and hesitations necessary to the simplest business deal.

Slyne said nothing.

'Perhaps you're thinking you might get the land for the deposit,' said MacDonnell quickly. He knew immediately he had hit the tender elbow, so often held rigidly close to the body, always protected, but vulnerable to the skilled archer.

'What exactly did you call to see me for?' said Slyne with almost perfect composure. The lack of knowledge of what MacDonnell knew came out of him in small areas of sweat, in something about the eyelids, in the way the trunk of the body was held. Otherwise, and to all others, he was absolutely impassive.

'Well, I really called to see Mrs Daly, but when I met you, I thought you might have something to say to me about the land you bought from her, and the old ladies in Connaught Street.' MacDonnell had settled himself a little too cosily in the crinoline chair — an appearance of relaxed ease always being useful in any tricky discussion — for now he began to feel it creak a little under his weight, as if he had plumped down on the well-padded knee of a woman, who is suffering from rheumatism and whose joints suddenly crack.

'I see.' Slyne stroked his cheek with his forefinger, and looked at MacDonnell blankly for a moment.

He's very good at this he should be in the government but I suppose the ones they have are even smoother than he is if that's possible and then that awful Tammany unction they were always like that greasy oily and dangerous I wonder what he has up his sleeve he knows something of course but what well I was warned I had it all mapped out for me but I should have listened more carefully to that last quotation I heard about the German general who told his officers that the enemy have always four methods of attack open to them and they always use the fifth I suppose I should be friendly to this man after all he could be useful but if I was would he like it don't think so not that it's ever possible to know what they like or don't like really they are the most tiresome people always putting on an act always preserving face always choosing the weaving way between two points such a bore

'I don't think you're going to get away with the deposit,' MacDonnell said gently. He might have been pointing a gun at a pretty young girl he much admired who had sold some trade secrets; or, more likely, some arch rival he had been longing to get for years, and who was now cornered, with Macroom or someone else behind, pointing a gun at him. MacDonnell never shouted on these occasions, and there had been at least three memorable ones in his career. It was so much more satisfying to speak in a low, soft voice, very well mannered, very unconcerned. Yes, there was real pleasure in that.

'We shall have to wait and see. I have no absolutely definite plans at the moment,' said Slyne.

'I'm concerned about my neighbours, especially the old ladies.'

'I see.'

'They're naturally worried.' MacDonnell had been told years before in Boston by a retired Mafia godfather, that one should always take great care not to sweat, and for this reason he used a powerful deodorant, which could only be had in America. He was to hold his body in a certain way, a little slumped from the beginning, so as not to allow an involuntary start, and above all, to give his level, honest, open-eyed look into the other's eyes full on at the opening of discussion, and, thereafter, to use the direct stare with economy. In this game he was rather more experienced than Slyne.

'And so they ought to be. It was a disgraceful fraud,' said Slyne, showing signs of well-controlled anger.

'Do you think so?' was all MacDonnell said, as he gathered his big body together for the take-off. It was said lightly, as an aside, and a quick glance at Slyne indicated, and he had taken note of it. But further discussion was impossible just then.

'They will get the letters tomorrow,' said Slyne, rising also, and suddenly coming out with something he had already passed over in silence. But MacDonnell now knew the form: this was a pleasant minor addition to his store of knowledge. Slyne would do nothing hasty. But he was still in the ring.

'Poor old women,' murmured MacDonnell when he had collected his hat and gloves. 'Two of them really are poor, I don't know how they are — oh, well, of course none of that is your business, but that sale meant so much to them; a little nest-egg for their real old age. No one likes to think of the County Home. It terrifies the old, and indeed can we be surprised? Oh, dear. Well, goodbye for now Mr Slyne, and thank you.'

MacDonnell called into Fenny's on his way back from the hotel. He had spent some time with Mrs Daly and Maud after leaving Slyne, and since neither had mentioned the sale of the land, or Slyne's presence in the hotel, he, who always waited for the other person to draw down any subject, had said nothing. He was given tea, and Maud had chatted amiably with him for some time, saying nothing that might give him the faintest hope that she would receive his addresses on a more serious issue with enthusiasm. On the other hand, she had been friendly, flirted a little with him and looked more beautiful than ever. But they had talked of nothing for half an hour; a subject on which the three of them were experts. It is amazing how much tact, skill and wit are expended on nothing. It is a subject which requires the greatest experience and social confidence. Nevertheless, he had come away, as so often, feeling a little disappointed.

The O'Farrells were sitting behind their respective

counters, with the empty floor of the shop between them. At the back, facing the street door, the stove gleamed wickedly with blazing coal, and Ellen even had a small fireplace behind her grocery counter, which she often lit on particularly cold nights.

MacDonnell moistened his lips with the ritual glass of whiskey, so as not to insult the house. Fenny always poured out one when a friend called. Even his regulars were treated on special occasions: the illness of a relative, the death of a friend, after a long absence due to illness, or a journey which took them out of the town for some days. This did not happen often, as many of Fenny's clients had never been out of Bridgeford in their lives; one man had never even crossed the bridge into Leinster in all his eighty-eight years, but was promising to do so for this ninetieth birthday, a dangerous expedition.

'Well?' said Benny, when all the rituals had been carefully observed.

MacDonnell told them, quite accurately, just exactly what Slyne had said to him.

'Yes, yes,' said Fenny, 'but is he prepared to go through with it?'

'I don't know. I think so. You know what the English are like.' MacDonnell seemed to cherish deep thoughts within him, like a camel with humps bulging for a desert crossing. The weight of his expression was certainly camel-like, and he appeared to be taking the situation with great seriousness; something which Fenny had never been able to do.

'No, I don't know what the English are like,' he said with a small smile, knocking his pipe on the ledge behind him, 'No one does, not even they themselves. Besides they vary.'

'Slyne is a type,' said MacDonnell slowly. 'He has a deep faith in the law, and somehow always manages to keep on the right side of it. Easy enough, since it was people like him who made it in the first place.'

'So you think he'll bring the old ladies to court?'

'I have little doubt that's his intention.' MacDonnell coughed into his fist, and looked at his half-empty glass. It was a bore having to consume all this booze, and tea, whenever one had anything to do with the neighbours. At the same time he remembered the words of a famous Boston bootlegger; 'Mac, never refuse a drink, you may need it to take the place of your blood some day.'

'And you have a plan?' said Fenny quite naturally. For old MacDonnell always had a plan, and the whole situation surrounding the sale of the water-logged acres, seemed to be very much his sort of problem. For occasions like the present was he born, reared to pass under, over and around every law of the land, silently and without fuss.

'If it seems likely to come off. Of course, I'll think about it.' This was his standard reply, and with it, a gallant bow to Ellen, a firm, square handshake for Fenny, he was gone.

The O'Farrells were silent for a few minutes, listening to the muffled breathlessness of the stove, the few footsteps outside, and the blessed silence which they knew reigned behind the passage door. Gummy was out at the moment, and not expected back until closing time.

'God forgive me,' said Ellen, shaking her head, 'but I can't warm to that man.'

'You mean you don't like him. Well, neither do I.' Fenny, re-established on his bum-boat, with his shoes comfortably tucked in on one of the wooden rungs, puffed on his pipe, holding his elbow in the other hand. 'I doubt if anyone really does. I think it's because MacDonnell has a finger in every pie, all over the country. He has never done anything practical himself for anyone. He gets them jobs by wheeler-dealing, he gets a doctor to see them, because the doc owes him a favour, youngsters are got into school for the same reason, grants got from the County Council, and so on. But never does he dip into his own pocket, and he has no real, deep-down sympathy for anyone. It's curious, but I think he's a very lonely man and probably doesn't realize it. He's too busy fixing deals — I suppose a spider is reasonably content weaving alone in the middle of its web.'

Ellen laughed. She had always been her husband's best audience.

'Is it true what I hear, that he's asked Maud Daly to marry him?' Ellen leaned down comfortably on her arms over the counter, the solid, well-seasoned wood providing a welcome support for her present condition. She remembered her mother saying that women who served in shops could go on working until the very last minute, because of the counter, and also because most of them lived upstairs. She was very conscious of that protection now.

'At least twice, if not three times. Maud hasn't committed herself.' Fenny chuckled, and looked at his wife from under his reddish eyebrows.

But Ellen was not disposed to joke. The subject of Maud Daly's boyfriends, and her eventual marriage, was one that was discussed hotly by the mass women, and she could not help overhearing it from time to time.

'But hasn't she another fellow, that big farmer from Westmeath?' Ellen reached down under the counter to the shelf where she kept the teapot. She felt the open lid and the spoon and sighed with relief.

'Willie Wickham? Yes, she has him too. But he's not as cool as the old boy, drinking himself into an early grave, I hear. And now he's taken to gambling.'

'Oh dear. That'll be the end of him, if he isn't careful.'

'He isn't careful.'

'A fine-looking man, I saw him come out of the Duke several times, dresses well too. I wonder Maud doesn't make up her mind. I mean, at the moment both men are good matches, and she must prefer one to the other.'

'Maud prefers Maud, that's her great love, Maud Daly. She spends hours admiring herself in the glass, and always did.'

'Well, she's lovely-looking, a real beauty, I don't wonder. But I don't believe she has no preference, I think she'll save Wickham from gambling, cut down on his drink and marry him.'

Fenny gave his wife a small, wry smile and shook his head. Then he turned aside and busied himself with his pipe. Ellen felt for her teapot, took it up and popped two spoonfuls of cold tea leaves into her mouth; then she put the pot away again, wiped her mouth with a handkerchief, and took up the open packet of tea — finest quality Indian, five shillings a pound, and sniffed it long and lovingly. Since her pregnancy Ellen had developed a passion for used tea-leaves, which Gummy collected for her, thus making it possible to have the pot brewing all day, a job very much to Gummy's taste. The tea for smelling, a secondary craving, Ellen was naturally able to prepare for herself: all she had to do was take down one of O'Farrell's specially blended high quality teas, made up in pound and half-pound bags, with 'O'Farrell and Son, Quality Grocers and Tea Importers', imprinted on them. Every

Monday, Fenny made the blend from two chests of Musgraves, and Ellen weighed the different mixtures and put them into paper bags. O'Farrell's had a name for tea.

'I wouldn't be at all surprised if Miss Maud Daly ended up as an old maid, pretty and all as she is,' said Fenny.

'O Benedict, such a beautiful girl — ' Ellen in her happiness thought the single station in life, for women at any rate, a really dreadful fate. That anyone should seek it voluntarily was beyond her.

'Yes, indeed. Very good-looking, but wouldn't it be awful if she turned out like her mother — '

'I still think she'll marry Mr Wickham.' Then, with one of those post-lightning changes of mood, she remarked that it was queer that no one had come into the shop so far that evening.

'They must have heard the news by now, Benedict. I thought we'd have them all tonight.'

Fenny shook his head, adjusted his trousers to ease the tightness in the groin, and settled comfortably into his bum-boat.

'They'll wait until they get the solicitor's letters in the morning. I never knew anyone, in these parts anyway, to take any sort of action while a law letter was pending. It's part of the defence to pretend that you never, ever expected one. That state of mind starts early.'

'Poor old things,' said Ellen sadly as she thought of Hosannah, Mrs Pig, Miss McLurry and Donie's poor unfortunate wife, although a large family did not appear so very dreadful to Ellen as it once had. 'Anyway, Donie's wife has the children, but the others, apart from Mrs Daly, have nothing. I'm really worried about them.'

'Don't,' said her husband with a grin. Then he busied himself with his pipe again, and Ellen helped herself to another spoonful of leaves.

'I hope to God whatever dey have, boy, girrel or tewins, it isn't de colour of an injun wid all de tay she's eatin',' was Gummy's comment to her gossips.

The next day was foggy, and it was not easy to follow the progress of the postman on the opposite side of the street. But

he delivered in O'Farrell's a little after ten, and looked at Ellen
with a gleam in his eye.

'Is de boss down yet?' he said with a tip of his head in the
direction of the door leading to the stairs.

'Did you want to see him?' said Ellen, who had learned at
least some of the tricks of survival which Bridgeford natives are
born with.

'Dey all got dere letters from Fair this mornin',' he said
slowly and ponderously, as if the mailbag had weighed down
his voice also. 'Thank God, dere isn't a dog here, ma'am. Me
leg is as bitten as a polisman.'

Ellen was also getting used to Piddle the Post's sudden
non-say-quitters, as they were known locally. His real name was
Biddle, a British army legacy, and Piddle was at least better
than Diddle, or Fiddle, which would have been a professional
slur on his job. Nevertheless, Fenny often called him
Fiddle-de-Diddle because he never had the right change for
anything, and it was his habit to buy a little something in each
shop to which he delivered a fairly heavy post, or a long screed
from America or Australia.

'Would ye ever have a half pound a tay?' he now said quickly.

Ellen reached back and took down the half-crown mixture,
for which she supposed Piddle owed her one-and-threepence.
He produced exactly one-and-three half pence, after a great
deal of puffing, his bag to one side, and searching all his pockets
inside and outside his uniform, ending up in the rim of his cap.

'I'll give ye de penny-half-penny next time round. Miss
McLurry didden get wan,' he remarked, as he secreted the tea
in some pouch on his person.

'Didn't get what?' Ellen always fell for Piddle the Post's red
herrings.

'A letter from de solicitor, a course. Dere's letters for the two
odder aul wans, but none for Miss McLurry.'

'Why is that?' Ellen lifted her bag of tea and sniffed it. She
assumed innocently that as she sold tea, no one would see it as a
'craving', of which she was ashamed.

'De sorter, aul Ennis wid de wan hand dropped it, she'll get
it on de second post. Mrs Daly didn't get wan eidder, at least
nod through de post office. Isn't dat queer?'

'Good morning Shaun,' said Fenny, suddenly appearing in
the doorway. This was an important day, and he had got up

early, at ten, to be ready for the land-owners when they received their letters. 'None for Mrs Daly, eh? I suppose that 's because he's staying there. She might turf him out.'

'Well, indeeden she might, sir. Dat wumman is fit for annyting.' He backed skilfully to the door, an old and perfected hand, bearing his cut-price tea, which he preferred to get from Mrs O'Farrell, who was a real lady, and had no sense at all. Fenny was uncertain. 'I tole de missus all, an' ye have a letter from the Canon about the bazaar. Mornin'.' And he disappeared into the fog outside, like a villain in a melodrama.

Ellen told Fenny the news about the letters, as he was arranging his bum-boat for the day.

'Um,' he said as he hoisted himself up. 'Sarah Jane will be in all the same. She'll know about old Ennis dropping the letter.'

'Why didn't somebody pick it up?' said Ellen, without thinking.

Fenny looked at her in amazement. Then he relaxed, remembering that she was pregnant and subject to odd notions.

'What does Canon Sharkey want for his bazaar this time? Open the letter, love, and tell me.'

'Just a request for support. It's a circular, but signed on the bottom by himself.'

'That means two bottles of everything for the St Jude stall, and two pounds of tea of the best for the St Martha stall, also two Christmas candles, red, a half pound of real almonds, and at least half-a-dozen pots of jam.'

'They say he has more than half the money for the new church already, isn't that wonderful?' Ellen looked at Canon Sharkey's letter with affection.

'Wonderful, only the angels could have done it, to be sure, and thank God you don't have to have a stall this year.' Fenny looked at his wife and smiled as he might at an anniversary. No twinkle was permitted. Ellen was very sensitive about her condition, and hated having it spoken about. Part of this, he knew, was not simply prudery, although she possessed a surprising amount of that, but to a genuine fear that, after twelve years, it was asking for trouble to talk too much about anything so precious and unexpected.

'What did the Piddle do you out of this morning?' he said quickly.

'Three-halfpence.'

'He had a good story the last time he did for me, about Mrs Larkin down the lane. Did I tell you?'

'Is it a dirty one?' Ellen fingered the Canon's letter gently.

'Not in your sense.'

Ellen was not able to express any opinion on this one, for just then Mrs Pig loomed out of the fog, as large as a statue, and crashed into the shop — Fenny had a sudden vision of a great carved stone figure toppling over into his door. She was holding up her letter in one hand.

'Well, I got de summons,' she exclaimed, waving the letter as if it were a flag. 'Did anywan ever get anythin' else from a bloody Englishman? Oh, God Almighty, de treachery of them, de double-dealin', de cunnin', de cuteness, de trickery, de divil himself is only half in them, because dey have nothin' to learn from him. There,' she said, slapping her letter down on the counter in front of Fenny. 'What did I tell ye, didn't I tell ye a hundred times dat dat fella hadn't a straight bone in his body? How would he, and he an Englishman from the time they were swingin' from tree to tree, and we havin' our own kings and queens, and royal princesses, and a whole holocaust of monks to hammer Christ into the heathen French, Germans and de rest o' dat foreign crew? O sad is the day and bitter de night when I ever had anything to do with dat Slyne — Sly is his name and no mistake, the end stuck on to cover him up, like the English are forever doin', when decent people are walkin' naked — '

Here she paused for breath, giving Fenny time to put out his hand and ask her if she would like him to read the letter.

'A course, a course,' she said, thrusting it across the counter, and, remembering her manners, even in her extremity, she turned to Ellen, nodded to her with a sudden smile, and asked her how she was that morning.

'Very well, thank you, Mrs Prendergast, except that the fog is awful, I wouldn't like to be out — '

'And take very good care dat you don't, girrel, now listen to me,' and Mrs Pig wagged a large finger to emphasize her absolute insistence on Ellen's taking good care of herself. Ellen turned the open tea bag round in her hands, as if she were about to close it. Mrs Pig pretended not to see.

'Well, it's the usual, or at least what I expected,' said Fenny, gravely looking up over his spectacles, which he used for reading, especially when it was something important. He was often asked to read letters for others who could not read them, and he found that putting on the specs produced a soothing effect. They made him look ten years older, and Ellen hated them, but they were part of Fenny's public image, something which everyone in the town understood, even if only subconsciously.

'Fair says that the land was sold by misrepresentation — '

'Did ye ever hear such gall? Didn't Slycie Sly foot de land inch by inch with meself?'

'Well, yes, I know,' Fenny allowed the glasses to slip down his nose, something that helped when the going got rough. 'But he claims that he bought it unaware that it was flooded in winter, that that was never explained to him, that the land was useless to him for a large part of the year, as a result of the flooding and the after-effects of it, and that he is requesting his deposit back, after which he would decide whether to sue for fraud or not.'

'Fraud! Misrepresentin'! Useless! The finest site south of de town! An' askin' for his money back! Is he mad?' Mrs Pig had thrown off her husband's big frieze coat, and she now slung it round from her shoulders with the air of a torero worthy of the poker school. She thrust out one arm, then the next, as if she were flexing them for battle, into the sleeves, settling the whole thing about her shoulders with an expert twist of her body, followed by a fine shaking of the shoulders to make the garment fall in the proper place for business transactions of a weighty nature. Then she clapped the palm of her hand on the top of her head as if she were fixing a hat, paused for an instant, and decided to do business in her hair.

'He's not goin' to get away with dat,' she announced.

'What about the deposit, Mrs Pig?' Fenny said gently, like a very old prelate indicating a difficult spiritual exercise, to a mother superior with the will of a Teresa of Avila.

'The deposit!' roared Mrs Pig suddenly, flailing the air with her arms, and jumping on the boarded floor with a thud that shook the bottles on the shelf behind Fenny. Elllen clutched her tea bag. At that very moment, as if she had been waiting for a cue, the door to the kitchen opened and Gummy staggered in bearing a bucket of coal for the stove.

Mrs Pig turned to her and threw out her arms. Here was a

woman, to be avoided in everyday affairs, but of priceless worth in a row.

'D'English! d'English!' panted Mrs Pig. 'Miss Hayes, what would you do to a low-down, sly, twister of an Englishman, if he was trying to get money out of you be false pretences?'

'False pretenshuns is it!' Gummy dropped the bucket with a bang, threw back her head and planted her smoky hand on her hips. 'Twistin' d'inside of yer purse is he? O de villain, de curse-o-God traitor an' hangman. I'll tell ya wad I'd do wid him, I'd hang, draw and quarter 'im, an' pay a butcher to scatter his guts up on de barrack wall, an' sell his head for greyhounds, dats what I'd do. O Mother a' God, only let me at em —'

'Miss Hayes, Miss Hayes,' murmured Ellen faintly. Gummy looked as though she was going to have a fit there and then.

'Gummy,' said Fenny stoutly, taking off his glasses, a monumental gesture which meant finality. 'That's enough, now, you'll do yourself an injury. Leave the bucket there, we don't want coal yet, and go back and make a cup of tea for Mrs Prendergast. She must be parched on a morning like this. Better bring along the big teapot and a few cups, I'm expecting visitors.'

This call to order, accompanied by exact instructions concerning hospitality, and the awful delight of more visitors with lovely letters, had the effect of bringing Gummy back to normal, with as swift a change of attitude as if it had been done with lights and a quick curtain. She raised her hand in solidarity with Mrs Pig; then turned and marched back into the passage, closing the door with intention behind her.

'Dat's the kind of talk dat's needed now,' declared Mrs Pig, taking a big check handkerchief out of her overcoat pocket, and wiping her red and sweating brow. 'Miss Hayes is one of dem Irishwomen, quiet and retirin' in dere ways, and livin' lives devoted to others, who answer de call of Ireland when needed. All honour to her.'

Fenny looked across at Ellen with one eyebrow faintly raised. He had heard Gummy called many a thing in his life, but this inclusion with the heroic women of Ireland was new. Had they been harbouring a Maud Gonne in the kitchen all these years? Fenny didn't think so. The moment was charged, the atmosphere tense, and passions high. 'Charge the moment, fence the atmosphere, and buy the passion', as his father once remarked, when that famous three-phrased sentence was used at least ten times by a politician on a platform in the square.

'I think early as d'hour is, Mr O'Farrell, I'd prefer a drop of whiskey, if you don't mind,' said Mrs Pig with confidence. Everybody knew that she was a woman who could hold her liquor and had a strong head. She took money out of her purse and put down the price of a small one on the counter. Fenny took it with a shopkeeper's smile as he handed her a glass. To offer Mrs Pig a free drink at this stage in the proceedings would have been a grave breach of etiquette. Hosannah, who was now in very difficult circumstances, might have to be subsidized and the drinks chalked up to save face, but the rest would pay. Never let it be known that they had been beggared by an Englishman.

'He can prosecute,' said Fenny gently.

'Let him,' declared Mrs Pig with a sweep of her arm, the other hand holding the glass in a rock-steady grip. 'Let him have us rounded up be de polis — all stinkin' Free Staters anyway — and let him try to throw us in jail. O let the Shannon flow backwards and churn into butter, before we let dat happen!'

'But surely,' said Ellen timidly, for she held Mrs Pig in a certain kind of awe, although she admired her, and had always found her friendly and kind, 'you're not going into court, Mrs Prendergast? You know the old saying, "out of court into harbour." It's a terrible thing to face judge and jury.' She shivered and grasped her bag of tea so tightly that it nearly burst.

Mrs Pig was about to make a spirited reply, but again her regard for Fenny's gentle wife, especially in her present condition, held her back, and she spoke quietly.

'I hope to God dat you never have to face it, Mrs O'Farrell, but of course you never will, but it has no fears for me. I'd take on a judge and jury anytime before I'd face a chargin' bull, or a mad dog, or a cornered rat, oh yes, I would. And dat Slycy-Slyne-boots will get de whack of his life when I get up into de witness box.'

'Oh, pray that you won't have to,' said Ellen, who was so upset that she helped herself to a heaped-up spoon of cold tea leaves, right in front of Mrs Pig, and did not even think of it.

Mrs Pig turned away and caught Fenny's eye. She smiled a special little smile that normally she kept for her cat, but it denoted true affection and a kind of strong-armed gentleness. Fenny nodded politely and returned her signal. Something unspoken, understood and shared passed between them, on a deeper and more permanent level than all the rhetoric that both of them were capable of.

'The present courts as constituted by the Free State are not recognized by me,' said Mrs Pig, quietly and with great dignity. 'When dey signed dat cursed Treaty with Lloyd George, an agent of the Divil, and a freemason if ever dere was one, dey took over de whole English dog's dinner of laws, courts, judges, wigs and all — de whole maze dat was set up year after year to serve d'English in power, and blind d'eyes of de poor with confusion. Laws like dat are not binding on my conscience, so why should I be afraid to go into court, I can tell dem anything I like, and come out with me conscience clean as a nun's nose.'

'Oh, but your Mr De Valera is in power now, Mrs Pig,' said Fenny, with a glint in his eye, 'and he's using the courts just as Cosgrave did. Won't that trouble you?'

'I know you and your father before ye were Free Staters, and I'm saying nothing against ye. Ye're wrong, and ye're doin' an injury t'Ireland, but we're neighbours, and I don't believe in lettin' politics get between neighbours. Anyone can be wrong. But,' and here she drew herself up, and looked about her with the air of someone in a lofty trance, 'as far as Mr De Valera is concerned, he can't be expected to change de law back into de real Gaelic Brehon code overnight. He's a statesman, and a great one, an' it'll maybe take years before he has all de laws — unjust down to de last comma, with never a full stop in case dey'd have to rush an emergency wan through parliament to keep de poor and downtrodden in dere place — dat was England's policy now and forever from the past, and remember dey keep down their own poor, just as dey ever tried to break us — but Dev'll show them, he'll knacker dem in time, but for now de laws is null and stinkin' well void, and I can say what I like up dere in de dock of shame.'

'What about the oath, Mrs Pig?' said Fenny, who was genuinely interested in this turn of events. He leaned forward on his arms over the counter, and out of the corner of his eye saw Ellen helping herself to another spoonful. Gummy would have use for all the tea she brewed that day.

'You mean it's on a Catholic bible?' Mrs Pig held her glass close to her collar and frowned. 'Well, I'm not one of dose ignorant people dat think de bible was invented by de Protestants, but dat's to de back of de point. What matters when ye go into de witness box is not the bible ye swear on, but yer conscience. And if yer conscience tells you dat de law is unjust, and forced on ye be foreigners, den d'oath on de bible is a prayer merely to give ye strength to stand up for yer rights. And besides, of course you take it with mental reservations, just like Dev did when he had to enter the Dail, to save de country from de Free Staters. So dat's not worryin' me one single bit.'

Ellen listened to all this with kindling amazement, and was so startled by what she heard that she forgot all about her tea leaves for the moment.

'Oh, Mrs Prendergast, Mrs Prendergast,' she moaned softly, 'stay out of court like I said, for God's sake.'

Mrs Pig looked round at her, and her expression softened. She was about to say something pacific to Ellen, when she caught sight of a wavering figure outside the shop window. It weaved in and out of the fog like a wraith, and a moment later Hosannah staggered into the shop, with her hands clasping a letter to her bosom, and a rag of a scarf tied round her thin, matted hair. Her stockings were awry, full of holes, and her slightly swollen ankles bulged out over worn and dirty shoes. The piece of rabbit skin, that was stitched onto the collar of her coat, was almost as bare as her face, and seemed to belong to some dim, ageless past, when it had been a half-creature, half-developed and dead from natural causes. Hosannah looked a fright.

'Oh,' she croaked, beating the letter against her breast, and holding onto the wall of the Cafe Royal with the other, 'hauld me up, for God's sake someone, I'm on me lass legs, and me mind is not hereabouts. O o o o, may de Blessed Mudder a' God intercede for me a poor sinner, an tricked on me dyin' bed, for dat's what I rose from dis mornin', when I got dis. O Mrs P, oh Mr O'Farrell, show me a chair in d'honour a' God —'

Fenny had come out smartly from the back of his counter, and Ellen from hers, to lend a hand in case Hosannah fell down in a dead faint. But the partition was sufficient support for her, and having regained her breath, she thrust her letter at Fenny, and they all waited silently as he read it. It was the same as the one received by Mrs Pig, but protocol demanded that Fenny should give it the same attention as if he had never seen it before. Hosannah was watching him like a buzzard.

'Well,' she gasped, when he had finished reading, and glanced up over the rim of his specs, 'did ye ever hear de likes a' dat in yer entired life, an' before id? Who would tink dat wan a' de Braidens, an' we rooted in de soil a' dis place forr hunners a' years, an' me fadder an' mudder in heaven, and me granfadder an' me granmudder in heaven, an' all me brudders an' sissers an' uncles an' anties back ta Cromwell — God bless us — all prayin' in heaven for me, an' where are dey dis minnit, when I want dem? An' all de candles I lit, spent every penny a' de money on candles ta de Moss Pure Hard a' Mary, an' where is she now when I need her, dat's wad I wand ta know? — '

Mrs Pig took a firm hold of her arm, and steered her into the Cafe Royal, where she collapsed like an old curtain taken off its rings, dusty and rigid, surprised by freedom, then slowly folding in angular lassitude to the floor.

'Tea, I think,' said Ellen, going off to fetch Gummy. Once in the kitchen, she would be able to refill her own pot, for Gummy kept a perpetual brew on for her convenience.

'Shurely ta God, he's nod goin' ta drag us inta court?' moaned Hosannah, 'No wan belongin' ta me ever stood in de dock — '

'De best blood in Ireland stood in de dock, an' weren't ashamed of it,' declared Mrs Pig stoutly. 'Remember Lord Edward! An' bauld Robert Emmet, de darlin' of Erin!'

'Lord Edward wus a man, and well able ta speak for himsel'. Didden I learn his speech from de docks when I wus a girrul? Bud I'm ony a poor lone wummin, failin' in me bones, an' de blood barely able ta make ids way, tin as id is, between de hard aul alleyways a' me veins. Oh oh, me aul veins — '

'That was Robert Emmet's speech ye learned,' said Mrs Pig, a glazed look coming into her fine eyes. She gazed into space, and began in a fine resonant voice — indeed she did possess a lovely sounding voice, much disguised so far as Bridgeford was concerned, by her Kerry accent. '"Let no man write my epitaph; for as no man who knows my motives dares now vindicate them, let not prejudice or ignorance asperse them — "'

Suddenly from behind her, bringing a cloud of fog with him, as he held onto the handle to listen to Mrs Pig speaking, the voice of Donie Donnelly joined in:

' "When my country takes her place among de nations of d' earth, den, and not till den, let my epitaph be written." '

'Good man yerself, Donie Donnelly,' said Mrs Pig, who did not in the least mind his taking over her speech, especially as she had forgotten the middle part of the last great paragraph.

' "We have de shades of all dem dat died for Ireland hoverin' over us dis blessed day," ' he intoned looking up at the ceiling. "Never let it be said dat dey poured out dere martyrs' blood in vain." Did ye get yer ledders?' And he produced his own from an inner pocket, and held it out to Fenny.

'Close the door, Donie, please,' said Fenny, as he prepared to give the same attention to Donie's identical letter.

'Ah, sure I doan know whedder id's on de street, or out in de middle a' de river I am, and de fog all around me, like de legion of de lost. Oh, but begod it's terrible cold. Dat letter, by de way, Mr O'Farrell, is sent to me wife, bud of course I'm representin' her in all aspectations of d'estate.'

'Of course,' said Fenny, handing back the precious scroll with solemnity. 'What are you going to do, Donie, or advise your wife to do?'

'Deny it, a' course, isn't it a god-damned libel? We should be see-suing him. Didden I explain in great detail, counting on me fingers, one be one, d'extend a' de lands dat'd lie under water during de winter rains. I spelled it out for him, dere and den, an' we standin' at one side of a field, private like, and me mudder listenin' from heaven.'

'Are you going to swear to this, Donie?' said Fenny quietly. For Donie had boasted to more than one how clever he had been in selling waterlogged land to an eejit of an Englishman.

'A' course I am!' Donie looked about him, and glanced from eye to eye, a man counting his audience. He turned down the collar of the raincoat he was wearing over his working clothes. 'Haven't I to tink o' me wife an' childer, an' dey half-starvin', even wid all de bits and pieces o' money, de best bein' a half-crown, bitten and bent, an' raggedy aul ten shillin' notes, torn in the middle, dat has to be patched, or de bloody bank won't take it, a lot dey care for de poor, dem stuck up bank clerks, some o' dem not far outa cow manure?'

'Have ye a witness to dis, Donie?' said Mrs Pig who had a legal mind.

'Isn't me own word good enough for any Irish judge and jury? Don't I know ever wan o' dem comin' into de Duke, an' every wan odem knowin' me, since I was hardly higher dan de boots I was polishin'? I'm not ashamed, like some, a' bein' a workin' man, dat has to bend his back, and get down on his knees, to keep his wife and childer from stale bread not fit for pet mice, an' the County Home loomin' in fron' of us all —'

'Mudder O' God deliver us,' said Hosannah, crossing herself. She had turned paler than she was, and leaned back against the wall of the Cafe Royal, looking very much distressed.

There had been a silence all around, after Donie had made his speech. And as they now discovered, Gummy Hayes was standing at the door of the passage, with a tray of tea and cups in her hands. It was she who spoke first.

'I didden hear everything ye sed, Donie Donnelly, but de Lord forgive ye for drawin' down de County Home in the middle a' decent people. It was a shockin' ting to say, so it was. The work house!'

'Don't ever mention dat place in here again, d'ye hear me,' said Mrs Pig, in a low and menacing voice.

'I'm terrible sorry,' said Donie humbly, 'but it slipped out in de heat, and me half worried to death be de threat o' de law.'

'Let de law, so called,' said Mrs Pig beckoninng Gummy to come forward with the tray, for Hosannah looked genuinely weak, and had a very bad colour. But Gummy did not move. She made a slight motion of her head, which was immediately interpreted. Mrs Pig went over to her, and leaned forward over the steaming tray. 'Poor aul Hosannah was wans threatened be de County Home, it was awful.'

'I know,' replied Mrs Pig, 'I could trottle dat little rat. Such a thing to say. Howanever, bring de tea, for poor Susannah looks as if she needs it. And be quiet Gummy, be quiet.' She put a light but imperious hand on Gummy's arm, and the two of them went back to the Cafe Royal, in that close harmony, which can be even more effective when unsung.

'Ye poor faintin' craytur,' said Gummy, as she poured out a stiff cup of tea for Hosannah, who had raised her head, and was sitting up, more or less straight. But she looked very shocked.

'God bless ye, Annie Hayes, an' give ye a safe journey when de time comes, shure we'll all be haulin' you up over the rim a' heaven. I'm terrible weak. D'ye tink — ?'

'I do,' said Fenny, who was leaning in the hatch door, well aware of the effect that Donie's frightening reference had had on all. He signalled Gummy to hand him a cup. A few generous drops of brandy were added, and Hosannah, who could smell it across water, and knew exactly what the whispering meant, lay back again and closed her eyes with a dying sigh.

'Here,' she heard Gummy say loudly, 'here's yer cup a' tay.'

While the easing of Hosannah's fright was going on, and all of them were watching her closely, in case she became seriously weak, another figure passed the window outside, wavering in and out of the fog, opened the door smartly, and with a certain degree of professional finesse.

Miss McLurry was a shopkeeper herself, and knew how to manage a door in the middle of a thick fog.

'Did you all get letters from Fair?' was the first thing she said, not even pausing to take in the general atmosphere of the place. The question had been on her lips for the past two hours, and must be got out; a wasp on the tongue.

They all said 'yes', even Hosannah, who was sipping her tea noisily, with a trembling hand.

'You did?' Miss McLurry's voice was high and aggrieved. 'You mean to tell me that all of you – not *you* Miss Hayes — got letters this morning from the solicitor, and I didn't?'

'It's ony delayed in de post,' Gummy said, putting her finger in the stew prematurely, as she usually did.

'Who asked for your opinion?' snapped Miss McLurry. 'I never heard of such a thing. I'm as big a land-owner as any of you, and why should I be left out?'

'The mills of God — ' murmured Fenny, who had come round from his counter and touched Gummy lightly on the arm. 'Go in and see how my wife is, Annie please.' This saved face all around, and Gummy departed with a look at Miss McLurry that clearly indicated she was not in any way worthy of receiving a letter, even from an orphan at Christmas, much less a communication from the oldest established solicitor in the town, who had had a lord for a great-uncle.

'Didn't Piddle the Post tell ye?' said Mrs Pig sympatheti-cally. She had heard the same story from him about Ennis the sorter, and he might have dropped in and told Miss McLurry on the way back.

'He never as much as came within sight of the door,' replied Sarah Jane indignantly. 'And with the fog I couldn't follow his movements. I was waiting all morning.'

'Oh, you poor ting,' said Hosannah, much revived by the drop of brandy, and not too knocked down by the mention of the County Home to appreciate the pleasure of scoring off the stuckup Miss McLurry. 'I got mine first ting, as quick as d'aul Piddle could shuffle in. O me, bud he never as much as mentioned you, Miss McLurry.'

'Why should he?' snapped Miss McLurry, thoroughly aroused by being left out of the legal roundabout. 'Why should he mention *my* name to *you?*'

After this bulls' eye, there was a little silence, such as often follows a brilliant throw in the game of darts.

'It was dropped on the floor by old Ennis, one of the sorters,' put in Fenny quietly, eager to establish order: after all, no game can be played without it.

'I don't care if it was dropped on the floor by the post-master himself, big thick from Mayo that he is. I still think that old Piddle, to whom I often gave a full packet of Woodbines at Christmas, just to keep him up before the day, and a good handout, I can tell you, on his collection after Christmas, could've told me. Well, we'll see what he'll get this year, the old fool. Nobody would keep him in a job except the post office, which is filled with every dog and divil in the country, and not a brain to hand around on loan between them.' She paused, drew a deep breath, and looked about her with glistening eyes. 'I should have been told,' she exclaimed bitterly.

'So you should,' said Mrs Pig unexpectedly. She usually took a certain amount of grim pleasure in slapping down her friend's airier fancies, but in this matter of receiving what amounted to a summons, she could fully sympathize.

'It was an awful thing to happen,' went on Miss McLurry, and there was a general murmur of appreciation and regret, except from Hosannah, who had buried her nose in the tea cup.

'Would you like a cup of tea, Miss McLurry?' said Fenny in a soft and gentle voice, 'and a nice digestive biscuit? Nothing sets you up as well, my mother always said. Indeed, if she were here with us today, you would have been offered tea before now.'

Sarah Jane sighed and thanked him, her face expressing something like triumph, as she glanced at poor Hosannah, who was still sucking up her tea-and-brandy. But she looked up quickly, as if aware of the glance.

'An' Mrs O'Farrell, senior, wus a lady,' she said clearly and distinctly, before burrowing her nose in her cup again.

Miss McLurry looked uncertain, but this time Mrs Pig saved the day by leaning forward, and speaking into her ear one single magic word: 'Brandy'. Immediately Sarah Jane regained her confidence, and smiled her thanks to Fenny, who was standing somewhat anxiously half-way between his counter and the door. He slipped behind his counter when he had poured a strong cup of tea for the lady, and handed her the plate of biscuits brought in by Gummy.

'And now,' he said, restored to his high chair, 'what are you going to do about it, when you get your letter? After all, it's a blessing in a way, it gives you time to think, and advise the rest of us.'

The offer of advice was taken in good part, even if the rest of Fenny's remarks were not judged absolutely diplomatic by Miss McLurry herself. Everybody, she noted, seemed to be nervous, and not quite themselves this morning, except herself.

'Well,' she said after clearing her throat, and sitting down in a chair in the Cafe Royal, well away from Hosannah's red velvet bench. 'Well, the whole thing seems quite ridiculous to me. I can't understand it.' She paused, and nibbled on her digestive biscuit, and a slow inner smile, denoted by the relaxing of her face muscles, and a certain soft glimmer of the eyes, rose like a blush to her face from somewhere near her heart. 'Maybe it's because of that, that my letter has been delayed, or perhaps not sent at all — ' she paused for reaction, and Fenny responded immediately.

'Indeed, yes. That occurred to me too,' he said.

'Nod ta me,' commented Hosannah, with a sudden cackle.

'After all, the way I look at it is, that I've been defrauded by this Mr Slinn or Slynn or Slyne, or whatever his name is, he is of no account anyway, no gentleman at all. Well, as I was saying, no one in their right mind would have sold valuable land, bordering the banks of the Shannon, the most famous river in the British Isles, unless he or she knew it was only to be used as a sort of summer promenade. It never entered my mind that this Mr Whatever-his-name-is didn't know that the lands were flooded in the winter. If they weren't, I would have charged him ten times the price. That's what I think.' And, raising her head high over her tea cup, she gazed around her triumphantly.

They were all so struck by this brilliant piece of reasoning, that no one except Fenny, and even he only with a sideways glance, saw Ellen come back into the shop, and steal quietly behind her counter, with another fresh pot of damp tea leaves. She settled herself on her stool and lifted her tea bag to her nose.

'Well' said Mrs Pig with an admiring nod of the head, 'dat's de best one I've heard yet, isn't it, min?'

Fenny and Donie agreed that indeed it was.

'I tink dat's de defence we should all pud up,' said Donie.

'When I tink of all de candles I lit an de journey I made ta Dublin t'Adam an' Eve's,' moaned Hosannah.

'Have you been listenin' to what Miss McLurry has bin sayin?' said Mrs Pig, who was sipping her second whiskey, and had money for yet another in her purse.

'And didn't you go to Tralee, Marcella?' said Miss McLurry, pleased with the general reception of her idea.

'Faithen I did, and went up de mountain in a hired car, decked out like de captain's bride in an opra, and not wan o' me school mates left to admire me. There wasn't such a scatterin' from d'auld street since de famine.' She shook her head. 'Connaught Street is me home now. I'll never leave it, because if I did I'd have to come home again, and ye can't do that. Something'd happen while I was away, and me contentment'd be blown off like a spider's web. I learned dat from Mr Slyne and his land grabbin'. If I went away again, he might have de roof taken off from over me head, and de Guards waitin' outside for me return. O very likely.'

'Surely to God, Mrs Prendergast, ye doan expect de Guards ta drag ye be de hair a de head down into de barracks, do ye?' said Donie, coming back into the arena with a good deal of spirit.

Mrs Pig ignored him. She was subject to these sudden fits of black depression. The dark cloud descended on her, whenever she thought of the bleakness of her old mountain home, and nobody left but old crones she did not recognize; all her lovely companions, boys and girls, scattered over the face of the earth, and many a one of them under it, and under a foreign sky too.

'Well,' said Fenny, who knew all about these black moods, and was devoted to Mrs Pig, 'what are we all going to do now? Nothing?'

'Nudden,' intoned Hosannah, as it is were the 'amen' of a hymn.

'Oh, begod nudden,' said Donie, standing up on his toes.

'Nothing,' said Miss McLurry firmly. 'Let him make the next move.'

'He won't, you know,' said Fenny calmly. He looked at Mrs Pig, and took down a special bottle of very old brandy, which was as good as a vision of light for those plunged in darkness. It was a malady he well understood. He poured a finger of it out, sniffed the large glass he was warming, and leaned in through the hatch to give it to Mrs Pig. To mix this potion with even the best whiskey would be a disaster with ordinary people, but there were a special few, who could take it and recover their sense of life: and he judged Mrs Pig to be one.

'Here,' he said in a low voice, touching her shoulder with his finger, 'this is something special. It's not everybody's dose, but it'll set you up.'

Mrs Pig took the glass, held it firmly in her own grimy palms, swirled it slowly, and sniffed deeply. She expelled a breath of pure satisfaction, and began to sip with her dark eyebrows already beginning to draw apart. It was a pleasure for Fenny to watch her.

'An' ye never got to Paris, didya?' said Hosannah, looking at Miss McLurry.

'I decided as a patriotic Irishwoman, with a stake in the country — not like some, with barely a camp to their name — to buy my fashion in Dublin. Switzers, and Leons in Grafton Street, are every bit the equal of any Pawris house, and as for Miss Doran in Dawson Street, well she's way ahead of even the best French houses. I can go to Pawris, Miss Braiden, anytime I like.'

'So can I,' said Hosannah, recovering her old form. Fenny had taken good care not to mix any more brandy with her tea. 'I have a powerful imagination, though not, I'd be de first ta admit, anytin' as game ball as yours.'

Miss McLurry opened her mouth to make a full-lit reply, when the blast was taken out of her lungs by a sudden flurry in

the fog outside, followed by the opening of the street door, and
the entrance of half-a-dozen men all talking at the top of their
voices.

'We heard what happened — '

'So we came at wanst — '

'True for ye, Larry — '

'Does anywan want a pair o' hands with guns at the end o'
them — '

'Faithen I'd used a rope — '

'Such a way to treat decent, honest people that have been —'

'Hullo there, Fenny, set us up — '

'Good evening, Ladies — '

'Arrah, howarya, Donseen — '

'We're here to tell ye that the whole of Connaught Street — '

'And beyond — '

'Are behind ye in yer struggle with a foreigner, that's tuk the
law into his own hands — '

'What law — '

'True for ye — '

'Three Guinness is it, Larry?'

'Make it four, Fenny, we're parched with de damp, yah
yah — '

In they came, in little groups of two and three, until the shop
was full of men, all talking, drinking pints and shouting to
Fenny and Donie over the shoulders of one another. The smell
of cigarettes and pipe smoke began to take over from the cold,
clammy, bog-soaked scent of the fog; sweat was indicated, and
the curiously haunting smell of damp tweed.

'Let him do his worst, we'll see him.'

'They tried it in '98 — '

''98? For God's sake, they've been tryin' it since that aul
bitch that built the chapel in Clonmacnoise, the Devils-gill,
isn't that what she was — '

'They drove the earls out in 1603 — '

'An' very nearly did for us all be de famine — '

They milled about, some clutching glasses close to their
chests, others flourishing them aloft as they remembered 1916.
A few listened, nodding their heads now and then, as the talk
grew louder, and the dates more frequent.

Donie had joined the crowd of men, and was adding his voice
to the general din, shouting that he died for Ireland, like many

another in 1916. In the Cafe Royal, the three women sat in silence. Mrs Pig listened to the battle cries with a grim smile, and kept her eyes on the closed door. Miss McLurry closed and opened her eyes at intervals, sighed and shook her head. Hosannah had taken out her rosary, and was rattling it in her lap, occasionally muttering a prayer, and darting a quick eye at the hatch, behind which Fenny was hard at work, pulling pints, serving whiskies, and opening and closing the till. One of the neighbours had come behind, and was helping him with the serving, taking good care to hand the money for each to Fenny.

'Ye know,' said Mrs Pig quietly, speaking almost to herself, 'Donie is goin' to repeat all of this, dat he can remember, to someone in the hotel, who will then pass it on to Slyne. It's not a bad idea, it might frighten him off taking further action — not dat I think he'll take it anyway.'

'Why, Marcella?' said Miss McLurry anxiously.

'We haven't heard the whole of this yet, Sarah Jane, me bones tell me.'

'What do dey tell ye?' said Hosannah, with a last imploring look at the hatch. An answer to prayer, Fenny glanced in and caught it, he held out his hand for her cup, disappeared with it, reappeared a few moments later, to find that Hosannah had got to her feet, and was waiting at the hatch. When he handed her the cup, with a decent slosh of whiskey in the bottom, she invoked prayers on his head — 'provokin' heaven' she always called it herself — and promised him payment on her next pension day, and two candles to Our Lady.

'Thank you, thank you, said Fenny, with a sudden private smile for her. 'I know, I know.'

'Could I have de teapot please?' said Hosannah, still standing up when she turned from the hatch. By no manner or means was she going to bring the cup down level with the eyes of her two companions.

'Here,' said Mrs Pig, handing it up to her, 'it's a bit cool now, but I don't suppose you'll mind.'

'Cold tea is the best ting in de wurruld for ye,' said Hosannah, putting her cup down on the ledge, and taking her two slightly shaky hands to the large teapot. 'I always have it dis way meself.'

'Do you mean the tea, or the — ' Miss McLurry was

beginning, when she was silenced by a look and a tap on the arm from Mrs Pig. This was no time for petty spite.

'I can feel me heart and me soul swellin' within me, when I hear dem dates, and all the long litany of de martyrs of Ireland,' she said, in a low chanting voice. 'Me own brother dat was kilt in 1916, and all his comrades, even Connelly the communist, murdered be d'English only seventeen years ago. Sure de tears o' de widows an' mothers is hardly dry on their graves yet.' Then she listened to the voices of the men outside for a few moments, while Hosannah was able to take her place on the red plush bench, with her hard-earned cup of whiskey-tea clasped lovingly in her lap. She was delaying the pleasure of the first sip.

'An' yet,' went on Mrs Pig, 'me heart, and me eyes, and something in me guts is sad, for always we were got de better of — '

'Oh, no,' cried Miss McLurry, 'Ours is the first Catholic state in the whole world, since we got the running of it ourselves.'

'True for ye,' said Hosannah, having taken her first sip, 'shure, 'tis heaven on earth dat d'Irish do be lookin' for.'

'I never heard such rawmaeesh in me life!' said Mrs Pig, standing up. At that moment some one backed against the door, which swung in. Mrs Pig put up the palms of her hands, and buffered him skilfully, giving him a fine push out into the midst of the men outside. But while the door was open, she caught a glimpse, through a sudden parting of the drinkers, of Ellen alone behind her counter at the other end of the shop.

'Excuse me,' said Mrs Pig, going out of the Cafe Royal, and pointing a well-aimed shoulder at the mass of men outside. She cut through them like the prow of a powerful ship in thick, oily waters. Not a glass was spilled, not a drop driven to the rim, hardly a body was touched, as she made her way effortlessly towards her goal.

'Mrs O'Farrell,' she said in a low voice, leaning forward over the counter, 'I don't think ye ought to be here. No one is goin' to buy groceries at dis time of night. Are ye all right?'

'Oh, yes, Mrs Prendergast, I am, truly I am.' Ellen smiled, but she looked pale and blank, and had been staring in front of her, quite detached from the patriotic slogans and sentiments whirling in the air about her.

'All the same, ye ought to be outa dis. De smoke alone is bad

for ye, and dat awful fog outside. Here, give me dat teapot ye
have beside ye, and I'll bring it in to Gummy, she'll get you a
new pot, and you carry your tea bag with ye, come on now.'
Ellen got down slowly from her stool, heavy-eyed with
weariness, yielded up her precious pot to Mrs Pig and came
out from behind the counter, the big woman holding up the flap
to allow her to pass. Then she took her firmly by the arm, and
steered her to the door leading to the passage, the kitchen, and
the breakfast room.

Gummy was, as expected, in the passage, having retreated
from behind the tiny slit of door-and-post she always kept open,
to keep an eye on the shop whenever it was crowded.

'Oh, Mrs, ma'am,' cried Gummy, throwing up her hands, 'is
it tired y'are? Why didden ye call me, an' ida come out, here
gimme dat pot an' I'll get ye anudder.'

'I'm perfectly all right,' said Ellen, who had been taken a bit
by storm, and had been merely staring ahead blankly out of
sheer boredom. But now she suddenly felt very tired. 'Just a bit
tired. It was very good of you, Mrs Prendergast — '

'Ye must take care o' yerself, and rest plenty,' said Mrs Pig. 'I
know dere's nothin' wrong with ye, or I'd have one of dem
boyos out like spout for the doctor, but ye're better off in your
own room, especially as dis meetin' will go on all night.'

'Did ya ever hear such landwich?' said Gummy, looking
longingly at the door of the shop.

'Yes,' said Mrs Pig, making off.

When she got back to the Cafe Royal, Fenny was waiting for
her at the hatch, his head coming through, like a man in the
stocks.

'Is there anything wrong with Ellen?' he inquired anxiously.

'Nothin' dat couldn't have been put right be you at de time,'
replied Mrs Pig. 'She's all right, just tired. And who wouldn't
be, with all dis noise goin' on?'

'I thought you were enjoying that, Mrs P,' said Fenny with a
grin.

'Haven't you noticed dat God is always on the side of
d'English?' she said suddenly, her face dark and sad.

'Frequently,' said Fenny, who had heard his father say the
same thing.

'He has abandoned us,' went on Mrs Pig, 'turned His face
away.'

'That's a shockin' ting to say,' squealed Hosannah, taking her last sip of fluid. 'God is here beside us in de snug.'

'Think of our pure Catholic state,' said Miss McLurry in a shocked voice.

'I'm thinkin' of it,' said Mrs Pig grimly.

'Have another,' said Fenny, putting out his hand.

'Me, me!' screamed Hosannah.

'I suppose so,' said Mrs Pig, with a sigh.

The fog drifted away to be followed by rain. It was hardly possible to see one end of the bridge from the other, and people went about shapeless, turning their bodies this way and that to avoid the welting wind, and the thriving rain. Those who could, stayed indoors, and among the fortunate was Mrs Katherine Anne Daly, who had sat most of the day at her window, looking down at the less fortunate thumping by. It was now three days since Fair had written his letter to the people who had sold land to Slyne, and as yet Mrs Daly had not received one.

She knew of their contents, of course. She had had that from Donie, while pretending not to hear the recital, which included details of the measures to be taken by the land-owners to protect themselves. His own defence seemed a little crude, after hearing what the three Connaught Street women intended to do, so he suppressed it and gave their plans only, claiming naturally that it was he who had thought of them in the first place.

'About that booking from the Middletons of Harrow, who come every year, are you sure they wrote last week?' said Mrs Daly, as if she had never heard of her land being sold, or anyone else's either.

'Yes, ma'am,' said Donie sulkily, remembering that he had handed the letter to Mrs Daly himself, and had then taken it downstairs to Miss Mutton for a typed reply.

'Such nice considerate people, the Middletons, always write in November for next May. I wish there were more like them. By the way, Donie, if he's still in the hotel, would you knock on Mr Slyne's door, and ask him that I would like to see him with a cup of coffee.'

Donie, who had just brought up the coffee, knew that Mrs Daly would use her Crown Derby cups and saucers in the cupboard in her sitting-room. She rose from her chair, and took out another cup for the tray, while Donie was about his business.

The day after the letters had been sent out, Slyne had gone to Dublin, telling the office that he would be back in a few days, and had arrived just the night before. Everybody commented on the fact that he appeared completely unmoved by the whole affair. No sign of irritation, or worry, or a secret inner doubt — which Maisie Hound claimed to be able to divine — was seen or sensed by anyone. He remained calm, polite and unruffled. 'D'English never get cuffuffled', was Mrs O'Flaherty Flynn's verdict. 'Calm as bog water, wid three corpses beneath it.'

'Ah, Mr Slyne,' said Mrs Daly, after he had knocked and come in, 'I thought you might like to have a little cup of coffee — Bewley's best, you know — with me. You must get quite weary sitting in your own room, working at your papers.'

'I never get bored with figures,' said Slyne with a smile. He had a charming smile, which gave his pink face, lit by bright blue eyes, a guileless look. In spite of his heavy shoulders and slight jowl, he still retained the appearance of an over-grown schoolboy. Mrs Daly did not trust him even the seventh part of an inch. 'They're my hobby as well as my business, I really enjoy them.'

'How wonderful for you. Black or white?'

'White please, and one sugar. What lovely china you have, Mrs Daly.'

'My mother-in-law's. They do have a certain usefulness — mother's-in-law I mean.'

'Ha ha.'

He sat down lightly on one of her fine chairs, and gazed at her mildly for a moment, as he stirred his coffee. Mrs Daly, who could not bear the sight of such guile, looked out the window and shook her head. Then, fixing her features in a bland smile, which she believed was absolutely British, she shifted her seat a bit, and also changed her way of speaking. For some time now Mrs Daly had been reading a series of English novels by contemporary writers, dealing with the upper-middle, and lower-upper class strata of British society. She felt completely easy in the idiom, and had no doubt that it was the proper and only way to deal with her guest.

'Too tiresome, this business of the bog-land,' she murmured, using only the upper register of her voice, so that she sounded as if she had a bad chest cold, and was getting her voice through only with considerable shoving.

Slyne looked at her, and put down his cup. There was little else he could do, for the change from her normal, rather pleasant way of speaking was startling. He felt safer with his valuable cup — and Slyne knew the exact value of everything in that room — out of his hands. One never knew with the Irish: they might spring.

'I, of course, knew nothing at all about it, until Donie, who is such a *dreary* little man, positively shame-making at times, told me that he had actu-ally sold his wife's bit of bog to you. Is this correct, Mr. Slyne? One does so much want to know.'

Slyne blinked, and pressed the knot of his tie between his plump finger-tips. Mrs Daly was drawing the side of her hand, the one with the big ring, languidly across her forehead, sighing with half-closed eyes. All she needed, he thought, was a long cigarette holder. Curious that she had overlooked this prop.

'Yes,' he said.

'And, to my horror, he also informed me that he had sold a bit of land, the backside of my mother's estate, to you also.'

'Yes,' Slyne did not know quite where to look. He was not aware that the 'English upper classes' were so daringly frank in their language.

'Which, of course, the little off-sider had no authority from me to do. Too tiresome.'

'Oh.'

'So you *do* realize, don't you, how embarrassing all this has been for me. I am *rather* peeved with the little sod.'

'Yes, yes, of course.'

'That's pipping.' Mrs Daly laughed gaily, as all her tennis-playing heroines did, although she was apt to get their lingo just a little netted occasionally. 'So I'm off the list, mmn?'

'Mmn,' said Slyne, nodding his head sturdily.

'It's such a *bore* being reminded of poor Mummy's misfortunes. The less said of *that* the better. *Such* a story of rotten luck, an old family estate running down and down, until nothing was left, but nothing, except that blithering bog. Rather tragic don't you think?'

'Oh, yes rather.' Slyne shook his head, waited for the blood to leave it, and watched Mrs Daly looking at him with the tragic eyes of one who has seen well-bred, and properly registered horrors.

'So you are *not* buying this dotty piece of bog? Yes? No?'

'No.'

'Jolly good. Too kind.'

'Not at all.'

'I'm completely out of it?'

Slyne was now fit to speak again. He took out his handkerchief, dabbed at the corners of his mouth, and would have done the same for the corners of his eyes, if he had been alone.

'You mean that Donie sold the land without your consent, and you didn't sign the contract or receive the deposit?'

Mrs Daly looked at him with what she hoped were huge eyes of dismay, but she did not break; she held her head high, and was gallant.

'What contract?' she asked blandly.

'Oh, I see.' Slyne was getting more used to the idiom — not the English slang, which he thought peculiar — but the entire Irish idiom. Mrs Daly was quite prepared to swear that she had not signed her contract, had never received it, that it had been signed by Donie, who had obviously pocketed the money. When a claim as bare-tongued as this is made, Slyne knew that there was little one could do about it.

'Did you actually get a contract signed in my name?' demanded his hostess.

'I thought it was your name, naturally.'

'What cheek! What infernal cheek! Really one does not know what to say, does one?'

Slyne nodded.

'I rely upon you to see that I am not annoyed further by this tiresome business. Too silly.'

That daughter of hers everytime I see her I can feel myself weakening but I doubt if she sees me much taken up with herself besides she thinks I'm too old too old at thirty-five what age is she twenty twenty-one I'm really mad about her and it's utter madness I'd have to take her back to England and make her learn some sense and it'd never work besides what would old Marjorie say we've been together now eleven years and she doesn't want to marry me good old Marjorie fifty this year and not looking a day over my own age we're like an old married couple this lech for the Daly girl is pure middle-age and simple too I wouldn't stand her two months she's silly fundamentally but gorgeous absolutely gorgeous like a ripe peach an unfolding rose the first narcissus of the year all that and more and I'd be an absolute idiot to have anything further to do with her pity she's chaste that's the word not used much nowadays but my mother often said it pure she used to say too I don't know about Maud being pure that's a different thing I think she knows what it's all about and she had quite a corrupt little mind her mother's daughter in this and oh then there's the mother no I couldn't take that that's enough a tumble with Maud that would be nice but she'd have to be different and perhaps I'd like her less then what a lot of silly people me included for the moment

'I'll see Fair about it. You won't have to bother anymore.' He smiled and nodded, and Mrs Daly touched the rim of her cup with a spoon, listening to the clear little tinkle, with her head delightfully inclined as English ladies do. She smiled back, a gay wistful smile. Or so she thought.

'Are you absolutely set on keeping the land?' said Slyne casually.

'Why, is there something under it?' she snapped back, all gentility forgotten. 'Why do you ask that?'

'I'm just trying to save you from embarrassment,' said Slyne smoothly.

By jove that was a near one fast she is and keen I should have known that the speed of it.

'What sort of embarrassment?'

'Well, I suppose the others believe that you've sold your land in the same way as they did — well, not in the same way, since you had nothing to do with it personally — but they might think it odd if you repudiated it now. And then, to be tricked by Donie — ' he let his voice drop on the name, giving the effect of being too embarrassed to go on. There was no need to look at Mrs Daly. Her furnishings would do. The carpet alone was worth a fortune, and he would have loved to own the eighteenth century break-front book case, and all of the other George III furniture. He was not interested in china or delft, however English and old, but his soul lusted for the brass-studded library chair.

'Of course Donie must be spoken to, and severely. The stinkin' little cur, you could twist his backside up a round his neck, and no one would know the difference. Holy God!' Mrs Daly was *'ruz'*, as Donie himself would say, and as a result became far more vocal, and infinitely more colourful.

'He was very anxious to sell the land, his wife's land, and no doubt he thought it a good price. Perhaps unthinkingly he might have suggested that you do the same with your end of the estate.'

'Faithen, you might be right.' She looked at him sharply. He was gazing at the library chair, and gently stroking his blond moustache, something he almost never did. He might have been a connoisseur of women, admiring a beautiful face. 'Half the time I don't be listening to him at all — how could I, and all I have to do!'

'Indeed Mrs Daly, you carry a heavy responsibility.'

'Heavy? It isn't even a load. It's pullin' me down from the front, and blindin' my eyes with dust. It's a vocation, that's what it is, a charge from God, and sometimes I feel like a camel dragged along the desert — with the hump under her chin.'

'I think perhaps it might be better for you to let things lie as they are,' said Slyne softly. 'I'll go ahead with the charges —'

'You mean you're going to issue writs? The Lord save us.'

'Yes, I've given them seven days' notice to return the money.' He paused for a moment to let that sink in before going on in his flat, toneless business voice. 'You will have noticed that you have not got a letter from Fair —'

'I should think not indeed, and you staying here with every luxury for half nothing.'

Slyne looked at the blue-white cut glass hanging from the centre of the ceiling, old Waterford, blinking with ease like cats lying in a warm hall. He thought of his own room, and the table that shuddered and collapsed under his eyes. He said nothing.

'Am I to get one?' said Mrs Daly, when the silence had become ominous, as Slyne intended it should.

'No, of course not. I wouldn't embarrass you for the world. And besides, perhaps I half-guessed the circumstances. So for this reason, it might be better to leave very well alone. We'll just let the matter drop.'

'Could I have the contract back?' said Mrs Daly eagerly.

'I doubt if Mr Fair would agree, while the others are under threat of writs. Besides — ' he paused and flicked a crumb from his trouser knee, 'there is the question of the money paid. You know how solicitors are about that. He will expect it to be repaid.'

'Well, let Donie dribblin' Donnelly pay it, he has his pocket well lined for years from the hotel, and all that's in it. I only keep him outa charity, and his poor demented wife, and the onrush of children she has.'

'Of course, of course. You must keep out of it. I'll speak to Fair.'

'And I'll knock the table you broke off your bill,' responded Mrs Daly generously. 'And give you commercial rates, although you represent no company.'

'A private person merely,' murmured Slyne, touching his moustache again. Mrs Daly had not noticed this growth much before, so fine and delicate it was upon his ruddy face, but now she found it fascinating, and began to think that Slyne was a fine figure of a man, and had never mentioned a wife. It had always been her ambition to get Maud married to an Englishman of property, related if possible, to the land.

'Too kind,' murmured Mrs Daly, her wits now cool again after the first principle, that of money, had been set to rights. But she was not left in possession of herself, an ancient and favourite burden, for very long. She was working her way round to Maud — 'sweet child' — when there was a sudden thudding at the door, as if someone were scrabbling at it, instead of knocking. Before Mrs Daly or Slyne had time to do anything, it burst open to reveal Donie, with his hair on end, his hands hanging down beside him, with the fingers spread out stiffly, and his face as pale as that of a white horse.

'Donie!' Mrs Daly crossed her hands over her heart, while horrid thoughts ran through her head. A fire, a plague of rats, a gunman found asleep in one of the rooms, with a machine gun beside him on the pillow, a wall collapsed, Mrs O'Flaherty Flynn abducted —

'It's Hamlet,' gasped Donie, taking a few tottering paces forward, and appearing very unsteady on his feet.

'Have you been drinking, Donnelly?' said Mrs Daly crossly. Such a figure to make, while she was engaged in such delicate negotiations.

'I wish ta God I wus, oh me heart me heart, what colour am I?'

'What is it?'

'Oh, missus, ma'am, it's Hamlet, poor liddle Hamlet, I'm after findin' him in his hole — dead!'

'What!' Mrs Daly shot up out of her chair as if she had been propelled. 'He couldn't be, the Brothers assured me he was healthy. Did he do himself in?'

'No, no, he jus' died. He's curled up down dere in his liddle hole, as stiff as a gun, wid his head on his hands as peaceful as a liddle angel, O God forgive me for ever sayin' a hard word agin' him.'

'I'll go down and see,' said Slyne, as he walked quickly to the door. Mrs Daly made no effort to stop him. This was something she would prefer not to see, until the cause was ascertained. She went to her cabinet and took out a bottle of whiskey, filled a glass and handed it to Donie. He was shaking so hard that he had to grasp it in his two hands, but even this did not prevent him slopping a few drops on his brown jacket, when he took the healing mixture from his lips.

'God bless ya,' he gasped.

'How did it happen? Sit down, Donie, not on that chair, it's too delicate, on the strong one inside the door. Well?' Mrs Daly remained standing, nor did she join Donie in a drink. Death or no death, that was unthinkable.

'He wus all ride dis mornin' cos I called him, an he did de shoes, an' brought up de breakfasts to you and Miss Maud.'

Mrs Daly nodded. Guests were not served breakfasts in bed in The Duke of Clarence.

'He seemed all right then,' she said. 'I didn't notice anything. Of course he's a silent boy.'

'Wus,' corrected Donie mournfully. 'He'll never be silent agin, or run messages, or do all de tings he used to do — '

'Well, obviously,' retorted Mrs Daly, adding quickly: 'Lord have mercy upon him.'

'Amen, amen, and may de Lord forgive me all the tings I said to him, for he wus a strange boy.' Donie sniffed and took another magic draught. Mrs Daly's private whiskey was famous, and generally only available at funerals, or visits from friends who had had a death in the family. Mrs Daly's death potion.

'Amen, amen,' said Mrs Daly impatiently. 'But how did it happen?'

'Oh, missus, ma'am, I open de door of his hole — '

'His quarters,' snapped the mistress of the house.

'His quarters ony half an hour ago, less, lemme see, id wus — '

'Yes, yes, and you saw?'

'Ad first I tot he wus asleep, lyin' curled up dere in his liddle hole — '

'Yes, yes,' Mrs Daly was beginning to despair of ever getting anything out of Donie. He was probably waiting for another glass, before descending to sober terms. Just as he opened his mouth there was another knock on the door. Mrs Daly said 'come in', and the door opened to reveal Maisie Hound, standing with her hands clasped over her stomach and her eyes rolled upwards.

'The Angel of Death has entered into this house,' she intoned.

'I know,' said Mrs Daly, 'but how did it happen?'

'Oh, oh, murder, murder, mudder — ' moaned Donie.

'Be quiet, Donie.'

'For death is come up into our windows,' went on Maisie. 'It is entered into our palaces — '

'Where is the boy now?' said Mrs Daly.

'To cut off the children from without,' went on Maisie, 'and the young men from the streets.'

'Oh, for heavens sake — ' burst out Mrs Daly, pushing Maisie out of her way. 'I'll go and find out for myself.'

Going downstairs she found Maud ready for her. She had waited for her mother, and now they came down into the hall together.

Slyne had been on the Western Front in 1916, and when he saw Hamlet, lying as Donie had described him, in his little cupboard under the stairs, he knew he was dead, but not probably for very long. He touched his wrist, his forehead and the side of his neck. The boy was lying on a heap of newspapers, overlaid with an old coat, fully dressed and with his eyes closed.

Misses Mutton and Cutlet were behind when Slyne turned around.

'I saw him go down this way about an hour ago,' ventured Miss Mutton. 'The Lord save us and bless us and preserve us and — '

'How did he look?' said Slyne.

'The same as usual,' put in Miss Cutlet, who had been at the reception also when Hamlet passed by. 'Oh, the poor child, God help us all. What are we going to do?'

'Ring for the doctor and tell him to get the ambulance, and inform the police. Hurry.'

The two girls were gone on their errand when Mrs Daly and Maud arrived. Mrs Daly took a quick look and turned away in the direction of the office. Maud came forward, a curiously eager look in her eyes. It gave Slyne an opportunity to grasp her arm, firm and plump and delicious under his grasp. As he leaned, he felt the rounded edge of her breast: it was for him a moment of sheer ecstasy, which he felt might have extended into a sort of trance-like state, if the contact had lasted longer. But after looking down at Hamlet for what seemed all too short a time, during which Slyne could feel her heart beating fast, and her whole body shiver and tremble under his arm, she turned back and took her arm away.

There were tears in her eyes, and her small red mouth trembled.

'Oh, it's so terribly sad,' she whispered. 'I shall remember this all my life.'

Slyne thought that a curious remark to make, but he was interrupted by the flurry of Mrs O'Flaherty Flynn's arrival, followed meekly by a trembling Maureen Cox. Large as she was, and forever complaining of pains in her legs, among other spots, Mrs O'Flaherty Flynn dropped to her knees with the agility of a young nun, leaned into Hamlet's cupboard, and began to whisper into his ear.

'What's she doing?' said Slyne, touching Maud's superb arm again. He had never felt so totally entranced in his life; it was rather like a spasm of pleasure, indefinitely prolonged. He would never forget this moment either.

'Saying the Act of Contrition,' whispered Maud, allowing his hand to warm against her arm.

Then Mrs O'Flaherty Flynn drew back, a rosary bead appearing miraculously between her fingers, and let out a long, shivering wail, the like of which Slyne had never heard in his life before, not even on the Western Front. It was the beginning of the age-old Irish caoine, the keen for the dead.

Mrs Daly suddenly reappeared when the wail reached her ears.

'That's enough of that,' she said in a voice she had never used to address Mrs O'Flaherty Flynn before. 'We don't know how long he's dead, and the spirit may not have left him yet. That keening will frighten the angels away, so stop it.'

Mrs O'Flaherty Flynn stopped it abruptly, and gave her employer a rare apologetic look. Mrs Daly acknowledged it with a slight inclination of her head, and left again immediately.

'Lord forgive me,' whispered the cook to Maureen Cox, who was at her side, 'I never taught, I didden tink. O pray God I didden disturb de spirrut.'

'Of course you didn't, Mrs O'Flaherty Flynn,' whispered Maureen gently in her ear, 'Wouldn't the Lord know yer grief? An' spirruts are not that aisily frikend.'

'God bless ya, Maureen, for yer a good girleen, an de Lord will answer yer prayers.'

There was a bustle at the bottom of the stairs as the doctor arrived, accompanied to everyone's amazement by Willie Wickham. He followed Dr Dobbs, a small energetic man of hard on eighty, with thick grey hair, a limp from a bullet in Egypt, and a pair of very bright green eyes.

He knelt down by the body in the cubby hole, conducted a brief examination, stood up, took his stethoscope from his ears, and shook his head.

'The Guards are on their way with the priest. He's been dead about two hours. Better have him removed when the Guards are finished with him.'

'What are they goin' to do wid him?' said Maureen Cox with great courage, the inspiration of fright, ignorance and fondness. Everyone looked at her except Dr Dobbs, who was looking at his watch.

'They will want to know whether he was murdered or not,' Willie said wildly.

'Merciful hour,' whispered Mrs O'Flaherty Flynn.

'Ah,' said Maureen wisely, looking at the thin body curled as if in sleep, 'He was never murdered, but be life.'

Dr Dobbs put back his watch, and touched the great gold chain that hung from one waistcoat pocket to another.

'What's your name, child?' he said kindly.

'Maureen, Doctor Dobbs, sir.'

'Well, Maureen, you're a wise young woman. Ah, here come the police, and Father Raft.'

The two policemen spoke briefly to the doctor, and then Father Raft, a young thin man with a dark thin face, and very small feet and hands, moved towards the corpse, put on his stole, and took out the little silver box in which he kept the sacred oil for anointing. Suddenly, before he had time to begin, Mrs O'Flaherty Flynn whispered into Maureen's ear, and the girl got up and ran towards the kitchen. The priest began the abbreviated anointing, which is given to the lately dead, but before he had finished, Maureen had returned with a lighted candle in a silver holder. She stood by the cubbyhole, with the flickering candle in her hand until the priest had finished.

He took off his stole, rolled it up, kissed it and put it in his pocket together with the silver box.

'Good girl Maureen,' he said with a sudden wide grin, which gave his thin, Italian-like face a curious but very potent charm. 'It's nice that the poor boy should have a candle, God rest him.'

'Amen,' said Mrs O'Flaherty Flynn, still muted, but a little more at ease than she had been with Dr Dobbs. 'We allas keep wan in de kitchen in case any of us die sudden like, and see how it came in useful, be de grace a' God. O de poor, poor craytur, to come inta life unwanted, an to lave it unloved. Oh God grant he's wid his mudder in heaven dis day, an' she reformated.'

'And if she isn't — in heaven I mean, she may still be living — there is the Mother of us all waiting there for him,' said Father Raft.

'True for ye, Fadder,' nodded Mrs O'Flaherty Flynn.

The two policemen, who had taken off their caps and knelt on one knee while the priest was anointing the dead boy, had got to their feet, replaced their caps, and were again talking in low voices to Dr Dobbs. He turned round after a few minutes and spoke to Maud, who all this time had been standing against the wall of the passage, with Slyne by her side. He had withdrawn his arm from hers, but was standing very close to her.

'Natural causes,' said Dr Dobbs briskly, 'Heart failure — consumption — whatever. Now, where is he to go, the hospital or here?'

Maud looked at Slyne, who responded immediately.

'I'll go and ask Mrs Daly.'

'Don't be long. Stephen and Larry here — ' indicating the two guards — 'will carry him wherever you want.'

Slyne hurried off, while Mrs O'Flaherty Flynn began a

decade of the rosary. Maud took a tiny handkerchief out from her breast, where it had nestled cosily inside the opening of her frock, and pressed it against her mouth.

For a few moments the little group stood there, quiet and still; the small white-haired doctor, the two tall policemen, Mrs O'Flaherty Flynn on her knees with her rosary, murmuring the Hail Maries, with Maureen standing beside her, holding the lighted candle in one hand. A little to the back, Maud stood with tears in her eyes, while she gazed as if hypnotized at the frighteningly still figure, curled up in the cupboard surrounded by the junk of years.

Slyne came back just as Dr Dobbs was beginning to fidget.

'Well?' he demanded.

'The hospital,' said Slyne, 'and before the ambulance comes, he's to be put in the downstairs bedroom, at the end of the passageway there.'

'Do you two men need help?' said Slyne to the Guards.

'No, sir, he's not stiff yet, the doctor says. We'll carry him easily on the level to the Lock Hospital.'

'The what?' said Slyne.

'A nickname for the downstairs suite with the bath,' whispered Maud.

'Oh.'

The men went forward and lifted Hamlet out of his 'quarters', wrapping an old coat round his middle, which one of them supported, and made off slowly with their pathetic burden. Mrs O'Flaherty Flynn began to cry, silently except for a few suppressed sobs, and Maureen, still holding the lighted candle, followed the procession with her eyes, and when it disappeared around the corner, left her post and followed it, carrying her candle. Mrs O'Flaherty Flynn got to her feet, holding out a hand to Slyne who assisted her.

'Thank ye, sir,' she said.

'Does this mean he's going to the morgue?' said Slyne.

'Yes,' said Dr Dobbs, again looking at his watch. 'I must be off. Keep an eye on that fellow Wickham: I was down in the club for the past few nights playing billiards, and I managed to sober him up yesterday. He came in here with me, oddly enough. Will someone go and see that he's not drinking again in the bar? He promised me.'

The doctor went off, firm-stepped and sturdy; as kindly and

generous a man as ever lived, as they all knew there, and all through the town.

'God bless 'im, and keep 'im, an lave 'im active for a hunread,' said Mrs O'Flaherty Flynn, as she waddled off in the direction of the Lock Hospital.

Maud moved away from Slyne, but before she left she gave him a smile, small but infinitely touching, rested her fingers on his forearm for a moment, and was gone.

She found Willie in the bar, standing in the middle of the floor looking down at his shoes.

'Where is the poker school?' he said to Maud, as she came in.

'Shut down, I suppose, when they heard of the death.'

Miss Mutton, who had slipped into the bar to get a drink for the Guards, could not help interrrupting. She prided herself on her knowledge of the history of the hotel.

'The moment they heard it, they laid down their cards, ordered a double brandy each, stood up and toasted the dead in silence, as is correct, and then went off. It has happened six times since the school began. Two British officers died here, one a suicide in 1891, the other in the dining-room, of a stroke in 1905. Then of course there were Mrs Daly's father and mother-in-law, 1920 and 1922, and two guests, one out there in the hall, of heart failure, in 1908, and another, an American, of the same, at the bottom of the stairs. The school toasted them all and adjourned. Isn't that nice? I must be off now, terrible about poor little Hamlet. I'm not believing it yet, see you in a minute, Mr Wickham.' And off she went to serve the Force.

'What are you doing in here, Willie?' said Maud, rather severely.

'It was the only place I could think of coming, when I heard of what happened. Then the school left.'

'Not to have a drink — ?'

'Oh, no, Maud, I'm cured for good. Dr Dobbs did it down in the club, talked me out of it, and he *elephants* himself. But he said something no one ever told me before.' He blushed, as he did fairly easily, and fiddled with his tweed cap.

'And what was that?'

'Well, he told me I'd never be able to have children, if I continued to drink. I mean to say — '

'Imagine! Don't you want to see Hamlet, Willie?'

'Oh, no, no.' Willie moved back from his beloved and stared at her with frightened eyes.

'But Willie, Mrs O'Flaherty Flynn will have him laid out beautifully in about twenty minutes, you must go and see him, we're all going. You mustn't miss it.'

'No, Maud, no thanks, I'd rather not.'

Maud was silent for a moment, then she gave Willie a very curious look. Saved from drink he might be, and that was good, but it was beginning to appear to her that he had a much worse fault than that.

'You don't mean to tell me, Willie Wickham, that you're afraid of a corpse?'

'Of course not.' Willie gave his Lock's cap some of the roughest mauling it had ever received, crushing and uncrushing it between his sweating palms.

'Then come with me and say a little prayer for poor Hamlet, before he goes off to the morgue.'

'The morgue!' Willie shivered, and backed against the wall.

'You *are* afraid, Willie,' cried Maud with reddened cheeks, 'Oh, my goodness, I never heard anything so awful in my whole life. Why I was brought to see my first corpse when I was six years old, and I wanted to sit up on the bed beside it. I never *heard* of a man being afraid like that. You can't mean it, Willie, it must be the lack of drink.'

'No, it isn't, that doesn't affect me at all. But my English aunt — '

'The one that married the Lord and became a pervert?'

'She was *not* a pervert. She did *not* change her religion, she remained a Catholic. Well, she told me that it was extremely bad form to make a habit of visiting corpses. She said it was an insult to their peace of mind, trooping in around them like that. She said that they should be treated with more respect.'

'Willie Wickham, you *are* scared, I know you are. Are you coming in to see Hamlet, or aren't you?'

Willie twisted his cap again miserably; he had gone quite green in the face, and knew that if he saw the remains he would be sick.

'Dr Dobbs told me — ' he began. But Maud had seen and heard enough to turn away in disgust, and was just about to hurry away from the bar, when Willie made one last desperate effort to retain her.

'But I'm sober Maud, I'm sober and enjoying it. I mean, I feel absolutely no interest in drink at all. It was Dr Dobbs did it, and it's a kind of a miracle.'

Maud turned and looked at him. Certainly he looked well, and was, except when rotten drunk, always a fine figure of a man, but not, in her mind, finer than Slyne, who most certainly was not afraid of the dead, in spite of being English.

'If you're feeling all that well, it's a wonder you wouldn't spend a few minutes at the half-cock wake of a poor, harmless boy, who is gone so suddenly and so sadly to his Maker.'

'I hardly knew Hamlet,' said Willie truthfully. 'I can't be expected to feel anything but — ' he paused to search for a word, but it was not necessary.

'Heartless too, as well as being afraid,' said Maud scornfully. She looked at Willie slowly from the top of his head to the toe of his hand-made shoes, contempt following her gaze like an evil spirit.

'Dr Dobbs told me I wasn't to subject myself to anything that might upset me. That was very important, he said, and — '

'Are you, or are you not coming to see Hamlet? Mrs O'Flaherty Flynn and Maureen will have washed him and set his face, and laid him out proper by now. I'm sure he'll look lovely.'

The description of the process of laying out a corpse made Willie want to be sick. He turned pale and opened his mouth, but it was too dry. He closed it and swallowed. But Maud was already walking from the bar. She had learned her lesson. English aunts, with a title and loads of diamonds, were no good to her, neither were Willie's broad Westmeath acres and thoroughbred horses, if he was so unnatural as to be afraid of a corpse.

She did not go immediately to the Lock Hospital, but ran upstairs to be with her mother, as she always did in moments of crisis.

Mrs Daly was sitting in an armchair beside the fireplace, not as usual by the window. What she had to decide upon was not something she wanted to be seen doing.

'Ah, Maud, I've been thinking about poor Hamlet.'

'Willie — ' began Maud.

'Later, later, dear. First of all Hamlet has to be buried, hasn't he? And a mass said for him.'

'I suppose so, I never thought of that.' Maud's excitement subsided, and she sat down on a low chair near her mother, full of attention and interest.

'When the Brothers of Mercy were handing him over to me, they said they had no knowledge at all of his parentage. He was picked up in a doorway in Mullingar, and brought to their House outside the town.'

'Mullingar,' murmured Maud, 'a wicked, wicked place.'

'Be that as it may, he has no one belonging to him, not even in Mullingar, so far as we know. So, who buries him? Who has to pay for the mass?'

'You, I suppose, Mama dear,' said Maud, completely at sympathy with her mother, as she was more often than not. She only called her 'mammy' to tease her, and worse when she was out of humour with her.

'Yes, of course, it's your poor old mama who has to foot the bill, as she has to always, you'd think I was made of money. And I hardly got more than a few years work out of Hamlet, Lord have mercy on him — '

'Amen,' murmured Maud, closing her eyes and joining her hands.

'Then he drops dead like this, after all the good food he had access to in this place. The Brothers, holy and all as they may be, took me in. They sold me a pup, that's what they did. And since I'm an honest woman, I say what I think and not wait, like one of the hypocrites, until after the funeral. I'm stuck with the cost of the whole thing.'

'People have to be buried by the County,' suggested Maud gently.

Mrs Daly shook her head slowly, and gave Maud a meaningful glance, which could, as is always the case with such looks, mean anything.

'That wouldn't do,' she said, patting her pearls, 'People would talk. Besides, I was never mean.' She paused here for a nod from Maud, but did not get it. 'No, he will have to be brought to the church from the morgue, and a proper mass said. Not a Requiem High Mass, of course, since he has no relatives. A low mass will do quite well.'

'But where is he to be buried, Mama dear? He has no plot, and no one will let him into theirs, and the cost of a new plot — '

'Well, that's something I'll have to see the Brothers about. I

wired Brother Angel this morning to come at once, and he rang
up — Miss Cutlet took the call — to say he'd be here
tomorrow.'

'Brother Angel,' said Maud, with a faint smile. She had
never forgotten the glimpse she had got of Brother Angel of the
Brothers of Charity, as a young girl, when he had called to
collect for the orphanage. A flash of pure gold, white, and light
tan: he was outrageously handsome, and when she met him
socially in her mother's room, just before Hamlet was delivered
to them, he was even more beautiful. She sighed and looked at
her mother with a tender little inclination of her head.

'I know all about that, Maud. I was even a little bit taken
myself, besides they're not ordained, the Brothers, you know,
and I must confess that never in my life have I seen such a
charmer as Brother Angel. But he'll bury the boy nevertheless,
or I'll know what for.'

'You mean send him back to Mullingar? That's an idea.
After all, the Orphanage was his home, more or less. But who's
going to pay?'

'Oh, me, of course, yours truly, Katherine Anne Daly, who
pays for everything, all the time, for everybody. But I'll make
him get a special price from an undertaker in Mullingar, where
the Brothers have the eejits over there strangled with appeals,
tickets for stale geese, and ordinary daylight robbery, hand to
hand. If I get one of the Bridgeford undertakers, they'll see me
coming, and charge the earth. The ambulance will take him to
the morgue, and I'll pay for the hearse to the church, but from
there on the Brothers will have to take over. It isn't good
enough. By the way, did Mr Slyne say anything to you?'

'Anything what?' Maud opened her eyes wide, and dropped
her lower lip, a loose, sliced cherry.

'I don't think he's married,' said Mrs Daly, patting her
pearls again. She had, earlier, almost immediately after she
could get away from Hamlet's body, changed into a dark frock
and, of course, she would not think of wearing anything but
pearls with it. Gleaming softly, pink-white and comfortable,
heavy and expensive, warm and companionable, diamond-
clasped and well insured, they made up to her for many of the
misfortunes and disappointments of life: easier to keep than a
dog, warmer and closer than a cat, and representing money
appreciating, instead of leaking out as might happen with a pet

orphan, over which she could always do a deal with Brother Angel. Plenty of widows had dependent, clean and well-behaved young men about the place, who greatly lightened their days. No, pearls were best.

'I expect he'll tell me,' said Maud, giving her mother all the information she needed.

Mrs Daly rose, and picked up a small hand-sewn purse from the table beside her.

'I'm bringing down my beads to say a decade for Hamlet. Mrs O'Flaherty Flynn and Maureen will stay of course, and the two girls from the office will stay also, until the ambulance comes, but you and I must also do a little vigil. It's only fitting. Have you your beads, my love? Good.'

In the Lock Hospital, the cook and her assistant were sitting at either side of the bed, admiring Mrs O'Flaherty Flynn's handiwork. Fortunately Hamlet had died with his eyes closed, but his mouth had been open, and an expert job of modelling the still warmish skin with the utmost care had produced a fine result.

'Issen 'e a lovely corpse, ma'am?' said Mrs O'Flaherty Flynn, as her employer and her daughter came in. Immediately, Mrs Daly realized that the dead Hamlet had scored over her once again.

'Beautiful,' she replied, holding back the tears, which like all the other women in the hotel she was able to shed at will. She had intended to weep for exactly three minutes at Hamlet's bed: more would have seemed a trifle insincere. 'But the habit — ' she looked at Mrs O'Flaherty Flynn, who clasped her hands over her heart and inclined her head to one side, while the tears started to form in her eyes.

'De Third Order, ma'am. I always keep wan in de kitchen, in case anywan drops dead in d'otel, doan I, Maureen? Dat's right. An' isn't his mout' beeootfully closed an' all — '

'But the ambulance, Mrs O'Flaherty Flynn, it'll be here any minute, and you have laid him out as though for an all night wake here.'

'Oh, miss, ma'am, shure ye wudden grudge de use of a room to de poor misfortunate boy dat's dragged up ta heaven in his sleep. No mudder or fadder to mourn him, nuttin' in dis wurreld, an nowan to give 'im de love of a mudder, O me heart is hangin' down wid grief for 'im, so id is, issen id, Maureen?'

'Yes, Mrs O'Flaherty Flynn, indeeden it is.'

Mrs Daly might have sensed Maureen's feelings, for she immediately gave in to Mrs O'Flaherty Flynn, and allowed a few tears to cloud her sharp eyes. It was bad enough for Hamlet to die in the broom cupboard, but to keep him in one of her best rooms, with bath, laid out in a correct habit, and covered with fine linen, with two holy candles burning in heavy silver holders, all this would do much to quench the bog-fire talk that would spring up about his death. She would keep him here until the following afternoon, when he would be brought to church at her expense, but after that, Brother Angel would have to take over.

Mrs Daly got down carefully on her knees by the side of the bed, touched her rosary against Hamlet's bone-cold hands, and murmured in a prayerful voice:

'Of course he must be kept here, the poor boy, when I think of the way those Brothers must have brought him up to leave him so delicate, but someone will have to telephone and cancel the ambulance — '

At that moment Maureen, Maud and Mrs O'Flaherty Flynn glanced at the door, behind which the murmur of male voices could be heard.

'They're here,' said Maureen, tripping round the bed to open the door. When she did, the two ambulance men, carrying their stretcher, walked into the room.

'Well,' said one of them, a craggy veteran of the Boer War and the Connaught Rangers, 'ye have him greatly tarted up for lyin' down on a slab in de morgue. Harry, will ye look.'

'Very fancy, George,' commented Harry, who had not seen Mrs Daly yet, and was just about to remark that the auld bitch was losing her marbles, when that lady got to her feet.

'It's all right, men,' she said quietly, 'I'm sorry that you should be brought out prematurely, indeed brought out at all, but Dr Dobbs ordered the deceased to the morgue, and the message had been sent out before I heard about it. Naturally, I want to give the poor boy a decent send-off, so we're keeping him here in a prayerful wake. It's the least we might do. And Maureen,' she said, lowering her voice out of respect for the dead, but not too low, since the ambulance men were meant to hear it, 'bring in two drinks for the men, whiskies of course.'

The men put aside their stretcher, and each went down on one knee. Then Harry got up suddenly, took the sprinkler from the bowl of holy water on the night table beside the candle, shook it vigorously all over Hamlet, and handed it to George, who got up and did the same. Then they both went down on one knee again.

Presently Maureen returned with two well-filled glasses of whiskey, and Mrs Daly judged it a good time to excuse herself and Maud for a short while. The ambulance men got to their feet as the ladies went out. The two girls from the office, as Mrs Daly always called Misses Mutton and Cutlet, had not yet made their appearance. They would fill in on the watch, when the cook and Maureen began to wilt.

George and Harry seated themselves on two chairs pulled up against the wall. For a long time they sipped their whiskies, and stared at the corpse. Mrs O'Flaherty Flynn and Maureen did the same, all of them having a trancelike look in their eyes. This was going to be a real wake, and every ritual must be observed.

'Well,' said Mrs O'Flaherty Flynn at last, and with a little hesitation, for she knew she was speaking to experts, 'wad do ye tink a him? Me an' Maureen laid 'im out.'

'Mmn, not bad,' said George holding his head to one side. 'What would you say, Harry?'

'The same. How old is he, Mrs?'

'Barely seventeen, de craytur, a poor orphant.'

'Looks a bit seedy to me,' said George. 'Musta died of a weak heart.'

'Imagine, an' we never knew,' ventured Maureen.

'I saw young fellas die of fright in Spion Kop, and even in Mafeking,' said George, holding his glass on his knee and inspecting Hamlet's face closely. 'Well, maybe not fright, but a kinda over-excitement, and eagerness. Ye get a lotta dat in d'army, in my day anyways. I dunno if dey're as eager today. So he died in his health, did he?'

'Yes,' said Mrs O'Flaherty Flynn, 'an dussen he make a beeootiful corpse? I fixed his mout' mesel'.'

'Not bad,' said Harry.

'I've seen worse, and dey were healthier than him, when dey conked out, young soljers with red cheeks, and dey'd lie like dat for a coupla hours, lookin' like dey wus asleep. But dis fella doesn't look very healthy to me.'

'He wus always pale, an' he had dem sunken eyes, dark like, if dat's what ya mane,' said Mrs O'Flaherty Flynn, a bit nettled in spite of the men's superior experience. After all, she had laid out, washed and habited a good many corpses in her own day.

'His temples is sunk in,' said Harry. 'Sometin' awful.'

'He had them hollows always,' said Maureen loyally. 'I tink he looks lovely.'

'Well, tastes differ,' said George, knocking back his glass. 'Come on Harry, d'aul bus is parked outside, people will be wonderin'.'

'Will we tell dem there's a wake on?' said Harry, putting down his empty glass on the floor with a regretful sigh, 'Ye'll want somewan to let ye sleep for an hour or two during de night.'

'Yes, a' course, tell anywan ye see, and come back yersels if ye can. We'll have de sideboard a bit better organizered in a few hours. Dis took us be surprise, but when de girrels in d'office come in, me an' Maureen will set at makin' de sanwitches and cold mates.'

The two men picked up their stretcher and made off. They were too experienced campaigners to make a reply to Mrs O'Flaherty Flynn's invitation. But from the look in Harry's eye, it was clear to the women that if it got about that the refreshment was good, they'd be back to pay their respects.

Mrs Daly went over to the office and told Miss Mutton to write to their principal tea suppliers, Barry's of Cork and Musgraves of Belfast, requesting a half-chest each for several charities that were expected that winter. The same letter went to Jamesons, Powers, Williams, and Lockes of Kilbeggan, all distillers, and another, of course, to Arthur Guinness. Mrs Daly was a good payer (in cash), and she did not often make such requests which the brewery and distilleries received in their hundreds every day. When asked to contribute to the local bazaars and sales-of-work, Mrs Daly invariably sent some article of clothing belonging to her mother-in-law, who had a large wardrobe, and occasionally something of her own which she did not like. And she had taken the trouble of going on a few of the principal committees which ran these charitable affairs — attendance even at a few meetings a year saved her many donations. It was well known that committee members did not contribute anything to charity, beyond their work around a table, and occasionally at a parish kitchen, where tea was brewed and handed around, while tickets were being sold. But it was a long time since there had been a death at The Duke of Clarence; those of her husband, his father and mother had not required a wake, since her spouse had passed away in a Dublin nursing-home, and had come straight to the church, while her in-laws had both died before him. Hamlet's death, she knew, was a very special occasion; his youth, the circumstance, the necessity of not appearing mean, savage or hard-hearted was urgent. The whole street must be allowed to sit about his death bed, and the whole street, if necessary, must be offered refreshment. And there must be no stinting of it.

'Will I type the letters now, ma'am?' said Miss Mutton, who had not been a bit surprised by the order. After all, Mrs Daly was in effect still providing the tea and spirits. If she had not been such an old customer, with very good credit, these gifts would not be forthcoming in the first place. It was keen practice, but not exactly sharp.

'I think so, before people start coming in, I mean the neighbours.'

'Very well, ma'am.'

'Tell me, Miss Mutton, did you ever notice any signs of weakness in Hamlet?' Mrs Daly's relations with her office girls, who were also bar-maids, part-time cooks, and waitresses when the occasion demanded, was good. She was always careful to address them formally, and treat them with consideration whenever they wanted a day off, which was not often, since they had no place to go, and very much preferred to stay in the hotel in their free time, washing their undies, darning their cardigans, and shampooing their hair. A room of one's own with a bathroom down the corridor, together with the honour of being an official 'Miss', meant much to them, as Mrs Daly knew well.

'I thought he often looked very pale, and he sweated a lot sometimes,' said Miss Mutton after some thought, 'but he never complained of a pain or anything. It's very strange.'

'Very. The Brother in charge is coming tomorrow. They must know something, but they never told me. I don't think that was fair, do you, Miss Mutton?'

'Oh, no, ma'am, I do not.' Being taken into the confidence like this was very refreshing. But their conversation was interrupted by the arrival of two neighbouring women, Mrs Macken and Mrs Moore.

'You must have got a terrible shock, Katherine,' said Mrs Macken sympathetically.

'I could hardly believe it,' said Mrs Moore.

These two ladies went everywhere together, and always echoed each other's remarks. They were members of two of Bridgeford's oldest merchant families, very rich and very conservative. They understood Katherine Anne's dilemma perfectly, and were here to support her, if necessary; and also of course to perform one of the most important of the corporal works of mercy.

'He's in the new suite downstairs, I'll bring you along myself. Yes, of course I'm shocked. Completely unexpected. He must have had a weak heart.'

'A dreadful thing to do to you,' murmured Mrs Moore.

'Those Brothers —,' said Mrs Macken, shaking her head.

But others were moved in another way by the death of Hamlet. As in folklore, a figure with a lighted torch seemed to run down the street, touching each door with fire, to indicate in the depths of December that winter is on the turn, and the shortest day already gone; so too in Hamlet's case, something seemed to leap from house to house in Church Street and the narrow lanes leading off it, which touched the hearts of all the women and some of the men who lived there. To die so young and so unexpectedly, without ever knowing a father or a mother, struck a chord in the echo chamber of their memory. December was on them, and the shortest day still to come, but this boy had already served his shortest day, and the people responded to it.

And so, as the day wore on, heavy and dank and still, they came, all the names from that part of the town: the Hogans and the Sheffields and the Brownes and the Foys and the Curleys and the Maddens and the Prices and the Flemings and the Larkins and the O'Briens and the Campbells and the Farrellys and the Molloys and the Timons and the Burkes and the Horans and the Connells and the Sweeneys and the MacManuses, and this one, and that one, and dodder flowing, who were not born in the town.

But there was another aspect to Hamlet, which gradually became known, and which partly explained the large numbers who came to pray and watch by his bedside.

In the low archway of Court Devanish in the middle of the street, and leading to that lane behind the hotel, which Hamlet had negotiated so often in his errands to and from Connaught Street, which led also, straight back into the seventeenth century, Mrs Murphy said to Mrs Kelly —

'Lord have mercy on him and us all, and may he go flyin' through purgatory on a first-class ticket.'

'Amen. But wasn't he the boy, Lizzie, who used to run for old Mrs Collins of the Strand?'

'That's right, Bridie, d'ye know I never thought of it? 'Tis him, surely, and many's the message he ran for me too.'

'And me. Are ye going up to see him? I hear she has him grandly laid out in the Yanks sweetie downstairs.'

'The least she might do. Come on.'

It came out that Hamlet had indeed never refused to 'run a message' for the various old ladies who saw him passing, and called him to their doors. He was known as 'the boy from the Clarence', and few people outside the hotel called him Hamlet.

They gathered round now, as they had always done, to pray and pay honour to a departed one, who had done them all a good turn in his time; to touch his clasped fingers with their rosaries, and many to touch his white-cold forehead with their thumbs.

'So young, the creature, he might be an old man.'

'It's his eyes, those big dark sockets.'

'Like a Spanish painting.'

'Such an obliging young lad, God bless him.'

'May he open his eyes to the light.'

In the early hours of the morning, with a packed semi-circle of mourners seated round the bed saying the rosary, Mrs O'Flaherty Flynn and Maureen went back silently to the kitchen. It was lighted by one paraffin lamp, which the cook preferred to gas, and which gave off a low and flickering, but soothing glow. With the range damped down but alive, the kitchen was a place of friendly and well known shadows, comforting smells and, little creaking sounds, and a big stuffed sausage to keep out the draught from under the back door.

Maureen made tea, as they always did, straight into the cup, handed Mrs O'Flaherty Flynn's to her, and sat down on a stool beside the big old cane armchair. The table was littered with unwashed tea cups, and Maureen knew there were more in the dining-room, where Donie was dispensing the tea and spirits.

'Funny how much tea has gone, an' very little whiskey,' said Maureen after a suppressed yawn.

'An some aren't goin' to de dinin'-room ad all. I never taught dey'd turn up like dey did, ta honour him on his lass. Some a dem took noddin' ad all, it's a rale sign of honour.'

'Isn't it wonderful the way he ran messages for all,' said Maureen. The two women were whispering, and their voices sounded like the rustling of mice in the great kitchen, with its flickering paraffin light, and the one-eyed glow from its range. They had drawn close together instinctively, spoke between long silences, and when at last their tea was drunk, Maureen put the cups on the table, and took Mrs O'Flaherty Flynn's great rough hand in her own, as she perched on her stool.

'Old Mrs Collins had no pennies to give him, Maureen, dat's certain, nor a good many more I heard he ran messages for.'

'Old Mrs Browne gave him sixpence,' whispered Maureen proudly.

'Yes,' sighed Mrs O'Flaherty Flynn, and began to doze off.

Maureen sat open-eyed beside her and stared ahead, seeing nothing, thinking little, except that the image of Hamlet's gaunt little white face on his gleaming white pillow, lingered in her imagination, but she was bone tired and slump-backed. And presently two tears formed in her eyes, and rolled slowly down her face as it glimmered in and out of the feeble light.

The next day, the day of Hamlet's funeral, two men arrived in Bridgeford, one of whom, from Dublin, was to have a profound effect on the owners of the flooded fields, and on Slyne himself. The other was Brother Angel, who went directly to the hotel. He prayed for some time over Hamlet's body, and layed on his breast an envelope containing one hair of the founder of the Order's head, a privilege extended only to the Brothers themselves, and any orphan who happened to die in their care, or soon afterwards in tragic circumstances. He then asked for Mrs Daly, and was shown upstairs directly.

It was already afternoon, and he had timed his visit well. Mrs

Daly had slept late, after such a harrowing night, and did not appear in her sitting-room until after lunch. Hamlet would soon be coffined and brought to the church.

Brother Angel, named after Angelo Ralbo, who had been partly raised to the altar by Pope Pius X in 1908, was indeed a glamorous figure, tall, slim, and possessed of a face which would have made him a matinee idol, if he were that way inclined. He was in fact a strict celibate, a hard worker, a man of prayer, and in more ways than one an ornament of his Order.

After the preliminaries were over — all that could be said about Brother Angel's health, the general state of the Brotherhood, and the sadness of Hamlet's sudden death — they got down to essentials, like a dog burrowing through a sack of grain to get to a bone at the bottom.

'You must have known he had a weak heart when you gave him to me,' said Mrs Daly reprovingly.

'Yes, we did, but the doctor said that he was to lead a normal life; that he might live quite a long time —'

'How long?'

'Ten, twelve years, maybe more,' Brother Angel's brilliant blue eyes clouded a little. 'I was fond of the boy — we all were, but he was anxious to leave. And this was the best we could do at the time. You found him satisfactory?'

'Oh, quite, but if I had known — ' she pressed her lips together and frowned. 'It was a very big risk to hand him over to me.'

'Life is full of gambles, Mrs Daly. He might have lived. I can say no more for myself.' He looked at her with a fairly bold meaning in his face. It was not lost on Mrs Daly.

'Well, there's no use crying about spilled milk. I'm sorry about Hamlet — ' she suddenly stopped and turned aside, caught unawares by a ridiculous onset of tears, and a sudden palpitation of the heart.

Brother Angel looked at her mildly and waited for a minute to allow her to reset her face, a very important matter for Mrs Daly, as he well knew. And for all of us, alas, he said to himself.

'I put a small envelope containing a relic of Blessed Angelo into his hands, while I was downstairs,' he said presently, spreading out his large brown hands with fingers outstretched, like an amateur actor who feels he should mime everything he says. It was rather a habit with the good brother.

The effect on Mrs Daly was pre-electrical, more like a gas jet, hissing a little before lighting up.

'What sort of relic?' she said without any attempt to appear disinterested. She knew what Brother Angel was capable of doing.

'A hair from his head. Unfortunately they are very rare, since Angelo was quite bald when he died.'

'Is it going to be buried with him?' she inquired eagerly.

'I think it is only right, don't you? After all, the boy was brought up under the patronage of Blessed Angelo, and of our founder Saint Pius Arlotti. I intended it for burial with poor Hamlet, and our Provincial gave permission.'

Mrs Daly made no further comment. The church had spoken. But she had a plan forming in her head.

'About the funeral,' she said gravely, weighing her words like clods of earth. 'I have arranged for the mass, not a High Mass of course, as poor Hamlet has no relations. Then,' here she paused as a grave-digger is apt to do halfway in his task. 'Then, there is the burial.'

'Ah yes,' said Brother Angel quickly, 'I assume he is coming back to us.'

'Well, it would be quite impossible to buy a plot for him here. He is not a native, and — '

'Poor lad, he was not a native anywhere, but he will be buried with our community.'

'It's quite a distance to Mullingar,' said Mrs Daly with a sigh.

Brother Angel did not appear to hear her. Instead, after a moment's silence, he looked at her earnestly and began to speak in a slightly hesitant voice.

'You mentioned — I mean, I mentioned a relic a few minutes ago,' he murmered almost to himself, looking down at his outspread fingers again. Although he worked on the farm with the rest of his community, Brother Angel's hands, strong, brown and hard, still possessed the fine shape and slender wrists he was born with. A superior once told him he was vain, although not necessarily of his hands, which were merely used as a sign to draw attention to his general appearance. The young brother had agreed with his mentor, but had never got out of the habit. He was aware of it; aware also that it was slightly silly, but over the years it had become part of his outer personality.

'Yes. Blessed Angelo. So kind of you to think of bringing it for poor Hamlet.'

'I have just received a relic of the True Cross from Rome.' He dropped his hands, and remained quite still as if posing for an old-time photographer.

'Oh.' There was no need for him to look at Mrs Daly. He knew the expression of greed and appetite — a look almost prurient in its intensity — that passed across her face. The very sound she made was breathless and impatient. Then, as she looked modestly to the floor, he could sense her changing gear, as it were. He was reluctant to raise his eyes: they were already heavy with shame.

'Really,' she said in a very different tone. 'A genuine one?'

'Of course. It was sent to me by the Provincial.'

'For your own use?'

'Yes.'

Pause.

'Oh, dear, poor Hamlet, such an errand for you. But you have a relic of Saint Pius. Already?'

'Yes.'

'I do envy you. It must be wonderful to have all those relics in the same house.'

'Yes.'

Pause.

'About the funeral. Have you any means of getting the remains to your house in Mullingar?'

'No, I'm afraid not.'

It was not usual for the Brothers to bury any of their orphans, when they died outside the institution.

'Do you think you could get a True Cross relic for me?' The question came rather sooner than he had anticipated. But there were all kinds of imponderables to be taken into account in this case of Hamlet and his employer. The orphanage depended largely on the patronage of persons like Mrs Daly. It was necessary for Brother Angel to get his boys placed in what seemed to be good positions. He had another boy ready to take Hamlet's place. Several who had been 'placed' by him in lowly positions — for what else could an unknown orphan expect —

had done well for themselves in Bridgeford and the other towns nearby. Hamlet's death could be exploited against Mrs Daly, especially if she suspected that people were thinking that the boy had died as a result of over-work and ill-treatment. When the emotion of the funeral was over, this sort of talk might easily begin. Brother Angel could not take the risk of being involved in it.

'I could,' he replied slowly. 'It might take some time, and of course, no one can guarantee such a grace. That is why relics are so difficult to get. They have to be passed by the Office in Rome.'

'Of course, of course.' Mrs Daly now saw the way clearly before her, and she did not hesitate. Only *two* people in Bridgeford possessed relics of the True Cross. Old Mrs Browne, whose daughter had married into a great English Catholic family, and had been given the relic as a wedding present. Stories were told as to how the mother purloined it. The fact remained that she had it. So had old Mrs Lyster, who had got it from her brother who was a bishop. As a result both ladies enjoyed enormous esteem in Bridgeford, and might be said to dominate the place socially, so far as Catholic society was concerned. To break into this tiny privileged circle, Mrs Daly would have risked anything short of murder. To pay for Hamlet's funeral cortège to Mullingar, and give her seal of approval to the Brothers and their orphan boys, was a bargain price to pay for such a reward; even when she had also given the Brothers a large contribution towards the upkeep of their institution.

'I will arrange with Reilly, the undertaker, to go to Mullingar after the mass. You will stay for it, Brother?'

'Well, I do have some business to do in Bridgeford — '

'Naturally. He goes, as you know, to the church this evening, and the funeral is after the ten o'clock mass in the morning. I have a room prepared for you. And now tell me, have you a good boy you can give me?'

'Well, as a matter of fact I have, and — I could, of course, let you have a loan of the True Cross relic, until I manage to get another from Rome,' he said carefully, smiling at her a little ruefully, an expression he knew was particularly potent with middle-aged women, indeed with all women.

'Oh, Brother Angel,' she breathed, closing her eyes to the

light which broke upon her. She was about to enter into the ecstasy of a real social position, unchallenged and for life.

'I have it with me,' he went on, like a man prolonging a partner's particular pleasure; this especial agony was not shared by him.

He took out his wallet, extracted the tiny silver box with its glass front, and put it down gently on a table equidistant between him and Mrs Daly. She joined her hands and looked down on it with a yearning look, opening and closing her eyes slowly and heavily, as if the very sight of it were too much for her.

Quietly he left the room. He did not want to witness the awful greed, the claw-like gesture with which Mrs Daly would snatch up this relic, which she believed to have been touched by her God and Saviour. Brother Angel went quickly, and made for the kitchen.

Mrs O'Flaherty Flynn, who had had to lie down and get some sleep in the mid-morning, was now up again and standing in the centre of the kitchen, staring at the dirty window. She had put on a dark frock and black stockings, and looked quite impressive in them. When she saw Brother Angel come in she turned around, threw out her arms and wept silently. He and the cook were old friends.

'Oh, Brudder Angel,' she sobbed, 'I wus wishin' an' hopin' an' prayin' and lookin' out for ye ta cum, an' be wid us in our hour a greef. Oo ooo de poor harmless gossoon wudden hurt a fly wid its legs hangin' off, or tell a lie before a gun, an' he wus dat obligin' dat if ye were halfway to Moate he's pick ye up an' carry ye on his bended back — o weary, weary — '

As he patted Mrs O'Flaherty Flynn's arm, Brother Angel tried to picture Hamlet carrying her all the way to Moate, a distance of ten miles. But he understood the feeling behind the talk.

'An' he wus a good boy, Brudder Angel, none o' dat chasin' after de women like some, an' he wus always runnin' messages for d'auld wans — now, what boy'd do dat?'

'He was a good boy.'

'An' a lovely corpse, God bless 'im. He reminds me a' some statyah saint in the Friary. Why did ye call 'im Hamlet? I was meanin' to ask millions a' times?'

'One of our brothers had a signed photograph of Sir Henry

Irving, a famous actor of fifty years ago and more, in his costume as Hamlet, and he was so like — '

'Dat ye called 'im Hamlet, well issen id great dat he wus called after a lorrd? There was plenty o' them here in d'auld days. Ah, dere's Maureen, Brudder, Maureen salute de priest.'

Maureen, who had come in from the pantry, went scarlet and made a little bob as Brother Angel took her hand. Then, with a scared look at Mrs O'Flaherty Flynn, she hurried out of the kitchen.

'De best liddle girl dat ever wus, Brudder,' said the cook, nodding her head after her. Mrs O'Flaherty Flynn could never get the hang of Brothers, and always saw them as priests. She thought of Brother Angel as a kind of a high priest of orphans.

'An' she muss have de grace a' God in bucketfuls, because the family background is somethin' awful.'

'I have a new boy for you, Mrs O'Flynn.' Brother Angel was one of the few people allowed to shorten the cook's name. More than one person had been chased out of the kitchen for trying it. Mrs O'Flaherty Flynn's sense of ancestry was strong.

'Tanks be ta God. Is he strong, willin' and afraid a women?'

'He's everything you might require, Mrs O'Flynn. His name is Eddy — '

'Oh, after de Duke a Clarence, he wus Prince Eddy, is dat it?'

'No, I'm afraid not.' Brother Angel smiled to himself as he thought of Brother Eddy. 'No, after a holy man of our Order.'

'Tanks be ta God. I never heard of a Saint Hamlet, but a course dere wudden be if he wus a lord.'

'I hope you'll look after him, Mrs O'Flaherty Flynn. He's a strong growing lad, and needs all the food he can get.'

'Doan you werry Brudder, he'll get all de left-overs an' more dan a fair share of what's hot. I'll stuff 'im, you'll see. Is his heart sound?'

'Oh, absolutely. He's a very strong lad.'

'An' ye're sure he's pure?'

Brother Angel cleared his throat and nodded.

'Because dat odder fella, Tommy whatever, dat ye gave to de Hickey's wid de pub, is after gettin' a liddle girl inta trouble, an' he's nod sixteen yet, nod dat I blame him. De Hickey's Cork people, ye know, keep a very mixed house, soljers an' all, and de girl is two years older dan him, and as bauld as brass teet'. Still,

he wus named, an' de Hickeys say it wus him and no odder, I
tink — '

'I'm going there directly, Mrs O'Flaherty Flynn. I'm staying
the night — '

'Tank de Lord,' she clapped her hands with delight. 'I'll tell
Maureen ta make it up special for ye, an open de winda for a
while, maybe half an hour. Id'll be aired ta perfection for ye.'

'I want to visit the other boys too that are placed in
Bridgeford. Tommy of course, then — '

'I can tell ye all about dem, each an' every wan o' dem.
Now — '

The other visitor to the town on that day was already with old
MacDonnell. Macroom had cooked them an excellent lunch,
and they were sitting in the study afterwards, relaxing with
brandy and cigars, before any reference to their mutual affairs
was made.

'Yes,' said old MacDonnell, 'Roosevelt will do well. He has
great self-confidence, a powerful voice and more friends among
the bankers than he ever admits. He will serve their interests in
his own way — the only way at present.'

'You don't like him,' said MacDonnell's visitor. He was a
young man of about thirty, with a massive head and
enormously broad shoulders, very well dressed in a fine Harris
tweed, tailor-made suit. When he stood up even his excellent
tailor could not disguise the fact of his two sturdy, but slightly
bandy legs. His strength of frame, his low forehead, tight,
receding curls, flattish nose and deepset small eyes, all revealed
him as a type often seen among Rugby players. In his case this
was true. Charlie Kennedy would, if his legs had been in
proportion to the rest of him, have been a first-rate full back: as
it was he played hooker.

'That's quick of you,' smiled MacDonnell. 'I don't. Neither
do I trust him. And of course he doesn't really like the Irish, and
his wife actually hates us. But he'll be a great President. The
Democrats are lucky.'

'Do the people involved here know anything about me?' said
Kennedy, when the short discussion on American politics
ended. This question was followed by a quick flick of the clasp
on his briefcase — an elaborate model with his initials in gold

```

above the clasp — which indicated that he was ready for business now.

'I called in on the man who's more or less acting for them, and told him you were coming, and why. They'll all have heard by now.'

'Acting for them?' Kennedy's voice had an upward inflection at the end, a rising whip-lash behind the tone.

'Oh, he's not a barrister — you're the only one in all this business, Slyne has only a solicitor — no, Ben O'Farrell is a publican, people exchange news and views in his place.'

'I see.' Kennedy played with the clasp of his briefcase, which he held in the crook of his legs, having put one large well-shod foot on his knee — a habit of his. 'Did he believe you?'

'Fenny — that's his nickname around here, Fenny O'Barrell instead of Benny O'Farrell, you see?'

Kennedy nodded, and gave a slightly ironic smile to indicate that heavy forms of provincial humour were not lost on him, in spite of his superior Dublin wit.

'Yes, he believed me,' said MacDonnell. 'Or at least he gave that impression.'

'Oh, why?'

'Because Fenny is a publican, first, last and all the time. He agrees with everyone and keeps his own council, which I have never discovered. He is very well thought of round here, always friendly, always ready to do a good turn, so long as it doesn't cost him too much. He's a witty enough fellow, and has a nice little wife, who's expecting for the first time in twelve or fourteen years, I forget which, and I think he is genuinely attached to her.'

'Can he be trusted?' Kennedy tapped his gold-lettered initials with his short blunt fingers, which were quite capable of squeezing the life out of a man.

'Yes, he's involved in the thing himself. Sold a piece of his upland meadow to Slyne, but not the whole of it, I tipped him the wink, but I don't think he'd have sold it all anyway. Shrewd fella.'

'Is the land, this Barrelly fellow's, important?'

'No, only mine is, for access and exit. Fenny's plot will add to the opening, and that's desirable, but not essential. He says he wants to keep it for his pony.'
```

Kennedy looked up at the old man, but no hint of irony crossed his expression; he was as poker-faced as ever. Kennedy, although he was part of his organization, did not trust him an inch. But so far, he had done well out of the old boy, made the right contacts, established them, and saw his way plain. Soon he would be setting up on his own, and MacDonnell would be merely one client out of several.

'Eamon knows you're here of course,' said MacDonnell in a very low voice.

'Of course, he's following every move. I was with him last night.'

'Any chance of anyone near him, or you, having friends or relations in these parts?'

'Not that I know of. But just in case, we take precautions. I go to a block of flats in an old house in Clyde Road, slip out the back garden, and into the next house, which, like most of the big houses on Clyde Road, is owner-occupied: Eamon's. We meet there.'

'Good idea.' MacDonnell paused. 'Everybody saw you coming in here, that's why I dropped the hint to Fenny last evening, coming back from the wake in the hotel.'

'The Clarence?' Kennedy indicated some interest. On a visit to the hotel in June with Eamon Kelly, the politician, he had seen Maud. He had always wanted to pay another visit. Perhaps it could be worked this time. 'Who's dead?'

'The boots, a young fellow, barely seventeen, who used to carry messages for me. Sad.'

'Yes,' said Kennedy, opening his briefcase. 'I have all the documents here. How long do you think this meeting in O'Farrell's will go on?'

'Forever,' said MacDonnell drily, and Kennedy laughed dutifully. 'Well, I told Fenny you'd be here and ready to meet them at half-two, and it's nearly that now. However, it's only two minutes walk down the street. How's Eamon's electioneering doing? He had a great meeting in the square here a few weeks ago. The other lot had theirs at the same time.'

'I heard about that, FitzClarence and Co. Is it true that Fitz or his father is a royal bastard?'

'Very likely. They were certainly right royal boot-lickers, Eamon is to win of course?'

'He's the man, yes. Almost a cert.'

'And then — ' smiled MacDonnell, leaning forward over his big desk and stubbing out his cigar.

'We can get on with this,' said Kennedy tapping his briefcase again. 'Does anyone suspect?'

'Not the old women certainly, not Donie, not even Mrs Daly. She's not taking any interest in it, or pretending not to, and the others are too anxious for the dough. They need it, but badly.'

'Good. What about this Farrell fella?'

'It's impossible to tell what he's thinking about anything. Castle Catholic family, of course, and a Treaty man. Very shrewd. Knows his own interests. I tipped him the wink, or gave him a blink as Macroom says, to keep him happy about his own interests.'

'Suppose he suddenly — today — starts making difficulties? Putting things off?' The small, keen eyes glittered in their fleshy depths, the low forehead wrinkled, the tubular nostrils flared, and the square jaw jutted. This was a ball that was going to emerge from the scrum, his, and his only.

'Tomorrow the processes will be served,' said MacDonnell, flicking ash from his waistcoat. 'None of them wants that; too complicated, and besides, Donie and the old women have spent the deposit money.'

'I know that, of course, but I wanted to make sure there were no late developments.'

'I see what you mean,' said MacDonnell, not imagining for a moment that anything could have happened unknown to him. 'Communications are difficult.' He glanced at the telephone, 'It's just possible that something might have turned up, and I mightn't have been able to contact you in time. Yes, you're on the ball.'

'I was wrapped round it at one time,' said Kennedy, with an easy laugh in which the older man joined. He was well acquainted with this form of wit.

'Well, shall we join the ladies?' said MacDonnell in the same strain. 'Of course, Fenny will be there, but officially we're only dealing with the ladies. Donie won't be there on account of the funeral, but he'll hear it almost before the sound reaches the door of O'Farrell's.'

'As a Dublin jackeen, I've never been able to understand this bush-telephone, or telegraph,' said Kennedy, springing to his feet, and drawing himself up by tucking in his belly and hunching his shoulders. MacDonnell was four inches taller than he, and it seemed all wrong somehow to Kennedy. The old buffer was shrewd, and still a power to respect, but he was old, and living as he did in this God-forsaken hole, was more or less out of the Dublin racket, which was all that counted in Ireland. The provinces were strictly for the floating votes.

'They have it in Africa and India too,' said MacDonnell as they went into the hall, where Macroom stood ready with the boss's overcoat in his hands. 'It's a sort of telepathy, I think. Never to be discounted, Mr Kennedy, even by the shrewdest of city men, isn't that right, Macroom?'

'City men in Ireland is like Hoosyerasses in the States,' said Macroom, with a sour look at the gleaming Kennedy.

'That means Hoosiers, and all other hill-billies,' chuckled MacDonnell, who had perfectly understood the look Kennedy had given him during his 'Dublin jackeen' routine. These young tigers of the party had to be taken down a peg now and again, and made to realize that it was the old men who were running things now, as they had always done in the past.

Kennedy laughed his hearty rugby laugh, which sounded like the tearing apart, by over-muscled fingers, of a big leather ball.

'OK,' he said, 'Let's go.'

There was a sudden chilling silence. MacDonnell stood quite still in his overcoat, holding his hat in one hand, his stick and gloves in the other. Macroom stood with his back to the door, equally rigid, but glaring angrily at the visitor. For a moment Kennedy felt disoriented, as if someone had sat on his head, and pushed it into the ground during a match. He had never experienced anything like this off the field in his life. And it lasted nearly thirty seconds or more.

MacDonnell was the first to relax. He looked at Macroom, moving his head a fraction of an inch.

'Is everything OK, Macroom?' he said quietly.

Macroom moved quickly to the old man's side and whispered something in his ear, which the visitor could not catch. He was being instructed in the ways and means of protocol.

'I'll attend to it when I get back,' said MacDonnell softly.

Then he looked across at the drab houses with eyes that were alert with a new inquisitiveness.

'And,' said MacDonnell in a low voice, 'they'll know all about you, your family, business, habits and any hidden vices, before the night is out. A sobering thought, isn't it, Mr Kennedy?'

The three ladies had arrived in O'Farrell's nearly an hour early. Hosannah, who was first, immediately asked if she could go behind Mrs O'Farrell's grocery counter, and sit on a stool where she could say her rosary in peace.

'Of course you can,' said Fenny, throwing out his arms with a wide smile to match, 'what kind of a stool do you want? There is a high one, and a low one.'

'De low wan, please,' said Hosannah humbly. 'De two others is sure to be jabberin' away like starved infants, an' I can't say a prayer wid all dat noise goin' on. Oh, Mr O'Farrell, isn't it shockin' about dat young fella dead in his boots in de hotel? In a hole in the wall, I hear she had him, like a dawg.' Hosannah clasped her hands together and rolled her eyes upwards. Standing in the centre of the shop, alone with Fenny while Ellen was finishing her lunch, she felt the need of a prayerful attitude to protect her.

She scurried behind the counter, holding her hand against her middle in case of a mishap as her elastic had snapped, and lowered herself onto the low stool, where only the top of her head, with its mass-hat, could be seen over the counter. Fenny, she thought, would not after all pursue her here, with Ellen expected at any moment, and the others too. But Hosannah had a firm belief that if you let yourself be alone in a shop, or any other place with a man, he's bound to assault you. So she crouched over her stool muttering prayers, and clasping her waist as if she had a bad pain.

Fenny went behind his own counter, smiling and shaking his head.

'Are you all right now, Miss Braiden?' he called out, more for devilment than anything else.

'I'm sayin' me prayers Mr O'Farrell. Terrible long prayers dat has de power.'

'Good. Would you like me to go over and say a few with you?' Fenny climbed up on his boat, and appeared fixed for the afternoon, but this did not reassure Hosannah.

'Mother a'God, I hear yer wife comin' up de passage, Mr O'Farrell.'

'I doubt if she's finished yet.' Fenny looked at his watch, and Hosannah cowered lower.

'She carries a rosary wid her, dussen she?'

'I think so. Are you sure you're all right over there?'

'Oh, God Almighty, yes, I'm for annuder year in Purgatory.'

'Purge yer tory,' said Fenny, repeating a favourite word of his father's.

'What's dat? Our Fadder who art — '

Before she could finish the street door opened, letting in a blast of cold, damp air, followed by Mrs Pig Prendergast and Miss Sarah Jane McLurry in a great state of suppressed excitement and expectation. Mrs Pig stopped inside the door and looked around, while Sarah Jane, with a little nod and smile to Fenny, made for the Cafe Royal.

'Where is Susannah Braiden?' demanded Mrs Pig, 'I saw her duckin' in here a good ten minutes ago.'

'I'm here,' squeaked Hosannah from behind the counter. Mrs Pig looked and saw the top of the mass-hat, and a pair of red-rimmed eyes peering at up at her. 'On a stool.'

'What else?' said Mrs Pig with a laugh, 'I didn't think dat Mr O'Farrell kept a jerry in de shop.'

'God forgive ye, Mrs Prendergast, an' we aitin' for news dat could make us, or forsake us. I'm prayin' like mad.'

'You do that, Susannah, it makes a great difference with lawyers, Englishmen and aul lags like MacDonnell. What d'ye tink is goin' to happen?' she said to Fenny.

Fenny sucked at his pipe and closed one eye, while his jawbones could be heard chewing the stem of his pipe. His silence was for once pregnant, for at that moment the door opened again to deliver old MacDonnell and the smart young Mr Kennedy, who entered in the proper exercise of protocol: Kennedy first, to hold open the door for his companion, as MacDonnell, after the slightest of pauses and an affable nod to his man, walked slowly and weightily in first.

'Good day, Mrs Prendergast,' he said with great respect,

taking off his hat, 'may I introduce you to Mr Charles Kennedy, a partner in a most distinguished firm of Dublin barristers, not one of them a freemason.'

'Thanks be to God,' said Mrs Pig, holding out her hand to the young man, who took it and shook it firmly. A villain, thought Mrs Pig.

Sarah Jane came out of the Cafe Royal to be introduced, but it was rather more complicated with Hosannah. She stood up, pressed her stomach against the edge of the counter, and put out her hand, with the arm laid heavily on the top of the counter. Kennedy was hardly able to do more than touch the tips of her fingers.

'What's the matter with you?' said Mrs Pig, coming over and leaning across the counter.

'Lastic. De band o me knickers is gone soft, an' I'm in fear o' me life dat id'll fall down, Lord save us.' Hosannah whispered.

'D'ye think you're the only wan dat's had that affliction, aye, an' often in the middle o' the church, an' couldn't go to the altar? There's plenty of twine in dere under the counter. Tie yourself up with the string, you're not the only wan dat's had to do it.'

But Hosannah pursed up her mouth, and frowned. How was such a complicated operation to be achieved squatting down behind the counter, with Mrs O'Farrell due at any minute. No, she'd hold herself together with her hands until she got home. String indeed, they might be down to that in Kerry —

'Well, now,' said Kennedy, standing with his back to the wall between the Cafe Royal and the street door. That way no one passing could see him, he could stop dead the moment anyone entered the shop, and slip into the snug if necessary, and finally, he was facing all the people with whom he was dealing. But before he began, he thought he'd make doubly sure of his privacy.

'Is there anyone likely to come in suddenly while I'm speaking?' he asked, looking first at MacDonnell and then at Fenny. Both of them shook their heads.

'No one from the street certainly, it's unlikely anyone from Leinster will be in here — an odd one comes to drink in the evening, to see how the other half lives — no, we're private, except for an unforeseen foreigner. And,' he went on, looking at Mrs Pig, who was leaning against his counter with her arms folded across her chest, 'Ellen is staying in the kitchen keeping Gummy busy.'

Mrs Pig chuckled and nodded, and Hosannah's head popped up from behind her counter, like a sniper behind a ditch.

'Is yer wife nod comin' in?' she squeaked.

'No, Susannah. You just sit down there and make yourself comfortable. Something tells me that Mr Kennedy has a very interesting, if not sensational report to make.'

'Hardly sensational,' said Kennedy, wrinkling his low brow. 'This is in the nature of a legal document. Well, is everyone ready?'

Silence descended on the shop like heavy curtains over a window. Fenny, who was used to it, could hear the house creaking with age, and remembered his father's saying that all old houses have arthritis of the wood, just like elderly people have it in the bones.

'On Tuesday the 2nd of June 1933, Mr Hector Slyne, giving his address as The Royal Hibernian Hotel, Dawson Street, Dublin, and permanently, as he instructed me later, of — Hamilton Terrace, London NW8, made an appointment with me to visit me at my office — 2 Dame Street, Dublin, on the following afternoon at 3, Wednesday the 3rd June, 1933.

'Although I was not directly involved in subsequent negotiations for the purchase of lands in the vicinity of Bridgeford, County Westmeath, the lands being in the townland of Buggawn and Courraghnabul, in the Barony of Towey etc. etc., he instructed me to write to Mr Patrick Joseph MacDonnell of 92 Connaught Street, Bridgeford, Co. Westmeath, making an appointment to see him at any convenient time during the following week, it being necessary for the successful completion of Mr Slyne's business that their meeting should take place at my office at the afore-mentioned address.

'Should Mr MacDonnell be unable to attend, Mr Slyne gave me full powers to deal with him on the matter of his — Mr MacDonnell's lands — in the Queen's Meadows, Bridgeford, Co. Westmeath. I subsequently got in touch with Mr MacDonnell, and he agreed to see Mr Slyne at The Duke of Clarence Hotel, Bridgeford at a time and day to be appointed when Mr Slyne visited Bridgeford.'

Kennedy paused in his reading and looked up.

'I met him,' said MacDonnell, who was seated on a chair Fenny had fetched for him, and placed in the middle of the shop near the stove. 'And, as you know, no sale took place.'

'Yes,' said Mrs Pig, looking at Kennedy as if he were an intruder in her backyard. 'But what has de meetin' in your office — Dame Street, what a name, why don't they change it to something decent and Irish — to do with us, an' our land?'

'Our herediatage,' piped Hosanannah, peering over the top of her counter, which she was grasping with her fingers, as if she were hanging from a wall.

'Yes,' said Miss McLurry, 'our proud heritage,' emphasizing the correct pronunciation, so as to teach Hosannah. That lady smiled and wagged her head over the counter in reply. Well she knew that Sarah Jane was as ignorant as a tinker's grandmother, and was always pronouncing words wrong.

'Ha, ha,' cackled Hosannah, 'Listen to dat, Mister Kennedy, our proud herediatage. Write dat wan down Mister Barrister.'

'Well, you see,' began Kennedy with a patient air, 'subsequently we had a general chat about his business interests, there were some points he wanted cleared up, and during this talk he mentioned that it was his intention to buy land along the Shannon just south of Bridgeford.'

'He must have seen the land,' Fenny said, who had been looking at Kennedy with a curious air of detachment, and an occasional ironic twinkle of the eye. 'How did he get down here to see it, unknown to us all?'

'Did he?' said Mrs Pig looking at MacDonnell.

'No, he didn't. He sent on an agent, who didn't even walk the land, just looked at the site from the bridge, and Burgess's Park, across the river from your land.'

'And what did d'agent tell him?' said Mrs Pig, looking a little confused.

'Well, he told him what was common knowledge, and not only in Bridgeford, that all the lands, except for Mr MacDonnell's, were flooded every winter.' He paused, and looked about him. Hosannah was now almost standing up, clutching the counter, with her mass-hat a little askew. He had his audience, something which gave him intense satisfaction. 'I told him the same myself. But he assured me that it did not matter, that he only wanted the place as a sort of summer moorings place. He intends to build two jetties at either end of the lands, and enjoy some boating during the summer.'

'Oh, de villain,' cried Hosannah, her voice cracking with
agitation, and the strain of holding herself together while she
spoke, 'and he wants to get his summer high jinks outa us for
ony depose-it money. Oooo, murder!' And she brought down
one clenched fist on the counter, causing some jars to jump on
the shelves behind her, and her own underwear to slip a further
inch down. She grabbed at herself and ducked behind the
counter again. Kennedy looked at her in astonishment.

'Have you any witness for this statement of Slyne's?' said
Fenny, always near to the point.

'Yes, of course. My clerk, Harry Meehan, a south
Roscommon man himself, who knows all about the flooding. I
called him into my office to tell Mr Slyne this.'

'A good thing you did,' said Fenny, with a little smile.
Kennedy, who was used to such smiles, grinned right back at
him. 'So what this means is dat — ' Mrs Pig held out one palm,
and tapped it with her forefinger as she scored her points, 'one,
Mr Slyne was with you in yer office on de 3rd of June last, two,
dat he asked you to write to Mr MacDonnell about de sale of his
land in the Meadows?'

'Correct, ma'am,' said Kennedy, nodding his small, flat
head.

'Three, has Mr MacDonnell de letter you wrote him?'

'Yes,' said MacDonnell quickly, 'of course, but not,
unfortunately, the envelope. I didn't think it necessary to keep
it at that time.'

'Why the envelope?' said Sarah Jane, who had pulled her
chair forward, and was sitting at the door of the Cafe Royal.

'To prove dat it came from Dublin,' said Mrs Pig quickly.
Kennedy caught her eye for an instant, then smiled and went
on.

'There is no question of that,' he said smoothly. 'My clerk
posted it, and we keep a letter book. Not that anyone is going to
question it.'

'And where does all this leave us?' said Miss McLurry, who
was feeling a bit bemused.

'It means, madam, that Mr Slyne knew, before he made you
his offer for your lands, that they were flooded in the winter, but
since he only wanted the foreshore in summer, the flooding did
not worry him.' Kennedy flicked open his briefcase, put in some

papers he had been holding in his hand, then snapped it to again.

'Does this mane dat we keep de depose-it?' piped Hosannah, who had bobbed up again.

'Of course,' said Kennedy with a smile. For a man who looked as though rugby had been the main occupation of his leisure hours, he had a remarkable repertory of smiles, grins and movements of the lips, that indicated anything from a slightly ironic agreement to a reasonably serious disagreement. For absolutely serious matters, he preserved a rigid expression that would have made him a great poker player.

'A man of many talents,' said Mrs Pig to herself. 'Horns on Monday and a halo on Sunday, as me father used to say.'

Kennedy heard her say something, but beyond a quick glance he did not ask her anything. Old ladies were given to muttering, murmuring and other obscure internal sounds.

'Does that mean that he will go ahead with the purchase at the price agreed on?' said Miss McLurry.

'He will have to, madam. He has no other choice.'

'Can we sue him for tryin' to get it off us for de price of de deposit?' said Mrs Pig, who was all for attacks of every kind.

'I don't think that would be advisable. It would lead to legal costs on your part, and you might not be able to sustain your case. In my opinion, I would advise acceptance of the offer, which is not bad at £60 an acre. You won't do better.'

'Prayer is powerful,' said Hosannah, putting her hands on her hips, and thus discovering a posture which she could keep up with reasonable safety. 'If I lid enough candles to de Blessed Virgin, I'd ged a hunnered pound for me lan'. In de fambly since Cromwell, de curse o'God on 'im.'

'Amen,' said Mrs Pig. 'He never ventured as far as Kerry. De kingdom was fur King James — '

'Undoubtedly so, it was always given up to it,' said old MacDonnell, who felt that things were spreading a bit, like a mound of sand under many boots. That was Irish history, and the sand was all over the country by now.

'Well,' said Fenny, taking out his pipe, and giving Kennedy a knowing smile, 'you've certainly pulled a fast one on Mr Slyne. But I have a feeling he won't object too much.'

Kennedy and MacDonnell both looked at him, and their combined looks indicated prudence.

'He has no choice,' repeated Kennedy. 'Like many another shrewd business man, he exploited a situation which was ready to hand. He would have got the land at a tenth of its price, if he could, but he reckoned without my own connection with Mr MacDonnell for one thing.'

'It certainly came in very handy,' remarked Fenny, drawing two further warning looks from the old man and the barrister.

'Tanks be to de Lord God Almighty,' intoned Hosannah, hands on hips, 'an' His Mudder, an' His faster-fadder St. Joseff, an' all de saints of Ireland includin' them dat's not canonicated or ized — yet — like me own fadder an mudder dat's always prayin' in heaven above fur me an' me friends — '

'Dats very nice a' them to be sure, Susannah,' put in Mrs Pig. 'Dey must be havin' wan hell of a' time up dere.'

Kennedy covered his mouth with his fist and closed his eyes, while Fenny laughed outright.

'You're a terrible woman, Mrs P,' he chuckled.

'By the way,' said Miss McLurry innocently, for she felt that a lot of this business had been done without much contribution from her, 'why did Mr Slyne go to your office in the first place? How did he come to hear about you?'

Kennedy took his hand from his mouth, and looked at her with a sudden searing glint in his hot little eyes.

'I had done some business for colleagues of his in England, people who have property over here. I don't think he knew of my business connection with Mr MacDonnell, or if he did, which is quite possible, he may have thought that it would be a help rather than anything else. And so it would have been, if he had not attempted to make capital out of the flooding. Mr MacDonnell got in touch with me when he heard about it, not on his own account, since he was not interested in selling, but for the sake of his neighbours and friends.' And he turned his burning eyes on every one of them, except MacDonnell, who was modestly looking into his lap.

'We owe you a debt of gratitude, Mr MacDonnell,' said Fenny, leaning forward with an inclination of his head.

'Indeeden we do,' said Hosannah, 'May ye grow to be ninety widout dung spots, an' may de seein' in yer eyes, an' de hearin' in yer ears, get sharper be de year, an' may ye live ta see yer great-grandson grow into a bishop, amen.'

'Amen, indeed,' said Mrs Pig, with an admiring glance at

Hosannah. That lady had more in her than Mrs Pig, who was certain she knew the best blessings in Kerry, and therefore in Ireland, and the bitterest curses also, had suspected. 'Are ye prepared to go inta de witness box and swear t'all this, if Slyne turns nasty, English dat he is?'

'Of course, madam,' said Kennedy, raising his thick eyebrows. 'The truth must be served.'

'Something must be served,' said Mrs Pig darkly, but almost immediately grew merrier. 'Oh, Lord above,' she said gleefully, rubbing her hands together, 'isn't dis great, above all tings?'

'Great,' said everyone in the place, except Kennedy, who smiled.

'D'you know, you all have a sort of glint in your eyes,' said Fenny, scratching his chin with the stem of his pipe, and looking from one to another. 'Very much the same expression, sort of happy and excited, and up to God knows what mischief.'

'The mischief is done already,' said Mrs Pig with a smile at Kennedy. He did not exactly wink, but he blinked and made a clown's mouth with his lips.

'Thanks be to Our Lady of Mount Carmel,' said Miss McLurry fervently, with clasped hands, the gleam of excitement not quite faded from her eyes, 'If only I had a bow and arrow that I could shoot up a 'thank you' message, beyond the clouds —'

'Mrs P, Mrs P,' called out Hosannah in a husky undertone. 'Come over a minnit, please do, me treasure.' She was leaning across the counter holding a length of twine in her hands, and her face was more alive than anyone's, her little eyes popping with glee.

Mrs Pig needed no explanation. She stalked over, held up the flap of the counter, and went in behind. Hosannah whispered something at her, Mrs Pig nodded, and simply turned her back on her, facing the company in the shop, and providing ample shelter for Hosannah with her height and her broad back, as the little lady behind her pulled up her skirts, and tied the string round the erring top of her knickers. When she was finished, she sighed deeply with relief, and stepped out from behind the massive shelter afforded her.

'Now I'm all ridio,' she announced cheerfully, 'and God save Ireland from de hooks, crooks an' starspooners dat's tryin' ta buy 'er up.'

'Why harpooners, Miss Braiden?' said Kennedy easily.

'She said starspooners, Mr Kennedy,' said Mrs Pig, as she held up the flap for Hosannah to pass through after her ordeal. 'Miss Braiden has her own word for almost everything, haven't ye Susie?'

'Have I?' said Hosannah with some puzzlement.

'I think all this deserves a drink, and it's on me,' said MacDonnell, rising from his chair and bowing gallantly to the ladies, one after another.

'Oh, tanks be ta God an' His Blessed Mudder,' cried Hosannah, 'De muscles a' me jaws is stiffenin' wid disusery, and I'm affeared if I doan get some sorta drink soon, me passage'll be blocked, like de canal below wid dead cats.'

'Rightio,' said Fenny, setting to with a will, and the evening, which had witnessed the triumph of the land-owners against the wicked stranger began. For, not five minutes after MacDonnell had ordered the drinks, Connaught Street began to come in, in twos, and threes, and singles, every man that had a leg on him, all of them prepared to join in the wonderful work that had been done that day.

When Slyne heard later that evening from Mr Fair, the solicitor, himself, on whom Kennedy had called while the party was still on in O'Farrell's, he realized that something very extraordinary had happened.

'Will I go on with the summons?' said Fair, not entirely without irony.

'No, no, of course not. But do go ahead with the sales as quickly as you can. I want to have this matter settled before I go back to London. It has been hanging fire rather a long time now.'

'Yes, it has,' said Fair with a curious look, which did not escape Slyne. 'Do you think it a good thing to have good will in these matters? It may seem small and unimportant to you, but to the people involved here the whole thing is a great event in their lives.'

'What do you advise me to do?'

The two men were sitting in the commercial room, in the same chairs which had served for Slyne's interview with Fenny. The room was as cheerless as ever, and not for the first time Mr

Fair, a native of the town and a man of high intelligence, wondered how the luckless Duke of Clarence managed to enjoy himself in that stinking little court outside the window. Of course that was over forty years ago, and he knew from his father that the hotel had been well kept then, with fires in all the public rooms, and some good furniture even in the commercial room; but he had long come to the conclusion that the British were rather suspicious of luxury, or even comfort, and felt quite at home in any kind of room, so long as the place had an atmosphere they felt secure in. And this was exactly what The Duke of Clarence had. Mrs Daly treated her guests, no matter how eminent, exactly like a Victorian hostess managed her bachelor visitors: like grown-up schoolboys. This was an attitude the British, in particular, were completely comfortable with, and could understand. He thought he would put his theory to a further test.

'I would advise a delay of some days, during which you will, or at least I suggest that you will, go to Dublin, and I will let it be known that you are thinking about it. Then, when I judge the moment is ripe, I will call them in to sign.'

'Sign?' Slyne looked at him hard, and saw an amused but honest man, and he was hardly ever wrong in this.

'They'll sign.' Fair sipped the drink that Slyne had bought for him, and was silent for a few moments.

'What exactly do you think of the hotel here?' Fair, a great man in court, could put more point into a simple sentence than anyone else within forty miles of Bridgeford.

'The hotel?' Slyne was taken aback, but recovered. He was beginning to get used to this Irish habit of flicking from subject to subject, as if they were dusting a precious table, which they never intended to use. 'Oh, I rather like it. I imagine one could grow to like it very much. It has one great luxury.'

'Has it?' said Fair, a little surprised.

'Yes, it doesn't belong to the twentieth century. It is stuck irretrievably in the nineteenth, and that was Ireland's greatest period. Morals here are still Victorian.' Slyne sipped his glass as sparingly as his guest. They were two men who felt at home with each other. Slyne always made sure of securing honest solicitors. They were rare, but not impossible to seek out.

'I hadn't thought of that,' said Fair thoughtfully. 'Do you mean — '

Fair could not help smiling one of those ironic smiles for which he was famous in court. One such had once had a sensational effect on a hardened wife-beater, who was setting forth all the religious clubs and organizations he belonged to, when he saw Fair smiling at him. To everyone's intense surprise, he broke down and sobbed out that he was entirely in the hands of the Devil.

But the old solicitor had much more success with this subtle weapon in private: when a client was piling the evidence up to make an impossible junk heap, he was often recalled to the cold, clear waters of reality by Mr Fair's expression. Slyne now recognized it at once for what it was.

'I suppose you're thinking I'm hardly in a position to discourse on morals, Irish or any other,' he said genially. 'English hypocrisy, no doubt.'

'When it comes to morals no one has the floor to himself,' Fair replied smoothly. 'But I do see what you mean about the moral climate. You're quite right, of course.'

Slyne bowed and smiled. When the Irish were well-educated and intelligent, they were irresistible.

'I've begun to think philosophically,' he said ruefully, 'I'd better stick to my last. I'll be at the Hibernian in Dublin from tomorrow. You can send the deeds to me there for signature.'

'I will bring them up myself,' said Fair, who went to Dublin once a week, 'if Thursday will suit you?'

'It will. How kind. Thank you so much. Would you, ah, like another?'

'No, thank you. I will give myself the pleasure of getting one for you when we meet in the Hibernian. A fine old place.'

'Yes, indeed,' said Slyne, seeing him to the door.

That evening, after settling his bill, for he intended to make an early start in the morning, Slyne sent for Donie in the commercial room, which was becoming quite pleasant to his eye, as he got used to it. That smell of candle-grease, tobacco, stale beer and potted hyacinths was unusually and slightly nostalgic, as everything in this country, he told himself, always turned out to be, as one prepared to leave it.

'You've heard about the land settlement,' he said grandly to Donie, using the style he knew the old fox favoured.

'Indeeden I have, sir,' said Donie, not yet quite recovered

from Hamlet's sudden passing; and the thought of a new boy within the next few days was unnerving. 'Bud I wasn't ad de meetin' where dey tried ta pull a fast wan over ye. I'd never be associated wid de like o' dat, so I wudden. I played straight wid ye, sir, from de start.'

Slyne was a little confused as to what particular turn of the screw Donie was referring to at the moment: there had been so many. But he accepted the statement in good part.

'Of course not, Donie, I know that.' He paused for a moment. 'You'll have the rest of your money very shortly after you sign the final deed.'

A shadow of suspicion passed over Donie's face like the wing of a bird of prey; that fatal word 'sign' had been used. Slyne realized his blunder at once.

'Well, it's not a final signing of course, you've signed already, now it's just a formality, then you get the money.'

'Oh, fine, fine, de wife'll be pleased,' said Donie, brightening up.

What children they are, all the same, thought Slyne. Clever, quick-witted and eager, but obsessed by words. Use 'formality' instead of 'signing' and they're happy. No wonder we made such a mess of things with them. Ah well.

'I'll be back again quite soon, of course, Donie,' he said easily, 'so I won't say goodbye, besides I hate the word.' Instead he took out his wallet, pulled out a five pound note and gave it to Donie, who looked at it as if someone had hit him between the eyes.

'Oh, sir, whad'll I say in me tanks? Shure you're a law among men, an' ye don't keep de same time as the world ad all.' And he looked up at the tall man, who had entered all their lives in so dramatic a fashion, and was now leaving like a gentleman. It was so unexpected that tears welled up like swollen eaves in Donie's tired and sleepless eyes, and he wept silently, pushing the tears away with the back of his hand.

'Now, now, Donie,' said Slyne, finding himself quite near to tears for the first time in many a long year, and feeling how extraordinary it all was. He would have something to tell dear old Marjorie when he got back to Hamilton Terrace. He had never brought her to Ireland with him, partly for business reasons, but even more so because he felt that his Marjorie would take to Ireland like cocaine, and become an incurable addict.

'I'm sorry sir,' spluttered Donie, digging out a large handkerchief from his pocket and wiping his face with it. Then he blew his nose, and the little season of sentiment was over. 'Is dere anything I can do for ye? I'm better movin' dan standin' dis last while.'

'Would you ask Miss Maud to spare me a few minutes in here, if she would be so kind?'

'I will indeed, Miss —' then it dawned on Donie whom he was supposed to fetch. He gave Slyne a startled look and toddled quickly, like a fast infant, out of the room.

Surprisingly, Maud was not long in coming. She had heard on the bush telegraph that Charlie Kennedy was in town, and Maud already knew that particular gentleman and wanted someone to throw his name into the ring for her. Slyne would do that very effectively, she felt, whether present or absent.

'I'm so sorry to hear that you're leaving us, Mr Slyne,' she said in her best drawing-room manner.

'Do please sit down, Miss Maud,' said Slyne, pulling forward the best chair for her. She accepted with a graceful inclination of her head, then looked up at him with an expression of amused attention. It was a look she had often practised before the glass, and one which she knew particularly became her. 'Witty eyebrows' she had read somewhere about somebody, and she felt this applied also to herself. It was a measure of Maud's instinctive good manners that she never 'overdid' the various personae she invented for herself in her own room. She possessed the great art of simplicity, and, although she longed to be complex, her nature did not agree.

'We haven't met or talked much, Miss Maud,' began Slyne with a dry little cough, as he inclined towards her, bending the upper part of his body, like a surgeon at a rich hypochondriac's sick-bed: any moment he might be expected to extend a reassuring hand and take her pulse. 'But I hope, I very much hope that when I am next in Ireland, you will do me the honour of coming to dinner with me?'

Maud looked at him in astonishment; pure and simple, maidened and long-haired, lily-white and dove-direct.

'I should love to, Mr Slyne. But — ' she paused, and he

leaned forward another inch, 'but where are we to go?'

Slyne was taken aback. To be taken so literally, in this hotel of all places, was something he was not prepared for. There was in fact, except in The Duke of Clarence dining-room itself, no public place where a lady could be brought to lunch, dinner or any other meal, late or early, for the simple reason that only men dined out.

'Now, I have several friends who have nice houses,' went on Maud smoothly, enjoying herself thoroughly, 'girls who were at school with me, senior girls, of course, who have married men with houses fit for entertaining, but they are all some way from here.' She paused and looked at him gravely. 'Do you know Clara?' she said.

'Yes,' said Slyne, who had studied the map of the midlands intensively before coming to it, had noted Clara among other places. 'It's about sixteen miles from here, isn't it?'

'Yes, through Moate. Well, a girl who was at the convent with me married a man who has a lovely old house outside Clara, in the same family since 1700, and they entertain quite a lot. I'm sure she'd give a dinner party for me, if I asked her. She's always asking me over as it is.'

'That would be lovely,' said Slyne not showing his disappointment. The great thing in any enterprise was not to force it. 'Do you ever come to Dublin?'

'Yes, in August for the Horse Show, and in November for the Christmas shopping.'

'You haven't gone this November yet?' Slyne felt a sudden, almost hurtful little glow inside. Lucky, lucky, lucky . . .

'No there was, well, your business with Mummy. She thought she ought to be here until it was completed. By the way, is it completed yet?'

'Everything, except the final signatures. Mr Fair was over to see me earlier.'

'Yes, I saw him coming out of Hamlet,' said Maud quite casually.

'How do you mean?' Slyne was puzzled.

'I mean he went in to see Hamlet laid out, before he saw you. It was only an hour before they coffined him. He went off to the church an hour ago. Donie is terribly upset, more than we expected.'

'Yes, he was in here with me — '

'Yes, just after coming back from the church. You know, people are brought to the church here the day after they die, in the evening, and buried after mass next morning, or in the afternoon, if relatives have to come from a distance. Hamlet will be going to Mullingar after eight o'clock mass in the morning.'

'You mean he's left the hotel already?' said Slyne, who was feeling out of his depth and did not like it.

'Oh, yes, he was coffined at half-six, while you were talking to Mr Fair, and brought out the back door to the hearse. Mummy didn't like the idea of him going out the front door. That's kept for the family, when they die. Guests and staff go out the back; it's always like that in hotels. Poor Hamlet, I was dreadfully upset by it all. Everybody is, even Donie who was always bullying the poor boy, even Mummy is. I don't know why, but Hamlet got around people in a peculiar way. He was a strange boy in many ways, but everybody liked him. Mrs O'Flaherty Flynn is in a terrible state. Funny isn't it?'

'Oh, I don't think so. The sudden death of a young man is always upsetting. Even in wartime. Some people never got over the death of young soldiers in France in the war. It's not so strange.'

All that side of life and death all those customs their way of thinking their everyday behaviour not to speak of their unusual behaviour is all so different from ours no wonder we could never make a fist of them and they must think we're as foreign as Chinamen and I suppose we are that coffin and all the people going in to see it and Fair coming along to me just after and the coffin carried through the hotel without even suspecting a thing it's really rather frightening weird too even macabre or is it are they more sensible than we are about this whole business I remember the time I had with poor old Marjorie when her mother died a few years ago she wouldn't go to the cremation or even admit it had happened and she became quite hysterical when I brought the matter up I don't want to think about it that sort of thing doesn't exist as far as I'm concerned the moment you begin to think about it it begins to take over your life I've seen it happen I don't want to know about it it's the only way of course it exists but so does murder do we take murder seriously or think about it or let it influence our lives not bloody likely I'm going to live all the way darling and you're going to help me do it everything else is morbid and I simply don't want to hear about it so please darling make me a drinky-winky and let's go to bed that's what Marjorie said

'I have to stay on in Dublin for a week or so,' he began, 'Perhaps you'll be in town while I'm there.'

'We're going up next Monday, Mummy says.' Maud smiled, and stroked the backs of her hands lovingly.

'I stay at the Hibernian,' he said slowly.

'Oh, do you? We often have our tea there. It's awfully handy for Grafton Street, and Mummy spends hours in Switzers, and Leons, and Walpoles in Suffolk Street. But we stay in the Gresham, in O'Connell Street. Mummy knows the manageress, Miss Mullen, very well.'

'I've been in the Gresham, fine place, always full of clergy.'

'And bishops, I've seen the Cardinal there several times.'

'Do you know Jammets?' he said after a pause.

'Oh, yes,' Maud turned a radiant face to him, glowing in that shabby room like a bird's wing in the dust. 'It's marvellous, oh I do love it so.' Willie Wickham had brought her there several times, and she had never forgotten the air of quiet and expensive luxury which it exuded.

'It's as good as some of the best restaurants in London,' said Slyne solemnly.

'It's as good as some of the best restaurants in Paris or Orleans,' said Maud. 'Several of the nuns in Mount Anville were French, and one of them had a brother who owned a famous hotel in Paris. She said she heard him saying that about Jammets.'

'Would you like to have dinner with me there?' he said slowly, and with some apprehension. He need not have worried. Maud had been expecting something of this kind for quite some time. It was a delicious feeling to know that Willie Wickham was ready to rush in and admire her anytime she asked him; that old MacDonnell was every bit as admiring, even if more restrained; she knew that this new Kennedy fellow could be added to the ranks, if he behaved himself properly. And now, there was Slyne also, equally soft-eyed and soppy. It was most gratifying.

'Oh, Mr Slyne!' she exclaimed joyfully, for Jammets was one of the summits of her ambition. 'That's far too much.'

'Surely not too much for you,' he added gallantly. 'You would be an ornament to the place. Do come.'

'Oh, you are kind, yes, of course I'll come.' She paused and

placed a finger against her cheek and glanced at him sideways.
'But you must promise to do something more for me. Now you
don't really have to promise. I know that isn't right, but you
might do it for me?'

'What is it?' smiled Slyne, straightening his shoulders and
sticking out his neck.

'Send me a postcard from London,' said Maud promptly.

'Oh, my dear Miss Maud, of course I will. What'll I send,
London Bridge, Buckingham Palace, the Tower, there are so
many . . .'

'Send the best ones, one by one. You see I love getting
letters.'

'I'll write too.'

'You will? Oh you are a dear, kind man. You have no idea of
how wonderful it is here in this cold, damp place to get a lovely
coloured postcard during the winter. All the girls I knew, when
I was in school, have sent me postcards, usually when they were
on their honeymoons, but some live in these places. I have
postcards from Paris, and Rome, and Venice, and Madrid, and
Lisbon and New York and Chicago. Oh, some of them were
sent by the nuns as they were transferred, and remembered
their old pupils. It's strictly forbidden, but they always
managed to get them sent. But I've never had a postcard from
London. Queer, isn't it?'

'Well, we'll soon put that right. I'll send you postcards of all
the London sights.'

'It'll go through the post office here,' said Maud, 'and it'll be
read. What will you sign it as?'

Slyne paused and drew his breath in sharply with delight; he
had achieved conspiracy, and was atingle.

'Just "H" for some, "S" for others, and if the series runs on
we'll start on the ABC. You'll know who's sending the cards
from London, won't you?'

Maud wriggled with delight. This was just her choice of
feathers, perfectly plumed and coloured.

'Of course. Oh, this is exciting. And if you write?' she looked
up at him sideways.

'You'd like me to write a letter?' he dropped his voice as low
as a fluting dove.

'Oh, I hope you will. I love getting letters too. All the girls write to me, and I keep their letters faithfully, I really do. But — ,' she paused and smiled at her gleaming nails, 'I never get letters from gentlemen.'

'Oh, Miss Maud,' he breathed.

'Nice, chatty, informative letters, and,' she turned and smiled brilliantly at him. 'I promise to reply. I'll write and give you all the news, would you like that?'

Epilogue

Young Andrew O'Farrell ran to open the second half of the shop door, the top bolt of the heavy oak leaf having been pulled down by his father. Outside, on the dusty pavement, Mrs Pig stood waiting to wheel the perambulator into the shop, and home.

'See how quiet your little sister is, Andrew, an' she after a two mile walk down de bog road.' Although the day was sunny and warm Mrs Pig was well wrapped up in her light woollen coat, which she had bought out of the sale of her land to the Englishman. It was bright green and totally unsuited to her large, angular frame; but it had been bought in one of the best fashion shops in Tralee, and was hors concours.

'Yeah,' said Andrew, giving his sleeping sister a brief, condescending glance, 'rolling down to Rio all the way in her chariot, I don't think.'

'Andrew,' said his mother sharply from behind her counter, where she was looking through her accounts book, 'I told you not to speak like that to Mrs Prendergast, and don't say "yeah", you hear me.'

'Yeah,' said Andrew, strutting towards the back door, which he was hoping some day to open himself; but he had not yet achieved it. Just as he was about to grab the handle, with a light in his eyes, the door opened, and out popped Gummy Hayes. She was not now as quick as she used to be, but she was still able to time the return of the youngest member of the O'Farrell family from her daily outing, wait behind the door to prevent that bold Andrew from opening it right under her very nose, and scuttle across the shop mid-way to take control of Elizabeth and her pram away from Mrs Pig. It was a ritual, long established, and followed by both women, down to the last inch and minute: taking the O'Farrell baby out of the house, out of Gummy's control, and its eventual return and ceremonial handing-over, in public, to the child's lawful and acknowledged nurse, Gummy.

'Tanks be to God an' 'is Blessed Mudder dis day dat yer back safe ensoun' in yer own safe an' comfortable house, an' out the ways a' de wickedy worruld, an' all dem dat take delight in id!'

Gummy made this speech, not much varied from day to day, as she unloosed the elaborate cover of the pram, and gathered the sleeping Elizabeth out of the rich depths of her splendid carriage, an equipage, which with its rubber wheels, elaborate springing, and heavily fringed hood had once carried Benedict himself in the slow, burnished, last decade of the nineteenth century. No sooner was the baby in Gummy's arms, held triumphantly aloft, like the prize capture she was, than she began to cry.

'Ooh, aah,' moaned Gummy, 'a course yer sick an' sorry after de sights yer after seein', an' de company yer keepin', me poor, half kilt liddle doat. Come on now, doaty.' And she disappeared through the back door with her screaming bundle. It was Andrew's part to wheel the pram after her. But recently he had been showing signs of some reluctance to perform this task which, a year earlier, he had insisted in taking out of Mrs Pig's hands. That lady did not mind in the least who wheeled the pram in, so long as it was not Gummy, and she had been delighted when Andrew had first taken it into his head to relieve his old nurse of this part of her daily ritual.

'A fine young fella, see how he loves his liddle sister,' was Mrs Pig's comment. But now she stood in the middle of the shop, and watched him walk slowly towards the front door, close the usual half of it, and then suddenly disappear into the street.

'Well, upon my word, but we're gettin' very big and independend for our age,' she pronounced, as she turned back to look at Andrew's parents. Fenny, who no longer sat up in his high carved chair, since it could no longer accommodate the width of his seat, was leaning his fore-arms on the bar counter. Behind him, in place of the famous bum-boat, stood a plain kitchen chair, heavily covered with cushions, but not restricted by arms. Fenny now spent more time leaning on his counter, when he was not serving customers; but he still sat down to smoke and read his paper.

'And bold,' said Ellen, looking at the front door. 'Wait till I get him back.' She frowned and pursed her lips.

'Well, I suppose I'd better be going home,' said Mrs Pig, a little nervously, for she was not at her best in these moments after she had yielded up her charge, and the O'Farrells allowed the silence to lengthen, as they so often did since the little girl was born.

She turned to go, and suddenly came back with all her old energy and spirit. 'Maybe it's time I leff de chile to Gummy. I doan want to cause trouble in the house.'

'Oh, no, Mrs P, no, no,' said Fenny with a genuine note of pain in his voice. He stood up from his leaning position, and waved a hand to emphasize his denial.

Mrs Pig stopped, while Ellen put her pencil in her accounts book and closed it. She had been very glad when Mrs Prendergast had taken over from Gummy for the outside trips. Gummy would have stopped to talk to everyone — a baby is as good as a dog for introductions, as Fenny remarked at the time — and would have had the poor child out half the day. Mrs Pig spoke to all she knew, but did not stop, ever.

Ellen was about to add to Fenny's protest, with a more reasoned explanation of her own; but they were all stopped short, and their preoccupation completely banished by the sudden entry of Donie Donnelly, out of puff, and obviously bursting with news.

'Arrah, Donie, is it yerself?' said Mrs Pig, much relieved that the porter had arrived in time to break up a sticky situation.

'A pint, Donie?' said Fenny, putting his hand on his beautiful delft handle.

'Me tongue is hangin' oud,' gasped Donie, 'I'm in mordal danger from de wasps.'

Fenny laughed and poured out the pint. Donie nodded his head, and saluted Ellen respectfully. She nodded curtly, and opened her book again.

'Miss McLurry muss be doin' a grade bizniz,' he panted, as he watched the poetic rise and topping of his pint, of which art Fenny was a master. 'She has a girrel in de shop, attendin'.'

'Maureen Shine, from Clonown, a cousin of her own,' said Mrs Pig. 'Sarah Jane put the bit of money she got from dat English twister into stock, and now she has a real good quota.'

'An' good luck te'er,' said Donie, taking up his drink

religiously, bowing his head over it to Fenny, and looking down at his glass with an expression of reverence. But before he bent his head to partake of the holy fluid, he looked at Mrs Pig with a private glint.

'Nod dat she'd lay in much stock, wid all she got from dat boyo. *Slainte* all, and may yah never wash yer — ah — foot in anyting bud water.' He tipped back his head, and swallowed with all the flare of a fire-eater.

'God outa heaven, bud dat was grease to a pan, amen.' He replaced his glass on the counter, cleared his throat, looked at Fenny, and was turned half-way to look at Ellen, when he stopped, and they all heard the slip-slop of Hosannah's old shoes outside. Gone were the days of the tap-tock-tap-tock. They all waited until she appeared.

'I saw ya come in here, at de top a de lane, Donie Donnelly,' she said in her old voice. Apart from her feet, which were giving way on her, Hosannah was much the same as she had always been. 'Ye have news.'

'Indeeden I have.'

'Wait till I get a chair under me,' said Hosannah, opening the door of the Cafe Royal and tottering in. Donie waited until he heard a chair creak, and then lowered his head, backed away to the end of the bar, so that he was facing all of them, and cleared his throat. So rapt were they all that Miss McLurry managed to slip in the front door without a comment from anyone. She had seen Donie go by, and followed him as quickly as she could.

'Miss Maud is back, wid de two childer, she's left him.' Donie closed his eyes and sighed deeply, after making this pronouncement, which created the sensation he had expected. They were all, even Fenny, speechless for a few moments. But it was he who found his voice, cracked as it was, first.

'You mean she's left Slyne?'

'Yah, an' never goin' back. Arrived be car ad d'otel ad twelve a'clock lass night, and spent two whole hours wid 'er mudder, tellin' all. Tom was lissenin' to every word. Oh, Lor' wad a story.' He sighed deeply and closed his eyes as if in prayer.

'Who's Tom?' screeched Hosannah from the snug. Since her feet gave out she had not been going to the seven o'clock mass, and was out of touch.

Donie looked at the others and shook his head.

'De fella dat came from de Brudders in place a Hamlet, God rest 'im for the dacent, willin' craytur he was. Dis Tom has a wicked temper, an' he's as idle as a bundle a bones. Bud he's a powerful lissener ad doors. Dussen miss wan word.'

No one believed this. Tom may have been a budding genius on the jungle telegraph, but for such an important occasion as last night, no one but Donie himself would be allowed the key-hole of Mrs Daly's drawing-room.

'Well, what happened?' demanded Miss McLurry. 'Why did she leave the twister?'

Donie sighed again and lowered his eyes.

'She found oud dat dere was anudder woman.'

'What did she expect with de English?' said Mrs Pig.

'Ah, bud Mrs Pig, ma'am,' said Donie, opening his eyes wide, 'id was worse dan dat. Dis woman was mixed up wid 'im, even before he came here, de Lord save us.'

'No English man is faithful to his wife,' said Mrs Pig. 'Tis well known.'

'An',' said Donie, pausing to hold the moment, 'she's an aul' wan, fifty or someing, called Marjarine, no Marjorie, I tink, an' he tole Maud dere was nuttin' between dem, ony aul friends.'

'A likely story,' said Mrs Pig. 'An' ye may be sure dere's more than Marjorie in his life, dirty twister.'

'Ah ha,' called out Hosannah, with a cackle, 'd'aulder de fiddle de sweeter de tune.'

'So that's the end of Maud Daly,' said Fenny softly, almost in a whisper. 'It's not what one would have expected, somehow.'

'Didden she marry him in a registerry office?' said Mrs Pig. 'Like she was bein' sent off be package.'

'Or baggage,' put in Ellen unexpectedly, from behind her counter. The women all murmured assent to this. None of them had any sympathy for Maud Daly. Only Fenny had his inner memory of dark, shining curls, milk-white skin, and the loveliest figure in all Bridgeford.

'So,' said Miss McLurry, 'he double-crossed the whole lot of us, everyone in the end.'

'The ink was hardly dry on the Treaty of Limerick before de English broke it,' said Mrs Pig.

'Ah ha, bud I knew when 'e came crawlin' upta us, and hidin' himself in a dark doorway, de night a de meetin' in de square, dat he was a twister,' called out Hosannah from the Cafe Royal.

'I never trusted him from the beginning either,' said Miss McLurry firmly. 'Not ever, not once.'

'Got our land off us, and den disappeared,' said Mrs Pig.

'Right, Marcella,' said Sarah Jane. 'A strange Englishman arrives in town, makes an offer for land, and we sell it to him for half nothing.'

'It'd be worth a fortune now, de wife is always ad me aboud id,' said Donie, reaching for his drink and comforter.

'Oh, Lord God above, juss tink whad id be worth now,' yelled Hosannah. 'A tousen' an acre.'

'Ad de very least,' said Donie, pausing with the glass to his lips. 'We were robbed, cheated outa our inherididge dat men died and faught for ad de Battle of Aughrim.'

'In 1691,' put in Mrs Pig, who knew about these things.

'Harmless eejits dat we were, too innocend for de kinda worruld he came outa, livin' wid two women an' he nod married ad all — he took us all for a ride on a tinker's pony.' These reflections came from Hosannah, who was beginning to feel the strain of speaking without a drink to ease her vocal muscles. Fenny poured out a tiny drop of gin, and topped it up with orangeade, while the other women looked on approvingly.

'Diss 'ill be remembered as long as Ireland holes up her head among de nations of de earth,' declared Mrs Pig, looking around with a superb gesture, that would have greatly impressed any crowd at a political meeting.

'As long as de people a Bridgeford lives and breathes,' put in Donie.

Fenny returned to his place, after putting Hosannah's drink through the hatch. Then, as the others went on about the various ways Slyne got around them, to get them to agree to part with their precious land, he began to make up a few figures on the edge of his newspaper. Mrs Pig had sold five acres and got paid at the rate of sixty pounds an acre, roughly three hundred pounds; Miss McLurry had received something over two hundred and sixty for her four acres, perches and roods; Donie's wife, roughly the same as Mrs Pig; Hosannah about two hundred pounds. He forgot what Mrs Daly received, but she had got it, and he had never been able to discover what old MacDonnell had held out for. He knew that Mrs Pig had done up her kitchen, put in an outside toilet, and still had a few bob in the bank; Sarah Jane had put her share into her shop, and paid Canon Sharkey a large sum for masses to get her brother into an institution; the masses — or the money — had worked; and now Miss McLurry had her house to herself, a thriving business, and was able to employ a helper at ten whole shillings a week; while poor old Hosannah, although she did light an enormous number of candles, also took to the bottle, and had to be taken into hospital, being discovered in her hovel unconscious, and surrounded by empty bottles of gin. Since then she had reverted to the poverty that had ruled her life for years; and her legs were very weak.

'When I was wheeling de chile down de bog road dis mornin' I looked across de meadows, where our rightful land used to be, before de English crook came, and a fairer sight ye never saw in all yer born days. An' to tink dat we were diddled out of it by a lyin', schemin', immoral twister of an Englishman, it make me blood run through me head like streaks of fire, and god if I could lay me hands on him, I'd shoot him.' Mrs Pig made another splendid gesture with her arm, her eyes flashing, and her whole face suffused by the flames that inspired her.

'Shootin' is too good for 'im,' shouted Hosannah, primed with what she thought was a good glass of gin-and-orange. 'Hang 'im ub, I would, be de saints I'd gut 'im, so I would.'

While this talk was going on, Fenny had torn out the sum he calculated the good ladies had received from the sale of their lands, and was now jotting down those notes he sometimes made when customers were in full flight at the bar, and he had time to interpret their higher truths. The river, he reflected, looked fine now. But last winter it was flooded just as high as ever it had been. It was true that the ladies did not know, as Fenny knew, having made discreet enquiries from his own local party man, that Kelly, the political candidate had been in on the deal, and had assured Slyne that the area would quickly be drained. He could only assume that Kelly went into the business with Slyne simply because he liked to be in on everything; just in case anything turned up in time. And backstairs politics was the breath of life to him. But as for draining the Shannon —

'Listen,' said Fenny, clearing his throat, and taking advantage of a lull in the oratory. 'My son Andrew is six and a half. In 1990 he'll be fifty-six, and I'm prepared to lay a bet that the Shannon, and our own meadows will still be undrained.

And in 2040 as well.'

They all listened to him in polite silence, except Ellen who had returned to her accounts. After all, he was an educated man, he knew a lot about history and politics and all sorts of things, and he was a decent son of decent parents. But he was tarred with the brush of West Britishness. Although he well knew how perfidious the English were, he was always prepared to do business with them. But his audience gave him a fair hearing.

'Dat's not de point,' Mrs Pig said patiently, after some moments of honourable silence surrounding Fenny's prophesy. 'Although Mr Kelly has said in public in dis very town square dat the time was comin' when de Shannon would be drained, and all the land on eider side of it turned into an eart'ly Paradise, and I believe him. How could he know dat we were fools enough to let ourselves be taken in like a bunch of gulls be a dirty, lying, God-forsaken Englishman. Now I ask ye all?'

Murmurs of assent greeted her speech. But Fenny was now bent down, reading his paper. Dunkirk, the headlines screamed.

'A man came into dis town,' went on Mrs Pig, putting the record straight, 'made himself as nice as pie to all and sundry, and got us, out of the innocence of our hearts, to part with de ony ting dat we have never yielded de right to, at any time, ever, in histry, our land. Issen dat right? Well, he tells us a whole pack of lies, an' gets us to sign a paper for dirty pennies, takin' our land away from us.' Here she paused, and took a deep, operatic breath. 'An' tries to get it for de price of the agreement money, wan tenth of what we were due. Den he goes off, marries a local girl, a Catlick, an' sends her back again with two children to support, while he spends his time gallivantin' with a whore, while we're left without our land, dat was stolen from us on false lyin' oaths.'

'Dat's rite,' squeaked Hosannah, 'dat's de trut, de whole an' ony trut'. We were swindled, diddled and culled be fine talk, an' big words be a hammerin' humbugger of an Englishman, and may de aul wan he's keepin', wid our profids, deceive 'im wid every dog and divil along de highroad. Oh, me lan', me lan', de lan' a' me fadders, dat we shed an oceanful a' blood to keep an' ta hauld forever, and along comes a common crook outa de ding-dong dung-dells a Lunnon, an' robs id from us ride uner our own noses. Sacred Hard a God haul' me back or I'll divide 'im.'

'Dat's right, every word of it,' said Mrs Pig, hitting her palm with her fist. 'Sure de half of it issen told yet.'

'No, indeed,' said Fenny, looking up from his paper. 'And it'll grow with the years. A famous case of macrooming, you might say.'

'Whad's dat ye say, Mr O'Farrell dear?' screamed Hosannah from the Cafe Royal. 'I didden hear id all. Say id again.'